A QUESTION OF LOYALTY

A QUESTION OF LOYALTY

Catherine Jones

This first world edition published in Great Britain 2005 by
SEVERN HOUSE PUBLISHERS LTD of
9–15 High Street, Sutton, Surrey SM1 1DF.
This first world edition published in the USA 2005 by
SEVERN HOUSE PUBLISHERS INC of
595 Madison Avenue, New York, N.Y. 10022.

British Library Cataloguing in Publication Data

Jones,   Catherine
    A question of loyalty
    1.   Great Britain. Army - Military life - Fiction
    2.   Great Britain - Armed Forces - Women - Fiction
    3.   Love stories
    I.   Title
    823.9'14 [F]

    ISBN 0-7278-6247-2

Typeset by Palimpsest Book Production Ltd.,
Polmont, Stirlingshire, Scotland.
Printed and bound in Great Britain by
MPG Books Ltd., Bodmin, Cornwall.

To Ian, as always

March 1985

Yvie was unconscious when she first encountered her future husband. She was at a party at another student's house, a poky two-bedroom terrace with lousy decor and worse ventilation, when she began to feel ill. That the room was overcrowded, coupled with the fact that she hadn't eaten since the day before, was not helped by the person next to her lighting up a foul-smelling French cigarette. Having Disque Bleu smoke blown in her face had proved the final straw. Her ears began to ring, she felt uncomfortably nauseous and light-headed in turns, and then, just as she felt her senses giving up and her knees buckling, she was aware of a pair of hands gripping her. After that, apart from a distant feeling that she was sliding, Alice-like, down a long, sloping tunnel, she was oblivious to anything for some minutes.

The first sensation to infiltrate her woozy state was an awareness of a soft, cool breeze caressing her face, like waves lapping over toes on hot sand. The air was so fresh and clear compared to what she had been inhaling inside the house that she breathed it in greedily.

'Hello . . . Hello . . .' said a voice just audible above the racket of the party throbbing through the closed window above her head. Culture Club, at full blast, drowned out partygoers, apart from the odd burst of laughter. She didn't think she wanted to cope with consciousness just yet. Then she felt someone patting her hand. She opened her eyes.

She found she was lying half on her side, on the ground, staring at a pair of men's shoes that gleamed in the pool of light spilling from the room behind. She moved her eyes to try and see the rest of him, but the light finished at mid-shin. The remainder of the figure was a black shape silhouetted

1

against the glow of a street lamp, so that her rescuer had a fuzzy amber aura.

'Hey, that's better,' the shape said. 'You were beginning to get me worried there.'

The effort of lifting her eyelids seemed too much for Yvie and she shut them.

'Don't faint again,' said the man, sounding worried.

'No,' Yvie mumbled. She felt awful, despite the cool air. She lay still, allowing the stranger to pat her hand. Slowly the feeling that if she moved she would either throw up or pass out receded and she was able to raise the energy to open her eyes again.

'Better?' said the man.

'A bit,' she replied. She pushed herself up so she rested on one elbow. The man was still just a black shape. She wondered what her rescuer looked like. Perhaps if she sat up she would be able to see more of him. Yvie shuffled her legs round until she was sitting upright.

'Not too fast,' said the bloke.

'I'm fine now, honest. It was the heat and the smoke.' She really did feel so much better. It was amazing the effect of fresh air.

'It was incredibly stuffy in there. Actually I was quite glad when you gave me an excuse to get out.' The shape shifted. He stood up and then sat on the low wall that separated the tiny strip of front garden from the road. Yvie could see him rubbing his thighs and then easing his shoulders.

'So did you carry me out?' she asked.

'Well, you didn't float out, that's for sure.'

'Sorry.'

'Hey, what's to be sorry for?'

'It wasn't drink.' She felt embarrassed about what had happened, and for some reason Yvie didn't want this man to have a bad opinion of her.

'You've lost me now.'

'I didn't pass out because I'd had too much to drink.'

'I never thought for a moment that you did.'

Silence fell.

After a few seconds, Yvie felt uncomfortable. 'Look, if you want to rejoin the party . . .'

'Not really. I wasn't enjoying it that much.'

'Oh.' The conversation, which had hardly been sparkling, died. Culture Club faded and for a second the full hubbub of dozens of voices competing against each other boomed into the tiny front garden. Then they, in their turn, were swamped by Cyndi Lauper insisting that girls just wanted to have fun. Yvie thought that having fun was the last thing she wanted right now. She shifted her position slightly but it didn't matter how she sat, the ground was still hard and uncomfortable. She made to stand up.

'Here, let me help you.' Her rescuer bent forward, grasped her hands and pulled her to her feet. Standing, Yvie decided in a second, was too big a step. The world reeled. She sat next to the man on the wall. Her head steadied again.

Now she was level with him, he stopped being a silhouette and Yvie saw that he was very good-looking in a clean-cut sort of way. She was struck by his hair, unfashionably short, and not the least like her other male student friends.

'You're not thinking of going back in?' He nodded at the curtained window of the house.

'Good God, no.'

'Right.'

'Right,' she echoed, at a loss for anything more original. Silence for another few seconds.

'Look, I thought I might go to the Swan and find myself a long cold drink. I don't suppose you'd care to join me?'

The thought of a long cold drink at the Swan, a particularly nice pub near the river, sounded unbelievably appealing.

'I'd love to,' said Yvie without any hesitation.

'Do you have a coat or bag or anything?'

'Nothing but what I stand up in,' she said, pulling her wallet from the pocket of her artfully slashed jeans to substantiate her answer.

'Come on then.'

'Umm . . . Do I get to know your name before you carry me off into the wild blue yonder and ravish me?' said Yvie with a smile.

'I'm Richard. And I *never* "ravish" on a first date.'

'Yvie,' said Yvie, holding out her hand and thinking that it might be a bit of a shame that 'ravishing' wasn't on the cards

3

after all. Apart from his looks, he had very good skin and teeth, she noticed.

Richard took her hand and clasped it warmly. 'Come on,' he said. 'I can already taste that cold beer.'

Yvie followed him out of the tiny garden and on to the pavement. She had been wondering how on earth they were going to get across town to the river when Richard stopped by a Ford Escort Gti convertible. He unlocked the passenger door and held it open for her.

'Get in,' he said.

Yvie didn't need telling twice. *Wow,* she thought, *a car and manners!* That was a combination she hadn't come across yet as a student. She settled down in her seat and pulled on her safety belt. She couldn't wait to tell her sister about this. Laura would be green!

By the time Richard had pulled up in the pub car park, he knew that Yvie was the first in her family to go to university, and she knew he was in the army – which explained the hair-cut and the fact he could afford a car. The pair of them drew stares from the mostly middle-aged regulars as they walked into the bar. It was hardly surprising, as they made an odd couple. In one respect they were well-suited, in that they were both tall and strikingly good-looking: Richard was athletically built, with short, dark curly hair, and dressed in cords and an open-neck check shirt; Yvie, on the other hand, although of similar height and build, had orange spiky hair, torn denim jeans and a skin-tight T-shirt over which was draped an outsized black string vest. Fingerless leather gloves completed the outfit.

Yvie took in the looks. 'I don't think the locals like what I'm wearing,' she murmured to Richard.

'Can't think why,' he said cheerfully, and eyeing her body with undisguised pleasure. 'I think you look fantastic.'

Yvie was touched by the compliment, and flattered, all the more because she felt that Richard meant it.

Over their first drink, she discovered that he was an only child of a military father and a doting mother, and that he was being paid by the army whilst studying for a degree in chemistry. So, instead of doing normal student things in his vacations, like working in McDonald's and getting drunk, he went

4

off to Cyprus on manoeuvres, or did winter warfare exercises in Norway. It seemed unbelievably glamorous and grown-up, and a world away from anything she had come across before. She wanted to talk more about him, but he insisted on hearing about her family, so she told him about her older sister who was married with a baby, and her father and her brother-in-law who worked in the local biscuit factory. Instead of being put off by her background, he seemed even more impressed by Yvie's achievements.

'So how come you are studying fine art?'

'I don't know. I can just do it. Painting and drawing is just something I don't have to think about.'

'How amazing. You must have *such* a talent.'

'Not really. I'm just lucky. I'm like those people who have photographic memories – they can't tell you how they do it, it's just an ability they have.'

'I'm still amazed.'

Yvie smiled shyly. It was nice to be appreciated. It wasn't something she was used to. Her dad certainly wasn't thrilled by his younger daughter's gifts, despite the fact that all through her school her teachers had gone out of their way to tell him how Yvie was 'doing well'. He was blue-collar and proud of it, and being academic didn't figure in his list of desirable attributes. To him 'doing well' meant having a job that provided enough money for the rent, food on the table, and left some over for the breadwinner to go to the pub on a Friday with his mates. 'Doing well' didn't mean going to university to study 'colouring in' (as he had put it) for three years. In his eyes, her sister Laura, older by three years, had done well. She'd left school, gone to work in the factory typing pool, found a man, got married and now had her first kid. And she'd achieved all that before Yvie had even made it into the sixth form.

'Don't worry, Yvie,' Laura had said. 'Why shouldn't you want to go into the sixth form? Can't see the appeal myself, but don't mind dad. He'll come round.'

But Yvie was now well into her second year at university, and her dad still hadn't come round. And Laura was doing even better, as she was pregnant with number two, and when Yvie went home all her dad did was mutter about what a waste of tax-payers' money her degree was going to be, and when was she going to give it all up, get a proper job and settle down. Not that Yvie thought that settling down looked like an option to aspire to. She watched her sister – run ragged with a toddler and pregnant with a second – battle with morning sickness and the drudgery of housework, and her mother – grey-haired, slightly stooped, and looking nearer fifty than forty – wash and iron and skivvy for a man who took it all for granted. And the depressing thought was that neither her mother nor her sister had anything to look forward to except more of the same. Well, decided Yvie, not for her. She wasn't going to have a job, she was going to have a career, and when she got married – *if* she got married – she was going to be on equal terms with her husband. Women's lib might have been lost on her mother and her sister, but it wasn't bypassing her. No matter what her dad thought of her.

By the end of the evening at the Swan, Yvie was besotted. Richard was mature, attentive, charming and witty. She tried not to let the fact that he was also well-heeled and guaranteed employment on graduating influence her further, but she did acknowledge that it certainly didn't detract from his appeal. She was completely made up when, as he drove her back to her flat, he asked if he could see her again the next day.

'Do you ravish on a second date?' she'd asked as they drew up outside her front door.

'I haven't yet, but I might be tempted,' he said. He leaned across the gear stick and kissed her on the lips.

Yvie was surprised at how clean-tasting his mouth was. And at the gentleness of the kiss. Perhaps, she thought, ravishing wasn't going to be quite his style. She felt rather disappointed by this thought. But no matter, you couldn't expect everything, could you?

Over the next months, Yvie and Richard saw increasing amounts of each other; they discovered they shared the same sense of humour and the same taste in films and music; their kisses became more passionate and 'ravishing' became a regular activity. They found fewer and fewer reasons to go home for weekends or holidays, and more reasons why they wanted to remain in each other's company. Their friends joked that they resembled a married couple, and Yvie began to wonder if one day the joke might not become reality. Apart from the fact that she was in love with Richard, she decided he was everything a girl could want; considerate, funny, steady, loving and good-looking. The trouble was, she also knew he was everything her father would dislike: educated, well-mannered, cultured and definitely not working-class. But then, thought Yvie, if her dreams came true, Richard would be asking her to marry *him*, not her father.

As casually as she could, when Richard took her to army functions, she tried to find out what it was like to be an army wife; after all, it was going to be a quantum leap from life behind the biscuit factory, or from being a university student. Much as she loved Richard, she was sensible enough to realize that if she wasn't going to cope with such a change she would just end up bitter and dissatisfied. Married life would have its ups and downs no doubt, but she hoped the ones in her life would be hills, not mountain ranges. If a future life with the colours looked hopelessly difficult and not the sort of thing she might be able to cope with, then she would do better to walk away now than get in deeper. So she got the wives to talk about themselves; not difficult, she soon discovered, which was lucky, as the last thing she wanted was to appear obvious and scare Richard off. The poor dears, thought Yvie, didn't seem to have much of a life; the tales of the constant moving, and cleaning quarters to an unimaginable standard, together with the endless litany of separation and unaccompanied postings just had to be exaggerated. And none of them seemed to have jobs, but had got on with the business of breeding kids. Some seemed to find things to do to pass the time, like running the unit's charity shop or teaching other wives how to arrange flowers, and Richard mentioned details on a similar vein, but Yvie was inclined to dismiss much of this talk as just so much embroidery. If it was as bad as that, no one would marry into the army – after all, living overseas, mess dinners and decent houses couldn't possibly make up for the ghastly details she'd heard described. Anyway, she was getting a degree; she was going to have a career. She could paint, she could do that anywhere. All it would take would be a bit of imagination and she was sure she could keep herself fully employed anywhere in the world. So Yvie listened to all that the wives had to say, and then promptly, despite her initial intentions of fact-finding, ignored all the information and the advice. It never occurred to her that she didn't want to hear the truth; that she had already made her mind up about spending the rest of her life with Richard, and she wasn't interested in the pitfalls of such a decision. The bottom line was that she couldn't imagine wanting another man as a partner, and she was going to take this one, warts, army life and all.

She was sure Richard felt the same way about her. Oh, please God he did. She didn't think she'd be able to bear it if he didn't.

May 1986

It was around a year later, just before their finals, that Richard asked her to marry him. It was at a ladies' guest night at his regimental mess. Although she had been scared witless at the first couple of do's she had attended, Richard had steered her carefully through most of the likeliest pitfalls, and had advised her on what to wear – a tricky matter given that her wardrobe had consisted mostly of punk-rock fashions. Now Yvie was far more at home in the formal and traditional atmosphere of the officers' mess, and had acquired a ballerina-length silk dress from Monsoon and had toned her hair down to a shade of auburn. She was still considered a little outré by some of the senior mess wives but she was 'coming along nicely', in the opinion of Richard's commanding officer. Yvie, despite her avant-garde take on fashion and art, discovered that she liked the comfortable predictability of mess functions. From the food to the music, from the uniforms to the topics of conversation, things rarely seemed to alter, and she came to understand why traditions persisted: no nasty shocks, no surprises, just an enjoyable evening. So when Richard produced a ring from the inside pocket of his bum-freezer mess-kit jacket, Yvie, besotted with Richard and dazzled by the candlelight and the glamour, didn't give any consideration to her answer. However, when she rang home with the news, the fact that her father didn't give any consideration to his reaction either took some of the gloss off her happiness.

'And how the bloody hell do you think we are going to pay for the sort of wedding Richard and his posh friends are used to? If he and his la-di-da friends think I'm going to beggar this family so they can get pissed at my expense, they've got another think coming. And furthermore, my girl, if you think that by marrying out of your class you're going to be happy

9

. . . well, let me tell you . . .' And her father had continued, ad nauseam and belligerently, in that vein until Yvie's money had run out and her father was left talking to the tone. Yvie blinked back the tears that her father's comments had caused and replaced the receiver.

Richard, waiting outside the phone box, noticed her tears instantly. 'What's the matter, sweetie?'

Yvie shrugged. 'Nothing.'

Richard put his arm round her shoulder and gave it a rub. 'It must be something. No one cries over nothing.'

Yvie sniffed. 'We'll have to wait a bit. Dad thinks it's going to be too expensive,' she said, paraphrasing and bowdlerizing frantically. 'If I get a half-decent job when I leave uni, I'll be able to save and help him with the cost.'

'It won't be that much,' said Richard, who didn't have the first idea how much a wedding cost.

The next day Richard tracked down Yvie as she was coming out of lectures.

'I spoke to the mess manager,' he told her.

'Congratulations,' said Yvie, looking bemused.

'No, silly. I spoke to him about getting married.'

'You mean you're going to marry him not me?' said Yvie in mock horror.

'Will you shut up and listen. I spoke to him about us getting married – you and me. He can do it for about three pounds a head. Do you think your dad can run to that? I shouldn't think that we'll have more than a couple of hundred guests at the most, probably less. Of course, the mess'll come for free. That just leaves the cost of your dress and the ones you want for your bridesmaids.'

Yvie was speechless. She threw her arms around Richard's neck and began crying all over again. Richard decided he really didn't understand women. They cried when they were unhappy and then when you made things better – they cried all over again.

Of course, Richard didn't tell her that the cost of three pounds a head was exclusive of both extra duty pay for the mess staff and any alcohol, to say nothing of the champagne that would be required. Put those factors into the equation and the cost more than quadrupled. But he was going to pay for all that, and the cake that the mess chef was going to make, and Yvie's dad need never know. So, with no other obstacles in the way, the wedding was planned for July.

However, despite discovering how little it was going to cost him to see his youngest daughter married, come the big day, Yvie's father still wasn't happy. Firstly, he wasn't stupid, and he knew that the reception was costing more than three quid a head, but he assumed that all officers' mess 'junkets' as he called them were subsidized by tax-payers like him. Secondly, his socialist leanings prevented him from enjoying the spectacle of his daughter leaving the church beneath the swords of a guard of honour. Nor could he relax in the understated opulence of the officers' mess. Yvie's mother, though, was in raptures and kept mentioning to Laura that, with all those uniforms, it was 'just like the royal wedding', which put Laura's nose right out of joint.

Laura had genuinely tried not to be jealous of Yvie's wedding, but it was exceedingly difficult. Deep down, Laura was proud of her little sister, getting a degree and everything, but when she had got married, she had had to make do with a reception in the local church hall, in which the smell of the previous day's jumble sale lingered, and a buffet of fish-paste sandwiches, scones and cheap white fizzy wine put together the previous day by her and her mum. Not quite the same league as this glamorous affair. Nor did it help that her children were letting her down. She'd been as pleased as anything when Yvie had asked if Lisa-Marie would be her bridesmaid, but even though she had looked scrumptiously sweet, the effect had been spoiled when she had picked her nose constantly during the service, and then had overindulged on pop at the reception and had been sick down the front of her dress. And Kylie, the baby, was teething and grizzled solidly throughout the afternoon. She might have found it easier to cope if her husband, Mick, had thought to help her with them, but he was too busy knocking back free champagne to notice – or care. Laura had tried to look happy for Yvie but, what with one thing and another, she'd just ended up feeling sorry for herself and wishing she could go home, put the kids to bed and have a drink herself. The only note of cheer, as far as she was concerned, was being chatted up by Richard's best man –

11

Adam Clifton. After five years of marriage to Mick, it was a novelty to be told she looked just like Bonnie Tyler and that she ought to try modelling. In her heart she knew it was flannel, but it didn't stop her from feeling like a million dollars – until Lisa-Marie was sick for a second time.

Not surprisingly, Yvie was also very conscious of Richard's best man. She hadn't met him before, even though Richard assured her that they were best friends. When, after Sandhurst, Richard had gone to university to study, Adam had gone to join a unit in Germany and had spent the ensuing three years either on training courses or on exercise 'to keep him out of the way until he knew what he was doing', according to Richard. Well, thought Yvie, he certainly seemed to know what he was doing at her wedding. He flirted with her female friends, complimented her mother on her outfit, joshed with her father, made a memorable and funny speech and danced with most of Yvie's female relations, including Laura, whom, Yvie noticed, he even induced to smile briefly. And to cap it all, he had been far and away the handsomest man in the room. In, fact, if Yvie hadn't just become Mrs Maxwell, she might have vied with the single women for his attentions. Even so, she felt a tiny pang of envy for the girls who did get his attentions, a pang that she quickly quashed. But she could have fancied a whirl around the floor with him, and was unreasonably disappointed when they left for their honeymoon before she had the chance.

Immediately after their honeymoon, Richard was posted to Germany, and married life in the army did not begin as Yvie had envisaged. For a start, she spent several months living in her parents' house while they waited for a quarter. During that time, she'd had to listen to her father's constant mutterings about the uselessness of the British officer classes, how Yvie should be getting a job, how supporting the army in Germany was a drain on the tax-payer, how Laura's kids were the apple of his eye and how Yvie herself would have done better if she hadn't given herself such high-fallutin' ideas as a result of going to university. It wore Yvie down. It might not have been quite so bad if Richard had been able to visit but, what with being abroad, together with the fact that his unit was involved heavily in the annual autumn exercises, his trips back to see

Yvie were rare. By November a quarter was found, the exercises were over for another year and Yvie assumed, as she disembarked at Hanover airport, that her married life was now about to roar into action – so to speak. If nothing else, she had got away from her father.

'You'll love the flat,' Richard told her as they sped away north on the main Autobahn to Hamburg. 'It's in this little village and it's so pretty. I know you'll adore it.'

Yvie thought that she didn't care where she lived, just as long as it was with Richard. Anywhere, even a trench on the ranges, would be preferable to staying with her parents for a day longer, so Richard's description of their first house bettered her expectations by miles. Yvie was not disappointed when they drove into the village of Bad Mannheim. Yvie had heard the word 'gemütlich' but had not really understood the full meaning until she saw the village centre with its church, tiny market square and brightly painted shutters adorning the surrounding houses, and there were winter pansies in the window boxes and hanging baskets by the doors, which added yet more colour to the pretty scene. Just down the road from the church, Richard drew the car up in a little car park behind a small block of flats topped by a pitched roof and dormer windows. It looked idyllic.

Excited, Yvie climbed out of the car and headed for the front door.

'You'll need the key,' said Richard with a smile, brandishing it tantalizingly. Yvie ran back to get it but Richard caught her and held her close. 'Not so fast, Mrs Maxwell.' And he picked her up. Yvie nuzzled his neck. Of course, she had to be carried over the threshold!

By the time they got to the second floor, it didn't seem such a good idea, or at least, it didn't to Richard, who was starting to buckle at the knees.

'Here,' he gasped, handing over the door key. 'You'll have to open it.'

Yvie leaned forward in his arms and worked the lock. The door swung open. The interior was surprisingly gloomy, which was slightly disappointing, but then it was almost winter. Richard, who deposited her gently on to a hall chair, went from room to room pulling up the roller shutters. Pale lemony light flooded in and the flat took on a different aspect. It wasn't huge – two bedrooms, a largish sitting room/dining room, tiny kitchen and even smaller bathroom – but what more did they need? And as they were on the top floor, up in the roof with the dormer windows, the ceilings were all interesting angles and corners, which appealed to the artistic side of Yvie. She ran around the flat exploring the rooms, opening windows and exclaiming over the view of the church and checking the contents of the cupboards. She was delighted to find a balcony running the width of the house, for which she instantly planned to have some real window boxes.

'It's perfect. I love it!' she announced after several minutes.

'There's an Aldimarkt in the square, down there,' said Richard, joining her at a window and pointing it out to her. 'Just a tiny one, but I'm told it sells pretty much everything. And a baker's. Shopping'll be a doddle for you.'

'Where's the Naafi?' Yvie knew enough about the British army to know that this would provide her with essentials from home, Marmite and bacon and the like.

'Oh, that's in the garrison. I'll take you there on Saturday.' Richard had warned her he was expected back at work for the remainder of the working week, but Yvie had been happy about that – after all, she had boxes of wedding presents to unpack and a home to make.

'Can't I get a bus?'

'I doubt it. We're a bit out in the sticks here.'

'Perhaps one of the other wives . . .'

'Oh, they all live in the garrison too. This is a hiring. We're miles from the patch.'

'Oh.' A tiny cloud of disappointment came over the horizon. 'Well . . .' Yvie shrugged. She hadn't expected to be on her own, but what the heck, she'd manage. She sent the little cloud packing. After all, wasn't living in a foreign country all about learning new things? New money, new language, new food. It would be exciting. But even so, she noticed that the cloud was still lurking because she wasn't in the thick of things. She'd been looking forward to meeting the other wives, getting a social life off the ground. Oh well.

It took less than a week for the novelty of living in Germany to wear off, and for loneliness to set in. She tried not to be

14

resentful. It was OK for Richard. He took the car every day and drove to the garrison, he had lunch with his chums in the mess, in the evening he could call into the bar for a drink before setting off home, he had access to people who spoke his language, and a job to do that occupied his day. But she was stuck in the back of beyond with nothing to do, no employment and no entertainment. She realized it wasn't entirely Richard's fault. If she had been able to drive, she would have been hugely better off, she could have got herself over to the patch and joined in the social life of the other wives. If she'd had German as a language rather than French, she might have been able to make friends with her neighbours, but with neither car nor a common tongue, she was on her own. Matters were made worse when, just before Christmas, Richard came home to tell her that he was earmarked for a number of training courses in the New Year. As Yvie marked them in her diary for the following year, she noted that she was going to see very little of him until mid-March. Privately she thought about going home for several weeks. Even life back with her cantankerous father would be better than staying put. But she put the thought behind her when Richard pointed out all the things they could do together during the few weekends that he would be around.

To try to keep herself occupied, Yvie looked at getting a job, but she was told that there wasn't much call for fine art graduates with the British army, and without a word of German she wasn't even able to stack shelves at the local supermarket. She tried to keep cheerful for Richard's sake, but it was hard going. Despite her best efforts, there must have been something in her manner which made Richard realize how very isolated his new wife was, so, as a sop, he arranged for a telephone to be installed in the flat, 'Then at least I can ring you up and tell you how much I'm missing you.' Big deal, thought Yvie a touch ungratefully, who knew that when he was away it was him she wanted – not his voice.

The telephone proved useful for keeping in touch with Richard but she barely used it to phone anyone else. If she phoned her mother, half the call seemed to be spent reassuring her that her daughter wasn't going to end up in Queer Street as a result of the bill. Laura wasn't much better. She seemed to be eaten up with jealousy at her idea of Yvie's new glamorous lifestyle. And when Yvie tried to put the record straight, tell her how lonely and bored she was, Laura accused her of patronizing her with lies. And as for ringing the other wives, she barely knew them. Certainly not well enough to while away time with chatting.

She dabbled in painting, but with only Richard to show her efforts to, it soon lost its appeal. She read anything she could lay her hands on, listened to the radio, rearranged the furniture in their flat, but still found that each day had more hours in it than she could possibly fill. If it hadn't been winter, she might have gone out walking or taken some form of exercise, but the bitter cold, snow and ice and lack of transport made going out a very unattractive prospect.

Christmas was fun, though. Yvie loved the German Christmas markets, with their smells of spiced biscuits and Glühwein, the glowing candles and pretty hand-crafted decorations. They spent the holiday together and, for a week, with Richard around all the time, Yvie thought that perhaps she had made a mistake about living in Germany.

Then he went back to work and the scheduled training exercises, and her sense of isolation reasserted itself. Some days she hardly felt it was worth the effort to get out of bed. After all, what was there for her to do once she was up? The winter passed slowly. The weather was atrocious; Yvie spent most of her days reading, trying to work her way through the entire stock of the garrison library. Richard was away more often than he was home. Yvie became less and less motivated to do anything, until, quite often when Richard was away, she didn't bother dressing properly for days at a time. What was the point? Who was going to see her?

It was in April, when Richard was back for a couple of weeks, that he came home from the barracks with some good news.

'Guess what?' he said.

'We're posted back to England,' said Yvie hopefully.

'Better than that.'

'We're posted to Hong Kong.'

'No, don't be stupid.'

16

Richard was right – that was too much to hope for. 'Tell me,' she said.

'Adam's being posted in.'

'Great.' *Oh, my cup runneth over*, she thought. If Adam was living in the mess, then Richard would be even later home in the evenings. Hoo-bloody-ray.

'And he and his wife are being quartered next door.'

'Oh.' Well, that was a completely different kettle of fish. With Adam and his wife in the vicinity, Richard might be home more. Yvie absorbed the various bits of information and digested them. Then she realized that she hadn't known that Adam was married, his wife certainly hadn't been at their wedding. 'What's his wife like?'

'Haven't a clue. A recent acquisition, I gather. All I know is she's called Pammy – Pamela, I suppose – and she's a modern language teacher.'

'Pammy!' What sort of name was that? God, how twee. Yvie didn't think it boded well for a friendship. But could she afford to be choosy? She thought not and determined to do her best to like her new neighbour.

When a shiny red sports car with the top down pulled up outside the little block of flats, Yvie knew instantly that it belonged to Adam. Trust him, she thought, to have such a flash car. She opened the door on to the balcony and called down to him as soon as he killed the engine.

'Hi!'

Adam looked up at her, squinting slightly against the sun. 'Hi.' Anything else he might have said was drowned out by the arrival of a khaki four-ton truck. It parked beside his car and several large squaddies vaulted over the tailgate at the rear.

'Shall I put the kettle on?' Yvie called down.

'Great. I haven't got that much stuff here. The lads and I should have it sorted in no time.'

Yvie left them to get on with hefting packing cases up three flights of stairs and went into the kitchen to make the tea. When the kettle boiled she loaded up a tray with steaming mugs, milk, sugar and biscuits, and then opened the door to her flat to see how the workers were progressing. A couple of burly soldiers were manhandling a large tea chest into the flat opposite, and Yvie could hear Adam giving instructions as to where he wanted them to put it. She waited until there was a lull and then called out that the tea was ready.

'Come in,' said Adam. 'Great to see you again. It's been a while since your wedding.'

'Not that long,' said Yvie.

'Perhaps it just seems like it.'

As they chatted, Yvie glanced around Adam's flat. It had already been furnished with army-issue basics, but was devoid of any sense of personality or comfort. Yvie picked her way through the half-dozen packing cases that barred her path across the hall, and put the tea tray down on the table in the sitting room. The two soldiers spooned vast quantities of sugar into four of the mugs, then they each grabbed a couple and the plate of biscuits, and, muttering thanks and something about a smoke break, they disappeared out to their mates at the lorry.

'I didn't want a biscuit anyway,' said Adam.

'I'll get some more.'

'No, no. I was serious. I really don't want a biscuit.' Adam laughed.

'Oh.' Yvie felt strangely sheepish. A small silence followed, which made her feel even more uncomfortable. To hide her embarrassment, she started to prattle on about the delights, or lack of them, of Bad Mannheim. Eventually she noticed Adam's eyes looking glazed.

'Well, I'll leave you to get on.' He didn't try to stop her. She felt rejected and gauche. She gathered up the mugs and tray. If she'd felt foolish before, it was nothing to how she felt now. The bloke must think she was verbally incontinent. 'If there's anything else you need to know . . .'

'I'll tell Pammy that you have the low-down.' He stifled a yawn.

God, how she must have bored him.

'Right. Well . . . I'll let you get on.' She backed towards the door.

'Thanks for the tea.'

'It was nothing.' She returned to her flat and shut the door. What a moron he must think I am, she thought. She sighed

18

and began to wash up the cups moodily. If he was Mr Cool, she was Mrs Dopey. She told herself that she didn't care what he thought of her, but then had to admit that that wasn't entirely true. If Adam told his wife that her new next-door neighbour was a complete thicko, would Pammy want to know? Probably not, and she did so want someone she could share a cup of coffee with, to chat to, to go shopping with, and Pammy, ridiculous name or not, was all that was on offer. And now she'd probably stuffed her chances. Brilliant. Absolutely wonderful.

She had just put the mugs on the drainer to drip dry when there was a knock on her door. She wiped her hands perfunctorily on a tea towel and went to open it. Adam was standing there with an empty plate and the mugs the soldiers had used.

'Oh, thanks. I'd forgotten about those.' She took them from him, but her hands were still wet and one of the mugs slipped from her grasp and shattered on the hall tiles. 'Damn and blast and buggeration!' she swore with some force as this minor mishap caused her frustration at her earlier behaviour to erupt.

Adam looked taken aback. 'It's only a mug,' he said. 'I'll buy you another one if it's so important.'

Yvie felt even more of a fool than she had done minutes earlier. 'No. It's me, overreacting.' She put the remaining mugs down on the hall table and bent to pick up the chunks of broken china. When she stood up, she noticed Adam was looking at her with some concern.

He thinks I'm potty as well as stupid, she thought angrily. 'Honest, I'm OK. I'm just having a bad day.' She wasn't going to admit to him, of all people, that she felt she had made a complete fool of herself, not once but several times.

'Do you want to talk about it?'

Yvie did, but she was aware of how she had bored him only a few minutes ago. She didn't want to look needy. So she said, 'Not really, thank you.'

Adam shrugged and left, shutting the door behind him.

God, she had sounded so haughty. It hadn't come out as she had intended at all. Potty, stupid and now rude. Damn!

When Richard came home from work, he dumped his stuff in the hall, kissed Yvie hurriedly, exchanged a scant couple of sentences with her about their respective days and then raced across the hall to see his old friend. It was only after he rang the bell for the third time that Adam, tousled, dishevelled and yawning, opened the door.

'Sorry, did I wake you?'

'Richard, you old bugger. Good to see you.' Adam's face split into a wide grin of genuine pleasure. 'Yeah, I was having a bit of a kip. I drove all last night to get here and didn't get any shut-eye at all. Yvie'll tell you what a zombie I was when I arrived. I could hardly keep my eyes open and no mistake.'

'No, she didn't notice – or she was too polite to tell me.' Richard didn't acknowledge to himself that he hadn't given Yvie time to tell him anything in his haste to get reacquainted with his old friend.

'Tactful of her.'

'Tell you what. Why don't you have a shower and come over to ours in about half an hour or so and have a cold beer and a bite to eat? How does that sound?'

'Ace.'

Yvie had started cooking supper when Richard returned to his own flat.

'Smells good,' he said, sniffing the aroma of frying meat appreciatively. 'I don't suppose there's any chance of stretching it to feed three instead of two is there?'

Yvie looked doubtfully at the mince in the frying pan. She knew exactly what Richard was angling for. 'I suppose if I did a mountain of mash,' she said, 'it might be enough to go round.' She knew that, regardless of what she said, Adam was going to be a dinner guest. If she said there wasn't going to be enough, Richard would just go to get bratwurst and chips or something. It was obvious that Richard was longing to catch up with his old friend and Yvie knew it would be churlish to deny him the chance. Just because she had messed up her re-encounter with Adam, it was no excuse to be a moo and stop the two friends from chewing the fat. Richard dropped a kiss on the back of her neck. 'Great. The last thing he wants to do after the journey and all that unpacking is to have to cook.'

No, thought Yvie. She doubted if he did. Cooking was, in fact, the last thing she had felt like doing when she had moved in, but she hadn't had a friendly neighbour to do it for her, so she had just had to bloody well get on with it. No, she thought, that was unfair. She *and* Richard had had to bloody well get on with it. But then she thought that probably, if the shoe had been on the other foot, Adam and Pammy would have looked after them.

It was less than twenty minutes later that their doorbell rang. Yvie, busy in the kitchen, ignored it. It was bound to be Adam, and as Richard was so keen to see him, he could stir himself and answer it. Over the sound of the radio in the kitchen, Yvie could hear voices and then a burst of laughter. If she was honest she was a little envious. She would have liked to have a friend to laugh with like that. Please God, she thought, let Pammy be my sort.

The two men, still talking and joking, bundled into the kitchen.

'Look what Adam's brought,' said Richard, waving a bottle of champagne.

'Oh, that's nice,' said Yvie, mustering a smile.

'It was on special offer on the ferry. I couldn't resist it,' said Adam. 'I bought a load.'

'Good,' said Yvie. She thought that it would probably be cheaper still in the Naafi or in the mess, but didn't say anything. It was a nice gesture anyhow.

'Get the glasses out, then,' said Richard.

Yvie turned the gas down under the potatoes and went to the cupboard to fetch them.

'We haven't got swanky flutes. You'll have to make do with ordinary wine glasses,' she said as she plonked three on the kitchen table.

'And I've got an apology to make,' said Adam as Richard busied himself with the foil and the wire cage over the cork. 'I was so rude earlier today. I'd been driving all night and was absolutely knackered. I'm really sorry. You must think I'm an arrogant bastard.'

'What's this? You been insulting my wife?' said Richard, easing his thumbs under the cork.

'Not at all,' said Yvie. She had to try to regain the ground she had lost earlier in the day with her crass behaviour. Perhaps if she was nice to him now he'd forget what a verbally incontinent and moody cow she'd been earlier.

21

The cork flew off with a satisfying pop and Yvie grabbed a glass to collect the foam already spilling from the bottle.

'Didn't waste a drop,' said Richard with satisfaction. He poured the fizzing liquid into the other two glasses slowly. 'So why all the humble pie, Adam?'

'Your poor wife was being an absolute honey, busting a gut to keep a gang of squaddies in tea and biscuits, making me feel welcome, and all I could do was yawn and look like some sort of mannerless git.'

'So, no change there then,' said Richard with a big grin.

Adam roared with laughter and even Yvie found herself grinning.

'Anyway, here's to being neighbours,' said Richard, raising his glass.

'Neighbours,' chorused Adam and Yvie.

By the time supper was on the table, the champagne had been finished and Richard had cracked open a bottle of Moselle. As Yvie dished up the food, she realized she was more than a little tipsy. Three glasses of wine on an empty stomach was probably unwise, especially as she wasn't an inveterate drinker. Twice she found herself staggering slightly as she carried the saucepans from the hob to the kitchen table, her feet not wishing to take the direct route but finding deviations of their own across the kitchen floor.

'Whoops,' she said, giggling slightly as she swayed towards the table with the plates.

'Whoops, what?' said Adam from the door.

Yvie giggled some more as she put the plates down. 'I think I'm tiddly,' she said.

'I think you are too. Do you want a hand?'

'Please.' As she said this, she took an involuntary step backwards. She grabbed at the table to steady herself, and sent a plate flying off the stack. Adam, with cat-like reflexes, grabbed it before it hit the floor.

'Tell you what. How about I serve the food?'

Yvie, even in her inebriated state, could see the sense of this. Using the kitchen table for support, she directed Adam to the serving spoons.

'Adam?' queried Richard from the doorway.

'Just making sure I can still do domesticity,' said Adam.

'Yvie?'

She hiccuped and giggled.

'Ah.' Richard understood. 'Best you carry on then.'

Adam finished slopping the mince and mash on to the plates and then carried both his and Yvie's plates through to the living room. Richard followed with his own and a large bottle of tomato sauce.

'I don't think I'm hungry,' Yvie said, slightly indistinctly.

'You need to eat,' said Richard firmly. 'Blotting paper.'

She slumped in her chair and picked up her fork in a desultory way, like a sulky child. She pushed the food around in a lacklustre way while Adam and Richard chatted and laughed. Suddenly the surfeit of alcohol, together with the smell of the food, proved too much for Yvie and she knew she was going to be sick. Mumbling an apology and clamping her hand over her mouth, she fled to the loo. She was vaguely aware of being grateful to have made the lav – the thought of leaving a trail of sick across the hall for Richard to clear up and for Adam to witness . . . Oh God, Adam!

After being sicker than Yvie thought possible, she slowly became aware that the worst was probably over. Kneeling on the floor, her head hanging over the loo, she began to feel marginally less ill. Well, perhaps 'less ill' was an exaggeration – less close to death was nearer the mark. She groaned, partly because she felt so utterly gruesome, but also because she knew she must have compounded the dreadful impression she had created. First of all she'd been this gushing do-gooder, then some sort of depressive who got upset over a broken mug, then a lush and now a vomiting slut. She slumped down, resting her cheek on the loo seat, feeling drained and embarrassed in equal measure.

'Yvie?' said Richard from the door.

'Go away,' mumbled Yvie.

'Are you all right?'

'What do you think?' The effort of talking was too much for her fragile state. She felt the bile rising again and spewed some more, coughing the last of the alcohol into the pan. Her ears were ringing, she was sweating and shivering, her stomach ached from retching and her nose and throat were sore.

'Come on. I'll put you to bed with a hot-water bottle and a bowl.'

Yvie felt too exhausted and ill to resist. She wiped her face and blew her nose on some loo paper, then she allowed Richard to help her up and assist her across the hall to their bedroom. She was so floppy with drink and the aftermath of being violently sick that he had to help her out of her jeans and top. Bringing her a bowl and the promised hot-water bottle, he tucked her under the duvet and pulled the curtains. Then he left the room and closed the door. As Yvie drifted off into a drunken, whirling sleep, she heard Adam laughing. Was it at her?

Yvie didn't see much of Adam over the next few days. He was busy at the barracks taking over his new job, and Richard, now he had caught up with his friend, was happy to spend his evenings in the company of his wife and let Adam get his flat straight ready for Pammy's arrival. Besides, on the couple of occasions that Adam appeared at their door to borrow a screwdriver or hammer or to beg some milk, Yvie let Richard deal with him, as she was still mortified at her behaviour at their previous meeting.

'Adam doesn't care,' said Richard when Yvie confessed.

'But I do.'

'Hell, he'll have forgotten all about it by now.'

'I haven't,' she said morosely.

It was obvious from the moment Pammy arrived that the two women were total opposites. The instant Yvie clapped eyes on her new neighbour, she wondered if Pammy was a vicar's daughter. Not that she had anything to base this assumption on – for all she knew, the majority of vicar's daughters were wild, fashion-obsessed and drug-crazed – but Pammy had this air of wholesome Englishness with a touch of aristocracy. Despite their differences, Yvie was determined to get on with her neighbour. Pammy was neat, petite and dressed in skirts and blouses with pie-crust collars, while Yvie was tall and gangly and favoured jeans and T-shirts. Furthermore, Pammy's long blonde hair was tidily arranged in a French pleat, while Yvie's short, spiky hair was dyed back to its old shade of red. Pammy was into home cooking and handicrafts, while Yvie took full advantage of anything the Naafi or the Aldimarkt could offer that made life easier and cooking less of a hassle. She wouldn't have recognized a crochet hook if it had poked her in the eye. And Pammy actually enjoyed ironing. Now that *was* weird, and even Pammy acknowledged that. After the first few days of making an effort to like her neighbour – and, Yvie hoped, encouraging her neighbour to like her – the two women soon became good friends. There was the small matter that there were no other Brits around for Pammy to pick and choose her friends from, so it was hardly as though Pammy was spoiled for choice, but, even so, Yvie felt a sense of gratitude that Pammy wanted to associate with her as much as she did. Judging by the look of Pammy, Yvie had the feeling that she didn't approve of strong drink, so Yvie fervently hoped that Adam hadn't told Pammy about her drunken evening a few nights previously. Now things were looking up, she didn't want them spoiled. In somewhat less than a week, Yvie discovered that she really didn't have to make an effort to like Pammy, she genuinely did. And judging by the way Pammy seemed to like Yvie's company, to actively seek it out, it seemed that the feeling was mutual. Yvie had had plenty of friends in her time, but none with whom she had hit it off so effortlessly, or so well, so quickly.

The best thing about the arrival of Pammy and Adam was the advent of a second car. And because Richard could give Adam a lift into work in the morning, it meant Pammy had access to Adam's MG. If Yvie didn't give a tuppenny hoot about Pammy's other talents, there was one thing about her that she did admire – her driving licence. Suddenly Yvie's life changed. Now trips to cities like Hamburg and Hanover were possible, there were outings to art galleries and places of interest, and for a while Yvie's life was transformed. Besides, Pammy had relentless energy and wouldn't allow Yvie to slack for a moment.

'But we're not here for long and who knows when we'll get the chance to visit this bit of Germany again,' she'd say as she dragged Yvie out to see yet another Schloss or visit some museum or local beauty spot. When they weren't out and about in the car, Pammy tried to teach Yvie how to cook in return for Yvie giving her lessons in drawing. Both attempts at swapping skills transpired to be lost causes from the outset, as Yvie and Pammy found that they spent far more time laughing and chatting than on the tasks in hand. Outwardly the pair were diametric opposites, the vicar's daughter and the punk rebel, but underneath they seemed to have more in common than Yvie and Laura: they had the same quick sense of humour, neither could cope with the wives who wore their husband's rank on their sleeve, both loathed dinner and cocktail parties, and they both loved reading. They spent their days popping in and out of each other's flats, sharing coffee and secrets. However, there was one thing that dovetailed with Pammy's 'vicar's daughter' image: she was kindness itself. Yvie only had to think of something that she might like or enjoy or need – a cutting off one of Pammy's plants, a trip to a gallery or a lift to the doctor, and Pammy made it happen. It almost got to the point when Yvie was afraid to mention anything. In hardly any time, Yvie found that she had the energy to achieve more in a day than she had in a week and with Pammy's firm and relentless encouragement she took up serious painting again. Then Pammy commissioned a watercolour of a local beauty spot, which Richard framed, and Yvie found herself inundated with orders from the other wives. Now she was earning money on top of having a much more fulfilling life. Things were great, life was good. Yvie should have known it couldn't last.

July 1987

It was in the summer, not long after their first wedding anniversary, that Richard came home and told Yvie that he had some bad news. An acquaintance of his – they had trained together – had been killed in Northern Ireland. As a result, Richard had been earmarked to replace him and he was being sent on a two-week training course. Provided he passed, he would go out to Ulster straight away. He was destined to be the new bomb disposal expert for Londonderry.

'Oh no,' said Yvie, feeling as though she had been punched.

'Sorry,' he said. He said it as though he meant it, like it was his fault that this had all happened. But there was a glint of excitement in his eyes which Yvie spotted.

'How long?'

'Till I go, or that I'll be there for?'

'Both, I suppose.'

'The course starts on Monday. If I pass, I'll go straight from the course to Londonderry, and I'll be there for four months at least.'

Yvie sat down. It was the sort of thing that she had known might happen, but she had never expected it to become a reality – like flying and ignoring the possibility of being involved in a plane crash. Richard had told her when he married her that being an expert in ammunition meant that he might be picked to be trained by the army to defuse terrorist bombs, but Yvie had chosen to disregard that piece of information. After all, bomb disposal experts were heroic types, and even though she loved Richard to bits, there was no way she could describe him as potential hero material.

And it didn't help matters that he was replacing someone who had been killed doing the job.

'Damn and blast!' she said under her breath.

'It's a great career opportunity for me,' he added.

'Great,' said Yvie tonelessly.

'You'll be all right. You've got Pammy and Adam to keep you company now.'

'Yes.' That was going to make all the difference to those months of lonely nights – knowing that there were a couple of lovebirds canoodling next door. But Yvie put a brave face on it. She could sense that Richard was really thrilled to have been picked for training, and she didn't want to rain on his parade.

They spent the weekend packing his kit and early on Sunday morning he flew out of Hanover to Luton to start his course at a place near Leamington Spa that Yvie had never heard of. After he had gone, Yvie paced around the empty quarter wondering if her husband was going to come back in one piece, and trying not to think too much about the sort of dangers he might have to face in the near future. When the day drew to a close, and she went to bed, she lay restlessly under the duvet for several hours until she finally drifted off into a fitful, troubled sleep. When she woke, she didn't feel as if she had had any rest at all.

It was at about ten that Pammy came round to ask Yvie how she felt.

'How do you think?' was the rather sharp retort.

'I'm sorry,' said Pammy, a little flustered.

'No, I'm sorry. I'm sorry I snapped. I had a lousy night and I feel dreadful.'

'You poor thing.'

'It's my own fault. I kept imagining the worst, things that'll probably never happen. Anyway,' said Yvie more brightly, 'he might fail the course and not be able to go to Ireland at all.'

'Is that likely?'

'No, if I'm honest. But I can hope.' Yvie knew that she wouldn't earn any points, let alone receive any sympathy, if she went around looking like a wet weekend. Plenty of wives in the garrison had had husbands go off to do dodgy jobs and had got on with life without complaining – well, not publicly anyway. Yvie knew that form required her to put on a brave face, so she did her best. She dickered with the thought of inviting Pammy in for a coffee. It would be company and

28

would keep her from brooding, but she wasn't sure she could cope with Pammy's relentless cheerfulness. Mostly she loved Pammy's bright optimism, but today it might prove to be too much. She decided not to. 'How about coming over to mine for lunch?' offered Pammy as soon as Yvie had plumped for solitude.

Yvie considered this invitation for a brief moment. Solitude was all very well, but she knew precisely what was in her fridge – the square root of bugger-all – so she either had no food and no company, or Pammy's cooking and Pammy's bounciness. The second option was more appealing even if she felt that, under the circumstances, Pammy's kindness might push her over the brink into self-pity. She'd just have to brace up, she told herself.

'I'd love to come over,' said Yvie. 'I shall really look forward to it.' Well, it was only a little lie.

Of course, after that day, Yvie became very adept at lies – most of them not so little, because that was when her affair with Adam began.

She was in Pammy's flat, leaning against the door of the tiny kitchen and sipping a gin and tonic while she watched her hostess put together a quiche – all hand-made, not even the pastry was bought – when the doorbell rang.

'Get that, would you,' said Pammy, her hands all floury.

Yvie put her drink down on the hall table and opened the door. Adam was on the doorstep looking white and strained.

'Hi Adam,' she said, but he walked past her as if he hadn't seen her. Yvie stared after him, puzzled. She heard Adam's voice, low and urgent, and wondered what the hell was going on. She was about to return to the kitchen to see what was up when she heard Pammy cry out. She dithered. All was certainly not well, but Yvie wasn't sure what the protocols were in these circumstances. Should she make sympathetic enquiries or wait till she was told? She picked up her drink and took a gulp.

'Yvie,' said Adam. 'It's Pammy's mum. She's had a stroke and has been rushed to hospital. Pammy has to go back to England straight away.'

Oh no, thought Yvie. 'Right,' she said, hoping she sounded calm. 'Right, what can I do?'

29

'Can you help her pack while I get things organized? RHQ were trying to sort out a flight when I left. There's one due to take off at three, they're trying to get her on that one. Can I borrow your phone to find out what's happening?'

'Of course.' Yvie handed Adam her house key and went to help Pammy, the half-made quiche forgotten and abandoned on the kitchen table.

It was about an hour later that Adam drove Pammy away to the airport. Yvie let herself out of her friends' flat and into her own. She sat on the sofa feeling utterly drained. Grief, she thought, even when it's not your own, is exhausting, and, coupled with the sleepless night she'd just had, she felt completely wiped. She rested her head on a cushion and allowed her eyes to shut.

When she woke she couldn't get her bearings for an instant. Then the bell rang – literally. Yvie stumbled off the sofa and went to open the door. Adam stood there.

'Hi,' she said, rubbing her eyes.

'I'm sorry, I woke you.'

''S all right,' mumbled Yvie through a half-stifled yawn, glancing at her watch. Six! 'Good thing you did. I won't sleep tonight as it is. Did Pammy get away OK?'

'We got stuck in traffic on the motorway but they held the flight for her – only a few minutes but it's things like that that really help in this situation.' Adam looked at his watch. 'It'll have landed a couple of hours ago, but by the time she makes it to where her mum lives . . . Well, I don't suppose I'll hear anything tonight.'

'She will ring here, won't she? I mean, I did tell her to.' It was times like this that made Yvie realize how useful it was to have a phone. And taking a phone call from Pammy was the least she could do under the circumstances.

'I should think so, unless it's really late.'

'Well, when she does phone, you must tell her that it doesn't matter what time it is another evening. She's to phone when she wants. I won't mind, honest. I mean, it isn't as if I ever have to get up early for anything important, is it?'

'Thanks, Yvie. You're a true friend.'

As he finished saying that, Yvie's stomach gave a loud rumble. Yvie felt herself colouring with embarrassment.

'Sorry,' she said sheepishly.

'Goodness, you sound hungry.'

'Well . . .' It seemed, under the circumstances, churlish to mention that her lunch – or the makings of it at any rate – were still sitting on Adam's kitchen table.

Adam banged his forehead with the palm of his hand. 'Of course you must be. God, I'm sorry.'

'Hey, this isn't your fault, and I was more than capable of finding something else to eat.'

'But you didn't.'

'To be honest, after Pammy went, I just sat on the sofa for five minutes and the next thing I knew, you were ringing my doorbell.'

'Look, why don't I make it up to you? I've a fridge full of food. How about I cook something and you share it with me?'

'Umm . . .' It was a lovely offer and there was no denying that she was starving, and that her fridge was still almost empty. 'It's just I'm expecting Richard to phone.'

'That's no problem. I'll cook the food but we can eat here.'

Yvie smiled happily. Problem solved.

As she tidied up the flat and laid the table, she opened a bottle of Moselle and poured herself a glass. By the time Adam arrived with steaks, salad and baked potatoes, Yvie was into her third glass. However, this time she told herself sternly that she was not to have any more. Adam could drink the rest. He plonked the food on to the dining-room table and then disappeared out again. A minute later he came back brandishing an open bottle of red.

'Not for me,' Yvie said firmly. 'I don't want to do a repeat performance.'

'Ah,' said Adam, remembering. 'Well, do you mind if I do?'

'Go ahead,' said Yvie as she cut into her steak and noted it was done to perfection. They ate in near silence, both ravenously hungry.

'Didn't you get lunch either?' asked Yvie through a mouthful of salad.

'I was stuck on the Autobahn, then I went straight back to work.'

They ate on, enjoying their supper. It wasn't long before they had both cleared their plates and lounged back in their chairs.

'Better?' asked Adam.

'Much. That was yummy. I wish Richard could cook like that.'

'There's nothing to cooking steaks.'

Maybe that was Adam's opinion, thought Yvie a little disloyally, but Richard would run a mile if anyone suggested he should go into the kitchen and perform some household task. Yvie cleared away the plates and went to make coffee. While she was waiting for it to boil, she ran some hot water into the sink and put the dirty crockery and cutlery in to soak.

'Let me do that,' said Adam from the doorway.

'Indeed not,' Yvie protested. 'You did all the cooking.'

'So?'

'So, it's not fair.' Before Adam could do anything, she pulled on a pair of Marigolds and plunged her hands into the water.

'God, you're so masterful,' said Adam with mock admiration.

'Artist, dominatrix, bored housewife, you name it – that's me.'

'Multi-talented, and such useful talents too. I particularly look forward to seeing how expert you are at the second one you mentioned.'

Laughing, Yvie threw a tea towel at him. He caught it deftly and came to stand by her at the sink. He was so close that she could feel his shirt brushing against her bare arm. A frisson of desire coursed from her chest to her groin. It was like an electric shock. Yvie was so stunned by the power of the sudden burst of feeling that she almost dropped the plate she was holding out to Adam. How had things gone from a little light flirting to this? She couldn't remember ever feeling such a rush generated by Richard. It was bizarre. To cover up her confusion she concentrated on scrubbing the next plate in the sink.

She supposed that it was the fact that she was scouring an already clean plate that made Adam stare at her closely – which only added to her confusion.

'What's the matter?' he asked.

'Nothing.' But she could feel colour flooding into her cheeks yet again and knew that he must notice too.

'You were joking, weren't you?' He sounded anxious, concerned.

'What?'

'About being a dominatrix.'

'Good God, yes.' She tried to make her answer sound light-hearted.

'Well, that's something.' Then he added, with a note of disappointment in his voice, 'Heigh-ho.'

His comment made her laugh and gave her a chance to recover her equilibrium.

On the worktop behind her, the kettle clicked off loudly. 'Make yourself useful and do the coffee,' she said. She directed him to the jar of instant and the mugs.

'Sugar?' asked Adam.

'Not for me. Sweet enough. And no milk either, thanks.' Back to light flirting mode.

'Glad to hear it.'

She fished the last bits out of the washing-up bowl, emptied out the water. As she turned round, peeling off her gloves, Adam was holding out her coffee. She knocked his arm and boiling hot coffee slopped everywhere.

'Shit!' he said as some landed on his foot. As he was only wearing a pair of sandals, there was every chance he was in danger of getting a nasty scald.

'Sorry.' She grabbed the mugs off him and shoved them on the work surface. Yet more coffee splattered on to the floor, but this time well away from the pair of them. 'Quick, get your shoe off. We must get some cold water on that right away.' She ran the cold tap into the washing-up bowl.

'Don't fuss,' said Adam. But she wasn't paying any attention. She turned off the tap, yanked the half-full bowl out of the sink, hooked a stool out from under the kitchen table with her foot and told him to sit on it, and then knelt down in front of him. Gingerly he put his foot in the icy water.

'God, first she tries to fry me, now she's freezing me,' mumbled Adam.

'Stop moaning. How does it feel?'

'Cold, what do you expect?'

'The scald, stupid.'

'I can't tell. It's numb with cold.'

She hauled his foot out of the water and had a look at it. She pushed it back in. It still looked pretty livid.

'A bit longer, I'm afraid.'

'How much?'

She shrugged.

'This is ridiculous,' said Adam after a minute or so of silence. 'There's no reason why we can't sit in comfort, drinking coffee, and I can pretend I'm paddling at the seaside.'

Yvie felt foolish. Why hadn't she thought of that? She carried the bowl through and Adam hobbled along behind. He plonked himself on the sofa and she put the water down in front of him. She crouched beside him on the floor.

'How does it feel now?' she asked anxiously.

'Better, honestly.'

'Sure?'

'Stop fussing.' He lifted his foot from the bowl and examined the mark on his skin. 'I don't think it's going to blister,' he pronounced after a pause.

Yvie had a look at it. 'Even so, I'll put some cream on it.' She got to her feet and went to the bathroom, where she knew there was a tube of Savlon in the medicine cupboard. It might not be absolutely the correct stuff to put on a burn, but she felt it would be better than nothing. She took it back to the sitting room and began to massage the soothing cream into the reddened skin of Adam's foot. Suddenly she became aware of his gaze. He was staring at her with an intensity that was quite disconcerting.

'What, have I got a mark on my face?' she said, trying to lighten things a little.

'No,' said Adam. 'Your face is perfect.' He reached out and touched it. Again Yvie felt a bolt of electricity run the length of her body. It was devastating. It seemed to squeeze every organ in her body and stop her from breathing properly.

'Adam . . .' she began. But then, and she had no idea which one of them had moved, they were in each other's arms and they fell sideways together to the floor in a frenzy of kissing. Yvie was swept away by his ardour. In the back of her mind she knew she was betraying both her husband and her new best friend, but the passion was so strong, the feelings so intense, she was unable to resist. It was as if she had spent the last three years of her life in a desert subsisting on brackish, warm water, and she had suddenly found a delicious, ice-

34

cold spring. So, this was what real passion was like. What she had experienced before was a two-dimensional sham, a cardboard cut-out of the real thing, or a dull ante-room that preceded a splendidly Baroque chamber of gilt and mirrors and chandeliers. What she had discovered, now that Adam had shown her the way, didn't diminish what she felt for Richard, it just made her realize that her feelings for him had nothing to do with this sort of love – this explosion of feeling and desire. When she and Richard kissed, it was comfortable, warm and pleasurable, not explosions, fireworks, and heart-stopping lust. She had read about the power of love, but had assumed it was more to do with the overactive fantasies of frustrated middle-aged romantic novelists than reality. But she had been wrong, so wrong.

Between kisses they pulled and tugged at each other's clothes and in minutes they were lying naked on the carpet. Their love-making was swift and explosively fulfilling. It was wild and animal and abandoned. They reached orgasm almost simultaneously, and within what seemed like moments, but the reality had involved a much longer time. Spent, glistening with sweat and panting, they lay on the floor looking at each other.

After several minutes, Yvie whispered, 'What have we done?'

Adam shook his head and pressed his finger to her lips. 'That was amazing. You . . .' He paused and breathed out slowly, smiling at her. '*You* were amazing. I had no idea it could be so good.'

'Me neither,' said Yvie, truthfully.

Adam rolled on his side so he could look at her more easily. 'But there is a problem. This has made life difficult.'

'We don't have to think about it this minute,' said Yvie. She didn't want anything to spoil the delicious aftermath. She reached her hand out and stroked his arm, wondering if she could summon the energy for more.

The phone rang. Yvie jumped and instantly she was engulfed by a feeling that the caller knew what she had been up to. Caught in the act, she thought, as she shot Adam a horrified look. He just shrugged. Suddenly conscious of her nakedness now that everyday life had re-established itself, she got up,

35

pulled on her knickers and threw her blouse around her shoulders. She grabbed the phone.

'Pammy,' she said brightly on hearing who the caller was. She felt her face flood with colour as guilt and embarrassment in equal measures took her over completely. Adam signalled frantically not to let on he was in the room.

'No, of course you didn't disturb me. I just had a bite to eat.' Adam made a lewd gesture. She turned away, angry with him that he could make light of what they had just experienced together, and angry that he was trying to make her laugh in such a serious situation. 'Did you get home OK? Good. And your mother? Right, no, well, it is a bit late to visit, but at least you got there bef—' She stopped short. How crass was she about to be there? 'Do you want me to get Adam? No? Well, I'll tell him when I see him that you're home safe and sound. Will do, and love to you too. Bye.' She banged the receiver down and rounded on Adam. 'How could you try to make me laugh? I was on the phone to your *wife*, for heaven's sake.'

Adam grinned sheepishly. 'But she won't know.'

'But I *do*. I feel a heel.' The atmosphere altered perceptibly. A silence followed. Yvie was ashamed of herself. She had betrayed her new friend – a friend who was away due to a family tragedy. How low could you go, she wondered. Very, was the answer that sprang to mind. She felt disgusted with herself, but Adam had been horsing around, for God's sake. How could he make light of things? They had committed adultery, and not just with anyone – with their best friend's spouses. Hell, thought Yvie, as all the implications and complications suddenly became apparent.

'Hey, come here,' said Adam. Yvie shook her head. 'You were out of this world. You know that, don't you? I don't want to make comparisons, it wouldn't be fair, but you were sublime.'

Yvie felt surprisingly shy. She gave a small shrug, but she stayed out of reach.

'We were right together,' said Adam. 'It can't be bad when something feels that good. And we were obviously meant for each other.' He smiled, trying to reassure Yvie. 'Hey, just look at how well our names go together.'

Yvie wasn't going to deny that. And the sex had been electric, mind-blowing, a quantum leap from the sex she'd had with Richard, but now she wondered if the extra frisson had been provided by its illicitness.

And it didn't alter the enormity of what she'd just done. But neither did it prevent her from repeating the act again and again over the next weeks.

The affair was easy to continue. The other dwellers in the flats were all Germans, and neither Yvie nor Adam knew their neighbours at all. Visitors from the garrison were almost non-existent, and those who did venture out were invariably the wives, who tended to call around coffee time, when Adam was at work. There was no one to see which front door Adam and Yvie happened to be using, no one to witness their comings and goings. It was as easy as if they were both still single and available – a fact that they both sometimes forgot wasn't the case. And although they both knew it couldn't go on, they both ignored the issue that their affair inevitably would have to end one day, or both their marriages would. It was certainly easier to ignore the problem than to address it.

Pammy did not return to Adam for several weeks after her precipitate departure. Then, finally, her mother stabilized, was out of danger and was embarking on the long, slow process of rehabilitation. There was little Pammy could do: her mother's recovery was down to time, the healing process and regular physiotherapy. She was in a special unit of the hospital receiving the long-term care she would need for the foreseeable future. It was time for Pammy to go back to Adam.

'So where do we go from here?' Yvie asked Adam the evening before his wife returned.

Adam had sighed. 'It's not that easy, Yvie.'

Yvie had thought that it was. She had made her mind up. She would leave Richard, Adam would leave Pammy, there would be hurt and recriminations all round, but eventually things would settle down again.

'Why not?' She couldn't see the problem.

'I can't leave Pammy right now. Her mother . . . She and Pammy were – *are* – very close. With her mother being so ill, I can't make things worse for her. It wouldn't be fair.'

37

Yvie held her tongue about the unfairness to her.

'But suppose her mother gets better?'

'We'll see.'

Or supposing her mother dies, thought Yvie, but she couldn't say that. She wondered if Adam was thinking the same thing. It was Yvie's turn to sigh. She thought about being more assertive. Should she scream and shout and insist? Should she take a leaf from the book of *Fatal Attraction*? But it wasn't her nature and she wasn't going to demean herself by begging.

'So that's it then. The end of a beautiful friendship.'

'No, it needn't come to that. I'm sure we can still find ways to be together.'

Yvie rolled over on her side and curled up. What she was being offered was the proverbial half loaf. Was that better than the alternative? She knew that if Adam wasn't going to leave Pammy for her, all it was doing was delaying the moment when they would have to give each other up. They might be able to find time to be together with only Pammy on the scene, but when Richard came back too . . . Was that what she wanted – a stay of execution? She lay under the rumpled covers, thoughts tumbling through her head. It was one thing carrying on an adulterous affair when she didn't have to look her lover's wife in the eye each day, but she felt it might be quite different when Pammy was back, living next door. Was she really going to be capable of deceiving her best friend on a constant basis? Could she really live a lie, day in, day out? Could she be that devious? Did she love Adam enough to try? The answer to the last question was yes, she knew that for certain. What she didn't know for certain was if she could carry out the other strategies.

She decided that if she wanted Adam, then she would have to try, and if she failed . . . . If she failed, then Pammy would find out. She considered the prospect. She didn't want that. Yes, she wanted Adam, but not at the expense of other people's happiness. She decided she'd just have to try bloody hard.

Her thoughts were interrupted by the shrill warble of the telephone. She swung her feet out of bed and went to the sitting room to answer it.

'Have you managed to catch the news today?' said Richard without preamble.

'No.' No, darling, actually I've been in bed making love to your best friend. 'Why, should I have?'

'I'm on it.'

'No! Why?'

'Well, you won't recognize me. I'm all togged up in my bomb suit and helmet, but there's a shot of me walking in front of the law courts to deal with a car bomb.'

'Goodness, I'll have to watch.' Yvie checked her watch. 'I've missed the early-evening news. I'll catch it on the nine o'clock – assuming it's not been dumped for a more important story.'

'More important? I don't think so.'

'My hero,' said Yvie.

'So, what are you up to this evening?'

'Oh, you know. This and that.'

'Sounds fun.'

'Yes, well . . .' She could hardly tell him that the sex had been, but the post-coital talk with Adam hadn't. God, she was such a cow, she told herself. There was her husband risking life and limb – literally – defusing bombs in Ireland, and she was rolling around in bed with his best mate.

'Right, well, I'd better go. There's a queue for the phone. I'll talk to you again soon.'

'OK. Take care now.'

'I will. Love you.'

'Love you too.' And as she put the phone down she wondered if she really did. Surely, if she did, she wouldn't be having an affair?

When Pammy arrived back, Yvie tried to act as if nothing had happened during her friend's absence. She thought it would be incredibly difficult, but from the beginning the lying proved remarkably easy. Pammy asked about how Yvie had spent her days, which had reverted to hours of stultifying boredom relieved only by bursts of housework or painting. Yvie was able to tell Pammy with absolute honesty that most days very little had happened. Fairly naturally, Pammy didn't enquire about Yvie's nights, so she was spared having to lie through her teeth about them. But then Pammy insisted that Yvie spent time with them in the evenings, that she should come across to their flat and have a drink or supper rather than sit on her own and brood. Yvie's excuse that she wouldn't hear the phone was solved by the simple expedient of propping open both front doors. These times, Yvie decided, were her penance for her adultery, for now she could talk to Adam, smile at him, share a joke with him, but she couldn't hold him or kiss him or tell him how she felt while she had to watch Pammy doing just that. Frequently she would find that something that Adam said or did, a mannerism, a gesture, would send her into a reminiscence about the time they had spent together. At other times she would be suddenly overwhelmed by a feeling of absolute raw lust for her lover, to the extent that she found it hard to breathe. Unsurprisingly, both Pammy and Adam noticed her odd behaviour. She passed it off with excuses about missing Richard, and worries about his well-being, which Pammy accepted happily enough. But Adam guessed what was going on in her thoughts and, whenever the opportunity arose, he would let his skin touch hers, he would brush past her in doorways, would hold her hand for longer than was necessary when saying hello or goodbye. And Yvie would ache for him even more, and return to her lonely bed, where her hands would steal under her nightie until she found some sort of relief, but even then she would lie awake for hours trying to recall every moment she had spent with Adam, in case she forgot some of their precious shared hours.

Pammy noticed that Yvie wasn't her usual self, that she looked exhausted and thin.

'Do you want to talk?' she offered about a week after her return.

For a wild moment Yvie thought about telling her neighbour what the matter really was. Instead she made up a lie about finding it difficult to sleep in an empty house. Naturally Pammy was sympathetic and offered Yvie all manner of strategies that might help her to banish her fears, until Yvie was at screaming pitch and wanted to yell at her friend to shut up.

Her only solace was her telephone, which allowed her the occasional call to Adam in his office. Sometimes he couldn't talk, as there was somebody there with him, and she would replace the receiver almost crying with frustration, but at other times he was able to tell her what she meant to him, to reassure her that he thought of her as often as she did of him, and to keep her hopes alive that there was just the slightest possibility that he would leave Pammy for her.

It was about three weeks after Pammy's return that Adam came home with good news. The education centre wanted someone to teach conversational French and German to beginners on three evenings a week. Pammy jumped at the chance of some paid employment and relayed the news to Yvie.

'That's wonderful!' said Yvie excitedly, instantly realizing the implications of Pammy's future regular absences. 'When do you start?'

'They want me immediately.'

'But that's fabulous.'

'I know. I'm so looking forward to doing some teaching again. And best of all, because it's just evenings, it means we can still go out together in the day.'

Yvie didn't tell her about the other, even better reason she was excited about her friend's success in the job market.

Thus, on Mondays, Wednesdays and Thursdays Pammy left the flat at seven and returned at ten, giving Adam and Yvie more than enough time for whatever congress they chose to indulge in. But despite the rekindling of the physical side of their affair, it dawned on Yvie that that was all it was ever going to be. Whenever she even got close to broaching the subject of their future, Adam veered away from it. He loved her, or rather he loved the sex with her, that was not in doubt, but he didn't love her – or the sex – enough to leave Pammy. And as Yvie wasn't the sort of woman who could wreck lives for her own selfish ends, she knew that their affair was doomed to peter out when one or other of them was posted.

It was in November that Richard phoned with news of a move.

'I'm being sent straight back to Aldershot at the end of this tour. I'm to take over the bomb disposal detachment there.'

'That's awful,' said Yvie, assuming that it meant yet more separation, although her heart leapt at the thought of more months with Adam.

'No, you've got it wrong. It's great. It's a bit of a feather in my cap and I'm assured there's no waiting list for quarters.'

41

'Oh.' Yvie prayed to God that the disappointment in her voice was lost over the thousand miles of the phone link.

She told Adam the news the next time Pammy was teaching at the education centre. Yvie wanted to end the affair that night, but Adam persuaded her to see how things went. Yvie didn't really see the point. Their affair was coming to the end of its natural life – what was to be gained from trying to prolong it? His argument was that the adult education term only had a few more weeks to run, so they might as well make the most of the opportunity.

She spent Christmas with Adam and Pammy. She thought it would be an effort to appear to be excited at being reunited with Richard, but she found to her surprise that she really was. She also discovered that the prospect of never sleeping with Adam again wasn't as painful as she had expected it to be. Obviously it was time to move on.

In the New Year, she packed up the quarter and cleaned it to military standard. The activity kept her mind from dwelling too much on her reunion with her husband and her guilty thoughts about the past months. Would he notice any changes in her? Would she be able to keep her secret? Would he guess? And supposing he did? God, if he did, the fall-out would be appalling.

Pammy offered to help with the process of cleaning and packing. 'Many hands and all that.'

'I couldn't possibly let you. I won't be here to repay the favour when you go. Besides which, there's only me to clean up after. There isn't that much to do. God knows how women with kids cope, though.' Her refusal of help wasn't entirely down to the reasons she gave. She had another, very good reason for not wanting Pammy to help her dig out her flat – it was just possible that there might be some overlooked clues to the amount of time Adam had spent there, and she didn't want Pammy to stumble over them. The decent, moral bit of her knew that her relationship with Adam was about to sink without trace, but it wouldn't be right to take Pammy's relationship with him down too.

And when it came down to it, there was really very little to do. The packing was minimal. Apart from Yvie's painting equipment, a few books and stuff like bedding and towels, there was hardly anything to pack other than their clothes. Yvie looked at the handful of tea chests that she had filled, and thought that it wasn't much to show for her time in Bad Mannheim. In fact, as she looked around, the flat didn't look much different with all their possessions removed than it did with them there. Not much of a homemaker, are you, she told herself. Not like Pammy, with all the little touches she'd added to her flat to make it homely and welcoming. She would do better next time, she promised herself.

Adam drove her to the airport at Pammy's suggestion. Yvie was silent for most of the journey, letting her thoughts range back over the past months. She had enough maturity to look back over everything with dispassion. She had known from quite early on that the mad rush of emotion she had felt at the start had not been the sort of love that lasts for a lifetime. Passionate yes, explosive and exciting certainly, but not the sort of love cut out for the long haul. There had been an amazing physical attraction, but that had been all. Now, part of her wondered too if that attraction hadn't been fuelled by the fact that it was so very wrong. Had they wanted each other so badly because they shouldn't have an affair? The sex had been fantastic, there was no denying that, but really that was all their affair had been about. Then, when Pammy had returned and the dynamics of their relationship had changed, she knew that Adam felt much the same. The realization had been slow but it had not been painful, and now, in some respects, it was almost a relief that it was over. No more dissembling, no more lying, no more guilt. Yes, Yvie admitted to herself finally, yes, she was glad that it had come to an end. A tidy end too, with no rows, no recriminations, so even more reason to be grown-up about it all.

'So, it's goodbye then,' she said, her voice unemotional.

'That sounds so final,' said Adam. 'We'll see each other again, surely.'

'When?' But inside she was thinking, why? If they did meet up again, they would be accompanied by their spouses. There would be no opportunity for any sort of intimacy. Without sex there was nothing else, so what would be the point?

Adam unloaded her cases out of the boot and gave her a hug. Kissing was out – it might be a busy international airport but it was also a main one for air trooping, so goodness only knew who might spot them.

'It was wonderful,' he said, his hands on her shoulders. 'Richard is a lucky man.'

'And Pammy is a lucky woman.' She removed his hands gently. 'People might see us.'

'I love you, you know.'

'No you don't. You loved the sex. You were fond of me, but it's Pammy you love.'

'And is that all you feel for me?'

Yvie nodded. She noticed Adam hadn't denied what she had said.

'Perhaps one day . . .'

Yvie shook her head. 'No. I don't think so.'

Adam looked at her. 'Don't you want it?'

'Not now, no,' she said wearily. 'I think it's better if it all ends now.'

'Perhaps you're right,' he said.

Yvie thought she detected a flicker of relief on his face too.

Despite the fact that she was returning to England to be reunited with her husband, she felt quite morose. Morose and more than a little guilty. What about those wedding vows, all that stuff about forsaking all others? She decided on one thing though before the plane even took off from the tarmac at Hanover: whatever had happened in Germany was going to stay in Germany. She was not going to unburden herself on Richard. He need never know about what had happened. If she didn't tell him, then who would? As far as she knew, no one at all was aware of anything going on between her and Adam.

Having made that promise to herself, she then expected to be able to put her affair with Adam into a little mental box and forget about it. But it wasn't as easy as that, and by the time she stepped off the plane at Luton, her mind was still locked in thoughts and memories about her affair. She was looking forward to seeing Richard again, she knew she loved him, and part of her had missed him, but she was miserable at losing Adam. Adam had been such a dynamic part of her life for so many weeks. She knew that she was going to miss

44

desperately their wild hours of love-making, and that she wasn't going to be able to consign it to the past as easily as she had hoped, she would always have the guilt to contend with, and the memories, but she also knew that Richard was the man for her, even though it lacked the glamour and the pizzazz of her fling with Adam. What she had with Richard was the equivalent of a pair of comfortable loafers – she could slip in and out of it with ease, it didn't chaff or irritate, it just felt right. Her affair with Adam had been like a pair of high-fashion designer shoes with killer heels – a great wow factor but not good for the long haul. No, definitely not the love of her life. But she was still going to miss him. She knew she was still going to think about him when she and Richard were together, and she knew she was going to feel guilty for the rest of her life about ever having started the affair in the first place. But, as she picked up her case off the carousel and made her way through customs and out into the arrivals hall, she fixed a smile to her face and determined that Richard was never going to find out.

February 1988

A s soon as she had got the quarter sorted out, Yvie resolved to make some changes to her life. If nothing else, she wanted to keep busy to help her blot out the hole that the end of her affair was going to leave in her life. The less time she had to think and brood the better. For a start she decided to get a job, anything, something, as long as it gave her something to do every day. Secondly she decided to do more painting and to try to make some money from it, and lastly she was going to make a real effort with her new home. Perhaps not quite as much as Pammy had been wont to, but at least she would get in some plants and ornaments and make it a bit more personal. She hit the ground running as soon as she and Richard had settled into their new home, and Richard was both surprised and delighted with his wife's new-found energy.

'I was worried about leaving you in Germany when I went to Ireland. All alone in that flat with nothing to keep you out of mischief,' he confided in her one Sunday morning in bed after a marathon love-making session.

Yvie felt her chest constrict with guilt as she wondered if this was the precursor to him telling her that he'd guessed about her and Adam. 'Really?' she said, hoping her voice sounded normal.

'I thought you'd get even more bored. I know you had Pammy for company some of the time, but you sort of gave up on life, didn't you?'

'Hmm,' said Yvie, thinking that he didn't know the half of what had been going on. 'Well, there wasn't much to do in Bad Mannheim, was there?'

'No, maybe not. But you've got it all sorted out now you're back here, haven't you?'

'Speaking the same language as all one's neighbours is a

help.' Now that Yvie was certain that Richard was just chatting and not leading up to something, she turned towards him and snuggled against him. 'I'm going job-hunting next week.' 'Really? That's great. Actually, we could do with the extra cash. Now we've lost my overseas allowance, it's made quite a difference to my pay.'

'So you want me to cut down on the champagne and caviar?'

'Oh, I don't think things are that bad,' said Richard with a grin, stroking Yvie's nose.

'Phew, that's a relief.'

'So, what sort of job are you after?'

'I haven't a clue. I'd like to use my degree but I don't know what there is around here. Aldershot, "Home of the British Army", doesn't sound as though it's going to be home to aspiring British artists as well.'

'Put like that . . .'

'Still, there are plenty of other places round and about that I can get to easily. I expect somewhere like Guildford might have an opening for a fine arts graduate in need of a job.'

'You need to learn to drive if you're serious.'

Yvie considered this. 'Let's see if I land a job first. I'm sure I can cope with the buses for a bit.'

Over the next couple of weeks, Yvie was in a frenzy of job-hunting, home-making, painting, shopping and interior decorating. She packed more into a month than she had into a year in Germany. She went to the wives' coffee morning on the patch and got to know her neighbours, most of whom she liked but some she didn't, and discovered that most of the other wives worked; those without kids did supply teaching or agency nursing or other temporary jobs, while those with kids seemed to sell Usborne books or Cabouchon jewellery. It transpired that, but for a very few, very determined wives, to have a career and be married to a soldier was not an option. There were one or two wives driven enough to buck the trend, but the consensus of opinion was that they would either lose their husband or lose out in the long run on their hoped-for career path. Constant postings meant that it was nigh on impossible to dovetail the two ways of life together. Bearing that information in mind, Yvie lowered her sights a bit when she scanned the 'sits vac' column of the local paper. Anyway, she reasoned, she could still carry on painting in her own time and try to sell a few pictures via local galleries for extra pin money. Much as she had visions of being the next Bridget Riley, she knew in her heart that it was unlikely.

It was in mid-February she landed a job at a small art shop in Farnham, a nearby town. It was perfect, and although the pay wasn't brilliant, she knew she would enjoy it.

'The owner's called Miles,' she told Richard. 'And I'm sure he's gay.'

Richard looked horrified.

'Oh, come on,' said Yvie. 'Some people are, you know.'

'Not in the army,' he said forcefully.

'You don't approve,' said Yvie, grinning on discovering a side of her husband she hadn't known about.

'Of course I bloody don't. Raging bum-bandits!' This was said with real anger, which surprised Yvie. She had felt her husband was more liberal than that.

'Oh, lighten up. I'm sure Miles won't fancy you.'

Richard gave a snort of disapproval.

'For heaven's sake,' said Yvie, beginning to lose patience with his prejudice. 'What is it to you anyway?'

'It's not natural.'

'Of course it is. You're just brainwashed by the army.'

Richard shrugged. 'There's one good thing though. If he is queer, he won't be making a pass at you.'

'I could try and convert him,' said Yvie mischievously.

'Don't you even think about it. Anyway, he's probably got AIDS.'

'I doubt it. Just because one or two gay people have got it, doesn't mean they all have. I expect the stories we hear about it on the news are all wildly exaggerated.'

'Just you make sure you don't let him touch you.'

'Come on now.'

'I mean it.'

Yvie was startled. He sounded suddenly fierce. His prejudice, which had seemed amusing, began to annoy her. She decided not to say anything else on the subject, so that it would be dropped. She'd had loads of male friends at uni who hadn't been interested in girls. Everyone had known they were homosexual but no one cared. What they did for kicks was their affair. Why did the army get so uptight about it? Did Richard really feel that way, or was there some reason from his past for this ridiculous reaction – after all, he had been to public school. Perhaps stories of young boys getting buggered senseless by the prefects weren't as exaggerated as she had always assumed. There were some things about her husband that she was never going to get, she thought. But then she remembered that there were some things about herself that she wasn't going to share either.

Yvie loved her job and settled into it quickly and easily. Miles was undemanding, the customers were invariably pleasant and the work was enjoyable. It was about a fortnight after she had started work that she was downing her tea before belting out to get the bus, when she knew without a shadow of a doubt that she was going to be sick. She hurtled into the downstairs lav just in time to lose her early morning cuppa. Feeling slightly shaky but undeniably better, she rinsed her mouth out with cold water and wondered vaguely what the cause was. At least, she thought, she couldn't be sick again. She had nothing else to bring up.

On the journey to work the bus ground and bounced its way over the badly surfaced roads between Aldershot and Farnham. Every time the bus hit a particularly bad stretch, Yvie was aware that her breasts ached horribly. And in a deep recess of her mind she remembered Laura complaining that she knew she was pregnant with number three because her 'boobs ached like hell, the same as they did the other twice'.

'Shit,' said Yvie under her breath. Pregnant? Well, it was a distinct possibility. Scary or what? She got out her diary and began flicking the pages, trying to remember when her last period had been. For a couple of minutes, panic gripped her and she stopped thinking rationally. What if she was pregnant with Adam's baby? A cold sliver of fear raced through her body. Surely she couldn't be. She flicked through her diary faster. God, if only she had regular periods like other women did. Then she remembered. Yes, she'd had a period about four weeks ago, because she had been going swimming with Richard and had discovered she'd started as she was changing. So it was still possible that whatever was wrong with her was nothing to do with being pregnant. But then again . . .

49

And it hadn't been much of a period. Nothing much at all really, so had it been a proper period? Surely sickness didn't set in so quickly. Could it be Adam's if her worst fears were realized? The worry reasserted itself. She wished she knew more about pregnancy. What would she do if she found out her dates were up the spout? And what if the baby looked like Adam? God, it didn't bear thinking about. She told herself to calm down, that she might just be ill, but she had to clasp her hands together to stop them from shaking. She'd buy a testing kit in her lunch hour and try and find a book on the subject. There was no point in worrying if she only had a bug.

Her sensible advice to herself had no effect at all, and she was still thrashing everything around mentally as she got off the bus and made her way to the shop. The owner was already there. Letting herself in, she greeted him as cheerfully as she could and tried to banish her worries.

'You're deep in thought, ducky,' said Miles later on that morning, for, no matter how hard Yvie tried, her thoughts kept straying back to the matter that was really bugging her.

'It's nothing, honest.'

'You sure? I thought you looked a bit peaky when you came in earlier. I thought, that girl's not well. I thought, should she be at work? But then, you're not a child and you don't want an old man like me fussing and flapping over you.'

'You, old?' said Yvie, feigning incredulity, as if the fact that he was nearly twice her age had never crossed her mind. 'I bet you go to that disco in Camberley dressed as a punk and pogo with the best of them. Or is new romantic more your style?'

'Don't change the subject,' said Miles, trying to sound stern.

'OK, I did feel a bit off colour first thing this morning. But I'm much better now thanks.'

Miles raised an eyebrow.

'Really, I'm fine.'

'Off colour? In the morning?'

'Please don't even think it,' said Yvie with a note of warning in her voice.

'Well . . .' said Miles raising the other eyebrow.

Before Yvie could think of a suitable put-down, a customer came into the shop for some Daler board and Yvie went to serve. But Miles's reaction just seemed to underline her own suspicions. She decided to go to the chemist in her lunch hour.

The next morning, Yvie sat on the loo seat and stared at the blue line on the little white stick she held in her hand. She sighed. She felt she ought to be pleased. She knew there were countless women who would give their back teeth for a positive pregnancy test. But . . . there was still the scary possibility that it might not be Richard's. She'd glanced at a baby book in the bookshop and discovered two things: the onset of morning sickness varied and it appeared she could easily bleed after falling pregnant, so she was still no wiser than she had been. As she sat on the loo she sighed again. What a mess she was in. Quite apart from feeling completely daunted by the idea of motherhood, she was in turmoil that a minute cluster of cells might be about to reveal her adultery. For a mad moment she wondered if she could keep it quiet and nip off and get an abortion? Richard need never know. But then, she thought, it's a life. So this was payback time. This was her penance.

A bout of nausea swept over her and she threw herself sideways off the loo and wrenched the lid up just in time. Despite the violence of the bout, all she produced was a tablespoon of foul-tasting yellow bile. She sank back on her haunches feeling washed out. She was just about to tidy herself up and put on a brave face when Richard barged into the bathroom. In one glance he took in his wife, white and shaky, hunched by the loo, and the empty box that had contained the home testing kit, which was still on the windowsill.

'Yvie?' he said tentatively.

Yvie nodded before another wave of nausea overcame her and left her coughing and spluttering down the pan again.

'Are you sure?' said Richard when she surfaced for air again.

'Fairly,' said Yvie, spitting the taste out of her mouth. Richard filled a beaker of water for her so she could rinse her mouth out.

'But that's fantastic news! Oh, Yvie, how wonderful.'

'Yeah, well. It doesn't feel so wonderful right at this minute,' said Yvie tiredly as she struggled to her feet.

51

'No. Poor you. Why don't you go back to bed and I'll bring you a cup of tea.'

'No time. I'll miss the bus.'

'But you can't go in to work. Not in your condition.' Richard sounded horrified.

'I'm pregnant, not diseased. Of course I can go in to work.'

'But is it wise?'

'Richard, I'm not ill. It's a perfectly normal state for a woman to be in. I want to go to work.' Yvie thought that, if she went to work, it might also take her mind off how bloody awful she felt.

Richard still looked worried and sceptical. 'If you're sure,' he said, making it obvious that he didn't think she ought to be. Yvie shook her head, too washed out to find the strength to argue, and went to find some clothes for work. Behind her, Richard was grinning fit to bust.

Claire was born in October, three weeks prematurely, but weighing in at a reasonable six and a half pounds.

'Thank God I didn't go to term,' said Yvie, exhausted but buoyed up with elation and pethedine, when the midwife told her the weight. 'Think what a monster I would have had to push out!'

'Well, this is no monster,' said Richard, besotted with his new daughter and watching the midwife's ministrations to her like a hawk.

The midwife finished wiping down the newborn, put a nappy on her and then wrapped the baby in a flannelette sheet. Usually she handed the baby to the mother at this stage, but Richard looked so eager and anxious she put Claire in his arms instead.

'She's the image of you,' he said to Yvie. He bent down beside the bed so she could see her baby's face. As Claire was decidedly red and wrinkled and more than a little squashed-looking, Yvie – even in the proud throes of new motherhood – could only see a resemblance to a prune.

'How on earth can you think that?'

'Oh, but she does.'

And in the ensuing days, as a steady stream of visitors dropped by to admire the baby and congratulate Yvie, they all said that there was absolutely no doubt as to who the baby's mother was.

'So, apart from Adam and Laura, who else shall we have as a godparent?' asked Richard a few weeks later, as he idly played with Claire, lying on a rug in front of the gas fire. 'Oh.' Yvie hadn't thought about having Claire christened. And Richard's suggestion of having Adam as a godfather for Claire was distinctly unwelcome. Yvie had hoped that distance and time would allow the friendship to tail off. For her own selfish reasons, she didn't want it to continue. She didn't want reminders of her affair, her betrayal of her husband and her best friend, nor did she want the effort and responsibility of lying continuously. An occasional letter or phone call would be easy enough to cope with, but visits? Visits would be another matter entirely. And if Adam was Claire's godfather, then he and Pammy would be obliged to come to the christening, and she and Richard would be obliged to have them to stay. It just got worse and worse!

'Well, we'll have to think about it,' she said. She wondered if she would be able to talk him out of the whole idea, but she suspected that being the dyed-in-the-wool traditionalist that he was, she had no chance.

March 1989

'What is the matter with you?' Richard asked Yvie with barely concealed irritation. She was standing by the window, Claire on her hip, ignoring the room full of guests. 'I'm just tired, that's all. This reception didn't happen all by itself, you know. You try making a buffet for twenty people, as well as looking after a baby. I don't have a magic wand.'

Instantly Richard was contrite. 'I'm sorry, sweetie,' he said. 'You just look as though you're not enjoying yourself, and even my mother has noticed. Let me take the baby and you go and get a glass of champagne and circulate.'

Yvie forced a smile. Circulating wasn't what she wanted to do. Circulating would involve chatting to Claire's god-parents and she really didn't want to have a one-to-one with Adam. In the past few weeks, there had been a number of phone calls from Adam at times when he knew Richard would be at work. His excuses for ringing had been various: he'd needed directions; he'd wanted to know what to get Claire as a christening present; he'd wanted to check timings; he'd needed to know what he and Pammy should wear. And then there had been the way he'd stared at her in the church. Yvie had been terrified that someone else would notice, but luck-ily most eyes had been fixed on Claire. However, the last thing Yvie wanted now was Adam's company. She needed a reason to be excused circulating duties.

'Tell you what, I'll get some bubbly when I've changed Claire, I'm sure she needs a clean nappy. Then I think it'll be time to cut the cake and to drink her health. Give us five minutes and then you can get those bits organized. It might be an idea to get another couple of bottles opened. Unless, of course, you want to change Claire yourself.' She smiled at Richard, who she knew would rather have his fingernails ripped out than change a nappy. New man he was not.

'OK, sweetie.' Richard smiled at his wife and daughter indulgently. Yvie escaped upstairs. Great, she thought, Adam avoided for another few minutes.

Upstairs in the nursery she swiftly changed the offending nappy. Then she fiddled and faffed, playing peek-a-boo with Claire, tidying some of her clothes, anything to waste more time. However, it was inevitable that she would run out of things to do, and when she heard footsteps on the stairs, she guiltily picked up her daughter and made to look as though she was on her way down. Richard was, no doubt, coming to find out why on earth she was taking so long.

'Yvie,' said a familiar voice from the door of the nursery. Adam. Yvie felt a frisson of some sort of emotion pass through her. Guilt, she thought. And apprehension that if they were seen together, away from the party, Pammy or Richard might 'do the sum'. This was the confrontation she had been dreading. Perhaps 'confrontation' was putting it a bit strong – encounter might be more appropriate. Either way, in the last few weeks, she had spent countless hours going over how she should behave, what she ought to say. She hoped to God that she would stick to the script she had tried to drill into herself. Now was not the moment to show any signs of weakness, particularly as she didn't want to give any suggestion whatsoever that he had any cause to hope that their affair had a chance of resuming – ever.

She tried to sound nonchalant as she turned to face him. 'Hi. Have you come to see your god-daughter?'

'Not really. It's you I want to talk to.'

Yvie shifted Claire on her hip. 'Do you now? It's not a good idea.' Cool, calm.

'Yvie, what happened—'

She interrupted him smoothly. 'What happened is over, in the past, and that's where it's going to stay.'

Adam looked disappointed. 'But—'

'But nothing,' interrupted Yvie again. 'What happened never should have done. And now I've got Claire, there's a whole different set of rules I have to play by.'

'I thought you loved me,' said Adam with a hint of sulkiness in his voice.

'I was head-over-heels – now I'm not,' she said levelly.

'I had hoped—'

'Don't.' Brutal. Then she relented a fraction. 'Don't, there's no point. It really is over and I'm not going to change my mind.' She stared at him, willing him to believe her.

'I'll persuade you to come back to me one day.'

'Don't be so silly.' She dismissed this notion completely. How stupid was he being? Anyway, she'd had enough of this conversation and she'd made her point. She was afraid he'd start arguing, getting unreasonable. She couldn't cope if that happened. And what if Richard made an appearance? 'Look, make yourself useful. Take your god-daughter downstairs. Tell Richard I'll just be a couple of minutes.' She thrust Claire into his arms. He looked terrified.

'What if I drop her?'

'You won't. Go on, I've got to have a wee. I'll be down in two ticks.' And, leaving Adam with no chance to argue, Yvie dodged past him to the loo and shut the door.

By the time she returned to the party, Adam was in the centre of a crowd and looking much more relaxed as he showed his god-daughter off to her admirers. At least it had distracted him from his apparent obsession with her. When they'd parted in Germany they'd both agreed it was for the best. Now it seemed he had changed his mind. Why? Yvie wondered if it was because the arrival of Claire had made her more inaccessible. Was that it? Was he like some sort of spoilt kid who only wanted the things he really couldn't have?

Pammy was standing on the edge of the group with a strained smile on her face.

'Hi, Pammy. I've hardly had a chance to talk to you yet.'

'You've been busy. Delicious food, by the way.'

'All simple stuff. I just make sure every recipe is full of cream and eggs – that way, even if it goes a bit wrong it'll still taste scrummy.'

'Good idea.' Pammy's gaze drifted back to Adam and Claire. 'He'd make a great dad, wouldn't he?'

Yvie was caught on the hop by this statement. She'd only ever thought of Adam in the role of 'lover' and not as 'family man'.

'Umm, yes, I suppose so.'

There was a silence. Yvie glanced at Pammy and saw that her eyes were suspiciously damp. 'Pammy, is there a problem?'

Pammy shook her head and forced a smile. 'No, no. What ever gave you that idea?'

Even a halfwit wouldn't be taken in by that false tone, thought Yvie. She wondered about pressing the matter, but perhaps this wasn't the time or the place. Anyway, even if she had wanted to pursue Pammy's problem further, she wouldn't have been able to, as Richard called for a toast to be drunk to Claire's health. After everyone's glasses had been raised and the baby duly toasted, Yvie noticed that Pammy had slipped out of the room. She was about to follow her when Laura cornered her.

'You've done all right for yourself, haven't you?'

Yvie suspected that Laura had had an unwise amount of champagne. 'How do you mean?'

'This house.' Laura made an expansive gesture and wobbled alarmingly on her stilettos. 'Everything.'

'But it's not mine. We only rent it. We don't even own most of the furniture.'

'Yeah well, it's still bigger than the poxy little box Mick and I have.'

'But it's not a poxy box, and it's yours. I'd give my eye teeth to get on the property ladder, but what chance have we got, moving every couple of years? Besides which, even if we wanted to buy, have you seen what property prices are like round here?'

'It's still not fair.'

Yvie was beginning to run out of patience. Her sister had made her bed and now she must lie in it. She had been the one desperate to get married and have a family. She was the one who couldn't see the point of staying on into the sixth form and had opted to do shorthand and typing instead. She was the one who had applied for the dead-end job at the biscuit factory. And she was the one who had thought that Mick was God's gift to womankind and hadn't thought that she could set her sights a bit higher than Neanderthal Man.

'Well, life isn't fair, is it?' And with that Yvie made her escape. Why did her sister always manage to put a damper on everything? She'd been like the spectre at the feast on her wedding day, and now she was doing a reprise at Claire's christening. And as for her children . . . Yvie was thankful that Lisa-Marie had so far managed not to be sick but, presumably, that was only because investigating the contents of her nose was proving more enthralling than overindulging in Coca-Cola. Kylie had spent the entire afternoon grizzling that she wanted chips and throwing the food that she was offered on to the carpet, where it was ignored by both her parents, leaving Richard, Yvie or any of the other guests to pick it up. And Jason, being only two, hadn't yet acquired his sisters' social skills but was obviously heading down the same path, as he had spent most of the time lying on his back, drumming his heels and yelling 'No!' for no apparent reason. Yvie made a mental note that Claire was going to learn to say 'please' and 'thank you' – words apparently unknown to her cousins – eat everything she was offered, not see a chip until she was at least five, and get sent to her room if she threw a tantrum. Still, there was a bright side: as an object lesson in how not to bring up kids it was matchless.

By the time all the guests, apart from Adam and Pammy, had gone, it was after five o'clock and Yvie was shattered. She surveyed the debris of the buffet, the state of the carpet, the dirty glasses, and wondered if she could put off tidying up until the next day. Richard returned from seeing his mother off and stood beside her.

'They say the worse the mess, the better the party.'

'Do they? This one must have been a belter then.'

'It was.' Richard looked about him. 'Where's Claire?'

'She's having a nap. I think she found all the attention a bit much. And talking of missing persons – where are Pammy and Adam?'

'They've gone to fetch their case in from the car.' As Richard said this the doorbell rang. 'Ah, that'll be them.' He left to open the door and then show the couple to the spare room.

Yvie sank on to a chair in the dining room and tried to raise the energy not only to begin clearing up but also to make some supper for all of them. Sitting down was a mistake, she quickly realized. She ought to have kept going.

'You're exhausted.'

Yvie looked up and saw Pammy standing in front of her. She hadn't heard her come downstairs or enter the room. She must have dozed off for a second.

'A bit, yes.' There was no point in denying it.

'Right,' said Pammy. 'We're going to shut the door on this mess here. The sitting room isn't so bad. I'll give it a quick tidy, put all the plates and stuff in the kitchen, then we're going to send the boys out for fish and chips. You're not to lift a finger tonight – and tomorrow, when we've all had a good night's sleep, we'll get it all squared away in no time.'

Yvie was too knackered to argue. 'Sounds like a good plan to me.'

At that moment there was a wail from upstairs. 'You see to Claire,' said Pammy. 'I'll get going in the sitting room.'

Yvie dragged herself up the stairs and wearily lifted her daughter from her cot.

'It's OK for you,' she grumbled. 'You can sleep whenever you want. You wait till you're old and knackered like me.'

'Hardly,' said Adam.

Yvie jumped and turned round. She opened her mouth to make a pithy riposte when she saw Richard standing beside him.

'You haven't seen her when she wakes up,' said Richard.

Yvie shot Adam a look which clearly signalled that if he even *thought* about contradicting Richard, a cruel and unnatural punishment would await him – while she said, lightly, 'If you're going to insult me like that, you won't see me when I wake up ever again.'

'Now, now,' said Adam. 'Not in front of the visitors.'

Yvie changed the subject. 'Pammy has suggested we have a take-away tonight and we clear up tomorrow.'

'Sounds good to me,' agreed Richard.

'Is there going to be somewhere open on a Sunday evening?' asked Adam.

'The chip shop down the road never seems to shut.'

'Ah, I forget that in England the world doesn't stop at midday on Saturday like it does in Germany.'

When they got downstairs they discovered that Pammy had not only cleared the sitting room up but was about to start on washing up a stack of plates.

59

'Don't you dare,' said Richard, pulling her away from the sink and removing the rubber gloves. 'You lot are going to sit down with a glass of wine while I make up a bottle for Claire. Then, while Yvie feeds her ladyship, I'll stroll down to the chippy and get something healthy for the rest of us to eat.'

'I might come with you,' said Adam. 'Leave the girls to chat. Besides which, I could do with the exercise.' He patted his virtually flat stomach as if to prove his point. Yvie almost made a comment about how lean and taut she remembered it to be, but managed to stop before she dropped herself in it.

A few minutes later Yvie and Pammy were sipping their wine, Claire was glugging contentedly on her bottle and the boys had exited noisily in search of food – and, Yvie suspected, a pint at the pub they would pass en route.

'Not breast?' inquired Pammy.

'I do both at the mo. I'm getting her used to the fact that food comes in other varieties. I feed her myself at night and when we're out – just for the sheer convenience of it.'

'You look very fulfilled,' said Pammy, watching Yvie and her baby.

'Shattered would be a more accurate description.'

'Does she wake you up a lot at night?'

'No, she's pretty good really. Well, good compared to some of the horror stories I've heard. She sleeps about five hours at a stretch at night, so if I give her a last feed at midnight it's almost a civilized hour when she wakes me up again.'

'It doesn't sound very civilized to me.'

'I kip a bit when she naps during the day. I don't know how my sister managed with three, though. I mean, when you've got more than one, there's no chance of having them all zonk out at the same time.'

'So are you planning on more?'

'I think Richard would like loads, but I want to do something with my degree. I'd like a proper job. I have to say that Claire wasn't exactly planned, and I was hoping to find something a bit more stretching rather than work in the shop. I mean, it was fun, I liked the customers and Miles was a hoot, but it was hardly what I was aiming for when I graduated.'

'Claire wasn't planned?'

'Absolutely not. I got back together with Richard and bingo.'

'Lucky you.'

A noisy slurp alerted Yvie to the fact that Claire had emptied her bottle. She adjusted the muslin square over her shoulder and then lifted Claire up to wind her. After a couple of pats, Claire let rip with a resounding burp.

'Manners,' said Yvie indulgently.

'Adam and I have been trying.'

'Hmmm?' Yvie was concentrating on the baby.

'We've been trying for a baby.'

'Oh.' And . . . ?

'I don't seem to find it as easy as you did.'

Yvie finished winding Claire and turned her attention back to her guest. This explained her rather longing look at Adam when he was holding Claire. Yvie felt sorry for Pammy but wasn't sure quite what to say. 'Well, it's early days yet, isn't it?'

'We've been trying for a year. Adam and I have got to go for tests next week.'

Tests? That put a different complexion on things. 'Poor you.' Yvie didn't envy them. All that intimate detail that you'd have to share with total strangers. Ugh.

'I'm not looking forward to it.'

'No.' Yvie didn't blame her but didn't know what to say. There was an awkward silence. 'What does Adam think about it?'

'You can imagine. He's so convinced it's nothing to do with him that I'm quite worried he might not even turn up.'

'That's men for you.'

'Any possible suggestion that they might be firing blanks and they go into complete denial.'

'They think it's a slur on their masculinity.'

'Exactly,' said Pammy, with feeling. Then she made a small grimace. 'But in many ways I'm rather hoping it's me. I think I'd accept the problem better than Adam.'

Yvie patted the baby's back and had a sip of wine. 'Aren't things easier to solve if it's the bloke?'

'I don't know. We'll no doubt learn far more on the subject in the next few weeks than either of us ever wanted to know.'

Claire yawned contentedly. 'I think this one is nearly ready for bed. Why don't you pour yourself another glass of wine while I put her down?'

'Yvie?'

'Yes'

'Could I put her in her cot? I'll try not to make a mess of it and wake her up again.'

'Oh.' Yvie was a little surprised by the request. Besides which, this was the best bit of the day, when Claire, all sleepy and milky and soft and clean, was happy to be snuggled and cuddled and cooed over. But then she saw the look of longing in Pammy's eyes. 'Yes, yes, of course you can. Here.' She lifted Claire off her shoulder and placed her in Pammy's arms. 'Night night, poppet,' she said as she kissed her daughter's forehead. She watched Pammy leave the room and then took a thoughtful sip of her wine. She knew she ought to count her blessings for being able to have had a child so easily, and she loved Claire with all her heart and wouldn't change things now for the world, but . . . But, she thought with a sigh, it would have suited her better if she'd had just a few more years to get some sort of career sorted out before motherhood had come barrelling out of the blue.

Pammy returned downstairs just as the men tumbled through the front door accompanied by the unmistakable smell of the pub and the chip shop, demanding more beer and plates for the food.

'Give me a chance,' said Yvie, dragging them into the kitchen before their guffaws and horseplay woke the sleeping infant upstairs.

In no time, she had the food divided between four plates, two cold cans of beer out of the fridge, the tomato sauce out of the cupboard, and the knives and forks on the trays.

'Everyone grab a plate. I'll bring the sauce. Pammy, would you bring the glasses? Adam, I haven't enough hands for the salt and pepper, would you . . . ?' And then the party moved back into the sitting room. Between greasy mouthfuls of fish and chips, the banter bounced around the room. Pammy's earlier sad revelation was forgotten and the old friends picked up the threads of their happy time together in Germany as if they had been parted for a few days rather than nearly a year. Yvie noticed with relief that Adam seemed to have got the message and had stopped directing puppy-dog looks in her direction. Thank goodness, back to being friends with no other agenda, she thought as she relaxed, certain that Adam was not going to make some ghastly announcement about their guilty secret. She allowed herself to believe that their affair was indeed over.

It was gone midnight when they all trooped off to bed. Yvie popped into Claire's room and found her daughter stirring. She lifted the baby out of her cot and settled down in the rocking chair beside the crib to feed the infant, hoping that the two glasses of wine she had consumed during the course of the evening would ensure that Claire, too, would fancy a lie-in in the morning. Richard would have to go to work as usual but there was no reason for anyone else to get up at daybreak. Adam and Pammy weren't planning on leaving to catch a ferry until midday, so unless her ladyship demanded attention early on, Yvie had no intention of getting out of bed any earlier than was absolutely necessary.

As Yvie fed Claire, she let her mind drift back over the day. All in all it had gone well, or as well as any event could go if her sister and her grisly family were present. And at least Adam hadn't said anything untoward or made a scene, or worse, a pass, or anything else that Yvie had dreaded since Richard had announced that he wanted Adam as Claire's godfather. Yvie sighed in the silent darkness. It was a sigh of relief.

The next day, Claire woke on the dot of five, so Yvie was denied her lie-in. After she had fed and changed Claire and returned her to her cot for another couple of hours of sleep, Yvie considered creeping back into bed herself, but then she remembered the chaos left downstairs. It was tempting to ignore it and then rely on Adam and Pammy to help her clear it up, but it wasn't really fair. After all, they were visitors. Besides which, if she just washed up the glasses, they could be draining while she tackled some of the other mess. Anyway, she could murder a cup of tea. Pulling her dressing gown around her, she set off downstairs to get a head start on the day.

By the time Richard's alarm went off and he descended the

stairs in search of his wife and a cup of tea for himself, Yvie had almost finished the washing up.

'Gracious!' he said.

'Well, there didn't seem much point in letting it fester. Tea?'

'Please.' Richard sat down at the table, now covered with gleaming china and glasses instead of the smeared and stained debris that had been stacked there overnight.

Yvie pottered about, making the tea. 'Much planned for this week?'

'Dunno. Nothing specific, but it doesn't mean that something won't crop up. You know what this job is like.'

Yvie certainly did, although she tried not to think about it too much. 'So, if it's all quiet on the Western Front, you'll be home for lunch.'

Richard nodded and picked up his mug. 'Right, I'll take this upstairs while I have my shower.'

Another Monday, thought Yvie, another week. Once she'd seen her visitors off she'd have to think of some things to do so she and Claire had lots to occupy themselves. She was determined she'd never again get into the sort of doldrums she'd slipped into in Germany.

When Richard came home at lunchtime and told her his news, Yvie would have given anything for 'bored'.

She found she was shaking slightly as she tried to get to grips with what Richard had just told her.

'So, you've got to fly out to Belfast on Wednesday and appear in court to give evidence to put away some IRA bomber.'

'That's about it.'

'But these people are thugs. They have all sorts of supporters over here. This'll put you in terrible danger, not to mention us if they find out about you.'

'My name won't be given and I'll be behind a screen . . .'

'But there'll still be people in the court who'll know who you are. What if they pass the information on?'

'They won't. The authorities are very careful who they employ there. Lots of people do this sort of thing every day and don't have a problem.'

Yvie's face showed how much she believed that. 'Why so sudden?'

'To be honest, I've known for a while that I might have to go and give evidence. It was just a case of when and if they decided to use me.'

'You knew. And you didn't tell me!'

'I didn't want you to worry.'

Yvie snorted in disgust. 'You should have told me.'

'I might not have been called. It would have been pointless.'

'Can you refuse?'

'No. Anyway, I think it would be contempt of court if I did.'

Yvie knew that nothing she could say would make any difference. The system needed her husband, so the system would *have* her husband. No matter the consequences. She busied herself making scrambled egg for their lunch. 'So what's the case?'

'I defused a bomb outside the courts. You remember, the one where there was a shot of me on all the front pages the next day.' Yvie nodded. 'Because I defused it, rather than disrupted it, they got a load of evidence from it, including a couple of fingerprints – enough to nail the guy who made it. And because his bombs were quite distinctive, the way he made them was always the same, they can charge him with a whole load of offences. This guy is going down for decades, I shouldn't wonder. He's been responsible for dozens of deaths and injuries.'

'But if the other bombs he made exploded, how . . . ?'

'You'd be amazed the evidence they can get from just fragments. But a whole fingerprint, that's a different kettle of fish.'

'Oh.' She shrugged. The wonders of modern science were fascinating, no doubt, but she had other worries right now. Why, thought Yvie, was the fact that this guy was facing several life sentences almost more worrying than if he was looking at a few months in nick?

Richard was away for two days. While he was gone, Yvie scoured the newspapers for reports but found nothing. Not that she was surprised; Northern Ireland and the goings-on

65

there rarely made the national press unless something truly outrageous occurred. The trial of some bomber, no matter how prolific and deadly, was hardly news if it was related to 'The Troubles'. Of course, if he'd been operating on the mainland, if it had been citizens from Manchester or London who had been killed, it would be on every front page. Yvie sometimes felt sorry for the Northern Irish.

When he got back she quizzed him about how it had gone.

'Fine,' he said, which was no answer at all.

She asked if they were likely to be in any danger at all, to which he replied that they were in no more danger than any other army family. Not much comfort there either, thought Yvie. She took to checking the underside of their car before she used it. Some of her neighbours on the patch thought she was clearly barking, but Yvie thought grubby knees on her jeans were a small price to pay for peace of mind.

She sometimes wondered how long she was going to have to carry out this rigmarole. Was it a life sentence? Could she stop if Richard got posted to somewhere like Cyprus or Germany? Would she be safe if he just moved out of bomb disposal to an ordinary job? But, thinking about it, the only safe job would be one that didn't involve a khaki uniform.

Of course, as the following weeks turned into months, Yvie became slowly less assiduous about checking her car. The IRA threat didn't go away, but she felt that if nothing had happened then nothing was likely to. After all, if this bomber hadn't got his mates to track Richard down when the case was recent and, presumably, his resentment at a peak, then he was unlikely to suddenly take it into his head to give the order now.

October 1989

Yvie stuck the candle on the cake and tried to make a completely indifferent Claire pay attention.

'Look, Claire, look what mummy's made you.' But Claire was far more interested in the tray of her high chair, which she was banging loudly with the flat of both hands. 'Oh well, please yourself,' said Yvie, a tad disgruntled, as she was not a natural cake maker and she'd slaved for some hours to try and make something that would appeal to her daughter on the occasion of her first birthday. 'Let's hope you manage to show better manners at your party tomorrow.' Well, party was, perhaps, a bit of an exaggeration, as Claire's birthday celebrations were due to consist of two similarly aged friends coming over for cake and juice. Still, Claire didn't know what to expect. This was her first birthday when all was said and done. She picked her daughter out of her high chair and took her through to the sitting room to sit in her bouncy chair while she watched the early evening news and waited for Richard to appear. She had hardly settled when she heard her husband's key in the lock.

'Hi, darling,' she called.

'Hi.' Richard hurried into the sitting room. 'Good, I haven't missed the news.'

Yvie felt a trifle perplexed. 'Is something happening?'

'Happening? Have you had your head stuck in sand today then?'

The titles for the evening news rolled, together with a picture of a section of the Berlin Wall being pushed down by a gang of men, and others squeezing through the gap to be hugged and greeted by those on the other side.

'Blimey,' said Yvie.

They watched in silence as the cold war thawed in front of them.

There was little else on the news that night; nothing was going to match the importance of the imminent reunification of Germany.

'Do you think it'll be OK?' asked Yvie as the programme drew to a close.

'How do you mean?'

'Well, it looks like the world is going to be a safer place, but, presumably, there are some hard-line communists who won't approve of what's going on. What if they mobilize the Red Army?'

'We'll have to wait and see.'

If Yvie had been hoping for Richard to dismiss her worries, she was disappointed. She had a sudden urge to cuddle Claire, and reached forward to lift her out of her chair. 'Bath-time,' she announced brightly to cover up her fears and insecurities. Claire gurgled.

The normality of the evening routine helped banish Yvie's anxiety, and when she returned downstairs with Claire, pink and with slightly damp hair, she had decided that she must just hope for the best. Richard followed her into the kitchen.

'Nice cake.'

'I'm glad someone appreciates it. Claire was distinctly unimpressed when she first saw it.'

'Only because she's never seen one before. When was the last time you did any baking?'

Yvie laughed. 'True. Now, how about you make a couple of nice G and Ts while I get Claire's bottle ready.'

Five minutes later they were all settled in the sitting room again with their evening drink of choice.

'Of course, the Wall coming down is going to change everything one way or another,' said Richard.

Yvie felt another stab of fear – not for herself, but Claire was too vulnerable, too little to have to face a third world war.

'Well,' continued Richard. 'If the Red hoards don't pour through the fence in a final attempt at world domination, then there's not going to be much of a job left for us.'

'What do you mean?'

'I could be wrong, but the way I see things is that either we'll have war or peace. If it's war, which I really think is unlikely, then best I build you and Claire a nuclear bunker in

68

the garden, but if it's peace, I think I'd better start looking for a job.'

'Why?'

'Why the bunker or why the job?'

'Job.'

'Because there won't be any need for tens of thousands of British troops in Germany if we haven't got the Warsaw Pact to eyeball through the fence.'

'Can't they come back here?'

'And do what?'

'Well . . .'

'Exactly.'

Yvie thought for a second or two. 'But what would you do?'

'I'm not completely useless, you know.'

'I didn't mean it like that.'

It was about a month later that they went to the christening of a friend's child.

'Carchester Cathedral – how swish,' said Yvie when she saw the details on the invitation.

'His grandad does charity work for it – raises money for the roof or something.'

'Still, it puts Claire's in the shade.'

'Careful, you're beginning to sound like your sister.'

Yvie grimaced. 'Heaven forfend.'

'Tell you what, why don't we make a weekend of it? Carchester sounds a nice place and we haven't had a break for a while. We could do some Christmas shopping. Besides, I've never been there.'

'Why not?'

Yvie was smitten with Carchester as soon as she saw it: an ancient cathedral town based on a Roman fort, it had the classic crossroads in the centre, walls round the outside and a tumble of grey stone houses with stone roofs behind the shops that flanked the main roads.

'When I grow up I'd like to live here,' she announced as she stood at their hotel window and looked out at the bustling main street.

'I'm afraid it'll all rather depend on where I find work.'

69

'Still, we could think about it,' said Yvie hopefully.

'I think me getting a job must take priority over you finding a house. I mean, I shan't put in my notice until I get something but . . .'

'Yes, but you haven't done anything yet.' Yvie paused and turned to face her husband. 'You haven't, have you? Not even started to look.'

'No, well . . .'

'I think you should. I want to live somewhere like this. I want Claire to grow up with friends who aren't going to trickle away from her as they, or we, get posted. I want her to go to a local school and not end up boarding. I want a home I can call my own and not a succession of quarters. I want to settle.'

Richard was taken aback. 'You really mean that, don't you?'

'I know you were in the army when I met you. You told me what it would mean, what the life would be like, and I accepted it. It was fine when it was just you and I but there's Claire to think about now. She didn't ask to be born an army brat. The nomadic life won't be fair on her.'

'No, you're right.' Richard sighed. 'I'll think about it.'

'Promise?'

'Promise.'

The next day, Yvie got up early and took Claire for a walk in her buggy, before the service in the cathedral. Her excuse was that the walk would tire Clare out and she would be good and quiet for the main event of the morning. However, when, a couple of days later, the mailshots from estate agents started dropping through their letterbox by the dozen, Richard realized that Yvie hadn't been entirely straight with him.

'But there's no harm in looking, is there?' she said.

'But what if I get a job in Yorkshire?'

'Well, don't apply for one up there.'

'There may not be much choice.'

'Have you looked to see what's out there, down here in the south?'

Richard didn't meet her gaze. Yvie gave an angry sniff and stamped out of the room. For God's sake, she thought. At least he could *look*.

* * *

A month later, when the estate agents had realized that they hadn't had a single bite from Yvie and so the flood of house details had virtually dried up, Richard discovered he no longer had any excuse at all to procrastinate. The powers that be had decided that to keep a standing army of one hundred thousand men and women out in Germany was now a waste of money and they were prepared to offer a pretty generous redundancy package to those who wished to leave. When Richard realized that Yvie had read about the announcement in the *Telegraph*, he knew that his days in the army were numbered.

'Tell me if you really want to stay in,' Yvie said. 'It wouldn't be fair to either of us if you felt I had forced you into this decision.'

'I think I needed forcing,' said Richard slowly. 'The trouble is, life in the army is damn cushy. The pay's not bad, we get housed, I don't have to think about what to wear, the work's not too difficult and sometimes there's even the chance of the odd bit of travel. But . . .'

'But . . . ?'

'Well, Hong Kong won't be an option soon. Cyprus is only for the very lucky and the RAF, I might get a shot at an exchange posting but it's unlikely. Frankly, future postings seem to be a choice of Ireland, Aldershot or Didcot.'

'Wow!' said Yvie with a smile. 'Be still, my beating heart.'

'Exactly. And I've thought about what you said about Claire. I don't want her to go away to boarding school either. I don't want to miss her growing up. But you do realize that there's no guarantee that I'll get redundancy? It's not a done deal.'

'Yes,' said Yvie as she vowed to pray to every god available to grant her wish that they'd soon be civilians.

March 1990

'I don't know whether to be pleased or sad,' said Richard when he told Yvie his application to become redundant had been accepted.

'You may have doubts but I'm thrilled.' Claire came toddling into the kitchen, attracted by the sound of her father's voice. Yvie picked her daughter up and spun her round in the air. 'Just think, Claire, you and I can go house hunting. Won't that be exciting?' Claire gurgled and demanded another spin.

'If you say so,' said Richard.

Yvie put Claire back on the floor and looked puzzled. 'Aren't you excited at the prospect of finding somewhere of our own to live?'

'Come off it, Yvie, I haven't even got a job yet, have I?'

'That's a detail.' Yvie refused to see any clouds on the horizon.

'It isn't a detail. It's a major part of everything. I've been in the army for six years; I'm not trained to do anything in the real world. OK, I've got a degree, but so have lots of other people—'

Yvie interrupted him. 'You're great at man management. You're probably more mature than many of your contemporaries. You've got a grasp of current affairs. You've travelled . . .' Yvie petered out. She couldn't think of anything else. Damn. 'Well, I think any employer would be daft not to have you.'

'How many employers want someone who can defuse bombs?'

Yvie was stumped. Yeah, well. There probably wasn't that much of a call for an explosives expert in civvy street. Then a thought struck her. 'What about fireworks?'

Richard nodded. 'I'll grant you that. However . . .'

72

Yvie knew what he was implying. He might just have well have said, 'Go on, think of another mass user of explosives,' because it was patent that that was what he was thinking. 'I'm sure you'll find something soon enough,' said Yvie. 'But is it going to be something I'm really going to want to do?' Yvie couldn't answer that. But she suddenly realized that Richard wasn't so concerned about getting a job as about getting a job that didn't leave him tied to a desk doing something mundane just to pay a mortgage and put food on the table. She understood that he was feeling all the responsibility for this decision and would take a job, any job, rather than put his family in some sort of financial jeopardy. But the reality was it might be a short cut to purgatory for him. Oh goodness, she thought, what have I made him do? She decided that house hunting was not a good idea for the time being.

They had six months before Richard had to leave – the weeks began to pass scarily quickly and Richard was no nearer to finding something he wanted to do. Either the positions on offer didn't appeal once he had a chance to examine them in detail, or they were so appealing that he was almost killed in the stampede to get them. By June he'd been to four interviews only to find that he had been pipped at the post by another candidate – twice by people he'd known in the army. He tried to put on a brave face, but Yvie could tell he was getting increasingly worried. Yvie knew it wasn't just the matter of a job. Once he left the army, they would no longer be entitled to an army quarter. They would have to leave, and then what? Council accommodation? Go and live with Richard's folks, her parents, Laura? No, anywhere, but please not Laura. Actually, in reality, Laura was a non-starter. There was no way they could fit into her little house in Reading. Yvie knew that it probably wouldn't come to camping with family or friends. They would rent somewhere while they looked, but she worried about eating into Richard's precious redundancy payment, which was designed to keep them off the breadline if a job didn't instantly materialize. At this rate, it was looking like they were going to need every penny of it, which didn't suit Yvie: she'd planned for it to go on a decent house.

A week later, Richard came home even more down in the dumps. As he came into the sitting room where Yvie was watching Claire trying to fit bricks into a shape-sorter, she could tell he was fed up.

'Now what?' asked Yvie.

'Adam rang me at work today. He's gone for redundancy too, but he's really landed on his feet.'

'Oh?'

'He's got a job managing a country estate for some loaded yank. Somewhere up in the Lake District, I think.'

'Doesn't sound that great.' Yvie had never had Adam pinned as the hunting, shooting, fishing type.

'Sounds OK to me. Adam said that they get to live, virtually rent-free, in a wing of a stately home. The owner is almost never there. When he is, Pammy will be able to hire in staff to help her, while Adam will be expected to drive the lord and master. When he's not there, they will be expected to keep the house shipshape and make sure the estate workers do whatever they are supposed to do.'

'Cushy.'

'It certainly is, the way Adam told it. It sounds as though it is mostly supervisory and management, with the perk of living in a beautiful area and a fab house thrown in.'

Yvie tried not to feel jealous. Not that she wanted to live in the back of beyond, nor did she want a stately home as an address, but she did want the future settled. And they were very far from it. How come Pammy and Adam had all the luck?

'Mind you,' continued Richard. 'Adam told me he wouldn't have taken the job if there had been any chance of him and Pammy having kids. It's too far out in the sticks.'

'Oh, so it's definite?' said Yvie. 'I mean, definite that they'll never have children.'

'So you knew they were having problems.'

'Pammy said something at Claire's christening. She and Adam were going to have tests, but with medicine being able to do so much these days, I just assumed something would get sorted out. Besides which, I rather assumed it was going to turn out to be Pammy's problem. But it's terribly unfair, considering what a great mother Pammy would make.'

Richard nodded. 'Well, I don't know what all the ins and

outs were, but I got the impression from something Adam said that it was pretty much a certainty that it's never going to happen for them. But he didn't want to talk about it that much.'

'Typical man's attitude to gynae matters,' said Yvie ruefully. And she remembered her blind panic about the possibility that Adam might have been Claire's father. What she would have given to have known that back then . . .

'Well, if I were firing blanks, it isn't the sort of thing I would want to boast about.'

So, Yvie thought, it was Adam who had the problem, not Pammy. Perhaps that explained why they weren't going for treatment. Perhaps Pammy didn't fancy the idea of using donor sperm. Yvie thought that if she and Richard had been similarly afflicted, she mightn't fancy that idea either. Still, it hadn't come to that, thankfully.

'But, on the bright side . . .' said Richard. Yvie thought fleetingly that there didn't seem to be much of a bright side for Pammy and Adam. 'On the bright side, Adam told me about an opportunity that may be coming up. It'll probably come to nothing – knowing my luck so far.'

'Well . . .' Yvie didn't want to be too downbeat.

'There's a chap Adam knows who left a couple of years ago. He set up a sort of security firm. He advises people with commercial interests in funny places about how safe – or otherwise – they are. And he supplies bodyguards and the like. According to Adam, he's about to branch out into training courses, teaching people what to do if they get kidnapped or hijacked, what to do if the country you happen to be in is the subject of a coup, that sort of thing.'

'And?'

'And Adam thinks I should approach him and see if he needs someone to advise on how to recognize a postal bomb, how to recognize an under-car booby trap, how to cope if you get caught up in a terrorist bombing or bomb threat.'

Yvie nodded. She could see the sense – and need – for that sort of information if you had to travel to somewhere unsavoury. 'Go for it.'

'I don't know. I mean, it's a bit random ringing this guy up and saying I'm the world's leading expert in IEDs, you need to employ me.'

'What's the worst he can say? Shove off?'

'Well . . .'

'Have you got his name and phone number?'

'Yes.'

'And he knows Adam?'

'Yes.'

'Well then . . . You've always said it's who you know, not what you know, that counts.' Yvie walked over to the phone and lifted the receiver. 'Go on. Ring him now.'

Richard looked at his watch. It was after five. 'It's too late.'

'Bollocks. This bloke runs his own business. He'll be there till gone seven, I bet. Anyway, if he has gone home, what does it matter?' She waved the receiver at him. 'Go on.'

Richard took it from her. He pressed the button to free the line, while he searched with his other hand for the scrap of paper on which he'd scribbled the details. After a rummage in his wallet, he found it and began to dial. Yvie moved close to him so she could half hear what was going on. The connection was made and she heard the faint ringing tone.

'Hello,' said a woman's voice. 'Global Solutions. Can I help you?'

'Errm. Er, can I speak to Rupert Hayman please.'

'Who shall I say is calling?'

'Richard Maxwell. I'm a friend of Adam Clifton's.'

'Please hold.'

'There, I told you so,' said Yvie, triumphantly. 'And for God's sake try and sound more positive. Cut the ums and ers!'

'All ri— Oh, hello. Umm.' Richard nearly yelped as Yvie elbowed him hard in the ribs. He glowered at her. 'My name is Richard Maxwell and I was talking to Adam Clifton today. He was tell— Yes, he and Pammy are fine. He's moving to Cumbria. Yes.' Richard laughed. 'Yes, passports are probably mandatory. Anyway, he was telling me about your business. It sounds fascinating.' Yvie pulled a face at his obvious flattery. Richard scowled. He nodded and said yes a number of times as Rupert gave him the low-down. Even through the back of the receiver, Yvie could hear the smugness and pride in his voice as he gave Richard the details. 'Anyway,' said Richard determinedly when he could get a word in edgeways, 'I am leaving the army soon. I was in bomb disposal. I was

76

thinking that your proposed training package should include a phase for your clients on how to recognize postal bombs and other devices. High-powered executives are particularly vulnerable to that kind of attack. Especially if they have any sort of involvement in things that upset animal rights people and militant greens, or that might alienate powerful factions in unstable countries.'

At that moment Claire picked up her shape-sorter and promptly dropped it on her foot. She hollered loudly. Yvie raced across the room to comfort and quieten the child but, by the time calm had been restored, Richard was replacing the handset.

Yvie jiggled Claire on her hip. 'So? Tell me.'

'He wants to see me next Thursday.'

'Brilliant. Is he seeing anyone else?'

'I don't think so.'

'And where is his office?'

'Salisbury.'

'Oh.' Yvie said that single syllable with a nonchalance she certainly didn't feel. Salisbury! If Richard got the job, they could definitely live in Carchester. Oh bliss, oh joy! But she wasn't going to say anything. She wasn't even going to mention it to Richard. She felt that if she did, she might spoil things. She just hugged Claire and offered a silent prayer. Please, please let this all pan out right. She vowed to ring estate agents the next morning, as soon as Richard had gone to work, to see what they had on their books.

August 1990

The instant Yvie saw the details of the house in Hanover Close, she knew it was the one she wanted. It was perfect; built just like a doll's house, with a front door flanked by a tall sash window on each side, with three more similar sash windows above it. Above those was a pitched roof with two dormer windows looking across to the houses on the other side of the wide grassy strip that ran down the centre of the close. The front door was reached by a flight of four shallow stone steps that crossed the basement area like a bridge. Three bedrooms, three reception rooms, one bathroom, a basement kitchen and an attic. Perfect. Yvie mentally blocked out the sentence that read 'in need of major renovation'. And she knew that 'major renovation' was probably an understatement – that much was obvious from the price. She stared again at the fuzzy black and white picture at the top of the A4 sheet. It looked so beautiful. More than that, it looked a happy house, a comfortable house. Surely, anyone who lived there could not fail to be content.

She rang the estate agent and went to see it without telling Richard. She felt a tad disloyal, but there was no point in doing anything about it if the 'major renovation' was going to be more akin to rebuilding than refurbishment. She had already done the sums and knew they could afford it – just – but there would be precious little left in the pot for huge bills. Bearing that in mind, they would have to take on quite a bit of the work themselves. Which would be fine if it was a matter of painting and decorating, but if it was stuff like re-wiring, plumbing, plastering, stuff that they would have to bring in professionals to deal with, then the house was probably a non-starter. As Yvie strapped Claire into her car seat, she told herself that this was more than likely a wild goose chase, that she was wasting her time and that this perfect house, at a price they could afford, wasn't destined to be hers. But despite her sensible advice to herself, she couldn't help noticing that she was almost beside herself with excitement as she turned out of the patch and headed off towards Carchester.

The previous owner, the unexpectedly nice estate agent told her as he found the key to the front door, had done nothing to the house since moving in forty years before. She had then died and the children were selling it to split the proceeds. They all lived miles away and none of them had the time or the inclination to do it up before putting it on the market and realizing its potential value. Well, thought Yvie, their haste to get their hands on the cash was her good fortune.

She picked Claire up and held her close as the agent let them in. Lord only knew what state the house was going to be in, she thought as she stepped gingerly over the threshold.

'Don't worry,' said the estate agent cheerily. 'The house may be a tip but they knew how to build them in those days. It's pretty sound throughout.'

'Hmmm,' said Yvie non-committally. He would say that, wouldn't he? The agent bustled past her and opened a door to their right. Yvie peered round. The decor was dire but, underneath, the room was fabulous.

'Oh,' she said in surprise as she put Claire down so she could have a toddle around. The room, devoid of any furniture, was vast but fabulously proportioned. It ran from the front to the back of the house and had a high ceiling with a lovely central rose. The fireplace was obviously original, although the hideous gas fire patently wasn't. The floorboards were in a bad state, but Yvie didn't think that it was anything a belt-sander and decent varnish couldn't sort out. The plaster looked sound and the place didn't smell damp, but the wallpaper would have to go and the paint certainly needed sorting out . . . Then she noticed the lack of radiators.

'Central heating?' she inquired.

'Ah.'

'Oh.' Blast, she thought. That would be expensive. She wandered across to the French window that overlooked the garden and looked at the view. Claire toddled after her. Outside was a Regency wrought-iron balcony that ran the width of the back of the house, and a spiral stair led down to what should be a lawn but currently looked like a paddock. The garden was surrounded by a mellow stone wall, and behind that rose the twin spires of Carchester Cathedral. Even the garden was wonderful, despite the obvious neglect. A secluded, safe haven for Claire to play in. This house would be so perfect if it wasn't for the issue of the central heating. Her thoughts were interrupted.

'I think the details did say that this house needed work.' She turned round. 'Yes, yes they did.' And, thinking about it, the advert hadn't said anything about central heating, and she should have noticed the omission. She wondered what a new central heating system would cost – one thousand, ten thousand? She didn't have a clue. The house was going to cost every penny of Richard's redundancy payment, plus almost all of their savings. When they had discussed buying houses – although not this one, not yet – Richard had voiced the opinion that it would be good if they could get one for under the combined sum, so they could be without a mortgage and still have some rainy-day money.

'Then,' he had said, 'if anything happens and I lose my job, we'll always have our own roof over our head. We should be able to afford the council tax and utility bills and that sort of stuff whatever life chucks at us, but a mortgage – that can be a real millstone.'

Still, thought Yvie, a loan to sort this place out wouldn't be the same as a mortgage. Would it? Actually, she knew it would be. But it wouldn't be as *big* as a mortgage. And she already knew she desperately wanted to live here. But what if Richard said no? She'd compare every other house she ever saw against the yardstick of this one, and she didn't think she'd ever find anything she would like as she instinctively liked this. Oh damn, damn, damn, why couldn't it all be easy?

Yvie and Claire continued their trip round the house. Claire was oblivious to the turmoil that seethed within her mother. Part of Yvie thrilled at the potential of it, and part of her was fraught and anxious that it might never be hers. On the plus side, the estate agent wasn't lying when he said it was sound. It did look in pretty good nick. Obviously Yvie was no expert, but there were no sinister stains on the consistently vile and dated wallpaper, the floorboards were solid, the plaster remained stuck to the brickwork, and the sash windows all seemed to function. On the negative side, the bathroom belonged in a museum and the kitchen was so antiquated as to be a joke, but they were both just about serviceable and wouldn't need attention immediately if they bought it. They could wait and save up, perhaps. Then Yvie saw the attic and she knew that, whatever doubts or worries Richard might voice about it using up every penny they had, she had to persuade him it was worth it. Once Yvie had negotiated a narrow stair hidden behind a door on the landing, she discovered an amazing space lit through the two dormers that she had seen from the road, but which she now realized faced north. What a place for a studio!

Unsurprisingly, Richard was decidedly lukewarm.

'It's too much. It'll leave us exposed.'

'But it's so perfect. It's a wonderful size, the area is lovely, there's nothing major that needs doing . . .'

'Except the central heating.' Richard sighed. 'And I bet the wiring is in a desperate state. We agreed, didn't we, that we should look for something for less than a hundred and twenty thou. This is way over budget.'

'Yes, but it'll be worth far more than that if we do it up. It'll be a great investment.'

Richard shook his head. He wasn't the least bit convinced – that was patently obvious.

'At least look at it,' pleaded Yvie.

'What's the point? We can't afford it.'

'But we can. And it'll only be a little mortgage.'

'We agreed on no mortgage.' Richard had gone beyond unenthusiastic and was now verging on chilly. 'We don't even know if I've got the job yet, or what they might offer me by way of salary. To take on any commitments right now is daft.'

Yvie was tempted to throw a real strop, but she decided that Richard was under enough pressure, what with job-hunting and everything, and instead she stomped into the kitchen and took her annoyance out on a panful of potatoes with the masher.

Three days later, Richard rang her with the news that he'd got the job with Global Solutions.

81

'Rupert hired me on the spot. Said he'd been looking for the right sort of bloke to take responsibility for that sort of terrorist threat, so when I phoned him, he knew I was probably the man he was after.'

'That's wonderful. It's perfect. Clever, clever you for getting the job.'

'It's luck not talent. If I hadn't spoken to Adam . . .'

'Rubbish.'

'It's not rubbish, but who cares.'

'And what's the salary?'

'I'm going to be starting on about fifty thou.'

'Fifty? Fifty! But that's fantastic. And your redundancy money and your pension.'

'Thought you'd be pleased.'

There was a short pause, then Yvie said, 'Richard, about the house in Hanover Close . . .'

'I thought you would say that. I rang the estate agent to see if it's still on the market and it is.'

Whatever else Richard might have said after that was lost in the shriek that Yvie let out.

They put in an offer the next day.

April 2003

The low, bright early-morning April sun lit up the houses opposite as Yvie drew up the blind in her studio. Despite having promised herself the huge attic, so much work had needed doing before she could move into it that she had made do with the smallest bedroom at the front of the house to begin with, and nearly fourteen years later had not managed to move out. Actually, that wasn't quite true: she would have moved out about seven years ago, when they had finally finished doing up the house, but by then Claire had bagged the attic for herself and had moved up there lock, stock and barrel. Richard had been a co-conspirator in this, as, unknown to Yvie, he had promised to build Claire an en suite with a power shower in one of the corners, and had got the necessary planning permission for two skylights to be let into roof to supplement the meagre light from the dormers at the front. At the time 'miffed' hadn't even come close to describing how Yvie felt at being deprived of the attic, but now, what with Claire's predilection for mess and loud music, Yvie knew that it was a good thing that her daughter had a bolthole away from the adults.

She leaned on the windowsill and looked at the peaceful scene: the sky was opalescent and cloudless, the ornamental cherry trees that grew on the small green in the middle of the oval close of Georgian houses were just coming into flower, and beneath them the daffodils, all shades of yellow, from palest primrose through chrome, saffron and turmeric, were bobbing and nodding as a breeze wafted through them. The postman was also enjoying the fine morning. Yvie could hear him cheerfully whistling a recent pop hit as he propped his bike against the wrought-iron railings outside the house opposite and began his round. It had all the promise of a perfect day and Yvie felt utterly contented.

However, she hadn't come into her studio to admire the view, she told herself briskly, and she turned around and looked critically at the painting on the easel. For the past four years she had been working as a freelance artist designing jackets for a major London publisher. It was steady work which she enjoyed but which also gave her sufficient time to work on paintings for her own pleasure and profit that she sold through a gallery in the centre of Carchester. She knew she was never going to make the big time but, heck, she was happy working at this level. Stepping back from the current jacket she was contracted to produce she tilted her head slightly and studied it. She asked herself the question, was it what the publisher would want? She looked at the photo, pinned to the side of the easel, of an Asian girl staring warily at the camera. The author had sent it to her. 'It's the eyes that are important. I want that look,' the author had instructed her. Well, Yvie thought, she'd captured the look but was the rest of the picture OK? The publishers had sent her a plethora of instructions, mostly technical – to do with having uncluttered areas in the finished picture suitable for the title, author's name and the blurb, and a brief from the design department on details to be included. So she'd done all that, followed all the instructions and . . . ? Yvie considered her verdict. It was . . . satisfactory, she decided. Not great, but it would do. But then, considering what she got paid for jacket designs, the publishers didn't deserve 'great'. They were lucky, she thought, as she exited the room and headed for the kitchen, to get 'satisfactory' for that money. She had always promised Richard that she would get a job that earned a decent, steady income if they ever needed her to, but in the meantime he was more than happy to indulge her in earning pin money from her art. She was lucky in that respect and she knew it.

She left her studio and headed for the kitchen. Halfway down the broad curving stairs, she stopped and hooked back the heavy drapes in front of the beautiful tall window that looked over the back garden. Yvie paused and looked at the view – perfect as ever.

The back garden wasn't huge, and Carchester city walls, built of warm, weathered, grey stone and rising an imposing twenty feet above the herbaceous border, formed the bottom

84

boundary. Behind the wall soared the twin spires of Carchester Cathedral and the branches of the ancient copper beeches that grew in the Deanery garden on the other side of the wall. A hint of mist drifted across the roofs of the houses – just visible behind the wall, clustered around the cathedral precincts – and drained the colour from the scene. It was like looking at an old, faded, black and white photo. Not for the first time, Yvie thought that the view probably hadn't changed one iota since her house had been built. She loved this scene and every time she stood and enjoyed it she counted her blessings.

As always she had awoken early and without the aid of an alarm clock and had slipped out of bed without disturbing Richard, to make the tea. She knew she could lie in bed and doze till the alarm did go off – set for 'panic-time' in case she overslept, even though she never did – but she liked this bit of the day, when she could potter around the house, knowing she wasn't going to be disturbed by her husband or Claire, or the phone or anything else. She liked pottering at this time, tidying up, gathering up the previous day's papers, straightening the cushions, getting everything shipshape, ready for a new day. The sitting room sorted, she picked up the morning papers and the post from the doormat and then went down to the warmth of the kitchen. She flicked on the light switch and half a dozen spots and several fluorescent tubes turned a near-dark, subterranean space into a cosy but bright and inviting room. She chucked the mail and paper on the side, filled the kettle and plugged it in. While it hissed and fizzed, she perused the post. Bill, junk, junk, bill, postcard from a friend – put to one side to be read with her cup of tea – more bills, more junk. Yvie sighed. Nothing exciting. Well, the postcard was nice, but her own holiday was a long way off, so it was only going to make her feel slightly envious. She turned her attention to the paper. The front page was dominated by a depressing picture of a destroyed and blackened car. *Terror Hits Birmingham Suburb*, shouted the headline. *Prominent lawyer killed*, ran the smaller strapline. She ran her eye over the first couple of lines of the paragraph. The lawyer had, apparently, been killed by an under-car booby trap. The police didn't seem to know who was responsible. The smart money seemed to think that he might have upset a criminal gang – triads were mentioned. As Yvie looked at the picture, she thought that ten years ago, even less, such an act would have been put firmly at the door of Irish dissidents. Not now though. Others had discovered how effective a few ounces of high explosive were when it came to getting rid of an enemy. But no matter who was responsible, it was a grim, ugly act with grim, ugly consequences. Suddenly the lovely, bright, cheerful morning had a miserable cloud casting a shadow across it. Dispiritedly, Yvie chucked a couple of tea bags into two mugs, sloshed in the boiling water and stirred the brew until it turned a satisfactory colour. She finished making the tea and, tucking the post and the paper under her arm, she carried the mugs of tea back up the two flights of stairs to her bedroom.

She was almost at the top of the stairs when the memory of her affair and a concomitant rush of guilt assaulted her. It was so strong that it physically rocked her as though she'd missed her footing and had nearly fallen. As it happened, she knew what had triggered it – it was the car bombing. Subconsciously the picture in the paper had reminded her of the time when Richard had been in Ireland defusing the bloody things. The time when she had been left on her own in Germany. The time when she had let temptation and lust get the better of her.

The memory of that first night with Adam made her conscience cringe all the more – Richard had only been away for two days. Two days! She couldn't even keep faithful for forty-eight hours. Her shame was so strong that she felt almost dizzy, and she slopped the tea on to the floorboards. She leaned against the banisters. She could feel the colour rush into her face and then drain out again just as quickly – like a wave spilling and receding across a shallow beach. The fact that she had gone to bed with Adam *once* would have been bad enough, but it hadn't stopped there. God, she thought, why had she done it, why on earth had she let it go on for as long as it had? A tipsy one-night stand might be forgiven, but *four months*? What had possessed her? What had she been thinking of? If Richard ever found out, she could kiss goodbye to everything: Claire, marriage, house, happiness, the works. And no one would blame him if he divorced her. Frankly, thought Yvie, she wouldn't be able to blame him either. How would she feel if she discovered he'd been having an affair with *her* best friend? Yvie couldn't even begin to go there. Betrayed didn't come close.

Her eye lit upon the splash of tea on the polished floor-boards and she rubbed it in distractedly with the sole of her slipper. The banality of the action brought her back to the present, and she felt her heart rate approach something like normal. She exhaled slowly and heavily and pulled her shoulders back. Well, future punishment or no, there was nothing she could do to change past events, so she had better get on with living in the here and now, she told herself. She made her way to her bedroom and put Richard's tea quietly on his bedside table and placed the paper and post silently on the floor beside him.

Yvie thought about returning to bed but she was too wound up. Instead she made her way back to the studio. She picked up her palette and put it down again. There was no way she could concentrate on any work. The memory of her adultery had rattled her more than she had first thought. It had been years since it had been brought to mind, years since she had had an almost daily panic attack as to whether her secret might emerge. Since Adam and Pammy had moved up north, contact had diminished to Christmas and birthday cards and the occasional phone call. Yvie knew that, had she made the least effort, they could have organized a visit to the Lakes, but she had procrastinated relentlessly and selfishly. There was no way she was going to risk her past getting inadvertently raked up, and Richard finding out. The less contact they had the better, as far as Yvie was concerned, and, as keeping in touch was a female thing, she didn't think Adam or Richard noticed too much. Tough if Pammy did, but Yvie couldn't help that. She knew she was a cow in the matter but her priorities dictated it. Of course, if it was just her and Adam privy to the secret, then there wouldn't be too much to worry about, but the thought that Adam might have told a third party was quite a possibility. In fact, it was probably more than just a possibility – after all, Yvie had done just that.

Years ago, shortly after they had moved into this house, Yvie, having had a glass of wine too many in order to get through another excruciating visit from Laura and her family, had rashly confided her secret to her sister, swearing her to horrified silence. But then, of course, because her sister knew, the secret had stopped being quite so much of a secret. And had her sister kept her promise? What if Laura had told others? Laura still lived in their home town and still had countless acquaintances from their school days. Yvie could imagine Laura whispering gleefully to her friends, the ones who, like Laura, thought that Yvie had always been too big for her boots, too ambitious for her own good and too outré by far, and who might now know that she had overstepped the mark. Yvie could imagine her ever-so-slightly smug expression as she imparted that particular gem of gossip and implied that she wouldn't ever do anything so outrageous. Not that Laura was ever likely to follow in her footsteps, Yvie thought cattily. Laura, with her primness and sour expression, had been lucky to bag one man. Yvie couldn't imagine that there was another bloke out there daft, or desperate, enough to fall for Laura's dubious charms.

Yvie remembered the row she had had with Laura which had led to her stupid and reckless revelation. It was about a year after they had moved into the house and it had all happened in the kitchen, which was the first of the rooms they had tackled and which was Yvie's pride and joy. The rest of the house was like a building site, but the kitchen was a haven of warmth, order and beautiful fitted units. All the kids were in bed having had nursery tea earlier, the grown-ups had eaten lasagne and salad, had disposed of a couple of bottles of passable Chianti, and Richard had taken Mick to the local pub while the women got on with clearing up. Yvie stacked the dishwasher while Laura ran hot water into the sink to soak the lasagne dish. Yvie opened another bottle – if she was going to be stuck with Laura for the evening, she was going to need all the help she could get. She poured herself a glass and waved the bottle in Laura's direction. Laura – predictably – shook her head. All the more for me, thought Yvie as she took a slug from her glass. She knew she'd probably already had more than was entirely wise, but hell, she needed the boost with Laura's dreary take on life pulling her down.

'Trust you to have a dishwasher,' said Laura. 'Can't think you really need it, seeing as how there are only the three of you. I manage without and there are five of us.'

'Well,' said Yvie, not rising, 'I probably don't really need it, but I don't always run it every day. Besides which, it's jolly useful when we have a houseful like now.'

'Yea, but you've plenty of time to do chores like this. It isn't as if you've got a proper job. I mean, you can't call faffing around in front of an easel work. It's not like what I do at the office.'

At the office? thought Yvie. Making her sound as if she's some sort of tycoon rather than a typist. She took a breath. 'No. Obviously being creative is no sweat at all. And obviously I don't earn a bean doing it, either.'

The sarcasm was completely lost on Laura. 'Frankly you're lucky to earn anything from doing what you like doing most. I wouldn't mind getting paid for going down the play park with the kids or taking them swimming.'

'It's not like that. It is what I'm trained to do and I'm very professional about my painting. I do have a degree in fine art.'

'*I do have a degree in fine art,*' mimicked Laura in a babyish voice. 'Yeah, and what chance did I ever have to get a degree?'

Yvie began to lose it. 'You had exactly the same chances I did. If you cast your mind back, you may recall we went to the same school, had mostly the same teachers, we grew up in the same house and our parents gave us the same set of genes. It's just that I happened to decide I could make more of myself. I didn't want to settle for second best and a dead-end job in a dead-end town.' She nearly added, *and married to a dead-end husband*, but she managed to restrain herself just in time.

'Oh yes. Little Miss Perfect. Little Miss *I'm Too Good For Reading. I'm Too Good To Have An Ordinary Wedding. I'm Going To Have A Society Wedding And Show Up Everyone I Know, Including My Family.*'

'I didn't. That wasn't how it was at all, and you know it.'

'See!' Laura was starting to get shrill. '*See!* Even now you can't admit how it was like for us. You don't see how you showed us up at your wedding. You and your smart friends. We were mortified that we looked so shabby beside them. That we didn't know the right fork to use, the right glass to use, the right designer labels to wear. But you're so bloody

perfect you can't admit when you've got it wrong. Although
–' Laura's voice assumed a nasty, dangerous edge – 'I imagine you're so sodding perfect now, now you really have
outclassed even yourself, that you never make any mistakes
at all anymore.'

Yvie flipped. 'Just shows how much you know,' she yelled.
'I've made a really truly terrible mistake in my life. Just after
I got married, I had an affair and I am utterly ashamed of
that.'

The silence was palpable. Laura's mouth opened slackly.
'Bloody hell!' she said slowly.

Yvie shut her eyes. What on *earth* had driven her to reveal
that? 'Forget I said that,' she mumbled.

'Fat chance,' said Laura. 'You don't forget something like
that.'

'No.'

'How . . . ? What . . . ? W*hy?* Laura was floundering. Yvie
didn't really feel like going into details but, even so, her sister
deserved some sort of explanation.

'Boredom, loneliness. God knows. It was a stupid thing to
do. I've regretted it ever since. A day hasn't passed when I
haven't asked myself the same questions.'

'Who was it?'

'No one you know.' What was another lie after adultery,
thought Yvie. But she had the sense to realize that Laura knowing who it was would be no help.

'Shit, what a mess.'

'Something like that, yes.'

'Does Richard know?'

'Are you mad? And you mustn't tell him. Please, please
promise me you won't.'

'We may have had our differences but I'm not that much
of a cow,' said Laura coldly.

'No, no, of course you're not. I'm sorry. Forget I even
thought it, let alone mentioned it. It's just, I couldn't bear to
lose him.'

'And everything else,' said Laura dryly, looking around the
fabulous kitchen.

Yvie shook her head. 'I couldn't give a toss about anything
if I lost Richard. You know how the song goes, "You don't

90

know what you've got till it's gone"? Well, if nothing else, that business made me realize how much I love Richard and how awful my life would be without him.'

'You should have thought about that before you had your fling.'

'Don't you think I don't know that? But my punishment is knowing all that and not being able to go back and put it right.'

'And you think hiding it from Richard is the right thing to do?'

'I do. What happened doesn't alter how much I love him. And I've learnt my lesson. No matter what happens in the future, I'm never, ever, going to be unfaithful again.'

Laura raised her eyebrows and said nothing.

Yvie took another gulp of her wine. Let's face it, she thought, no need to worry about what else I might let slip from being in my cups; there's nothing else left to reveal. The evening could hardly get worse. Perhaps it wouldn't seem so bad through an alcohol-induced haze.

Upstairs, the front door banged loudly.

Yvie jumped so much her wine slopped. Guilty conscience or what, she thought.

'Hi,' called Richard. They heard his feet clattering down the stairs. 'Only me. I forgot my wallet. Couldn't let Mick buy all the drinks.' He appeared at the kitchen door. 'Ah, there it is.' He walked over to the dresser and put it in his pocket. 'Is it something I said?' he asked. 'Only, forgive me for mentioning it, but you don't seem very happy to see me back.'

'No, nothing like that. Not at all,' said the women almost together. Yvie tried not to exchange a look with Laura, but she knew Laura was studying her to gauge her reaction.

'Right, well, I'll leave you two slaving away. See you later.'

Yvie waited until she heard the door bang again and breathed out slowly. 'Now do you see what a mistake I made? No one can feel any guiltier than I do. I live in fear I'll let something slip, get found out and I'll wind up in the divorce courts.'

'Well, I won't put you there. Honest.'

But despite Laura's reassurance, Yvie knew that it could go horribly wrong. And it could do so all the more easily now she'd shared her secret.

91

And thirteen years on, Yvie knew it still could happen. She leaned against the window, her head resting on the cool pane. She consoled herself with the thought that, despite her catty thought earlier, Laura, as far as she knew, hadn't told anyone. Perhaps she had been unfair in thinking that Laura had broadcast her adultery around Reading like some sort of latter-day town crier. But that still left one other person who knew Yvie's secret, and that was Adam. Had he been completely discreet or had he let something slip? She knew she could find some excuse to phone him and ask, but what if either he or she were overheard? Besides which, it would mean digging up what Yvie hoped had been long buried by time. No, better to ignore the whole thing and trust to luck.

Yvie looked at her watch. Time to get Claire out of bed and to get the day going properly. She left her studio and crossed the landing to the door that led to the attic. She made her way up the spiral staircase that replaced the precipitous original, until her head emerged just above floor level. Between her and Claire's bed was a morass of clothes, CDs, underwear, schoolwork, paper, books, magazines, towels, dirty crockery, electrical beauty aids and God only knew what else.

'Claire,' called Yvie. 'Claire, time to get up.'

'Mmm,' was the indistinct response from under the messy bedcovers.

'Come on. It's seven thirty.'

That galvanized Claire. The covers were thrown back. 'Seven thirty! But you knew I needed to wash my hair.' Claire shot out of bed, grabbed a towel off the pile on the floor and ploughed a path through the mess to her bathroom. As she went, she shot her mother a baleful look.

Yvie couldn't remember any conversation about hairwashing that might have taken place the previous day. Obviously she was supposed to know by instinct.

She felt irritated by Claire's unreasonableness. 'And you can tidy your room today. Properly!'

Her only reply was the sound of Claire turning on her shower.

Yvie descended the stairs and returned to her room to get dressed. Richard was sitting up in bed drinking his tea and perusing the paper.

'I may have to go to the office,' he said.

Yvie nodded. Richard worked from home more often than not, but if something that had serious implications for Global Solutions or their clients occurred, then Rupert liked to have his staff at his head office. 'I thought you might have to. If you do, can you give Claire a lift in to school?'

Richard nodded. 'No problem. In fact, I'll take her in anyway if you like.'

Yvie finished dressing in her customary jeans and sweatshirt and went downstairs to get breakfast on the go.

She had finished making the coffee and was helping herself to a cup when Claire thundered down the stairs and into the kitchen, her hair still wet.

'Toast or cereal?' offered Yvie.

'Neither. I'm late.'

Yvie glanced at the clock on the wall. 'No you're not. Besides, Dad'll give you a lift to school.'

'Where's my sports kit?' said Claire.

Yvie shrugged. 'I haven't seen it.'

'You mean you didn't wash it? But I put it to the wash.'

'No you didn't. I'm up to speed on the washing, and no sports kit.'

Claire made a strangled wail and shot back up the stairs again. Yvie made a mental bet with herself that it was somewhere on Claire's bedroom floor. Well, if Claire got a kit mark from school for having dirty sports gear, it wasn't her fault. Although she doubted if Claire would see it like that. Yvie knew exactly who would get the blame if her daughter had anything to do with it.

By the time Claire reappeared with her sports kit, school bag and dry hair, Richard had disposed of a couple of slices of toast and was on his second cup of coffee. Yvie tried to persuade Claire to have something, but was tersely informed that if she hadn't had to spend hours looking for her school stuff, she might have had time. Yvie ignored the implied criticism of herself, and reasoned that Claire was unlikely to die of malnutrition between then and lunch time, so she gave up. Two minutes later the house was silent. Yvie breathed a sigh of relief, poured herself a fresh cup of coffee and went up to her studio determined to finish the book jacket.

* * *

Yvie painted steadily all morning. In the background the radio played pop music but Yvie was oblivious to it, lost in her thoughts about the past and what had happened in Germany. Every now and again she surfaced to reality to make a coffee or go to the loo, but mostly she painted on autopilot and replayed past events in her mind. She surprised herself at how little she now felt for Adam. There had been a time when the merest hint of his name was enough to send a whoosh of lust racing through her stomach and raise her blood pressure into the stratosphere. But not now. She came to the conclusion it wasn't just the effect of time and distance, but of maturity. She knew now, more than ever, that she was a one-man woman. There was no place in her life for anyone else. The knowledge came almost as a relief to her.

It was quite a while before Yvie stopped. The sky was finished and it framed the wary face well. She stood back to look at it. Yup, that was good. She wiped her brush on a turps-soaked rag, laid it on the easel and picked up her mug, but saw that the remains of her coffee were so cold that a sort of milky scum had formed on the surface. Time for a fresh cup, she thought. She made her way down to the kitchen and put the kettle on. As she made her coffee, she glanced at the kitchen clock. Lunch time. The morning had sped past – the upshot of all that hard work. She examined the contents of her fridge as she got the milk out. Cheese and pickle was all she was going to be having in her sandwich. She'd have to go shopping later. She put together a sandwich and took it into the garden to eat.

Holding her snack in her left hand, she wandered past the beds pulling up a weed here and there with her right. The garden was not looking at its best, she decided. It was unkempt – like an unmade bed – after the winter. She would have to make a big effort at the weekend, if the weather held. She wondered if she would be able to persuade Richard to cut the grass. That would instantly transform things, especially if she trimmed the edges too.

Out of the blue, the sun went behind a cloud and the temperature plummeted. Yvie looked up to see, not a small cloud as she had been expecting, but a huge thunderhead of apocalyptic proportions. Yvie shivered and it was not entirely due to the sudden cold gust of wind that ripped across her lawn and threw the copper beeches on the other side of the wall into a frenzy. Bewilderingly, she felt an unmistakable air of menace surround her. Common sense told her that it was just the electrically charged air before the storm broke, but underneath the application of good sense, she wasn't convinced, as she shivered and watched the goosebumps rise on her arms. Fat drops began to splat around her. Yvie ran indoors and had just reached the shelter of the kitchen as the storm broke.

Picking up her rather cool cup of coffee from where she had left it on the work surface, Yvie watched the storm from the kitchen window. It was a spectacular one, and no mistake. She drew a piece of scrap paper towards her and began to make a shopping list. She decided she would blast round the local supermarket as soon as the rain stopped – after all, Claire and Richard wouldn't thank her if they were only offered cheese and pickle sandwiches for their next meal. As the thunder crashed and the rain pounded down, Yvie checked the contents of her cupboards and her fridge and wrote down her requirements in her neat handwriting. She had about finished when the sky lightened nearly as dramatically as it had darkened, and the rainfall was reduced from a downpour to a light drizzle. Looking at the sky to the front from the basement window, Yvie reckoned it wasn't going to stop completely for a while, but, what the heck, she thought, skin's waterproof. She gathered together some shopping bags and made for the front door. She was just about to pull it closed when she heard the phone ringing. She returned indoors and picked up the receiver.

'Hello.' Silence. 'Hello,' she repeated. There was a click. Irritably, Yvie put the receiver back. How about an apology for ringing a wrong number, she thought. How much effort was that? She sighed and shook her head, then headed back to the car feeling unaccountably spooked by the call. She told herself to grow up.

By the time she reached the nearby supermarket, the rain had all but ceased, but it had had the effect of driving other shoppers away or keeping them at home – the car park was almost empty.

Yvie whizzed round the aisles in record time, loading up

95

her trolley with all the items on her list, plus a couple of others designed to placate Claire. She hadn't liked it that she and her daughter had parted on such unfriendly terms that morning, and she hoped that a packet of raspberry and apricot cereal bars and a bottle of expensive shampoo might heal the rift. She wasn't buying Claire's affection, it was just a peace offering, she told herself. And because she remembered how much time she had spent thinking about her adulterous affair, she threw a good bottle of red wine in for Richard.

When she arrived back home, she was surprised to see a sleek black limousine parked in her spot. Suppressing a little surge of annoyance, she began unloading carrier bags from the boot. It couldn't be anyone visiting her – there was no one in. How inconsiderate of her neighbours to let someone else park right outside her front door. It wasn't as though there was a shortage of parking spaces; the road around the green was almost devoid of parked cars. She sighed heavily as though each trip from the car to the door had been lengthened by yards instead of just a few feet. She piled all the bags on the top step by the front door before locking the car. Then she braced herself for the business of transporting the whole lot down the stairs to the kitchen. There were times, she thought as she began the first trip through the hall, that it would be a whole lot easier to live in a modern house.

She nearly jumped out of her skin when the door to her husband's study swung open. In her fright she dropped one of the carrier bags, which landed with a nasty splintering sound on the hall tiles.

'Richard!' she yelped when she realized her fright had been caused by her husband. 'What on earth are you doing home?' She hadn't noticed his car parked in the close. Perhaps that black limo was a company car.

'Umm, something came up,' he said non-committally, but seeming rather strained.

Yvie was only half listening and was certainly not looking as she rootled in the dropped bag to discover what, if anything, was broken. Not the jar of beetroot, thankfully – however, the marmalade wasn't looking too clever. Oh well, she thought, it could have been that decent bottle of wine. 'Right,' she said, picking up the bag again and heading for the kitchen.

'Umm, Yvie, could you leave that for a minute?'

Yvie stopped. This time she took on board her husband's serious tone and tense look.

'What is it? What, exactly, has come up?' As she asked the question, two other men materialized out of Richard's study. She jumped again. 'Oh,' she squeaked. 'Hello.'

'Hello, Mrs Maxwell,' said one.

'Is our car in your way?' said the other. 'Only, your husband—'

'Yes, it's fine,' said Yvie, not caring in the least about parking arrangements and impatient to find out just what the bloody hell was happening. She put the heavy shopping down. 'Could someone please tell me . . . ?' A sudden terrible thought stuck her. 'It's not Claire, is it? Tell me she's OK.'

'She's fine,' said Richard. 'This is nothing to do with her. Honest.'

One of the men, the older of the two, stepped forward. 'Tell you what, why don't we all go to the kitchen, have a cup of tea, and I'll fill you in on why we're here?'

There didn't seem to be much choice, so Yvie had to agree. The menace that she'd felt in the garden earlier seemed to have returned. She shivered again.

Yvie went down to the kitchen to put the kettle on. Richard and the men brought the bags of shopping down between them and dumped it all on the kitchen floor. She bustled around with mugs and milk, trying to keep her mind from going into overdrive, worrying about the presence of the strangers in her house and what it meant. She put the mugs of tea on the table and sat down.

'Right,' she said, hoping she sounded calm. 'Perhaps someone would now like to tell me just what is going on.'

'Mrs Maxwell,' began the older of the two men. 'I am Detective Sergeant Brian Gibbs and this is Detective Constable Jim Fairweather. We are from SO12 – Special Branch.'

'Oh.' Yvie was shocked. What on earth did Special Branch want with her?

'Mrs Maxwell . . .'

'Yvie, please,' she said. She couldn't be doing with this formality.

'Yvie,' said Gibbs, 'what do you know about the Carpenter?'

Despite the gravity of the atmosphere, Yvie was tempted for a ludicrous moment to reply that, although she thought some of the structures built by Handy Andy on *Changing Rooms* were an offence against good taste, they weren't so bad as to merit the intervention of Special Branch. But she restrained herself and looked for an answer that might be acceptable. From a recess in her brain, she remembered hearing the name before.

'Wasn't he an IRA bomber?'

'Exactly,' said Gibbs, nodding.

'And he was called the Carpenter because he always put the watch, or whatever, and the batteries—'

'The timer and power unit,' interrupted Richard, always a stickler for details.

'Sorry, he put the TPU –' she said TPU with heavy emphasis, cross with Richard for interrupting her – 'in a rather swanky wooden box with proper woodworking joins.'

'Absolutely right,' said Fairweather. 'And his name was Malachi Lynch.'

Yvie had forgotten his real name, if she had ever known it. But she still didn't understand what this had to do with them. 'But so what? He was sent down for ever once they caught him.'

'He was. But under the Good Friday Agreement he was let out again.'

'Oh. But what has this got to do with me – us?' she added, looking at Richard.

'Do you remember the Diplock Courts?' Gibbs asked Yvie.

'Not really.' Yvie wrinkled her forehead as she tried to drag some details of Ireland's political past to the forefront of her mind. 'Didn't they do away with juries or something?'

'Yes, and instead terrorists were tried by a panel of judges.'

'So?'

'Well, all the judges who tried Malachi Lynch are now dead.'

Yvie felt the penny beginning to drop. 'Did he kill—?'

'We don't know,' said Gibbs. 'We know for certain one of them died of natural causes. He had cancer at the time of the trial and he died about six months after Lynch was sent down. But the other two . . .' he paused.

'Just tell me,' said Yvie. She didn't want games or dramatic silences, she wanted all the facts.

'We really don't know. Verdicts of death by misadventure were returned at both inquests. One drowned. He had a boat on Strangford Lough. One night he fell overboard. It had been a fairly wild night, squally, and there was no sign of a struggle, so it was assumed that he'd taken a tumble, gone into the water and that was that. A tragic accident.'

'And the other?'

'An accident with a shotgun. He had retired to the Scottish Highlands and he went out on to the hills one day to bag some game. When he didn't come home, his wife organized a search party. They found him the next day. It seemed as though he had tripped in the heather and had shot himself in the leg. He was in the middle of nowhere and if he shouted for help no one heard him. He bled to death.'

'How awful,' said Yvie, appalled.

'Again, a tragic accident,' said Gibbs.

'But yesterday,' said Fairweather, 'the killing was deliberate.'

Yvie looked at both the policemen. 'That lawyer in Birmingham.'

They nodded. 'He was the prosecution lawyer at Lynch's trial.'

'Shit!' A cold fear began to creep through Yvie. Like a key turning in a lock and opening a door, her brain made the connection. 'And Richard defused the bomb that led to his trial, didn't he? Because of that, they found his fingerprint inside the casing, so they knew he'd made it. He went back to testify at the trial just after Claire was born.'

'Yes, that's exactly it. Yesterday's bomb, the one that killed the lawyer, was a carbon copy of the bombs the Carpenter used to plant in Ireland. We think he's back and he's out to get the people who put him away. It may be that the other deaths were just coincidental, but they were both in the last four months,' said Gibbs.

'And you think we might be next?' said Yvie slowly.

'We don't know.'

'But it's a possibility, isn't it? That's why you're here.' Yvie fiddled with her mug.

'Yes,' said Fairweather.

Yvie felt as though she was in some sort of surreal dream. This morning everything had been so incredibly normal, just a nice spring day with ordinary things happening, and now she was being told that she and her family might be blown to smithereens any day now. She looked at her hands and saw they were shaking slightly. She clasped them together and took a deep breath.

'So what happens now?' she asked. 'Presumably you know where this murderer is.'

'That's the problem.'

'You mean you don't.' Yvie's voice was high-pitched with anxiety. 'Why not?'

'After he was released from the Maze, he went to America. There are a lot of IRA sympathizers in the States, as you know. We think he was looked after by friends out there, that he changed his appearance, possibly even through plastic surgery, and got fixed up with a false passport.'

'Don't you know?' Yvie was aghast.

'Yvie, it's not that simple,' said Richard. 'They need to catch this man. They want him to make a move.'

The key clunked again in Yvie's brain. 'My God. You need some bait, don't you? And we're it. We're the tethered goats.'

'It's not "we",' said Richard. 'It's me.'

'What?' Yvie was losing the plot.

'Yvie,' said Gibbs. 'We can protect one person, we can be reasonably sure of doing that successfully, but with every additional person we have to look after, the risks go up exponentially.'

'I'm still not with this,' said Yvie.

'Brian and Jim want me to stay here and for you and Claire to go away to somewhere safe. Somewhere that no one will associate you with, so not your parents' place or your sister's or any of your close friends.'

'So, with that list of places I *can't* go, where do you suggest I *can* go?'

'We think you'd be safe with Adam and Pamela Clifton,' said Fairweather.

The names dumbfounded Yvie. After all the time that she had devoted to thinking about them this morning, now for

Adam and Pammy to crop up again . . . For a ghastly moment she wondered if this was all a put-up job; one designed to flush out the truth about her affair.

'Adam and Pammy,' she repeated to hide her confusion.

'Think about it, Yvie, they're ideal. They live on that vast estate and they have no neighbours to speak of for miles around, so no one need know you're there. It couldn't be better. Besides which, there is no obvious association with us, we haven't seen them in years. There's no way Lynch will track you there. Especially if we take sensible precautions.'

'Like?'

'You don't go telling people why you're there,' said Gibbs. 'Your daughter doesn't take a mobile with her, so there's no chance she can reveal your whereabouts by accident, you keep as low a profile as possible, that sort of thing.'

Yvie didn't doubt it was all sensible advice, but she wasn't sure how the confiscation of Claire's mobile would play. She decided she wasn't going to be the one to do it, at any rate. A thought struck her.

'But what about the owner?' Adam and Pammy might live in a huge mansion in the midst of hundreds of acres of the Lake District, but it wasn't their mansion or their acres.

'I spoke to Adam—'

Yvie interrupted him. 'Sorry, could I have a timescale here? I was gone for thirty minutes, maximum, just now. I was alone in the house when I left, and I come back to find all of you here, everyone fully briefed, and plans for my and Claire's immediate future already in place. I want to know just how long you have been privy to all this information, how long you've known that there's someone out there who wants to kill you with a car bomb and I've just been out in a car and . . .'

'Yvie, honest, I only knew about a couple of hours ago. We came straight back here to put you in the picture. As soon as I had all the facts, I rang Adam. Honestly, you've not been kept in the dark at all. And yes, I suppose we could have rung you and told you to stay inside, to lock all the windows and doors, but all we would have done was frighten you. The police think it's extremely unlikely he'll do anything in the near future. He'll keep a low profile for a while till the fuss dies down a bit after the last bomb.'

101

Yvie felt foolish. 'Sorry, sorry,' she mumbled.

'No offence taken,' said Gibbs. 'You're scared and worried. It's bound to make you upset.'

Yvie thought that 'upset' was a bit of an understatement, but she let it go.

'So, you've spoken to Adam?' she said, trying to keep her fear and worry under control.

'I didn't tell him all the details, but he got the gist. He says it's fine.'

'Meantime, you stay here and take your chances, is that it?'

'It's not a question of Richard taking his chances,' said Jim Fairweather. 'We will have a big operation to look after him.'

'What if it goes wrong?'

'It won't,' said Richard.

'How can you know that?' said Yvie, losing her battle with her feelings. 'How can you possibly be so certain? What was it the bomber who did the Brighton bomb said afterwards? "You have to be lucky all the time, I only have to be lucky once." Just suppose this one gets lucky once?'

'He won't.'

'You can't possibly be sure.' Yvie glared at the three men. They didn't answer. She'd made her point but it was a hollow victory. 'They can't make you do this, Richard,' she said as an afterthought.

'No they can't.'

'So why are you?'

'Because, if I help, they might catch him. If I don't, he'll get away with it. He's already killed and maimed God knows how many people, for which he's served about ten years in prison. I don't think it's justice of any sort for all those whose lives he wrecked.'

'And if he gets you – what about my wrecked life? And Claire's?'

'It's my duty.'

'Fuck duty,' shouted Yvie, seeing red. 'What about us? What about your family? What about your duty to us? Don't you have *any* sense of loyalty to us?'

'It isn't a question of loyalty to you,' he said quietly. 'As I said, it's duty. It's different.' He looked at the table. Anywhere but meet Yvie's stare. Brian and Jim shifted uncomfortably in their seats. The row between Yvie and Richard was a personal matter and they obviously were uncomfortable at witnessing it.

A shadow passed across the basement window. Yvie glanced up and saw Claire descending the area steps.

'Claire's back,' she said tightly. 'And just what are you going to tell her?'

'The truth,' said Richard. 'She's old enough to know and to understand.'

Yvie wasn't sure about that but she kept quiet.

Claire spotted there was something seriously weird going on the instant she walked in through the kitchen door. It wasn't just the two strange men sitting at the kitchen table, it was the horrible atmosphere and the look on her mum's face. For a second she thought perhaps that someone had died, but if that had been the case, then wouldn't her mum be looking sad or even crying? As it was, her mum just looked livid, as if she'd had a blazing row with her dad.

'Hello,' she said, not sure what else she could say. She shut the kitchen door behind her. Partly out of habit, but also it gave her another couple of seconds to try to work out what on earth was going on.

Her dad got up and came across the kitchen.

Blimey, thought Claire. This is bad.

'Claire, I'd like you to meet Brian Gibbs and Jim Fairweather. They're policemen.'

'Oh,' said Claire. Claire whizzed through her memory banks. God, was this about last week when she and Debbo had managed to get served in the Swan. She felt shaky and grabbed the back of a chair. It couldn't be that, could it? She tried to look all calm and natural but her stomach was churning.

'Guilty conscience,' laughed her dad.

Claire swallowed. Well, yeah, actually. Her heart was thumping. She wished everyone wasn't looking at her. What were they expecting? That she confess?

'Seriously,' said one of the blokes. Claire thought it was the one called Jim. 'It's nothing to do with you. Not directly, anyway.'

Claire swallowed again and exhaled. Until that moment she hadn't realized she'd been holding her breath.

'Come and sit down and we'll tell you what's going on,' said her mum.

Claire slid on to an empty chair still feeling nervous. Jim and Brian told her everything and why they were there. As the story unfolded, Claire felt increasingly angry and frightened. This wasn't the sort of stuff that happened to families like hers. This was a nightmare.

'But that's awful,' she railed when Jim and Brian stopped talking. 'Why should anyone want to kill dad?'

'He's a nasty man,' said her mum gently.

'Mother,' said Claire. 'He's not *nasty*.' Nasty, for God's sake! She wasn't a toddler. She could do big words. This was not the moment to get treated like some sort of special needs kid. 'He's evil. There's a difference.'

'Yes, well . . . The upshot though, Claire, is that we're going to have to go away.'

'Where?'

'Daddy thinks it best if we go and stay with your godfather in the Lake District.'

'You are joking, aren't you? The Lake District.' *The Lake District*? There was this really strange girl at school who went on holiday to the Lake District and did stuff like walking. Claire despised her for her frizzy hair – hadn't she heard of straighteners? – her underarm hair and her sensible shoes. What would her friends say when they heard that she was going there like Loser Lucy?

'Claire,' said her father sharply, 'this is no joking matter and there isn't any choice.'

'Yes there is. I can stay at Debbo's.'

'Not this time,' said Richard.

'But he's not after me,' said Claire.

'We don't know that for certain,' said Brian. 'As you said yourself, he's evil. There's a possibility that he might use you to get at your dad.'

Claire narrowed her eyes. 'How? He doesn't know who I am,' she reasoned.

'How do you know?' said Jim. 'He may know all about you already.

Claire felt her skin crawl. 'You mean he might have been watching us already?' Claire's voice dropped to little more than a whisper. She was horrified at the thought.

'We don't know one way or the other, but we can't take any chances.' Then her mum said something about a wrong number and how the caller hadn't said anything, just hung up.

'Has anyone else called?' asked Jim.

'Unless you took a call, no,' said Yvie.

Jim went to the phone in the kitchen and dialled 1471. 'The caller withheld the number,' he reported. 'It could just be coincidence. Chances are, if it is our friend, it'll be a mobile, and it'll probably be nicked or somehow untraceable. I doubt if we can trace anything from this. I'll get someone on to it but . . .' He shrugged.

Claire was wide-eyed. 'Ugh. It's awful, that he may know our phone number and all about us.' In fact it was horribly creepy. She shivered.

'So that's why we want to get you away to somewhere safe,' said her father.

Claire slumped in her chair. 'How long will it be for?' She was admitting defeat.

'We don't know. A month, maybe two.'

'A month . . .' She was appalled. 'What about school?' she said sulkily.

'Pammy is a teacher,' said her dad. 'And we'll get the school to give you work to do. Pammy will help you with it. You won't get behind.'

'Huh.' There was a pause, then she said, 'When do we go?'

'Tomorrow,' said her dad.

'No way. It's Debbo's party on Saturday, and I'm not missing that.'

'I'm sorry,' said Jim, 'but you're going to have to.'

Claire glowered at him. Just because he was a copper, it didn't mean he could tell her what she could or couldn't do. But it seemed that he could.

'And, I know this sounds bizarre, but we're going to want your mobile.'

'Oh no.'

'Claire, this isn't a joke, and this isn't some sort of game. Hand it over.'

Claire looked at her parents. Surely they'd tell him where to get off? Surely they'd back her up that she should keep it? But they didn't. Feeling anger and frustration boil up inside her, Claire reached into her pocket and pulled it out. She switched it off before she threw it across the table at Jim.

'There,' she said. 'Take the poxy thing.' Then, afraid that she was going to cry in front of them, she fled to her room.

The atmosphere in Yvie's car was thunderous as they crawled north on a motorway surrounded by nose-to-tail lorries and cars. The weather matched Claire's mood: the sky was leaden and every now and again the rain pelted down in angry squalls. Roadworks around Birmingham delayed them even more, and Yvie seriously began to consider the prospect of spending the night somewhere. She had banked on about six hours for the journey, but they had been on the road for over five already and they were only just nearing Manchester.

'I'm going to stop at the next services,' said Yvie. 'I need coffee and a wee. How about you?'

'No.'

'No what?' Yvie didn't know if Claire meant no coffee or no wee.

'No thank you,' said Claire with exaggerated sarcasm.

Yvie sighed. 'Is this a one-day sulk or a one-week sulk?'

'I'm not sulking.'

Yvie knew there was no point in contradicting her. 'I'm sorry about this, but please don't blame me. None of this was my idea.'

'You didn't even let me phone my friends.' Claire glared sideways at her mother. 'They don't know where I am, and Debbo'll wonder why I'm such a rude bitch that I don't even bother to turn up to her party.'

'Miss Hargreaves is going to tell everyone at school that you've had to go away for family reasons.'

'Like that's going to explain everything. If you just let me text Debbo . . .'

'No,' said Yvie more sharply than she'd intended. 'We've been through all this. For a number of very good reasons, the fewer people who know where you are, the safer it'll be for all of us.'

'But Debbo wouldn't tell.'

'It's a risk I'm not prepared to take.'

'So you're saying she can't be trusted.'

'No, and you know I'm not. Look, I haven't even told my own sister where we're going.'

'Like she'd care anyway,' said Claire under her breath. Yvie decided to ignore the comment. Apart from anything else, it was probably true. Laura resented everything about Yvie's lifestyle: her house, where she lived, her foreign holidays, the works. The fact that she and her family had been thrust into a crisis would probably only elicit a response of 'serves her right'.

They continued on in silence until they reached the next services. Claire refused to get out of the car.

'Well, you'd better not need a wee before we get to Adam and Pammy's, because I'm not stopping again.' Yvie left Claire and her bad temper and went to stretch her legs and to find a cup of strong coffee. Sipping her drink, she wandered around the bookshelves of the service area shop, refusing to be pressured into hurrying. If Claire wanted to sit in the car, hungry and thirsty, then she could. It was no skin off her nose if she wanted to sulk, and she was hardly likely to fade away for the want of one cup of coffee. But despite these thoughts, Yvie relented at the last moment and bought her a can of cola and a sticky bun. Claire didn't say anything when Yvie dropped them into her lap, but she tucked in all the same.

As they pulled out into the sluggish traffic heading north, Yvie flicked on her headlights. The gloom was partly due to the hour and partly due to the worsening weather, the rain was now pelting down steadily and Yvie began to be aware that it was turning to sleet. She hoped to God that it wasn't going to deteriorate further. She didn't fancy flogging across the Cumbrian moors in a blizzard. Did they get blizzards at this time of the year up here? Given the latitude and the elevation, it was more than likely. Oh, let joy be unconfined, she thought sourly.

'You are going to have to navigate for me in a little while,' said Yvie picking the book of maps out of the door pocket and handing them to Claire. 'Page ninety-five,' she added. 'I think we want junction thirty-six.'

Claire opened the book. 'Don't you know the way then?'

'Not really. I've never been up here. In fact, I haven't seen Uncle Adam since your christening.'

'I thought you liked him.'

'Well, he's more your dad's friend.' If you only knew the half of it, thought Yvie, thankful that her daughter most certainly didn't. The thing that worried her, though, was that only the previous day she had congratulated herself on how little she felt for Adam – which she hadn't then. But now there was the prospect of seeing him again, she felt undeniably excited, and each time she thought about him now, she felt a small surge of unmistakable lust in her stomach. She knew she had to keep it all under control and out of sight. There was no way she was going to let things start again. Not this time, no way.

The traffic trundled steadily north in three lanes, hardly anyone bothering to try to jockey for position by overtaking – there was no point. The rain fizzled out and stopped and darkness fell early. Barely five o'clock, thought Yvie, and it's already night. She thanked her stars they lived in the south. All this rugged isolation did nothing for her. The clouds cleared suddenly from the sky, revealing a cold, hard moon. The additional light was something to be thankful for, although its pale, bleaching gleam just seemed to make the surrounding countryside even bleaker. This is all I need, thought Yvie, my husband acting as bait for a revenge-driven psycho, me being stuck with the queen of the teen sulks, and the local countryside looking like the set of a gothic horror movie. Oh, she added to herself as an afterthought, and I'm to be closeted with my ex-lover and his wife, miles from anywhere, for the foreseeable future, and hope we can all behave impeccably. She sighed. Life had a habit of turning round and biting you on the bum, just when you thought everything was wonderful. Yesterday she had woken up and been filled with hope: the weather had been perfect, her painting career was going well, and everything had been coming up roses. Then, in the time it took to do a week's shopping, everything was topsy-turvy and she didn't dare look beyond the next couple of days at the most.

And what would the next couple of days hold? One thing was certain, and that was a reunion with Adam. Her thoughts flashed back to the moment in Claire's nursery, after the christening. God, she hoped he still didn't hold a candle for her. Please, she prayed silently to a God she never normally bothered, please let him have grown out of his fixation. It would be ghastly if he wanted to pick up where he had left off all those years ago. Yvie wondered how strong she would be if he did. It almost didn't bear thinking about.

'Mum! Aren't we supposed to be coming off the motorway here?' There was a note of urgency in Claire's voice.

Yvie, blasted back into reality, saw the first of the chevrons counting down to the slip road, just ahead of a lorry on her inside. Braking as hard as she dared, she indicated and began to ease her way into the nearside traffic flow. The car behind hooted.

'Mum,' said Claire, horrified.

'He'll get over it.'

Once off the motorway, Yvie pulled over, switched on the courtesy light and showed Claire the way to Adam's house. 'You see, we follow this road to this junction, then along this little yellow road, then we turn on to this one and finally on to this tiny white road.'

'You are joking,' said Claire.

'Why?' Yvie didn't understand.

'When you said we were going to be in the country, I thought you meant like in a village or something. But there's nothing.'

'Well, it is a bit isolated . . .'

'Isolated? *Isolated!* It makes Timbuktu look as though it's in the thick of things.'

'Don't exaggerate. I'm sure there'll be lots to do.'

'Like?'

'Um . . . Walking,' said Yvie brightly, trying to cover up that it was the only activity that she could think of at all.

'Oh yeah. Like that'll be so much fun.'

Claire's mood, which had lifted after the bun, was back into sulk mode. Yvie sighed and started the car. Apart from her trepidation at seeing Adam again, she couldn't wait for this journey to end.

'Thank God it can't be so far now,' muttered Yvie, more to herself than Claire.

'And how far is that exactly?'

'I don't know. You're the one with the map.' A thought struck Yvie. 'You do know where we are, don't you?'

'Yeah. I can map-read you know.'

It was about an hour later, after a tricky drive through increasingly narrow and precipitous lanes, that they spotted a monstrous pair of wrought-iron gates hanging from monumental stone pillars.

'I think we've arrived,' said Yvie, swinging the car between the gates.

'Bloody hell!' muttered Claire.

The avenue – there was too much of it to call it a drive – led through dense woodland. The moonlight made everything look eerily spooky. Yvie was immediately reminded of the opening of *Rebecca*. Every few hundred yards, there was a cattle grid. At the fifth one, the woodland abruptly stopped and in front of them was a vast expanse of parkland, dotted with ancient trees. The road led onwards through an avenue of beech trees and, at the end, standing proud on the brow of a small hill, was an enormous country mansion with a central tower rising above the front door, either side of which the many-windowed façade of the house stretched away.

'Good God!' said Yvie.

'Shit!' breathed Claire.

Yvie had known from occasional letters and phone calls that the place was big, but nothing had quite prepared her for this sort of scale.

They drove on in silence. At the top of the hill, the road opened out on to a vast sea of gravel. The car scrunched through it until Yvie drew up at the base of the flight of steps that led to the front door. It was in keeping with the house: huge, wooden and studded with black bolts. To the left was an old-fashioned bell pull.

'This is gross,' said Claire.

'I think it's rather swanky,' said Yvie, who had decided that it could be quite fun to experience such opulence for a while. She toyed with the idea of finding a postcard of the place –

110

there was bound to be one – and sending it to Laura, as it would wind her up no end. Then she remembered that such communication wasn't allowed. Claire broke into her thoughts. 'I'm just wondering what sort of creep would want to buy a place like this. Dracula perhaps?'

Yvie kept silent, as she didn't concur at all with Claire's assessment, but now was not the moment to embark on yet another disagreement. Apart from anything else, now her journey was at an end, she felt suddenly bone-tired. Wearily, she climbed out of the car. She stretched. It was so good to stop. Her back was beginning to give her gip. A gust of wind cut across the front of the house and sliced through her thin clothes. It was icy. God, she didn't want to be out here in this weather. It might be spring in Carchester, but it was still winter here, for heaven's sake! Yvie ran up the steps and yanked on the bell pull. She hoped Adam or Pammy wouldn't be too long trekking from the servants' quarters or wherever they lived; she was starting to freeze here. She waited on the top step, arms clasped across her body, trying not to shiver. A minute passed, then another. Had the bell rung? Perhaps the old-fashioned one was only for show. Perhaps there was a modern electric bell push somewhere. Yvie scrutinized the door frame. Nothing. She was just about to pull the bell again when the door opened and there, as the light flooded out, was Pammy, looking far more like the lady of the manor than the hired help. She moved forward to greet Yvie, and a pack of dogs of assorted sizes and colours rushed forward.

'Bingo, Trooper, Peanut, heel.' The tide of dogs turned and returned to the door, tails thumping, noses whiffling. 'Yvie,' said Pammy, extending both her arms. 'How wonderful to see you.' Yvie moved forward into the embrace. 'But how awful that it has taken something so horrid to bring you up here.' She hugged Yvie warmly. 'You haven't changed a bit,' she said. 'You look just the same.'

'The light's bad,' said Yvie with a grin. 'The wrinkles are there all right.'

'And Claire!' Claire shut the car door and moved forward. The dogs made a hint of a move towards her. Pammy saw her nervous flinch.

'Don't be silly,' she called. 'They're all as gentle as pussy-cats. They just want to get to know you.' Claire didn't look convinced. Yvie gave an involuntary shiver. 'You're frozen,' exclaimed Pammy. 'Come in, come in.' Yvie started to return to the car to get the cases. 'Leave the cases. I'll get Adam to drive the car round to the back. It'll save us lugging them through the house.' Pammy pushed the dogs out of the way with her foot, and Yvie and Claire entered the main hall. Yvie's eyebrows shot up in amazement and Claire gave a low whistle. Vast was the only word Yvie could think of that quite encompassed the scale. The ceiling must have been three storeys high, and a huge flight of stairs swept up from the far end, divided halfway, and then swept around to a gallery that ran the length and breadth of the hall. To Yvie's left was a fireplace big enough for her to walk in without stooping, and to her right the wall was covered with dozens of mounted animal heads – every species conceivable from every conti-nent. Yvie hoped that they were all antiques and not acquired by the current owner.

'Follow me,' said Pammy, who had bolted the door behind them. 'And don't worry about the temperature. The bit we live in has the heating belting away.'

'Am I glad to hear that!' said Yvie through teeth clenched to stop them chattering, as, even though they were now shel-tered from the biting wind, inside was as cold as outside.

Pammy led the way through the hall, followed by the three dogs, tails a-wagging, to a door set into the panelling. Yvie and Claire took their place at the back of the procession. As they passed through the door, the temperature soared, and the corridor and the rooms that led off seemed to have the propor-tions of a more ordinary house. They followed Pammy and the dogs onwards, taking various turns left and right, through a number of swing doors and then up a flight of stairs. Yvie gave up trying to remember the way. And it explained why it had taken Pammy a number of minutes to answer the door. They chatted as they went through the maze of corridors. Claire asked, a little nervously thought her mother, about the dogs, and Pammy told her that Bingo and Trooper were Springer spaniels and that Peanut was a border terrier. The spaniels were gun dogs, apparently trained to help with the shoots. Claire turned to Yvie to register her disgust at the idea of living creatures being blasted out of existence for sport. Yvie raised her eyebrows to signify that, whatever Claire's feelings on the subject, it would be polite if she kept them to herself.

Finally Pammy announced that they had arrived. She pushed open yet another door and they entered a perfectly normal flat – warm, cosy, carpeted and filled with ordinary, everyday furniture. The dogs peeled off, leaving Yvie and Claire standing in the hall.

And there ahead of them, waiting, was Adam.

Yvie felt a huge rush of adrenalin at seeing him again. She had braced herself for this moment but it still gave her a shock. She smiled. She hoped to God she looked normal. She certainly didn't feel normal. If anyone was monitoring her pulse, it would have given her away immediately.

He stepped forward, holding out his arms. 'Yvie,' he greeted her as he enveloped her in a bear hug. Yvie's knees almost buckled as she felt his arms around her again after so long. The electricity was still there. A surge powered through her, knotting her insides. No, knotted didn't do it justice. It was more like her intestines were involved in a game of cat's cradle. She noticed he still smelled the same. She had to physically check herself from burying her nose in his jumper and inhaling. Tentatively she returned the hug – hoping that she didn't look too eager. Then she disengaged herself.

'Adam,' she said somewhat awkwardly. 'Let me introduce you to your god-daughter.'

Claire stepped forward. 'Hi, Uncle Adam,' she said. She looked at her godfather. He looked like the pictures she'd seen, taken at her christening, but the pictures didn't really get his smile – or the twinkle in his eyes. Claire decided on the spot that she liked him. So why did her mum look so rigid when Uncle Adam gave her a hug? Perhaps she didn't like him much.

'Less of the uncle, please,' said Adam. 'I don't feel old enough. Besides which, I'm not a real uncle, am I? Just call me Adam.'

'And I'm Pammy.'

'Cool.' None of her mum's friends had made her feel like

113

an equal before. Claire reckoned that it was because these two didn't have kids.

'I expect you'd both like a cup of tea,' said Pammy.

'I think Yvie would like something stronger. That's a helluva journey she's just done.'

'Claire? Tea for you?'

'Yes, please.' She thought she'd exercise her newly acquired status, so she added, a little coyly, 'Pammy.'

Pammy smiled at her. 'You come with me into the kitchen. I expect you'd like a biscuit too. I made some today. Do you like shortbread?'

'You made biscuits?' she asked incredulously. 'Cor. Mum buys ours.'

Her mum grinned. 'As you can see, Pammy, some things don't change.'

Pammy grinned back and gestured to Claire to follow her. Claire went into the big kitchen, which was bright and light and smelt deliciously of home baking.

'Wow!' she said, eyeing the plate of shortbread and the chocolate sponge that was cooling on a wire rack. 'Mum never makes cakes.'

'No, but she paints beautiful pictures.'

'You can't eat pictures.'

Pammy smiled. 'Help yourself while I put the kettle on.'

Claire took a piece of shortbread and nibbled it. 'This is well nice, Pammy.'

'Glad you like it. So, I imagine you're not a happy bunny being dragged away from your friends and sent up here.'

Claire shrugged. 'Wasn't anything to do with me, was it?'

'But if it had been, you'd have stayed put.'

Claire nodded. She would have liked to have said that she would rather be anywhere than here, but she knew that would sound rude. She kept silent.

'I know Adam is offering your mum gin,' said Pammy, 'but do you want to see if she'd like something to eat?'

'OK.' Claire went into the sitting room. 'Mum . . .' Claire couldn't think why she should have surprised her mum so much, but she leapt out of her skin. Her drink slopped all over her hand and dripped on to the floor.

'Oh Claire! I didn't hear you.' She was as red as a beetroot.

What was the matter with her? And the atmosphere was weird. On the journey up, her mum had said that Adam was her dad's friend not hers. And then there had been her reaction to that hug. Perhaps they *really* didn't like each other. Well, that was going to make the stay even better. Just peachy. She remembered why Pammy had sent her to the sitting room. 'Pammy wondered if you'd like something to eat. You should try the shortbread,' she held out her piece so her mother could see the quality for herself. 'It's yummy.'

'Thanks but no thanks. The gin Adam poured me is all I need at the mo.'

'OK.' Claire left the room, wondering what on earth she could do to try to keep her mum and Adam apart. This was going to be a nightmare if her mum hated him as much as she seemed to.

'You see what I mean,' said Yvie in a low voice. 'There's no way we can even think about the past, let alone discuss it. And she's not stupid. She'd be bound to spot things. I might have got away with lying to Pammy but back then she hadn't known me for long, she knows me a whole lot better now. Anyway, I don't think I could lie to Claire. Sorry, I just can't go down that road again.'

'But I still want you, Yvie. The last time we met, at Claire's christening, I said you would come back to me. And look, you have.'

Oh, for God's sake, how deluded could this man get? 'No.'

'No, what?' asked Pammy from the door.

God, thought Yvie, can't anyone walk around noisily! Quickly she replied, 'Adam asked me if I was worried about Richard.' All these years, she thought, and I can lie to Pammy just as easily as I did before. They just trip off my tongue. What a fake I am.

'I do admire you,' said Pammy. 'I'd be a wreck if I was going through what you and Richard are. But you always were strong.' Yvie had the grace to feel embarrassed by this praise. Pammy continued, noticing nothing. 'Do you want to phone him? Let him know you've arrived safely.'

'In a little while. Perhaps when we've had supper.'

'Right, well, when you've had your drink, I'll show you

your room. I hope you don't mind, but I've put you and Claire in together. I wasn't sure how she'd feel about sleeping on her own in this huge pile, and anyway, my other spare room is a total tip and I didn't have time to sort it out.'

'For heaven's sake, Pammy, we're just grateful for anything. Sharing is fine.'

Yvie took another slug of her drink. 'This is really good of you, to take us in at such short notice.'

'Goodness, it wouldn't have mattered if you had just turned up on the doorstep. It's what friends are for. Besides which,' added Pammy, 'as I said, it's been far, far too long since we've got together, and I'm just so sorry it couldn't be under happier circumstances.'

'Yeah, well. I suppose I should just be grateful that the police found out about this guy before he got to Richard, not after. That lawyer didn't get this break.'

A silence fell as they considered that. Yvie put her glass down. 'Come on, why don't you show me our room?'

'Give me your keys and I'll get your stuff round,' said Adam.

Yvie handed over the bunch and Adam left the room.

Pammy gave them the grand tour of her flat, ending up with the guest bedroom. It was all pink chintz and frills – very Pammy – but spacious and warm.

'This is wonderful,' said Yvie.

'Bagsy the bed by the window,' Claire said, and plumped herself down on it.

'That's fine by me,' said Yvie.

'The bathroom across the hall is yours. Adam and I have our own, as you saw. And don't worry about the hot water. The tank in this place is the size of an Olympic swimming pool. I've never known it run out – even when Mr Big brings a houseful here.'

'Is that often?'

'About once a year. Usually for shooting.'

'Gross.' Claire grimaced.

Adam appeared with a couple of their cases and dumped them on the floor. He was noticeably out of breath. 'I'll go back for the rest in a minute. Haven't either of you heard of the concept of travelling light?'

Claire laughed. 'Sorry.' She sounded anything but. 'I wasn't sure what to bring. Apart from anything, we don't know quite how long we'll be staying.'

'Well, don't unpack everything, as you won't be staying here for very long at all.'

'Sorry?' said Yvie, not understanding.

'I mean, not here in this room,' explained Adam. 'If you'd rather, of course, you *can* stay here, but Pammy and I thought that you might prefer to be independent. Then you can do as you please. There's a cottage on the estate that's perfect. It's actually a holiday cottage, but we haven't had any bookings for it yet this year. It's yours if you want it.'

'Oh. That's, umm, very kind.' Yvie was fazed by this sudden change of plan. 'It's got lovely views,' said Pammy, encouragingly. 'And you're very close to the village. There's a shop there that sells almost everything. Once a week I do a shop in Keswick, but it's really handy for when I run out of things. They'll also deliver papers if you want.'

'Umm, no. The police said not to give our names out more than necessary.'

'Well, get whatever you want sent here. Adam can drop them over to you when he does his rounds.'

'We'll see.'

Pammy grinned at them brightly. 'Right, well, we'll leave you to get settled. Adam, could you get Yvie another gin and then bring up the rest of their stuff? If you want to freshen up, we'll be eating in about fifteen minutes.' And Pammy bustled off to the kitchen to finish the cooking. Behind her back, Adam gave Yvie a wink and tugged his forelock. Yvie, still angry about his earlier comment about her returning to him, ignored his attempt at humour. There was no way she was going to encourage him in any way, shape or form. If she did, God alone knew how he might interpret it and what it might lead to. She simply mustn't go down that route.

The next day brought driving rain and gales. Claire could hear it lashing against the window despite double glazing and the duvet pulled up to her ears. Just brilliant, she thought. She sat up and pulled the curtains back as gently as she could, so as not to wake her mum. However, the curtain track was an old one and the hooks metal, so it made a rattle despite her care.

117

She heard her mum stir. Claire looked out of the window and was so disgusted by the grey veil of rain that drifted across the view that she couldn't help a small snort escaping from her.

'You're not here for a holiday, so it doesn't really matter what the weather does,' she heard her mother say.

Claire shot her a look which was ignored. It didn't matter why they were there, the weather was still pants. Her mum heaved herself out of bed and crossed the room to kneel on Claire's bed and look out the window. Through the thick grey pall of unremitting rain and low cloud, it was possible to see a lake gleaming dully about a quarter of a mile away. The house appeared to be situated in the bottom of a U-shaped valley, with steep hills dotted with a few sheep rising on either side of them. The tops of the hills were, of course, obliterated by the lowering clouds. Between them and the lake there was parkland, dotted with huge mature cedars, oaks and beeches. In the sunshine, the spot was probably absolutely beautiful, but right now Claire thought it looked completely depressing. She just thanked her lucky stars she was nice and warm in a centrally heated bedroom and not stuck out on the fells like the poor bloody sheep.

There was a knock at the door.

'Come in,' called her mum. It was Pammy offering early-morning tea and wanting to know what they wanted for breakfast. She was horrified when Yvie and Claire declined bacon and eggs.

'But you'll starve!'

'I'm still living off last night's supper,' protested Yvie. 'Look, us soft southerners don't need as many calories to survive. We take cars and loaf a lot. None of this fell walking and battling against the elements for us!'

'OK. Toast and cereal it is. But I bet you change your ways once you've been up here for a couple of weeks. We'll get you out on the moors, you see if we don't.'

'Doubt it,' muttered Claire under her breath as Pammy left them to get washed and dressed.

She saw her mum suppress a smile. Yeah, she could see her mum tramping across the moors like Janet Street-Porter. Her mother didn't even walk to the newsagents at the end of the road if she could help it. What was it she said? If God had intended her to walk, He wouldn't have invented high heels. After breakfast, they all piled into Adam's battered old Range Rover for the trip to the cottage.

'I'll take you the short way,' he said as he turned the vehicle off the main drive and on to a dirt track. They bounced and jounced over several hundred yards of potholes and ruts before emerging on to a country lane that ran between the estate land and the lake. Adam drove along the lane for about a hundred yards and then swung the car through a gap in the drystone wall and pulled up in front of a tiny whitewashed cottage with a grey slate roof.

'Here we are,' said Adam cheerfully.

Claire leaned forward so her head was between her mum's and Adam's, so she could peer through the rain spattered on the windscreen. It looked pretty enough, but how efficient was the heating? And what about the plumbing? Picturesque was all well and good, but not if it came at the expense of modern amenities. And where was the village that Adam had assured them was so close?

Adam seemed unaware of his god-daughter as he leaned towards her mum. Claire flopped back on her seat, her view obliterated by Adam. Like her mum was going to enjoy Adam being so close. Obviously her godfather didn't realize that her mum didn't like him much.

'See that footpath there?' he said, pointing. Claire squinted, her mum nodded. Claire could imagine she could make out a stile leading over a wall. 'The village is over the rise and round the corner – about five hundred yards along the footpath. It's about three miles by car, as this track peters out by the lake. You have to go back round via the main gate to the estate. The walk is lovely. Even a soft southerner like you should be able to totter that far.'

Claire thought about telling Adam what her mother's views on walking were, but decided that it would be a bit cheeky.

'Right, well, why don't we get into the house instead of sitting here in the car?' suggested Pammy. 'I switched the heating on yesterday, so it should be as warm as toast in there now.'

At least, thought Claire, I needn't worry about freezing to

119

death. And if the cottage had heating, then the plumbing was probably efficient too. Thank God for that. A decent shower rather than baths in front of the fire.

Pammy jumped out of the car and ran to the front door. Claire and the others waited in the car for her to open it. 'No point in us all getting wetter than necessary,' remarked Adam pragmatically.

As soon as Pammy had the door open, they raced to join her. The three of them burst through it and into the living room.

'Feet!' Pammy yelled at them. They made a token effort on the large doormat. As Claire wiped, she looked at the interior of the cottage. The floor was stone flags but with bright rugs strategically placed. There was a huge fireplace at one end, with a black stove instead of an open hearth. In front of it were a comfy-looking sofa and a big wing chair. In the corner was a TV. Thank goodness for that. She had been worried that the sort of people likely to rent a place like this might be the likes of Loser Lucy and her family – all bracing walks and improving games on holiday, and no slobbing in front of the box. The other end of the living room was taken up by a spacious kitchen area. Not that Claire could see her mum making much use of that. After all, she had a wonderful show-piece kitchen back at Hanover Close, but she spent most of her time in it heating up ready meals.

Her mum was asking Pammy about various appliances.

'Don't worry,' she said. 'Dishwashers are available this far north, as are washing machines.'

'Phew,' said her mum. 'I was awake all night with worry.'

'Got them brought up by mule train specially.'

'More reliable than those newfangled railways,' added Adam.

Was her godfather having a laugh? Surely . . .

'Adam's joking,' said Yvie. 'They've had railways—'

'Since just after you were born.'

Claire's grasp of history didn't encompass the industrial revolution, it wasn't on the syllabus.

'Adam, do stop it. The poor kid thinks I've brought her to the back of beyond as it is. You're not helping matters, really you're not.' But Yvie's reprimand was spoilt by the fact that she was laughing as she said it.

'Can I go upstairs?' asked Claire. If the grown-ups were going to make idiots of themselves, she didn't think she wanted to be around to see it.

'Sure. I'll show you around.'

Pammy opened a door to reveal a spiral staircase.

'Neat. It's like my stairs to the attic,' said Claire. Perhaps things were looking up after all.

'You are made to sleep in the attic?' said Adam with a laugh. 'What cruel parents you have. Still, better than the cellar, with the cockroaches and the rats.'

Claire shook her head, rolled her eyes. She supposed he thought he was funny. Then she turned and followed Pammy upstairs. As she went, she hoped her mum would be all right with Adam. Well, she was an adult and she could join her and Pammy on the guided tour if she wanted to. Claire didn't feel it was her place to be her mum's minder.

Adam shut the door behind Pammy and Claire. 'And I'll show you around downstairs.' He moved towards Yvie and, before she realized what was happening, he had wrapped his arms around her and was kissing her. Yvie felt herself go weak as her resolve to keep a distance between them evaporated into nothing. She forgot herself, Richard, Claire, Pammy, and sank into his embrace. She so remembered his kiss and the feel of his body against hers. The floorboards upstairs creaked loudly and brought Yvie to her senses. She pushed Adam away.

'No,' she said breathlessly, her heart pounding.

'You're kidding yourself, Yvie. You want me as much as I want you.'

'No,' she lied. There was no way she was going to admit the truth, not even to herself. She got her breathing under control. 'You caught me off guard, that's all. What's past is past. We've both got too much to lose.'

'But Yvie . . .'

'No, Adam. I mean it.' She was cross. Cross at having been caught out and cross at her body for betraying her by responding.

'You can't deny that what we had before was special.'

'Yes, it was, to start with. But back then, when we could both have left our partners, when there wasn't a child involved, when neither of us had been married any time at all and we didn't have a heap of emotional baggage, we stayed put. Neither of us went for the divorce option then, and I don't think either of us would now. We were lucky last time, we got away with it. I'm not prepared to risk it all again. Besides, I may want you but I love Richard.'

'We could be discreet. No one need know.'

'No. I'd know, you'd know. And I don't want to start having to lie to Richard again. He doesn't deserve that, and what's more neither does Pammy.' The boards upstairs creaked again. 'Best you show me the downstairs as you said, otherwise they'll both wonder what we were doing with our time.' She stamped off into the kitchen area and began opening cupboards.

'Don't ignore me, Yvie.'

'I'm not.' She found the dishwasher masquerading as a unit and opened it. Small but perfectly formed. It would be more than adequate for her and Claire.

Adam squatted beside her. 'We can't just pretend there's nothing between us.'

'Why not?' Yvie shut the dishwasher and stood up. 'We pretended like crazy when Pammy came back from nursing her mother. I seem to remember we behaved as if we had hardly exchanged a word while she was away, when, as you and I were both fully aware, we had exchanged a darn sight more than that!' Yvie marched across the kitchen and opened the back door. Just at that moment the clouds parted a fraction and the sun came out. The valley was transformed from shades of sludge to a sparkling emerald jewel, and the lake shimmered like shot silk. Yvie stared, transfixed by the transformation.

'Beautiful, isn't it?' Adam said into her ear.

Yvie turned and Adam kissed her again. She tried to push him away again, but as they were both wedged in the doorway, there was nowhere to push him to. She knew she should struggle, she knew she should resist, but . . .

'There,' whispered Adam as he drew away. 'Now tell me it's over.'

Yvie felt defeated, but she still lied. 'It is, Adam, and you know it. And you're kidding yourself that we could let it happen again like it did before. I am not going to be unfaithful to Richard again.'

'I see.'

'I mean it.' But Yvie wasn't sure that Adam was going to respect her resolve.

Claire was delighted with the upstairs of their cottage. The rooms were in a converted attic space, so the ceilings were all angled and sloping and reminded her of home. As she was exploring, opening cupboards and checking out the shower, the sun came out and lit up the countryside.

Goodness, it is lovely, she thought. The nearby lake sparkled and glimmered, the hills turned all shades of green and russet and grey, and the patch of sky that had cleared was a deep sapphire blue. Perhaps it wasn't going to be so bad living here after all.

'Happy?' asked Pammy.

'Yeah. It's cool. I like all the cupboards. Usually when we go away there's never enough space to hang my clothes up.'

'I'm sorry there's no bath in this cottage.'

'It won't worry me. I only ever take showers at home. Dunno about mum though.'

'Well, it's not for ever. If she really wants a bath, she can always come up to the hall. Now tell me about your room at home.'

So Claire sat on the bed and described in detail her attic space at Hanover Close.

'Sounds great.'

'I think mum wanted it for a studio but she's got one of the smaller bedrooms.'

'We'll have to fix her up with something here. Come on, let's go down and join the others.

Claire opened the door at the bottom of the stairs and peeped round. Her mum was standing by the sink. She looked odd. Had she had a row with Adam? He was across the other side of the room like they wanted to put as much space between them as possible. Claire thought she ought to rescue her mum.

'You've got to see upstairs, Mum. It's so dinky. And you can see the village. It's no distance. And there's a power shower. My room is tiny but there's lots of cupboard space.

Come on, Mum. I'll show you.' And she dragged her mother up the stairs and wondered if she should ask if there was a problem. On balance, perhaps not.

'So, you think you could bear to live in the cottage till you can go back home?' asked Pammy when they returned down-stairs.

'It's perfect,' said Yvie. 'And, to be honest, I was worried about imposing on you for ages. You know what they say – fish and visitors stink after three days.'

'We have running water; you could wash,' said Pammy with a smile.

'Yes, but you know what I mean.'

'I'm afraid, though, this cottage isn't equipped with a studio. However, there are plenty of rooms at the Hall that you could use. I checked a few out earlier for light and stuff. There are rooms that are never used from one year to the next, so you won't be in anyone's way. I'm afraid we won't be able to heat it with much more than a portable heater, but see what you think.'

Yvie was suddenly startlingly aware that she was close to tears. All this kindness, on top of all the worry and the reawak-ening of her feelings for Adam, had caught her at an emotional weak point. She blinked rapidly in the hope that the tears would disappear and not spill. But Pammy noticed.

'Hey,' she said, moving forward and putting her arm round Yvie. 'I'm only offering you an empty room, not one of my kidneys!'

'I'm sorry,' said Yvie, sniffing. 'I'm tired and emotional.' She gave her daughter a wan smile, aware that Claire was staring at her intently. But then, thought Yvie, she hasn't often seen her mother cry.

'And you have every right to be,' said Adam, taking her hand and patting it. Yvie nearly snatched it away, then real-ized that would be more of a giveaway than not reacting. She pulled herself together and sniffed. She freed herself gently from Pammy's hug and fished up her sleeve for a tissue. At least, she thought as she blew her nose, at least in this cottage she'd be away from Adam. She decided to turn down Pammy's offer of a studio. Up at the Hall she might bump into Adam

124

more often than she cared to think about. Better to stay put in the cottage.

'Now,' said Pammy, 'all we have to do is work out where I'm going to teach Claire. To be honest, it would be easier for me to do it at the Hall, if that's OK with you, as I need to be near the phone. You could walk over in no time if you took the short cut that Adam showed you on the way here.'

Claire nodded and shrugged. 'I suppose,' she said.

'Yeah, I know. The idea of having a friend of your mum's teach you can't be great, but you don't want to fall behind. I'm not sure how good I'll be at the science and stuff, but I'll be OK at the rest. I do supply teaching locally, so I do know what I'm talking about – well, mostly, anyway. Your dad is arranging to have a load of work from your school posted up here. We'll sort it out. And I'll do other stuff with you – how about I teach you to cook too? And what about dressmaking? Even if you don't make your own clothes, it's a useful skill.'

Claire nodded. 'Yeah, sounds good. Well, the cooking bit does.'

'That's great.'

'Right,' said Adam. 'That's settled. I vote we get back to the big house, grab some lunch and then move you in over here.'

Yvie and Pammy decided that Claire wouldn't start her lessons until after the weekend, giving them time to settle in, unpack and explore their surroundings. On the first afternoon, Yvie braved the rain and trudged the quarter mile to the village, along the path that bordered the lake, to get supplies. It was only raining slightly when she set out wearing a thin jacket over her jeans and sweatshirt, but as she neared the village, the heavens opened. She sprinted the last hundred yards to the handful of houses and the shop. She tumbled in through the front door dripping.

As she shook the rain out of her hair, she looked around her. What a shop! The front half stocked basic necessities – bread, milk, some frozen meat and veg, tins and the like – but the stock at the back could have equipped a Himalayan expedition, together with a full quota of Sherpas. There were tents, cagoules, boots, lengths of rope, cleats, crampons, ice axes, Primus stoves

125

– name it and it was there. Yvie wandered round the emporium, stunned at the range. Not what you'd expect to find in most village shops round her usual neck of the woods. However, it was, she reasoned, probably what many tourists wanted. In fact, she thought, she might invest in a pair of wellies while she was here. Trainers, she noticed as she squelched around, were not designed to cope with these elements.

'Can I help you?' asked a fresh-faced lad with tousled hair and a faint Lancashire accent, who appeared from behind a display of sleeping bags.

'Er, no thanks. I was just looking.'

The lad's gaze travelled to Yvie's soaked trainers and soggy jeans.

'You've not come equipped for wet weather then?' he asked.

'No. I mean, I have, but I've not unpacked yet. I really just want a few groceries.'

The lad gestured to the shelves at the other end of the shop. 'Well, this isn't Tesco's, but I think you'll find we've most things if you're not after caviar or quails' eggs.'

'I don't think my Tesco's runs to those either,' said Yvie.

'And where would your Tesco's be?'

'Down south. Wiltshire.' Yvie didn't want to be more specific. The warnings from Special Branch had been perfectly clear on the subject of not giving away unnecessary information about herself.

'Are you camping?'

'No, staying with friends.' And Yvie moved determinedly to the food shelves. This was turning into the Spanish Inquisition, and she really didn't want to answer any more questions. She grabbed a basket and began to fill it with beans and bread and other staples.

'You walked here then?' said the lad chattily.

'Hmm?' responded Yvie, pretending she hadn't really heard.

'There's no car parked outside. You walked.'

'Yes.'

'So you're local.'

'Mmm.'

'Who are your friends?'

Yvie sighed and turned round. 'Look, I really don't think it's any of your business.'

126

The lad gazed at her completely unfazed. 'You're in one of the Cliftons' cottages – right?'

Yvie sighed with barely suppressed exasperation. 'Yes.'

'Had to be, really. If you were in the village, I'd have noticed. We don't miss much in a little place like this.'

'I can imagine,' said Yvie dryly. She moved around the aisles, stocking up on basics. She'd drive to Keswick on Monday, she thought, to get fresh meat, fruit and veg, but at least they now had enough to keep starvation at bay for a couple of days.

After she paid for her groceries, she made up her mind to splash out on the wellingtons. She was going to end up with trench foot if she didn't get some waterproof footwear sorted out.

'If you're doing any fell walking, you'd be better off with proper boots,' the lad advised.

'I don't think so,' said Yvie.

'You'll change your mind, you'll see. No one can resist when the sun's out.'

'Right,' said Yvie, thinking that she'd bet her last penny that she'd be able to. Richard might be into the great outdoors and being rough and tough, but the only contact Yvie wanted with the countryside was to be able to paint it – and in fine weather and journeying by car. She chose a pair of green wellies, paid for them and then, squaring her shoulders, she braced up for the wet walk home.

She hurried as much as she could, laden as she was with two heavy carrier bags, but she was still soaked through by the time she reached their cottage. She opened the door and there was Adam, lounging on the sofa and looking thoroughly at home.

'Oh, hello,' she said. She kicked off her wellingtons and took the shopping over to the kitchen area. Adam got up and came towards her.

'You're soaked,' he said.

'Ten out of ten for observation. Where's Claire?' She peeled off her sodden jacket and rubbed her hands to warm them.

'Pammy took her over to the Hall for a chat about school work. I thought I'd drop by and see if you needed anything.' He leaned on the breakfast bar and gazed at her. Yvie ignored him and busied herself putting her purchases away. Adam moved round the bar.

127

'Come on, Yvie. You know you're kidding yourself.'

'Kidding myself is better than lying to Pammy and deceiving Richard.'

'God, Yvie. I still love you, you know.'

Yvie stepped back but she came up against one of the kitchen units. 'No,' she said. 'What don't you understand about that?'

'But you know you feel the same way.'

It doesn't mean I have to give in to my feelings. I like chocolate but I can resist that as well. This is *wrong*, Adam. W.R.O.N.G.' She spelled it out. 'And I don't want you visiting me here when I'm on my own. This is a tiny place. People have already worked out I'm staying here—'

'Who?' Adam interrupted.

'The lad in the shop.'

'Mark?'

'I don't know his name. He asked all the questions. It was like being interrogated.'

'He means no harm. He's a nice lad. I should think he's bored when it's out of season as it is now.'

'Bored or not, he worked out I was staying with you, and I've no doubt that piece of intelligence is round the rest of the village by now. If you're seen over here too often, someone will do the sum and that will be that.'

'Come off it. The locals don't come this way. The footpath doesn't go anywhere they want to go.'

'You can't be sure of that. It seems everyone here is hell bent on getting out and walking – it's all anyone I've met so far seems to talk about. Well, when they're not finding out your Granny's maiden name.'

'Just because they all talk about it, doesn't mean they do it. Pammy only ever goes fell walking when we've got visitors and she's showing them around.'

'So maybe that's when the villagers do their walking. I'm not taking the risk, and that's that. Promise me, Adam, promise me you won't come round here when I'm on my own.'

Adam sighed. 'All right. If it makes you happy, I will.'

'Good. Now I shall make you a cup of tea and then you are to go home, back to Pammy, and stay away.'

'You're so masterful.'

'I mean it, Adam.' Yvie wasn't going to be distracted by humour. She put the kettle on and plugged it in. There was a slight pop and the power cut out. 'Shit!'

'See, you do need me.'

'No I don't. I can do fuses. All I need to know is where the fuse box is.'

Adam showed her the cupboard by the back door. 'In here.' Yvie opened it. 'It's only the trip switch,' she said, looking inside. 'I wonder what caused that to go?'

'Faulty kettle?'

'It's your kettle. You tell me.'

Adam flicked the kettle on again. The trip switch cut out. 'Yup. I'll get you a new one. The last lot of tenants must have knackered it and not bothered to tell us.'

'I'll make do with a saucepan for the time being. I'm going into Keswick on Monday to do a proper shop. I'll get one then.'

'Let me have the bill and I'll pay you back for it.'

'Really, Adam, I can afford a kettle.'

'But this is a holiday let. Things like replacing kettles are all tax-deductible.'

'In which case, I should be paying you rent.'

'We haven't had any takers yet this year. The place would only be standing empty.'

'But this is business, and it isn't as if I can't afford it.'

'And it isn't as if the owner can't either.'

'Well . . .'

Yvie's mobile began to ring. She crossed the kitchen to her handbag to answer it.

'Richard! Yes, fine . . . Pretty well settled now . . . Yes, Claire's over at the Hall talking school work with Pammy . . . Oh, he's fine. Do you want a word? He dropped by to fix the electrics.' Not much of a lie, she thought as she handed the phone over to Adam. She eavesdropped on Adam's half of the conversation, which was all mundane chit-chat, until he handed the phone back to her. Yvie was eager to know how things were progressing at Richard's end, but all he could tell her was nothing had happened over the last couple of days, that he was finding it difficult living under constant surveillance and that he was missing her already.

129

'And how's Claire getting on?' Richard asked.

'She says she feels like only half a person without her mobile. She's still bitching about the police taking it off her.'

'But she must understand why. It would be so easy for her to let something slip to a friend in all innocence, and we simply don't know how this guy operates, how he gets his information.'

'She says it's unlikely any of her friends would talk to an ancient creep like him. And anyway, why should I be allowed to keep mine.'

'Obviously because you're a trustworthy adult and she isn't.'

Yvie felt a pang of guilt at the word 'trustworthy'. How trustworthy had she proved to be in the past?

'Hmm,' she said.

'Well, that's as may be,' said Richard, misunderstanding Yvie's ambivalence. 'But we're not taking any risks. Give her my love when she gets home.'

Yvie put her phone back in her bag and then got on with making a pot of tea. It took an age for the water to boil using a saucepan, and Yvie regretted offering Adam a cuppa. She really wanted rid of him now. Apart from the fact she wanted to run a hot bath and change into dry clothes, she found his presence disturbing – but she wasn't sure if it was because she had rejected him or because she wished she hadn't. Either way, she felt relieved when he had gone.

On the following Monday, when Claire had gone over to the Hall for lessons, Yvie was tidying the house in a half-hearted way prior to setting out for the nearest town and a proper supermarket shop. She looked out of the window and saw Adam walk down the short cut towards the cottage.

'Oh no,' she muttered under her breath.

But then, when he turned on to the path that led to the village without a glance at the house, Yvie felt a stab of disappointment. It stunned her. It proved to her that it didn't matter how mentally determined she was to keep Adam at arm's length, her emotions, her basic instincts, were all set to betray both her and her resolve. Suddenly it became even more imperative that she and Adam were never alone.

* * *

A week went by, then two, and life settled into a routine. The weather improved, or more accurately it rained less. Richard phoned most days for news, and to let them know that he was still safe and well. Claire discovered that she rather enjoyed her lessons with Pammy – there was something to be said for one-to-one attention – to say nothing of the other skills that Pammy thought it was important for her to learn. And Yvie found herself, much to her surprise, actively contemplating buying a pair of proper walking boots so she could get out into the magnificent country that surrounded her. She mentioned it to Pammy one day when she went over to the Hall to pick up the newspapers and post.

'I knew it would happen. No one can resist the pull of the fells once they're here,' said Pammy, smiling.

'I really just want to take advantage of my stay here to build up a library of sketches. And I thought I'd take loads of photos too. So often the book jackets I get commissioned to do need this sort of landscape as a backdrop. It would be great to have some of my own original material to draw on.'

'Excuses, excuses,' said Pammy. 'You just want to get out there and roam.'

'Honestly not,' replied Yvie, but the fact that she too was laughing made a complete mockery of her words.

Pammy sensibly suggested that Yvie should only invest in boots.

'Boots,' she said, 'are personal, and it's terribly important that they fit really well. Other stuff, wet weather gear, maps and suchlike, we can lend you. There's no point in you going to a lot of expense only to find that you're going home in a few days.'

It made sense to Yvie, so that afternoon she and Pammy walked to the village shop to get her fitted for boots.

'Told you so,' said Mark, when Yvie told him what she was there for. 'How's the holiday going?'

'Oh, fine.'

'You here for long?'

'Mrs Maxwell is up here working,' said Pammy. 'She's an artist.'

Mark looked suitably impressed and went to get some stock to show them.

131

'Thanks,' whispered Yvie. 'He's relentless with his questions.'

'But he's very nice. Nice family. You ought to introduce him to Claire.'

Yvie was horrified. 'Pammy,' she hissed. 'I hardly think the circumstances are right, or appropriate, for matchmaking.'

Pammy shrugged. 'I was hardly thinking about matchmaking. But Claire needs company of her own age. She is stuck in the middle of nowhere. I don't know what the young do round here for amusement, but Mark will. It'd do her good to get out and have some fun.'

Yvie was unable to reply, as Mark came back with a selection of footwear. However, she thought about what Pammy had said while she tried on the hiking boots.

'Not stylish, but practical,' she announced as she walked up and down in front of the mirror at the back of the shop.

'I think you'll find that boots with kitten heels were last year's fashion,' said Pammy.

'I know. But you have to admit that they make my legs look short and stumpy.'

'Even if your legs were amputated below the knee, they would still look longer than most people's,' retorted Pammy with a snort of envy. Yvie did a half turn to see what the boots looked like from another angle. 'For heaven's sake,' said Pammy, 'it's the fit that's important, not how they look. By the time you've waded through a couple of bogs, they'll look a mess anyway.'

Yvie eventually made her mind up and paid for them.

'Yikes!' she said when Mark told her how much. 'Do you mind if I pay by cheque? I haven't enough cash on me.'

'That's fine,' said Mark.

Yvie wrote the cheque and rummaged in her bag for the card.

'Don't worry about that,' said Mark. 'You look trustworthy.'

Good grief, thought Yvie. She couldn't remember the last time a shopkeeper had trusted her like that.

'You'd better get plenty of use out of them to justify the expense,' said Pammy.

'Well, that rather puts me at odds with hoping I'll be able

132

to go home again soon.' Yvie regretted that little sentence as soon as she'd said it. Mark shot an inquisitive look her way from across the shop, which even Pammy noticed. 'I'll be so glad when the builders have finished,' Yvie added quickly.

Mark finished packing the boots up and Yvie and Pammy left the shop and walked towards the car.

'I am impressed,' said Pammy. 'Fancy being able to lie that fluently.'

'I don't know where it came from,' said Yvie, knowing full well that it had come from months of practice of almost constant lying.

'Even so, I really think you ought to relax. I mean, the folks around here probably hardly know what IRA stands for, let alone anything about them. You're paranoid.'

'Well, wouldn't you be, under the circumstances?' shot back Yvie with a flash of anger fuelled partly by guilt.

Pammy was contrite. 'I'm sorry. You're right, and I have no right to criticize. I can't imagine what you're going through. But you're probably safer here than almost anywhere on earth. And because the neighbours are so nosy, it's also a form of protection. Trust me, if there's anyone round here acting suspiciously, we'll all know about it instantly.'

'But there'll soon be hundreds – thousands – of tourists. No one will spot one stranger amongst so many, and I bet not all of them are model tourists. I bet any number of them cause raised eyebrows all over the place.'

Pammy shrugged. 'Yeah, but even if they're odd, they do touristy things. Your bloke is unlikely to. Honestly, if he does come up here, he'll stand out. I really *do* think you and Claire are as safe as houses.' Yvie nodded, but she didn't look convinced. 'And Mark isn't an IRA spy. You can put your foot down if you like, but I think he'd be a good companion for Claire.'

'Claire, could you nip down to the main hall and check if the post has come yet?'

'Of course, Pammy.'

Claire pattered off out of the flat, through the labyrinth of corridors and fire doors to the hall. She opened the door that

133

led out under the grand staircase, and a lad carrying a spirit level and a plank of wood nearly cannoned into her.

'Watch out,' she said.

'Oh, sorry.' He shifted the plank under his arm so he could hold the door open for her. 'You staying with Pammy?'

'Sort of. We're in a cottage by the lake.' Claire let the door swing shut behind her and began the trek across the vast stone expanse of the hall. The lad followed her.

'So your mum is the artist?'

'Yes, how did you know that?'

'She came into the shop the other day to buy a pair of boots. My dad owns the shop. I'm Mark, by the way.'

'Claire.' She stuck her hand out, feeling a bit awkward. Mark juggled the spirit level and the plank again so he could shake it. 'So, what are you doing . . . ?'

'I help out round the estate sometimes. Adam pays better wages than my dad. You here for long?'

'I don't know.'

Mark frowned. 'Not a holiday then.'

'No. Look, I can't really talk about it.'

'OK. That's cool.'

'I'd better get on. Pammy'll be wondering where I've got to.'

'Yeah. Me too. Perhaps I'll see you later. I need to talk to Pammy about some stuff.'

Mark wandered off and Claire watched him go. Then she ran across the rest of the hall, grabbed the post and returned to ask Pammy more about Mark.

'I'll give you the low-down when you've finished that piece of French comprehension I set you,' Pammy said with a smile on Claire's return.

'Slave-driver,' muttered Claire.

'Do you want me to tell you about him or not?' said Pammy with mock severity.

Claire knuckled down to her work while Pammy sorted out some holiday bookings on the other side of the table. They worked steadily for the best part of half an hour before the timer on the cooker buzzed.

'How's the French coming on?' said Pammy.

'I think I've done it all,' said Claire.

134

'In which case, you can get the cake out of the oven and put it to cool while I check your work. Oh, and put the kettle on while you're at it. I think it's time for a tea break.'

Claire busied herself with the cake, turning it out on to the wire rack, and made a cuppa for them both. She'd just finished mopping up the crumbs off the work surface with a damp finger when the doorbell rang.

'I'll get it,' she said as Pammy was still engrossed in marking her work.

'Fine,' said Pammy, waving a pencil vaguely in acknowledgement.

Claire opened the front door to find Mark on the threshold.

'Oh!' she said. 'Pammy's in the kitchen.'

On cue, Pammy called, 'Who is it?'

'Only me,' called back Mark.

'Come on through. We're just about to have a tea break.'

Mark seemed very at home, thought Claire, as she followed him back into the kitchen. Pammy was pouring the tea into mugs and Claire noticed that she didn't ask Mark if he took sugar – she just ladled in a couple of spoonfuls.

'There you go,' she said as she handed Mark and Claire their mugs. 'I gather you two met earlier.'

Mark nodded.

'I'm glad you have. There aren't a lot of young people around here, are there, Mark?'

'Not really. Mostly people seem to move out as soon as they can. It's better in the summer, of course.'

'So, what do you do for fun?' asked Claire. Carchester wasn't exactly the centre of the universe as far as clubs and stuff were concerned, she thought, but at least there was *some* nightlife. This place would make a morgue look lively. She was fed up with spending evenings watching TV with her mum.

'There's the pub,' said Mark.

'Wow!' said Claire in a voice heavy with sarcasm.

'Yeah, well . . .'

'But the weekend after next there's a gig over at Missenthwaite.'

'Oh yeah?' This was sounding more hopeful, but she wasn't having a problem keeping feelings of excitement in check.

'Do you like folk music?'

Claire's spirits plummeted again. 'Umm . . .'

'I don't know what the group's like. They're local kids but they've played at some big festivals. I could get us tickets if you'd like to go.'

'Well . . .'

'Why don't you?' said Pammy. 'It'll be an evening out. I expect you could do with one. I'll drive you both there, if you like.'

'That'd be great,' said Mark. 'Right, that's fixed.'

Claire drank her tea and wondered how she'd been bounced into going to a folk concert, while Mark and Pammy discussed the work he was doing in the library to replace some rotten timbers. The only good thing, she decided, about being in the back of beyond was that none of her friends would ever get to hear about this date. Mind you, she thought, Mark was all right. Not bad looking and decent manners. She guessed he was about seventeen, and if he was working in his dad's shop, then he must've left school at sixteen. Still, if he was earning, he could afford to take her out. Perhaps things weren't so bad after all.

'You look cheerful,' remarked Yvie, looking up from a sketch she was completing when Claire came home that afternoon.

'I met a guy today who isn't a geek or ancient.'

'Who was that?'

'He was doing odd jobs round at the Hall. He normally works in the shop though.'

'Oh, Mark.'

'You know him?'

'Where do you think I shop? Where did I buy my boots?'

'Oh.' Claire nodded. 'Anyway, he sometimes does stuff for the estate. He says it pays better because it's not his dad employing him but a proper person.'

Yvie laughed at Mark's take on the employment market. 'Is he nice?'

'Well, he's not—'

'A geek or ancient.'

Claire laughed. 'It does help, you know. I was beginning to think I was the only person round here under about forty.'

136

''Scuse me!' said Yvie with mock indignation.

'You're nearly forty. Anyway, you're my mum. You don't count.' She told her mum about Mark's invitation to the gig the next weekend.

'Do you want to go?'

Claire wrinkled her nose. 'I don't know, but it would be a night out.'

'And . . . ?'

'And do I really want to spend an evening shaking a tambourine and singing hey nonny nonny?'

'I take your point. But, as you said, it would be an evening out. And if it was truly awful, you need never go again, and I promise I'll never tell any of your school friends that you went to a folk concert.'

'Pammy thought I should go too.'

Yvie held her tongue. There's a surprise, she thought. But she wasn't sure if Pammy was acting in Mark's or Claire's interests, and, whichever it was, did it matter either way?

The next morning, after Claire had left to go to her lessons, Yvie pulled on her new boots, gathered her sketchbook and a case full of pencils and pastels, and stuffed them into a day sack together with a bottle of water and a waterproof top, and headed off round the lake. She'd been studying a map Pammy had lent her, and had spotted a secluded inlet along the lake, where a stream joined it. The contours were almost on top of each other at that point, so she figured there might be a waterfall of sorts, and she felt it might make an interesting place to do a few sketches of the scenery. For once the sun was shining and, although the weather forecast had predicted conditions deteriorating by evening, Yvie planned to be back by about one o'clock, two at the latest. She looked at the distance on the map. Only a few inches. Well, how long was that going to take her to cover? Half an hour? She folded it up and left it on the table. It was such an easy route, there was no way she was going to need it. The footpath seemed to run around the lake, so Yvie didn't think there was much chance of her getting lost. She knew her map-reading skills weren't fabulous, but she figured even she could cope with keeping water on her left and land on her right till she got to her destination.

It was further than Yvie expected to get to the stream, and the terrain was tougher to walk over than she had thought it would be. On the other side of the lake, she could see that the ground consisted mostly of sheep-bitten turf, small fields contained in a checkerboard of drystone walls, but, on this side, the moor, heather, bracken and a few wind-bent trees reached the water's edge. Amongst the vegetation were sudden outcrops of rock or boulders and once or twice Yvie found herself scrambling over the tail end of a scree slope. She dickered with the idea of turning back, but then figured that she had come this far, so she might as well continue on for another ten minutes or so. Ahead of her was a shoulder of land that ran from the top of a large hill on her right down to the lake. She decided she'd crest that, and see if she could see her objective. If not, she'd call it a day and give up. The climb up the small rise wasn't steep, but the sun was warm and she was perspiring quite heavily when she got to the top. There, about two hundred yards ahead of her, was the rocky outcrop she'd seen on the map, and the stream tumbling over it, sparkling in the brilliant, clear light, and spilling into a pool at the base. Yvie hurried down the other side of the hill and threw herself thankfully on to the small patch of grass that lay beside the water. She stripped off her jersey and stretched, revelling in the warm spring sun. The country was looking spectacular, with the grass a jewel-like green, the sky an opalescent blue, and the lake beside her shimmering in the lightest of breezes. The fells and hills rose round her and she felt as though she was being cupped in a protective hand. It was as perfect a scene as Yvie could have hoped for.

She glanced at her watch – eleven thirty! She'd have to get to work quickly if she was to get some sketching done and be home by three, especially as she now knew that it was well over an hour and a half's walking that lay ahead of her. Yvie found herself a flattish rock and got busy. She worked steadily, glancing up constantly to confirm the perspective or the way a shadow from an outcrop fell across the moor, but concentrating totally on the work she was doing, which was going fabulously well. She was utterly engrossed, only stopping a couple of times, once to take a drink of water and once to pull on her sweater as the breeze got a little stronger and the air a little chillier. When she stopped properly, her stomach complaining bitterly about lack of sustenance, she looked at her watch to see if it was time to be getting back.

'Half past three!' she exclaimed out loud. No wonder she felt so famished. She began to pack away her stuff, observing, as she did, that the breeze was now getting much stronger and the temperature was dropping. In fact, she felt noticeably cold. She looked at the sky. Over the fell behind her, a lowering mass of grey cloud was piling up ominously, and ahead of it streamed high wisps of cirrus. The weather was on the change and no mistake. She pulled on her dark-green waterproof. Not fantastic protection if the weather really turned dirty, but it would provide another layer and keep the breeze off her. She'd be all right till she got home, she told herself, after all, it was only a few miles, and if she walked briskly she'd be more than warm enough. For heaven's sake, it was May – hardly the depths of winter.

Yvie set off at a good pace. As she went, she pulled her mobile out of her pocket and dialled Pammy's number. Not a sausage. She looked at the little screen. Not a whiff of a signal. Blow, she thought. But what did she expect out here in the middle of nowhere? She tramped on. The wind was really beginning to pick up. Yvie was amazed at how quickly the weather was turning. She knew the forecast had said it would, but it was only when you were stuck out in it that you really noticed. Usually, she thought ruefully, she only looked at what the weather was doing from behind the protection of double glazing.

A few drops of rain spat at her then stopped. Yvie pulled the hood of her waterproof up and tugged on the cords so that it fitted snugly round her face. From some deep recess, she remembered that about seventy per cent of the body's heat was lost through your head. She didn't suppose a thin nylon hood was going to make much difference, but it would be better than nothing. It certainly couldn't make things any worse. Feeling increasingly cold – God, this wind was bitter – she pulled her mobile out of her pocket and looked to see if there was a signal. Zilch. She hoped Claire wasn't worried, but there was nothing she could do on that front. Best she concentrated on getting herself home.

The rain spat again, this time for longer, and it was markedly heavier. Yvie turned round to see if it was just going to be a passing shower, or if something worse was about to set in. As she did so, her foot turned awkwardly on a tussock of grass and she crashed over on to the ground. A pain shot up her leg. Yvie gasped in agony.

'Shit, blast, damn!' she swore through clenched teeth. She sat on the ground and clasped her ankle. It throbbed horribly. She began to undo the laces to get her boot off so she could assess the damage. It was tricky, as her fingers were almost numb with cold. She wished she'd thought to bring gloves. Actually, she thought, she wished she'd stayed indoors and never ventured out. Yvie felt close to tears with pain and worry. This was not a good situation to start with, and now it had just got a whole lot worse. She tried to ease her boot off, but she nearly passed out with pain. Hopeless, she thought, as she fought back more tears of pain, frustration and now fear. She decided there was nothing for it but to lace her boot back up again as tight as she could stand it, and try to carry on. Staying out on the moor wasn't an option. The rain was really starting to set in and her trousers were distinctly soggy now. Her chinos had offered little enough protection from the cold wind when they were dry, but now they were wet and clammily sticking to her leg, they were worse than useless. She began to shiver quite violently and she knew she really had to keep going. She took off her backpack. There was nothing in it that she needed or that could help her, and it was only an extra burden. She dropped it on the ground.

Yvie made the effort to stand up. The pain in her foot was almost unbearable but somehow she managed to get herself upright. Walking, however, was going to prove a whole other story. If she had a stick to take some of her weight, she might be able to limp a little, but there was nothing out here on this empty piece of moorland. Rain dripped from her face and found its way down the inside of her waterproof as she looked at rocks, boulders, marram grass, gorse, endless bracken and a few trees in the distance. Nothing, she thought, not a sausage that could possibly offer any support in any way. And the ground was so uneven it made things even worse. On the flat, she might have been able to hop and hobble, but doing that here only made it likely she'd knacker the other ankle too. She tried taking a tentative step but it proved hopeless. The pain was just too much. She wasn't going to make any sort of progress like that. She dropped on to her knees; perhaps she could crawl. She tried. At least she seemed to be able to manage that. It was going to take hours to get back to the cottage, but it just might be possible.

It was painfully slow progress, and all too frequently her palms or her knees encountered a sharp stone or a thorn. After barely a hundred yards, Yvie was almost in tears again. She rolled on to her side to take the pressure off her stinging and abraded skin. In her heart, she knew that, despite the fact that it was early summer, and she was only a couple of miles from safety, her situation was perilous. She was wet, chilled to the bone and injured. And it didn't help matters that no one knew where on earth to start looking for her. The only tiny glimmers of hope were that Claire would soon be raising an alarm, and that it wasn't due to get dark for a number of hours. She curled into a ball in a small dip in the ground that afforded a faint hint of shelter, turned her back against the weather and willed herself to find the energy to start again, but it was easier to stay in a foetal position than press on, skinning her hands and knees still further. She was so cold and tired, perhaps she would just stay there like this for a few minutes longer, she thought. If she had just a bit of a rest, she would be able to do better at her next attempt. Yes, that was the way to do it. Rest for a bit . . .

'Pammy, do you know where Mum is?' Claire tried to sound casual, but really she was feeling quite sick with worry. She'd had trouble dialling Pammy's number, her hand had been shaking so badly. She'd gone over all the options and she just couldn't make sense of her mum's disappearance.

'No. Has she gone to the shop?'

'I don't think so. I mean, I've been home over an hour now and there's no sign of her. And the car's outside.'

'Perhaps she's sketching somewhere,' suggested Pammy.

'Yeah, but it's tipping down with rain now. She'd have come home, surely. You don't think . . . ?' She couldn't bring herself to voice her worst fear – that the horrible IRA man had a hand in this.

'I'm sure she's fine. Perhaps she's sheltering somewhere. But Adam and I will come round and wait with you, if that'll make you feel better.'

Claire didn't think their presence would help much, but it would be better than being on her own.

'Thanks.'

'We'll be round in a jiffy.'

It seemed like an age before Claire heard the Cliftons' car draw up outside. She opened the door to let them in and was pushed aside by Trooper hurtling into the house, where he gave himself a vigorous shake to get the rain out of his coat.

'Sorry about that,' said Pammy, making a more sedate entry. 'But the rule is dogs first.'

Claire didn't smile. She was too worried.

'Right,' said Pammy, taking off her waxed jacket. 'Are you sure your mum didn't leave a note or anything?' She bustled over to the kitchen as she spoke, and put the kettle on. 'Tea?' she asked.

Adam and Claire nodded. Trooper flopped on to the floor in a corner with a resigned sigh, as if he'd been promised a walk and had been cheated.

'No. If she does leave notes, they're always on the table. It's the system we always use at home, so she wouldn't change it just because we're somewhere else. And I've tried her mobile, but all I get is a message saying my call can't be connected.'

'OK,' said Pammy. 'So we have to think that your mum planned to be home before you got back from lessons with me. And the fact that your call can't be connected means nothing. The network is hopeless round here.'

Adam was wandering around the living room. He stopped by the coffee table and picked up the map that was lying on it.

'Do you think she's gone out fell walking?' he asked.

'Dunno.' Claire went to the cupboard near the front door, where they kept their outdoor things. 'Her boots aren't here.'

Pammy made the tea and put three steaming mugs on the table. 'But she didn't take the map with her.'

'Nor the car, so wherever she's gone, it's local.' Adam picked his mug up and took a noisy slurp before opening the map and spreading it out. Pammy and Claire moved their mugs to make way for it.

Adam got a pencil and drew a rough circle around the Hall. 'I don't think she'd have planned to go miles. Probably she'd have followed one of the local footpaths.' Adam took another gulp of tea and peered closely at the map. 'Is this your map, Pammy?'

'Yes. I lent it to Yvie last week.'

'Have you marked any local beauty spots or anything on it?'

'No. I pointed out a couple of places that Yvie might like to visit, but that was all.'

'Well, someone's been drawing on it. Look.' He twisted the map round and pointed to a small pencil circle. 'I bet that's where she's gone.'

'But it's not very far. Why isn't she back?'

'It's further than it looks, Claire, and I expect your mum just got caught out by the rain and is holed up somewhere waiting for it to pass.'

But Claire wasn't a fool, and Adam's words didn't reassure her.

'Should I ring Daddy and tell him?'

'Not yet. No point in getting him in a stew over nothing. Have you got a thermos?'

'Yes, there's one in the cupboard.' Claire went across the kitchen and got it out.

'Good. Pammy, would you fill it with some hot sweet tea. I'm going back to the Hall to get my rucksack.'

He grabbed his jacket and left.The draught from the door opening blew the map off the table and on to the floor. Claire bent and picked it up.

'Do you think Mummy's going to be all right?'

'I expect so. I think Adam's right about where to look for her. And he'll take Trooper with him – he's a brilliant tracker dog.'

Trooper, on hearing his name, looked up from where he lay on the floor and thumped his tail.

'Shouldn't we get out mountain rescue or something?'

143

'If Adam doesn't find her, we will. But it's not going to come to that. It wouldn't surprise me if your mum doesn't come through that door any minute now, wanting a cup of tea and some dry clothes and wondering what all the fuss is about.'

Claire hoped so. It was cold now, as well as wet, and she didn't like the thought of her mum out on the hills, lost and alone.

Adam didn't return for about twenty minutes, but when he did, he told Claire and Pammy to go over to the estate office and man the radio there.

'Radio?' asked Claire.

Adam explained that it was one of the owner's toys. 'He likes to keep in touch with me when he's out playing lord of the manor.'

'How swanky,' said Claire.

'Come on,' said Pammy. 'Best we get ourselves over there. And we'd better leave a note on the table for your mum, in case she comes back while we're out. Don't want her having a panic over you, do we?'

Yvie awoke suddenly when a particularly violent squall drove icy-sharp, stinging rain into her face. The wind was backing and the dip in the ground was not protecting her any more. In fact, the opposite was true, as she realized that her discomfort was compounded by the fact she was now lying in a shallow puddle that had formed in the lower-lying ground. She glanced at her watch. She had been asleep or dozing for about thirty minutes, and she was colder and wetter than ever. Yvie knew that she had been foolish to let herself drift like that. It was only because it wasn't midwinter, and the temperature hadn't plummeted any lower than it had, that she wasn't now suffering from advanced hypothermia. Despite the fact that her clothes were wet through and sticking to her, ignoring the pain in her grazed palms, blocking out the still-nagging pain in her ankle, Yvie got on to her hands and knees and headed back towards the village again. Now the rain was really heavy and driving towards her, so she kept her head tucked down as she battled her way forwards. She decided to count the 'steps' of her shuffling progress. I won't look up till I've counted to a thousand, she promised herself, hoping that when she did

144

get to that total, she might be able to see the Hall or the village.

She began resolutely. 'One, two, three . . .' She struggled on, counting each laboured hand and leg movement, ignoring the pricks and stabs of the rough terrain, trying to pay no mind to the way the wet cloth of her trousers chafed her groin and the backs of her knees, blotting out the rain driving into her face. On and on she went, counting relentlessly and resolutely keeping her head down . . .

'Ninety-nine, one thousand,' she panted. She stopped and looked up. She couldn't see a thing, well, nothing apart from a sea of bracken and some gorse bushes. The hills were no longer protective, but threatening and lowering. Yvie felt as if they were like some wild creature, stalking her, waiting for her strength to fail before they finished her off. She looked eastwards. Surely she should be able to see the village from here. She knew she wasn't going the wrong way, because the lake was in the right place. Even through the veil of heavy rain, she could see its gun-metal shine. Perhaps she was a little further away from it than she had been when she'd strolled out this morning, but she was definitely heading back to the village. Why couldn't she see it? But the rain was sheeting down and the visibility was pretty hopeless. Perhaps on a clear day she might get a glimpse of it. But on a clear day she wouldn't be in this fix. She felt hot tears of frustration and exhaustion pricking at her eyes. She brushed them away. This was no time to act like a girl, she told herself sternly. She pulled her phone out of her pocket again and pressed the buttons for Pammy. Still no signal. How close to the village did you have to be to pick one up? She sighed and braced herself to crawl on again.

'One, two, three . . .' she began through gritted teeth. This wasn't getting easier. She concentrated on the counting. She didn't want to look up and see the countryside hardly changing. It would be too dispiriting, she might just lie down and go to sleep again. She got to twenty-nine and realized that she couldn't think what number came next. She shut her eyes to concentrate, but still she couldn't think. She started again at one. This time she wasn't so ambitious, she just counted in blocks of ten, then back to one again. On and on she did this. Oh God, she felt so tired. Perhaps if she stopped for a minute or two? If she rested, she'd find the energy to start again.

The wind picked up again and tugged and pushed her. She could hear it roaring across the moor, whistling through the grasses, which combined to make an eerie animal moaning. 'Like *Wuthering* bloody *Heights*,' she murmured. She could hear a dog barking in the distance. 'Oh, wonderful. Now I'm in *Hound of the Baskervilles* too.' She felt an urge to laugh growing inside her, but the feeling frightened her. She knew she was verging on hysteria. She felt as if her mind and body were both now out of her control. She pushed on again.

'One, two, three . . .' she counted.

The barking was getting closer, and slowly the significance began to dawn on Yvie. Even her fuddled, numbed brain managed to grasp the concept that this might mean someone was searching for her and using a dog to track her. With a massive effort, she pushed herself upright so that at least her head and shoulders were above the vegetation around her. With the wind swirling around, she couldn't be sure what direction the sound of barking was coming from. She looked about her, trying to spot the search party, but with the light poor due to the hour, the weather conditions and the black clouds overhead, she could make nothing out. She tried shouting but her voice sounded pathetic against the noise of the downpour and the wind.

There! A light. Yvie was sure of it. She stared through the driving rain, her body shaking with cold and exhaustion. Yes, there it was again. She tried shouting again. If anything, her efforts were even weaker than before. But there was another volley of barking. It was closer now, and then, bouncing and bounding over the tussocky grass and bracken, came Trooper. Yvie, not a dog lover, had never been so pleased to see any living creature before in her life. The dog stood beside her as Yvie hugged it with a desperation that sprang from sheer relief, and cried into its silky coat as the animal barked and barked.

Yvie could see the bright gleam of torch light come closer through the murk of the evening, and then she could hear someone calling her name. It was Adam. He'd found her and suddenly all her fear and worry and pain came tumbling out of her in noisy, gasping sobs as she collapsed back on the ground, overwhelmed by relief, completely exhausted and weak with cold.

'It's all right, my love. I'm here.' He knelt beside her. 'It's all right. I've got you now. You're safe.'

Yvie managed to find the strength to pull herself to her knees again and clasp her arms around his neck.

'Adam, Adam,' she murmured as she clung to him like a drowning swimmer to a rock. 'Adam, Adam.'

He'd found her. He'd rescued her. She was safe. She wasn't alone on the moors any more.

'Here,' said Adam, disengaging himself from her and rummaging in his rucksack. After a few seconds, he pressed something into Yvie's numbed hands. 'Here's some warm tea. Drink this.'

But Yvie was so cold, so shivery, that she couldn't grip the plastic cup from the thermos. Adam knelt beside her and put his arm round her.

'Come on,' he said, holding the mug to her juddering lips. 'Just a sip.' And he managed to pour a teaspoonful or so of the hot sweet liquid into her mouth. Then another and another, and slowly the violent, uncontrollable shivering died down. Adam poured some more tea into the mug and gave it to Yvie, who clasped her hands around it gratefully. Her fingers began to tingle back into life. Adam rummaged in his rucksack and pulled out what looked like aluminium foil. He wrapped it around Yvie so that she resembled nothing more than a Christmas turkey ready for the oven.

'You'll soon feel the benefit of this,' he murmured, as he made sure all the gaps open to the elements were tucked in.

The radio in the ultra-modern estate office crackled.

'Hello, Pammy, this is Adam. Hello, Pammy, over.'

Pammy grabbed the microphone and pressed the switch. 'Pammy here. Go ahead, over.'

'I've found her. We'll be back in about thirty minutes.'

'Thank goodness. I'll tell Claire.'

'Thanks. Out.'

Pammy sprang out of the swivel chair and ran round the

gravel path to the kitchen courtyard and then up the stairs to the flat two at a time.

'Claire!' she panted at the top. 'Claire, Adam's been on the radio. He's found your mum.'

'Oh Pammy. Thank goodness.' The sudden relief from the tension was too much for Claire, and two big tears spilled down her cheeks.

'Hey, honey. No need to cry. Your mum's safe, and that's all that matters. Adam'll have her back with us in no time.'

Claire nodded and swallowed, trying to control herself. 'It's just that Dad phoned a couple of minutes ago and I didn't know what to say to him.'

'Did you tell him?'

Claire nodded. 'He was worried. He'd tried Mum's mobile and the cottage and thought he'd ring here to see if we'd come to see you. I had to tell him. Did I do wrong?'

'Of course not, sweetheart. But ring him back now and tell him the news. He's got enough on his plate without this to worry about as well.'

Claire got dialling. Pammy went back to the estate office to man the radio until Adam reached the safety of the car.

'I didn't realize I'd caused so much trouble,' said Yvie, the words juddering out through chattering teeth.

'You haven't, yet. If I hadn't got to you before nightfall, we would have called out the mountain rescue. As it was, I had a fair idea where to look, and I had Trooper, who has come up trumps before.'

'But all this kit and the radio. It's like a proper mountain rescue.'

'Not yet it isn't. Of course, if I hadn't found you, it'd be a whole different story.'

But there was something Yvie still didn't understand. 'But how did you know where to look?'

Adam explained about the map and his detective work. He gave her a cuddle. 'But Trooper would have probably found you anyway. Better than a bloodhound is Trooper.'

Despite everything, Yvie was aware of their proximity, but she didn't have the strength or the will power to do anything but lean against him in gratitude. She sipped on the warm tea.

'You were so stupid,' said Adam, quietly. 'You could have lost your life doing what you did.'

Yvie nodded miserably. She'd been all too aware for a number of hours now that that was exactly what might happen to her.

'But I only went for a walk.'

'And you didn't tell a *soul* where you were going. You broke the cardinal rule of hillwalking.'

'I wasn't walking in the hills,' Yvie protested weakly.

'Don't split hairs. Have you any idea what you have just put us through? We've been out of our minds with worry. I was nearly beside myself when I found your day sack. I imagined all sorts of horrors had befallen you. Luckily Trooper here is a great tracker dog. If it wasn't for him . . .'

Yvie began to cry again. 'I'm sorry, I'm sorry,' she snuffled. 'I didn't think.'

Adam hugged her. 'The main thing is that you're all right now. I'm going to get you home, and Pammy'll put you in a hot bath and feed you soup and we'll get the doctor out and by tomorrow you'll be as right as ninepence. Now, in a minute we'll go and find the Range Rover. It's only a few hundred yards from here, but I couldn't get it any closer. Can you walk that far?'

Yvie shook her head miserably and explained about her ankle.

'So you crawled from where we found your bag?' Yvie nodded. 'My God, you've done so well. It must be about a mile and a half, perhaps two.'

'I tried to phone for help, but I couldn't get a signal.'

'Never mind that now. We must get you home.' Adam took Yvie's face in both hands and kissed her gently. 'What a plucky kid you are. You should be proud of yourself.'

'I might be if I hadn't been such a pillock to get myself into such a pickle in the first place.'

'Well, at least you're beginning to sound a bit better. Here, drink some more tea.' Adam refilled the mug a third time, and Yvie took it gratefully.

'Don't you want some?'

'I am properly dressed and I haven't been stuck out in the rain for hours on end. The top layer I've got on might be sodden, but underneath I'm warm and dry.' Adam radioed Pammy again to tell her to get the doctor out to look at Yvie's ankle. He packed away his kit and then he slung the rucksack on the front of his chest, taking the now empty mug from Yvie and tucking it in a side pocket. 'Right,' he said, kneeling in front of her. 'Climb on my back so I can get you to civilization.'

Yvie managed to haul herself up enough to grab Adam round his shoulders and hook her good leg and ankle round his waist. Adam tipped forwards till her weight was off the ground, and then, with a mighty heave, he staggered to his feet and clasped his hands under her bum to support her.

'Bloody hell,' he muttered as he lurched forwards. Beside them, Trooper trotted obediently as Adam stomped across the landscape. The rain began to ease off until it was not much more than a light drizzle. In the distance, at last, Yvie could see the shape of the Range Rover, parked by the stile near the lake.

'And it would have been easier to find you if you'd been wearing a bright cagoule too. I must have passed you earlier but neither of us knew.'

'How come?'

'Trooper followed your trail out to the stream, but when you headed back you took a different route. If you'd been wearing orange or yellow, there's just a chance I'd have spotted you earlier, you were only about fifty or sixty yards from the proper path. I might have been with you an hour earlier. If it had been much colder, that might have made a huge difference. As it was . . . well, not much harm done.'

'I can't thank you enough, Adam.' She resisted the temptation to kiss his ear, the little bit that wasn't covered by his woolly hat. 'I've been such a fool. And I've caused so much grief.'

'It happens every year,' said Adam, stopping and giving a little bounce to hitch Yvie's weight into a more comfortable position. 'Only, usually it doesn't happen to someone I care so much about,' he added.

Yvie felt even guiltier.

A few minutes later they reached the car. Adam managed to open the door and then swing round so Yvie could slide off his back and plonk her bum straight on to a seat. Adam eased his shoulders and stretched.

'I'm sorry,' said Yvie for the umpteenth time.

Adam turned. 'Hey, the main thing is that you're all right. Nothing else matters. Honest.' And then he kissed her. Yvie, weak, tired, vulnerable, and with her judgement seriously impaired, responded.

Pammy put down the microphone. A possibly busted ankle. That explained why poor old Yvie had got herself into such a spot. She switched off the set and then rang the number of the local surgery. The answer machine told her the number of the doctor on call for the night. When she got hold of him, he promised he'd come as soon as he could. He advised that Pammy didn't give Yvie anything to eat in case she needed treatment that night. Pammy locked up the office and returned to the flat. Claire was still nattering to her dad, obviously much happier about everything now she knew her mother was safe. Pammy tapped her on the shoulder.

Claire put her fingers over the mouthpiece. 'Yes?'

'Your mother's got a leg injury. That's why she didn't get back. But she's OK.'

Claire relayed the news to her father, and Pammy went into the kitchen to make up a couple of hot-water bottles, then she set about making up the beds in the spare room again. There was no way Yvie was going back to the cottage tonight, and possibly not for some time. She plumped up the pillows and tucked the bottles under the duvet. As she did so, she saw headlights coming up the track from the lake. She left Claire talking to her father and ran down the stairs to help Adam with the task of getting Yvie up the steep flight of stairs.

'Come on in, you poor dear,' said Pammy as Yvie climbed out of the car. She lent heavily on Pammy as she supported her through the door of the tradesman's entrance. Yvie stumbled into centrally heated warmth, dripping all over the carpet. 'You're blue with cold. We must get those wet things off immediately. The doctor will be here in about thirty minutes, so we've time to get you into a bath. I'm sorry I can't offer you a hot meal, but the doctor said not to, in case they need to set your foot.'

151

'I don't need the doctor,' said Yvie weakly.

'Oh, and your foot is going to heal itself. If it's broken, we need to get you to the hospital.'

Yvie was halfway up the stairs, making halting, painful progress, supported by Pammy and Adam, when Claire came flying down them.

'Mummy, Mummy, Mummy!' she cried. 'I thought you might be dead.' She stopped on a stair above the one Yvie was standing on, and bent to give her mum a big hug, tears of relief coursing down her white, frightened face. 'I was talking to Daddy. He was so worried about you, and I didn't hear the car draw up. Oh, Mummy, I was so scared.'

'But Pammy told you I was OK.'

'I couldn't believe it until I saw you.'

'Well, now you *can* see for yourself that I'm fine, so you can stop worrying now. And you have told Daddy I'm safe, haven't you?' said Yvie, returning the hug. Claire nodded so vigorously that she nearly sent her mother toppling. Yvie clutched wildly at Adam.

'Come on, Claire. Let's get your mum upstairs and you can give her a proper welcome home then,' said Adam. 'The stairs aren't a very safe place for all this, and we don't want your mum hurting her other leg.'

Weak though the joke was, they all laughed.

'Tell you what,' said Pammy. 'You go on ahead and run a bath for your mum. And get some clean towels out of the airing cupboard. There are some vast great bath sheets on the top shelf.'

Claire sped off, glad of being able to make a practical contribution. By the time they had got Yvie to the top of the stairs, steam was billowing from the bathroom and Claire was bustling about like head nurse. Yvie collapsed on to the hall chair. Pammy peeled off the space blanket that Yvie was still clutching around her shoulders, while Adam set to work with her boots. Whipping out a knife from his pocket, he sliced through the laces, then he pulled the tongue forward and began to ease it off her foot. Yvie winced.

'There's two ways of doing this,' said Adam. 'Slowly and gently, which will take a while and will still hurt. Or short and sharp, which will kill for a second or two.'

Yvie gritted her teeth. 'OK. Short and sharp.' She shut her

eyes and gripped the sides of the chair while Pammy held her shoulders.

Adam gripped the boot with one hand, and Yvie's leg with the other. He pulled it off as swiftly and as gently as he could. Yvie yelped and looked even more ashen, but the boot was off and that was the main thing. Adam didn't even try to peel the sodden sock off; he just got busy with his knife again and sliced it down the back so it fell on the floor by itself. Now it was revealed that Yvie's ankle had ballooned into a swollen purplish mess.

'No wonder you had trouble walking,' said Adam.

'I thought it was a bit sore.' Yvie gave a wry grin. It was a lot easier to be brave now she was safe. 'Do you think it's broken?'

'Dunno. If it isn't, it's a terrible sprain. You're going to be laid up for ages with this. Sprains can take almost as long as breaks to heal.'

Yvie looked as if she was going to cry. Not that anyone would have blamed her if she had. It had been an awful day, she was cold and exhausted, her ankle was a mess, to say nothing of the fact that she'd been very foolish and they all knew it.

Pammy gave her a hug. 'Come on, you're all right. You're safe now.'

It was too much for Yvie, and she gave in to all the emotion of the day.

About an hour later, Yvie was tucked up in bed, snuggled up next to two hot-water bottles and feeling deliciously warm again. She was in that limbo state between sleeping and waking when she was vaguely aware of the activity going on in the flat but also drifting in and out of bizarre daydreams involving trying to run through treacle.

Pammy popped her head round the bedroom door. 'Doctor's here to see you.'

Yvie roused herself. 'Oh,' she said sleepily. She pushed herself up so she was sitting propped against the pillows, and banished the treacly dream.

A middle-aged man strode into the room. 'Right, Mrs Maxwell. I'm Dr Dugdale.'

'Call me Yvie, please. And I'm so sorry to have caused you all this trouble.'

'Right, Yvie. Adam tells me you had a bit of a do out on the moors today.'

Yvie nodded, feeling more than a little sheepish.

'Don't worry,' said Dr Dugdale. 'I'm not here to make any sort of comment. I'm just here to see what damage you've done to your ankle.'

The doctor lifted the side of the duvet to expose Yvie's foot. He whistled. 'No wonder you couldn't walk back. That's nasty.' Yvie nodded. 'Does it still hurt?'

'It throbs like hell, to be honest.'

'Hmm.' The doctor cupped her ankle gently and manipulated it very slightly. Yvie winced and took a sharp inward breath. 'No need to ask if that caused pain.' He felt it as gently as he could, up and down the bone, then rested her foot back on the bed. 'To be honest, I'm not sure if it's broken or not. If it *is* broken, it's not a terribly serious fracture, but it'll need proper setting, and the only way to find out is to get you to hospital to get you X-rayed. However, I think a good night's sleep is what is required right now, so I'll strap it up for you and give you some painkillers, and Adam can take you to A&E tomorrow.' The doctor fished around in his bag and took out a small brown bottle. He dished out a couple of pills, then selected another container and handed Yvie a couple more. 'That should make sure you get a good rest tonight before the rigours of the casualty department and the fracture clinic tomorrow.'

Although Yvie had slept well, thanks to the painkillers and sleeping pills that Dr Dugdale had given her the night before, she was still tired the next day.

'An experience like that is bound to take it out of you,' said Pammy when she helped Yvie to dress the next morning. She lent Yvie a pair of trackie bottoms with side zips, because jeans were going to be useless if they had to put a plaster on her leg. 'And I'm sorry I can't offer you breakfast to help you get your strength back but . . .'

'I know. If they need to set it . . .' Yvie sighed. She was famished. She hadn't had anything since breakfast the day before, and that had only been a piece of toast.

154

'Adam'll take you for a big plate of pie and chips when you're all done.'

'At least there's something to look forward to.' Yvie wasn't relishing the idea of having her foot manipulated.

Before she left, she spoke to Richard and reassured him that Claire and Pammy had not lied the night before about her rescue, and that she was still very much alive and kicking.

'Promise me you'll never do such a foolish thing again,' said Richard sternly.

'Never. It's not an experience I want to repeat, believe me.'

'I was beside myself. I sent you to Adam and Pammy's to be safe, not to hear that you'd had half of Cumbria combing the countryside for you.'

'Don't exaggerate. It was one man and his dog, and you know it.' Yvie tried to make light of her ordeal.

Richard wasn't having any of it. 'But what if Adam hadn't found you?'

'But he did. And if he hadn't, then half of Cumbria would have turned out. But as it is, I'm all right, and I won't go out walking again unless the whole village knows my plans . . .'

'OK, OK, I believe you.' There was a pause. 'When Claire phoned to say you were missing, I was so worried, Yvie. I imagined all sorts of terrible things. I thought for a while that Lynch might have had a hand in it. Then when I heard you were missing on the fells, it seemed even worse. What do you know about surviving?' He added quietly. 'I thought I was going to lose you, Yvie.'

'I was scared too, Richard.'

'My poor Yvie. You must have been. I wish I was there with you.'

'I wish you were here too.'

She was subdued on the car journey to Carlisle, thinking about how close she had come to being in real danger, mixed with thoughts about how she felt about Adam and Richard. She stared at the sodden and gloomy scenery and wondered how it was possible to love two men in two different ways. She was in no doubt that she adored Richard: he was safe, warm and sensible. He cared for her and cared about her, but . . .

But it lacked the passion and the frisson of risk, the madness that existed in the relationship between her and Adam, that spark that Yvie had thought she had under control. And she *had* had the whole thing under control when she had kissed Adam in the kitchen. But out on the moor, there had been a perceptible shift. Sitting with him in the privacy of the warm car, she longed to reach out and touch him. Her loyalty to Richard, her sense of duty as a wife, held her back, but she wasn't sure how long she was going to be able to keep herself under control. She slid a sideways look at him.

Something must have alerted him that he was being watched. The primeval sixth sense, left over from the time when man was both prey and predator, kicked in and he met Yvie's gaze.

'Penny for them,' he said.

'Keep your eyes on the road,' she responded, not wanting to be drawn into revealing what was going on in her head.

Adam grinned and did as she had said. He steered the Range Rover expertly down the narrow road that led into Keswick, and then through the little town with its tea shops and gift shops, its bed and breakfast signs and its draggled hanging baskets. The town was busy with sodden-looking tourists in brightly coloured cagoules, which gave an aura of carnival jollity to the scene, which wasn't merited considering the weather.

'If we escape from the hospital in time, we'll stop for lunch on the way back. There's a pub I know – off the beaten track, so it shouldn't be heaving with trippers – which does great food.'

'Please don't talk about food,' said Yvie. 'I haven't eaten for twenty-four hours now.' And right on cue her stomach gave a loud grumble of protest.

'That takes me back,' said Adam.

And Yvie knew he was thinking about the evening after Pammy had made her precipitate departure to look after her mother. She reddened at the memory. Adam glanced across at her.

'We were so good together.'

Yvie nodded, not trusting herself to speak.

Adam picked her hand off her lap and took it to his lips.

Yvie let him kiss it, then gently disengaged it and let it rest on her lap again.

'All right, Adam, I admit it. I want you, I am still in love with you, I still fantasize about you, but I am not going to be unfaithful to Richard. I can't and I won't.'

Adam sighed as he took in the finality of Yvie's tone. 'OK. Well, I suppose I'll just have to be patient.'

They drove in silence the rest of the way to Carlisle – both preoccupied with their own private thoughts.

Silence still reigned in the car when Adam parked in the hospital car park some time later. He left Yvie and went in search of a wheelchair and a parking ticket. He had been gone several minutes when Yvie's thoughts were interrupted by a knock on the window. She was so lost in herself that she jumped. Looking round, she saw a brightly jacketed parking attendant. She wound the window down.

'You need a ticket,' he said.

'I know. My friend has gone to get one.'

'He's been gone a while.'

'He's finding me a wheelchair too.' The man looked at her disbelievingly. 'I think I've broken my ankle,' Yvie added, wondering why on earth she felt the need to explain things to this jumped-up little Hitler.

'I'll be back in five minutes,' he said, moving off.

Yvie shrugged. Did she care? But when Adam turned up with both the required ticket and a wheelchair, she felt a sense of relief that she didn't have to have a further encounter.

The inside of the hospital, like the huge, shiny, glassy exterior, was striking too. 'It won prizes for design,' murmured Adam. Yvie didn't mind if it had won best in show at Crufts, she just wanted to get her ankle sorted, as it was giving her gip again. She gazed about the vast atrium, more like an art gallery than a hospital, and wondered about the worth of the wasted space when balanced against visual impact. However, under the veneer of hanging textile banners, uniformed reception staff and the whiff of chocolate muffins and lattés emanating from the café, it was just like any other NHS hospital. Away from the reception, the hospital reverted to type: the standard smell was of disinfectant and medications, the seats were uncomfortable moulded plastic, the magazines on the tables were out of date and dog-eared, and the wait was predictably long. It was, after all, Saturday morning, and the A&E department was clogged with the results of the night before.

Finally Yvie was called, and after a perfunctory examination, it was deemed she needed an X-ray. Which, she thought dejectedly, was the reason she had come here in the first place. It was a pity they hadn't sent her for one of those straight away and saved not only the overworked casualty doctor's time but also an hour and a half's wait. She joined a long queue of other fed-up-looking patients outside the unit. Adam despatched himself to buy magazines for them both and a coffee for himself. 'There's no point in us both suffering,' Yvie had said when Adam had offered solidarity with her nil-by-mouth regime. He promised to make it up to her on the way home – a promise which Yvie was reluctant to accept, given what had passed between them on the way there.

It was nearly two hours before Yvie had her X-ray, and then another forty minutes before they got the results.

'A hairline fracture,' said the houseman. 'We'll get it set and you'll be as right as rain. But no need for any manipulation, you're very lucky. We'll just get you plastered up and then you can be on your way.'

'Too late for lunch on the way home,' said Adam.

'I don't care. I can have a sandwich now.' Yvie's stomach rumbled again.

'God, but that is the sexiest sound,' whispered Adam.

Yvie blushed vividly. 'Shut up,' she hissed, and shook her head. Adam was about as subtle as a poke in the eye. She sent him off to buy the biggest sandwich he could find, while she waited for the next event on the NHS conveyor belt.

Finally Yvie was free to go. The plastering, once it got going, was amazingly quick, and then all she had to do was sign for her crutches, get an appointment for the fracture clinic the following week, and that was it. She hobbled out into the car park, doing her best to make her way using the crutches she'd been issued.

'These are a nightmare,' she said, stopping and panting. 'I

158

always thought crutches looked quite simple to use, but it's impossible.'

'Stop there and I'll bring the car round,' said Adam.

But Yvie wouldn't hear of it. 'I've got to get used to them sooner rather than later.' But, despite her determination, she was shattered by the time she got into the car.

They were pulling out of the car park when Adam asked casually, 'How are you going to manage the spiral stairs in the cottage?'

Yvie looked at him in horror. She hadn't thought of that, and there was no way she was going to be able to get herself up and down that obstacle.

'There's nothing for it. You'll have to stay with us for a while now.'

'I'll find a way of managing,' said Yvie, gamely. There had to be a way, surely? She really didn't want to be in Adam's house, in the bedroom next door to his, constantly aware of his presence. There was too much chemistry and way too much history.

Adam raised his eyebrows. 'You'll wind up breaking your neck. I won't hear of it and neither will Pammy.'

'I could move myself downstairs and wash in the sink.'

'And the loo?'

Damn. The only loo was upstairs.

'And shopping and cooking? How are you going to manage crutches and hot pans? Face it, Yvie, there's no choice.'

Yvie sighed. Every time she seemed to find a way to put some space between herself and Adam, the gods seemed to find a way of closing it again.

As Adam had predicted, Pammy was horrified at the thought of Yvie trying to cope in the cottage.

'Claire can help me,' said Yvie.

'I've never heard of anything so stupid in my life,' said Pammy. 'This flat is ideal, there are no stairs for you to negotiate, you can have a bath – how can you possibly manage with just a shower at the cottage? I can do the cooking and the shopping.' Yvie opened her mouth to try to argue, but then shut it again, realizing that Pammy had an answer for everything. 'Anyone would think you don't want to stay with us,' said Pammy finally, wiping her hands on her apron.

I don't, thought Yvie miserably. I don't, because I'm terrified that if I do, I'm going to wind up in bed, bonking the brains out of your husband. But instead she smiled wanly and hoped she looked suitably grateful.

'Then that's sorted.' And she bustled off with Claire to gather together the essentials the two of them would need for the next few days. A big pack, to move them over properly, could wait until Yvie was well enough to supervise.

Yvie sat on the sofa in the cosy sitting room and tried to ignore Adam's presence. Instead, he came and sat next to her and took her hand.

'How are you feeling?'

'Like a traitor.' She took her hand back. 'Adam, please don't make this harder for me than it is already.'

'I meant, how are you feeling physically?'

'Oh, so-so. My ankle aches rather. It's better than it was.'

Adam brought her some painkillers and a glass of water. 'Here, take these. No point in suffering.' He then put her leg up on the sofa and rearranged the cushions behind her head.

'Just because I'm going to be living here, it doesn't change anything. I want you to leave me alone. What happened out on the moor . . . Can we forget it?'

'My but you blow hot and cold,' said Adam with an edge to his voice. 'Right, I've got work to do in the estate office. I've got a bit behind in the last couple of days. Here's the remote for the TV. Pammy'll be back soon. Do you need anything else? No? Then I'll be off.' He turned and left the room.

'Come on, Claire, I think we should go and do some shopping together.' Pammy had her car keys at the ready.

'Oh, all right then.' Brilliant, a schlep into Keswick and then trogging round a supermarket for an hour. Just how she wanted to spend Saturday morning. Still, it was probably marginally more exciting than a morning at the Hall with absolutely nothing to do. She fixed on a smile and tried to look enthusiastic, even though her heart really wasn't in it.

'I thought that, as you've worked so hard this week, you should have a treat. I thought you might like a new outfit to go out with Mark tonight.'

This was different. Pammy meant Shopping! Suddenly the day was looking up.

'There's a shop in Keswick that I hear has some neat stuff. Sort of ethnic and a bit retro.'

Claire jiggled with excitement. It sounded good – although it was a grown-up doing the recommending. She had to bear that thought in mind. Still, if it wasn't, she didn't have to buy anything there. 'Great.'

'Right, let's go.'

They ran down the back stairs and jumped in the Range Rover. Claire liked this car, as it was so high off the road she could see over the walls that tended to run along beside the roads. When she was in her mother's car, all she could see were blocks of stone and a glimpse of a field through the occasional gate. Claire asked if she could turn the radio on. She tuned it in to the local commercial station and looked questioningly at Pammy as if to ask permission.

'Mum only has Radio Four on in the car.'

'Well, so do I as a general rule, but I don't mind music for a change. Besides, this is supposed to be a nice day out for you. I can't think that starting it by forcing culture on you is going to go down a storm.'

Claire laughed. 'Well, I'd rather not.' They drove down the valley, music playing, towards Keswick.

'Is the shopping in Carchester good?'

'Not bad, but there's too many shops for old people – you know, Mum's age.' Claire stopped and put her hand to her mouth. 'Oh, I didn't mean . . . I mean, you're not . . .'

'Claire, I know exactly what you mean,' said Pammy, laughing. 'When you're a teenager, anyone over about twenty-five is ancient. You can't possibly imagine what it's like to be that age. Don't worry, I'm not offended.'

Claire looked relieved. 'Anyway, it's not bad. Well –' she grinned at Pammy – 'it's better than Keswick – what I've seen of it so far.'

'Claire, almost anywhere is better than Keswick. I didn't move here for the shopping. However, I'll bet you a slap-up lunch that you'll find something you like.'

'You're on. 'Cept Mum'll have to pay if I lose.'

'Then we'd better make sure that I win, hadn't we? Oh,

161

and no looking at price tags. I want you to choose stuff you really like, not the cheapo option.'

'Wow.' Claire looked at Pammy with genuine affection. What a great grown-up Pammy was. Claire could never remember going shopping with her mother when the question of the 'value' of a garment hadn't been questioned. Stuff like, 'How much for a skirt that short?' or, 'You paid *what*, for *that*?' had always been part of a trip out with her mum. At least, ever since she had had some say in the clothes being bought. This shopping trip was going to be fun, Claire could sense that. And she thought that Pammy wouldn't be critical of the fashions. That was supposing, of course, that fashion found its way this far north.

Pammy parked the car and led Claire to the shop that she had in mind. Claire wasn't sure initially, but as she searched the racks of clothes, she realized that this shop wasn't a chain, it didn't stock identical clothes to every other shop along any high street in any town, and it would be nice to have something different to wear from everything else in the fashion mags. She selected a couple of items that might look good.

'Try this on,' said Pammy, proffering a skirt that hung in a shapeless heap off a clothes hanger.

Claire grimaced involuntarily. 'Umm . . .'

'Look, I've a hunch this is the sort of thing that might look better on. Anyway, if it looks the same on you as it does on the hanger, then we shove it back on the rail. Just because you try it on, doesn't mean you have to walk around for the rest of your life wearing it.'

'I suppose.'

Claire took it and hung the skirt over her arm with a number of other outfits that she had picked out.

'And you'll need a blouse to try on with it,' said Pammy. 'What about this one – very tailored.'

'You have to be kidding.'

'No, I'm serious. It'll be very flattering.'

'Oh, go on then.'

'Shall I come with you into the changing room? Trust me, I'm horribly honest and I'll tell you if your bum looks big or it makes you just plain frumpy. After all, that would never do for someone of your age.'

162

'OK,' said Claire cheerfully. And she really thought that Pammy would be honest. Her mother might have been quite a rebel in her youth (Claire had seen photos and had logged the colour of her mum's hair, now a perfectly ordinary brown) but she was long determined, or so it seemed to Claire, to make sure her daughter was more conformist and conventional than a Victorian vicar's daughter.

The purple skirt was a wow. It hung beautifully, it moved as Claire walked, it made her look tall and slim and it was completely different from anything Claire had ever owned before.

'OK, Pammy, you were right,' she admitted. 'But the blouse sucks.'

Pammy agreed. 'Let me see if I can find something better.' She disappeared out of the changing room and went to raid the shirt section. She picked out several that caught her eye and returned.

'Here.' She shoved the first of her choices at Claire.

Claire looked at it suspiciously. 'There's not much to it, is there?'

'Don't be such a prude. It'll be fine when it's on.'

Claire slipped the soft white fabric over her shoulders. 'Is this silk?'

'Yes. Nice, isn't it?' Pammy showed Claire how to do the laces up the front of the blouse. 'No, that absolutely doesn't work.'

Claire looked disappointed. 'Oh.' She'd been admiring it in the mirror and thought it looked great.

'Oh, the blouse is OK. It's just your bra is all wrong. In fact, I think, with that lacing, you'd be better off not wearing one at all.'

'No bra?' Claire squeaked.

'Oh, don't be such a prude,' said Pammy. 'If you're that shy, I'll go out and you can tell me when you're decent again.'

Claire felt foolish. 'No, it's all right.' She slipped the blouse off and then her bra too. She did up the lacing and then looked at the blouse in the mirror again. Pammy was right. Now it looked sexy and provocative, whereas before there had been a hint of tarty. Much better.

'Mum will throw a fit,' said Claire.

'Can't think why. All it does is pretend you can see a lot of flesh. You can't really though, can you? There's nothing indecent about it at all really.'

Claire looked again. Pammy was right. It was only as if she was wearing an ordinary blouse with the top few buttons undone. It was just that the effect of the laces made it into something quite different.

'Now all we need is something to keep you warm and some shoes – or perhaps boots would be better.' Pammy stood back and contemplated the outfit. 'I'll see what they've got.' And off she went again, taking the unwanted clothes with her.

Claire sat on the stool in the corner of the little cubicle to await her return. How come, she thought, someone who seemed to wear nothing but tweeds and twinsets could suss out such great stuff for someone like her?

'Right,' said Pammy, returning with half a dozen jackets and tops on hangers.

'Excuse me,' interrupted a shop girl.

'Yes?' said Pammy.

'You can't take that number of items into the changing room.'

'Why not?'

'Well, you might . . .'

'Shoplift?' Pammy looked at the young girl with her eyebrows raised. 'Tell me, my dear, do I look like a shoplifter?'

'Well, no. But . . .'

'Yes, I know. You're only doing your job and its company policy.'

'Yes.' The young shop assistant looked relieved.

Pammy handed over three of the hangers. 'Look after these for me then, would you? I'll swap with these when Claire has tried the clothes on. Is that OK?'

'Oh, that's fine. Yes, of course.' She backed out of the cubicle hugging the excess clothes as if they represented some sort of prize.

Pammy handed Claire the first of the remaining garments. 'See what this is like on.'

Claire tried on the jacket, a black, classically cut number. It looked fine as a jacket but hopeless with the skirt.

'Dire,' said Pammy, handing her another choice. This was better but only marginally.

164

'And it makes you look an odd shape,' commented Pammy. Claire tried on a third top.

'Nope,' said Pammy with a sigh. She collected up the rejected clothes and went to swap them with the ones the assistant was minding.

'Not sure about that one,' said Claire, eyeing an elaborate purple and black creation. 'It looks like it's escaped from some sort of bodice ripper costume drama.'

'Go on, try it.'

Claire shrugged and took it.

'Stunning,' was Pammy's verdict.

'Do you think so?' Claire twisted and turned, trying to see the whole effect in the one mirror in the cubicle.

'Trust me. Have a look in the mirrors outside.'

Claire pushed aside the curtain and stepped into the area between the rows of compartments. She walked to the end, where there were three mirrors at angles to one another. She studied her reflections, her head on one side. Behind her, someone whistled appreciatively.

'Cor!' said a man's voice. Claire leaned forward to see further behind her in the looking glass. A youngish bloke – Claire reckoned he was about twenty – was leaning against the wall at the entrance to the changing rooms, staring unashamedly at her. 'If you want to pull,' he said, 'you have.'

Claire didn't know what to say. What was the right response? Gosh, thanks? In your dreams? I'm not that desperate? She stared back at the man and let the options flash through her brain. As she did, she saw something flash past the back of her head.

'Ow! Fuck me!' The man clutched his head and a shoe ricocheted off his temple and on to the floor.

'Fuck you? Fuck you!' a woman's voice bawled from the other end of the changing area. 'I wouldn't fuck you now if you were the last man on earth. How many times have I told you not to eye up talent when you're out with me?' And with that, a brassy blonde, a dead ringer for Barbara Windsor, stormed past Claire, limping unevenly on one shod foot and one bare one. 'Don't touch him with a barge pole. Nothing personal, dearie, but he'll shag anything with a pulse.' With that, she retrieved her shoe, shoved her foot into it and swept off.

Pammy watched the outburst from their cubicle and roared with laughter. The bloke glowered at her and Claire and slunk away.

'Blimey,' said Claire, utterly flummoxed.

'Well, at least that's two of us who think you look drop-dead gorgeous in that get-up.'

Being an invalid, Yvie discovered, was all well and good in the short term, but a complete pain after a couple of days. Over a week after her accident, Yvie was getting stir crazy. The novelty of being waited on had completely worn off, and while loafing was OK for an hour or so, Yvie had long since discovered that being a lady of leisure wasn't all it was cracked up to be. Sure, the hobbling around became easier, but she found the prospect of stairs terrifying, and hobbling and carrying anything except a book or the paper was virtually out of the question. Making herself a cup of tea was a non-starter unless she wanted to drink it in the kitchen, she couldn't help out round the house, she felt like a dead weight, and she or her crutch seemed to be constantly in the way or tripping people up.

Her proximity to Adam didn't help matters. She was inwardly adamant that she didn't want the sexual side of their relationship to start up again, but she wanted more than the crumbs she was being offered right now. She was acutely aware that he was making a point of ignoring her. All she wanted was friendship, nothing more or less. She would have liked that, though just because those were the terms that she wanted, it didn't mean that Adam did. But she only had herself to blame. She'd told him to leave her alone, so she could hardly complain that he now was.

She became increasingly frustrated, and that, coupled with the innate boredom that came from being housebound, made her ever more irritable. And she wasn't just imagining that she was alone and ignored. Adam was, according to Pammy, completely buried in estate work, while Pammy and Claire had lessons to get on with. When they weren't busy with their set school tasks, they went off shopping, or on errands to the village, while Adam had tenant farmers to visit and contractors to see, to say nothing of the day-to-day jobs that went with running a vast chunk of real estate. As a consequence, more often than not, Yvie found herself alone in the flat.

It was almost the final straw when the weather suddenly decided to take a turn for the better, and Yvie was forced to stare at the glorious May sunshine from an upstairs window. She had an urge to get out and paint, but that was pretty much a non-starter. Pammy and Claire were off on a shopping jaunt to Keswick – it would have been nice to have been invited too, but they'd bounced off without a second thought about her. Not that she was bitter, Yvie tried to tell herself. After all, she would have been a total hindrance and she would have refused, but it just would have been nice to have been asked.

Fed up, she flopped down on the sofa to see if there was anything on TV. Two minutes later, she'd switched it off again. Even she wasn't *that* desperate. She hopped over to the bookshelf and selected Dick Francis, but halfway through the first chapter, she realized it was one she had already read. With a sigh, she chucked it on to the coffee table, where it slid across the polished surface and landed on the floor on the other side. This was hopeless. She'd been rescued from near death on the mountain, only to die of boredom at home.

Making up her mind to stop being such a self-pitying wimp, Yvie decided that it was about time she tried to be more independent. Pushing herself off the sofa, she grabbed her crutches and made her way out of the flat. At the door at the top of the stairs that led down to the tradesman's entrance, Yvie stopped. The flight was long and steep. If she fell . . . No, she wasn't going to do that, she told herself firmly. She could do this, she said to herself. Yes, she could!

Taking her crutches in one hand, Yvie sat down at the top and, using her good leg as a brake, she flumped from one step to the next, dragging her crutches as she went. It was tiring but possible, and in less than a minute she reached the bottom. Triumphantly she opened the door and revelled in the smell of fresh air and basked in the warmth of the spring sunshine trapped in the kitchen courtyard. It seemed much longer than a week since she had last felt the sun on her face and the breeze ruffle her hair. It was experiences like the ones she had just been through, she thought, that made you appreciate the simple things in life all the more. She leaned against the warm brick wall of the house and soaked up the spring sun.

After a minute or two, she looked about her, unsure of which way to go. After all, she wanted to see more than just the back courtyard. Should she walk round to the side of the house and sit in the formal gardens, or might she be better off going round to the ornamental lake? She decided on the gardens – there were a couple of benches there. She wasn't sure that if she sat on the ground by the lake she'd be able to get herself upright again. How embarrassing would it be to end up like a beetle on its back, waving her legs in the air and shouting for help!

With her spirits soaring, Yvie felt a new burst of energy race through her body and she fairly swung along as she propelled herself along the gravel walkways, past the kitchen gardens and the stable block and towards the brick arch that led to the lawns and rose beds of the main garden. At the end of the stable block was a neat red brick Victorian cottage. The brass plate on the wall announced it was the 'estate office'. So this was Adam's workplace, thought Yvie as she stopped and stared at it. She'd wondered where the office was, but had always thought it was in part of the house. She imagined Adam at a desk within the building, sleeves rolled up, talking animatedly on the telephone perhaps . . .

The door opened. Yvie jumped. Adam stood in the doorway, sleeves rolled up as she had imagined.

'Yvie! What are you doing here?' Adam seemed angry to see her there.

She rocked backwards slightly, altering her point of balance on the crutches, putting another couple of inches between them. She wasn't used to this sort of reaction from him. 'I'm on my way to the garden,' she said defensively. 'I was going out of my head stuck in the flat, and the weather looked so wonderful and . . .'

'So you thought you'd risk your neck on the stairs.'

'I didn't.'

'So, what did you do, fly down them? Get Captain James T. Kirk to beam you down them?'

'No, I . . .'

'You should have phoned me. I'd have come and helped you, made sure you didn't come to any harm.'

'I can manage for myself.' Yvie's voice rose in annoyance that he thought her so useless.

'And it was your bloody independence that got you into this mess in the first place,' Adam shouted back.

'I . . . I . . . That wasn't "independence", that was lack of local knowledge,' she countered.

'Perhaps you should have asked advice.'

'Perhaps, when you were extolling the wonders of walking, you should have thought to tell me.'

Adam suddenly burst out laughing. 'God, it may be a cliché, but you are *magnificent* when you are angry.'

Yvie didn't feel like being so easily placated. 'And you are a bully. Now, if you'll excuse me, I want to carry on with my walk.' She swung round, trying to look haughty and dignified. As she did so, she got the rubber stopper of her crutch caught on the back of her good ankle, lost her balance and dropped both crutches. Adam caught her before she fell, grasping both arms and holding her steady.

'And where would you be without me?'

Yvie didn't look at him. She'd made a fool of herself and, what's more, she'd ended up in his arms again. She was aware that she was trembling. Part of it was from the shock and fear of nearly falling, but part of it was undoubtedly to do with the nearness of Adam.

'Hmm?' said Adam, wanting an answer to his question.

Yvie was thinking hard about where she would indeed be without him. Without him, she'd be flat on her face in the gravel looking even more foolish. Without him, she'd never have discovered the heights to which real passion could take you. Without him, she'd be in a very happy marriage with no outside temptations. (And, boy, was she feeling tempted right now.) Which was why she needed to be without him.

'I don't know,' she said sheepishly, as good as admitting he was right, that she did need him. 'You tell me.' She wriggled free from his grasp.

'Come on,' said Adam, bending down and picking up her crutches. Supporting her with one strong arm, he led her into the cottage. Yvie had just time to notice the ultra-modern office through the open door off the hall as Adam took her through to the back of the building, where there was a tiny but tidy kitchen and another low door. Almost before she knew what was happening, Adam, still clutching her crutches, led her through it.

'My bolt hole,' he said.

Yvie looked at the room; a state of the art stereo system, a plasma screen TV over the fireplace, a luxurious leather sofa, thick rugs on the floor, concealed lighting . . .

'What . . . ?' Then, 'Why . . . ?'

Adam lowered her on to the cool smooth leather of the sofa. 'OK, I'll come clean. This isn't my bolt hole at all. It's Mr Big's, my boss. When he comes to stay here, he always brings a houseful of guests with him. Up at the Hall he feels the need to be there all the time, playing at being mine host, dispensing largesse and drinks and bonhomie. It's what his guests expect, and he likes to make them feel special. But after a day or two it palls. So, he tells everyone he has to come down here on estate business and he escapes for a morning or a few hours, recharges his batteries and then goes back to being lord of the manor.'

'Doesn't he mind you using it?'

'He doesn't know that I do. Why should he? I leave it as I find it.'

Yvie looked at Adam steadily, a thought forming in her mind. 'So, how many women have you seduced here?'

'Do you want the honest truth?'

Yvie sighed heavily. 'We're both too old for stupid games. Why do you think I asked the question? Because I want you to lie to me? Get real, Adam.'

Adam shook his head. 'The honest truth is none.'

Yvie narrowed her eyes. 'What, not even Pammy?'

He shook his head. Did she believe him? He looked like he was telling the truth. Besides, who was there for him to seduce here? Some local village girls? Yvie suddenly had a picture form in her mind of Adam playing at being lord of the manor, in frock coat and frilly cravat, bedding a wench. How preposterous was that! She lowered her face to hide the smile.

The phone rang.

'Saved by the bell,' said Adam, raising his eyebrows. He left to answer it and Yvie wondered if he had really planned to seduce her here, or whether it was wishful thinking on her part. She gathered up her crutches and joined him in the office.

'That was Pammy,' said Adam, replacing the receiver, 'wanting me to organize yet another search party for you. She came back to find you'd done a runner and is worried. I told her you've just been out for some air and you're on your way back now.'

Yvie frowned. 'Why didn't you tell her I was here with you?'

'Well, we don't want her jumping to conclusions, do we?'

'Adam, there are *no* conclusions to jump to.'

'No. Whatever you say, Yvie.' His voice was thick with sarcasm.

Yvie gave a snort of annoyance and stumped out of the office, back to the house. It was a struggle to get back up the stairs. She did the reverse of what she'd done to make her escape, but then she'd had gravity on her side. Now she had to heave herself up a stair at a time using her arms and her good leg, then haul her plaster cast and her crutches up. Twice her crutches nearly slid back down the stairs, but both times she managed to grab them. Yvie decided she needed some sort of way of hanging them round her neck for manoeuvres such as this; she really didn't want to have to slide down to the bottom and start again like a player in a bizarre form of snakes and ladders.

Eventually she got to the top and opened the door to the flat. She was greeted by peels of laughter coming from the kitchen. She swung herself down the corridor to join Pammy and Claire and the fun. The laughter died as she got through the door.

'Hi, Mum,' said Claire. She was standing by the kitchen table creaming together cake mixture with a wooden spoon.

'You sounded like you were having a good time.'

'It was just something that happened while we were out,' said Claire. 'It was the sort of thing where you had to be there to see the funny side of it.' She giggled again.

'Tell me.'

Claire shrugged, still smiling. 'I don't think it would . . . I mean, it's not the sort of thing . . . You know,' she finished lamely.

But Yvie didn't know, not really, and what's more she felt excluded. She'd never minded in the past about the gales of laughter coming from Claire's attic room at home – that had been Claire and her friends, that had been teenage jokes and exchanges about their boyfriends, and Yvie hadn't expected to be a part of that – but Pammy was old enough to be Claire's mum. Pammy was *her* friend, not Claire's, and Claire was *her* daughter, not Pammy's.

'Well, glad you two had a good time,' she said lightly, trying to sound bright and cheerful. She went into the spare room and instantly saw a pile of carrier bags oozing clothes and tissue paper. She knew Claire didn't have enough money for a spree like that. Pammy must have been spoiling her. Yvie flopped on her bed, feeling a wave of more annoyance wash over her. Should she ask about their trip? Wait to be told? Should she be pleased at Pammy's generosity? Or cross?

She sighed. She was getting this completely out of proportion. She was being ridiculous. So what if Pammy wanted to spend money on Claire? It wasn't as if she had kids of her own to spoil. And so what if she and Claire found things to laugh about together? She should be glad that Claire was getting on so well with her friend. Wouldn't it be dreadful if they hated each other? She was being petty and dog-in-the-manger, and she despised herself for it. But, all the same, the niggle of jealously at Pammy and Claire's relationship refused to go away entirely. She got off the bed again, brushed her hair and returned to the kitchen.

'So, is there anything left in Keswick to buy?'

'Oh.' Claire looked a little sheepish. 'Well, Pammy thought that if I was going to this gig with Mark tonight, I ought to have something nice to wear.'

'What, like there's nothing in your wardrobe, right?' *Like I never buy you clothes?* was the follow-up question she wanted to ask, but the cattiness was uncalled-for, so she bit it back.

'Mum, this is a folk concert Mark is taking me to. I need something suitable.'

Yvie didn't understand. 'Jeans and a nice top wouldn't do, then?'

'Pammy showed me this really cool shop in Keswick. They

172

sell fab things, great textiles, all sorts of velvets and silks and stuff. And some of the jewellery is to die for.' Claire looked her mother straight in the eye. 'I bought the nicest belly bar you can imagine.'

'Belly bar? You haven't . . . ?'

Claire dissolved into fits of giggles again. 'Your face, Mum! Honestly.' She turned to Pammy. 'Didn't I tell you her reaction would be like that?'

Pammy smiled. 'I think your mother has a point. If I had a daughter, I wouldn't be too pleased at the idea either.'

Yvie was tempted to point out that that was just it, Pammy didn't have a daughter; that Claire was *her* responsibility, that she personally didn't find it very funny that they were taking the mickey out of her reaction, however predictable it was. And that being patronized as a result was just about the last straw.

'Well, I'm glad you both find the joke so funny.' She left the room again, aware that she had also ruined the mood. Well, tough.

Claire came to find her a few minutes later.

'I came to say I'm sorry. I shouldn't have made fun of your views on piercings.'

Yvie was still simmering but Claire was trying to make up, although Yvie suspected Pammy had a hand in this diplomacy. 'Apology accepted.' Yvie tried not to sound grudging, although she was thinking that perhaps one was due from Pammy as well.

'I didn't mean to upset you.' Claire sounded genuinely sorry and she looked utterly contrite.

Yvie began to feel a heel. Why shouldn't Claire and Pammy have a good time together? 'Perhaps this wretched ankle is making me a bit grumpy. I shouldn't take it out on you.'

Claire shrugged. 'It isn't as if things have been the easiest for you of late. And even if it gets better back in Carchester, we won't be able to go home, because you can't drive.'

'We will go back though. We'll get the train and come back to collect the car later. At the moment that doesn't seem to be something we need think about. Anyway, tell me about this date and show me what you're going to wear.'

Claire finished showing her mother her purchases and was

173

obviously excited at the prospect of her date with Mark. 'And Pammy's going to drive us to the gig and collect us afterwards.'

'But that's ridiculous. Can't you get a bus or something?'

'Mum, have you any idea about the buses up here? They run about once a week. This isn't Salisbury or Carchester.'

'Well, can't Mark's folks help out with the lift? It doesn't seem fair that Pammy is doing it all. After all, Mark asked you out.'

'Pammy offered.'

'I know, and it's very kind of her, but you can't expect her to put herself out for you like this. You should ask Mark to sort out something for one of the journeys.'

'Mum, I hardly know him.'

'You know him well enough to go out with him.'

'That's different.'

'I don't think so.'

'Oh God, Mum, you're so unreasonable. At least Pammy doesn't treat me like a kid.' With that, Claire flounced out and Yvie was left feeling even more resentful about Perfect Pammy and her relationship with *her* daughter.

The atmosphere at dinner that night was more than a little chilly. Claire swanned in, in her new outfit, after everyone had sat down and had started eating. Yvie was stunned. The outfit was unusual and beautiful, far more sophisticated than the sort of things Claire normally came home with from a shopping trip, and yet it looked quite casual. Certainly it would be great at a folk concert in a pub. Yvie detected Pammy's influence, although she couldn't think where Pammy kept this seam of fashion sense; normally her clothes were so staid and conservative she could have given Maggie Thatcher a run for her money. Claire sashayed to her place, oozing confidence. She looked great and she knew it, and Adam and Pammy both commented effusively. Yvie was still in such a mean mood that she had to force herself to make positive comments, but luckily Claire seemed to be oblivious to it, chatting away to Adam about her day, her trip to Keswick, and the shops she had been to, but Pammy noticed. She frowned at Yvie, which only succeeded in making Yvie more resentful.

And what have you to be upset with me about? thought

Yvie. You've had a great day out with my daughter, who obviously now prefers your company to mine.

And even as these thoughts entered her head, so did another one. If this was how she felt about Claire wanting to spend time with Pammy, how would Pammy feel about Adam wanting to spend time with her? The sense of betrayal that she felt about Claire, almost an adult, wanting to make a new friend, who was proving competition to her relationship with her mother, would be nothing, *nothing* to the sense of betrayal that would deluge everyone if she and Adam got found out. The thought made Yvie feel suddenly sick. She looked at the last few forkfuls on her plate and knew she couldn't finish them.

'Excuse me,' she said, rising from the table. 'I need to lie down.' She went to her bedroom and threw herself on to her bed. Pammy fussed in behind her. Not what she wanted.

'I'm sorry,' said Pammy. 'Have I done something to upset you? Please tell me if I have. I didn't mean to . . .'

'No, it's me. I'm just getting stir crazy. I was hit by the old green-eyed monster with all Claire's talk about your great day, and I felt sorry for myself being cooped up here.'

Instantly Pammy was contrite. 'I didn't think. I should have asked you to come too. I thought . . . Well, I suppose that's it, I didn't think. I imagined it would have been too much for you.'

Yvie put a hand up to quiet her. 'It would have been too much. I got knackered just getting to the gardens and back. You'd have had no fun with me in tow. But knowing that makes my envy all the more unreasonable. It's me who should be sorry. Honest, Pammy.'

'If you're sure?'

Yvie nodded. 'Now then, hadn't you better be getting that daughter of mine off on her hot date?'

Pammy looked at her watch. 'Goodness, is that the time? We must fly.' She abandoned Yvie and went in search of Claire.

A few minutes later, Yvie heard the car scrunching over the gravel and then Adam entered her room and in a second he was beside her bed. Yvie felt a frisson of apprehension. What did he want? After days of ignoring her, had her encounter with him that afternoon flicked a switch? He took her hand and began to kiss it.

175

'No,' she said, snatching it away. 'No.'

Adam drew back. 'Come on, Yvie, who are you kidding? I've seen you watching me. And you came to find me this afternoon. Why else were you at the estate office?'

'The only person kidding themselves here is you, Adam. I didn't come to find you at the estate office, I was out for a walk. Whatever was between us has to be forgotten. We've got to move on. And I'm not going to cheat on Richard again. What don't you understand about that?'

'But he needn't know.'

'It's still wrong.' Yvie was adamant.

'Is it? Is it so wrong if we really love each other?'

Yvie propped herself up on one elbow. She shook her head. 'But do we? We've been through this before. If we did, you'd leave your job and Pammy, I'd leave Claire and Richard. But neither of us is going to do that, are we?' She looked Adam squarely in the eye. 'Are we? Think of all the pain we'd cause, all the hurt. Do we really want to do that?'

Adam lowered his gaze. 'No,' he admitted, after a pause. 'No, you're right.'

'What you want is to have your cake and eat it, and I'm not prepared to be your bit on the side.'

'You make it sound sordid.'

'It would be, if that's what we did. But, Adam, this has got to stop now, totally.'

'OK.'

Yvie wasn't sure she could believe or trust Adam.

'Do you really mean that? I can't stay here if I feel you're going to keep trying it on with me.'

'But what would you tell Richard if you moved out?'

'The truth.' There was silence for a while as Adam digested this and all the implications.

'You mean that, don't you?'

Yvie nodded and swung her feet off her bed. 'Yes, I do. Now I am going to see what I can do in the kitchen to help clear up. You can help me or not, it's up to you.' And, grabbing her crutches, she swung herself through the door and away from Adam.

She found that she could manage a fair bit in the kitchen, as the plates had already been cleared through from the dining

176

room. She hopped and hobbled around, stacking the dish-washer, wiping down surfaces and generally tidying up. It took her much longer than it would normally, but she didn't mind. It occupied her and gave her something to think about other than how to cope with Adam. She had about finished when Pammy got back.

'You shouldn't have!' she exclaimed when she saw the tidy kitchen.

'It's my way of making up for being a cow,' said Yvie.

Pammy looked questioningly at Yvie. 'I don't understand.'

'I was in a vile mood and I took it out on both you and Claire.'

'It's because you've got lots to worry about. What with this business with the guy after Richard, and now your ankle . . .'

'Please don't make excuses for me, Pammy. Was Claire upset about the way I behaved?'

'No,' said Pammy, but Yvie thought she was lying. The answer was too glib and too pat. Yvie felt she could bet her bottom dollar that she and Claire had been talking about her all the way to pick up Mark – and afterwards too, perhaps.

Yvie felt another stab of annoyance. What right had they to discuss her? And Yvie had no doubt that Pammy had been offering wise counsel on how to deal with a stroppy mother. Like she was the great expert. Like she had brought up kids of her own. Just because she was a teacher, didn't make her the world's living expert on mother/daughter relations. But Yvie kept her views to herself and mumbled something about having a bath. She grabbed a plastic bag to shove her cast in, and stomped off to the bathroom to have a good long soak. She hoped that the steam and the hot water would put her in a more equitable mood before Claire returned home.

After her bath, she took herself off to bed with a book, but she couldn't follow the thread of the story. She kept going over recent events in her mind: getting lost on the moors, being found by Adam, Claire's growing closeness to Pammy, her feelings for Adam, his desire for her. She let the book fall from her hand and she gazed at the ceiling. There was no doubt that it was incredibly exciting to be desired by another man. Marriage was fine, it was comfortable and safe, but it was now lacking in passion. She loved Richard deeply, of course she did, but there were occasions, quite a few really, where she felt taken for granted. The way he assumed, on a Saturday morning, that she was as eager for sex as he was. The way he never kissed her properly any more; a perfunctory peck on the cheek was as good as it got. The way he no longer brought her little presents. The way he seemed to prefer to watch the TV rather than talk to her in the evening. Even at meals, he would rather have the radio on than talk. He never asked her about her work, he didn't even look at most of the paintings that she did, and when she asked him about his work, she was more often than not fobbed off with remarks about 'routine stuff' or 'the usual', hardly comments designed to make her eager to hear more.

But . . . but she couldn't imagine life without Richard. Maybe their life together had got prosaic, maybe they did take each other for granted, but wasn't that what happened to marriages in the long run? And, much as she still felt raw lust for Adam, she didn't think she could bring herself to betray Richard a second time.

'Was Mum still up when you left to pick us up?' Claire asked Pammy as she and Mark clambered into the Range Rover.

'No. She turned in early.' Pammy reversed out of the car park and on to the lane that led back up the valley towards the village and the Hall.

Claire didn't answer, but she wanted to say 'good'.

'I expect your mum gets tired having to use crutches all the time,' Mark observed, filling an embarrassing gap in the conversation.

Again Claire didn't answer.

'So, was it a good evening?' asked Pammy, just a shade too brightly.

'Yeah, it was, actually. The band was really good,' said Claire.

'You sound surprised,' said Mark.

'Well . . . I wasn't quite sure what it would be like. I mean, folk music is . . .' She took a breath and then said in a rush, 'I don't knit my own sandals, and I can't stand the idea of eating tofu, and I really don't want to play the tambourine,

178

and I thought I might be stuck for an evening with a load of people who do.'

'Is that what you think of me?' asked Mark.

'Well, no, obviously.'

'So why did you think everyone else might be like that?'

'Because there's so little to do round here, I thought you might clutch at any straw that came floating by.'

Pammy laughed. 'You make us all sound quite needy.'

'I don't mean to. It's just you've got to admit the night life isn't jumping, is it?'

A car came round the corner ahead of them, its lights on full beam. Pammy flashed at it to signal it to dip, but the driver either ignored her or didn't understand. Pammy squeezed the car as close to the wall as possible, to allow the oncoming vehicle space to pass. It didn't seem to be slowing down, and it vroomed past, bashing the driver's wing mirror as it went.

'Bastard!' said Mark, screwing round in his seat to try to see if he recognized the car, but all he could make out was that it was some sort of four-by-four.

Pammy opened her window and straightened the mirror. 'Never mind,' she said as it flicked back into position. 'Oh, damn. He cracked the glass. Adam will be livid. Spares for this brute cost a fortune. Still, it could have been worse. Whoever it was was driving like a maniac.'

'Not a local,' said Mark. 'Anyone from round here would drive with more care.'

Pammy shrugged. 'Maybe, maybe not. But they were in a hurry.'

'Or pissed,' said Mark.

'Anyway, the main thing is that we're all right. But that's the trouble with this place,' she said to Claire. 'As it gets towards the summer, there are dozens of visitors who are used to driving on wide suburban roads, and who can't cope with the sort they find here.' She slipped the car into gear and drove on slowly. Claire could see that her hands weren't as steady as before.

Claire tried to undress silently when she got in, but it was difficult in the dark, and she didn't want to switch the light on and risk waking her mother. There had been enough bad

179

feeling for one evening, and Claire reckoned that she didn't want another row. The mood her mother had been in earlier, Claire thought a bust-up would be inevitable if she woke her. However, the laces on her blouse were a nightmare without any light to see what she was doing. She moved towards the door to get the benefit of the glow of the hall light, but as she went she stubbed her toe against the leg of the dressing table. An involuntary yelp escaped.

'Claire?' mumbled Yvie from under the duvet.

'Sorry, Mum,' whispered Claire.

'What time is it?'

'About half eleven.'

'Oh. Do you want to switch the light on to see what you're doing?'

'Please.' Claire flicked the switch, and Yvie screwed up her eyes against the sudden brightness.

'Why are you so late?'

'Mum, the gig didn't finish till eleven. We came straight back.' Well, apart from the few minutes they stopped after the close shave, but Claire wasn't going to mention that. That was *bound* to cause upset, and all she wanted now was to get to bed. She was knackered.

'It's not right that you dragged Pammy out so late,' grumbled Yvie.

Claire sighed. Not this again. She finished undressing and folded her clothes up on a chair. Then she grabbed her nightie and went to brush her teeth. When she returned, her mother was sitting up looking wide awake.

'I hope this isn't going to be a regular thing,' said Yvie. 'I don't want to stop your fun, but it's not fair on Pammy. If I could drive, I'd run you to things, but I can't. I know it's a pain for us both, and it's not your fault that I'm out of action, but I really don't want you taking advantage of Pammy's good nature.'

'Mum,' said Claire, the exasperation obvious in her voice. 'Can we leave this till the morning? I'm tired and I want to go to bed.' She switched off the light and hauled her duvet back.

'OK, we'll talk about it in the morning then.' And, with an angry little sigh, Yvie turned on her side.

180

Claire lay awake in bed, cross that her mother had spoiled what had been a fun evening. Why shouldn't she have some fun? And why shouldn't Pammy drive her – after all, she said she didn't mind. Why did her mother have to interfere? Life was so unfair. It was all her dad's fault. If he hadn't got mixed up with the blasted IRA, she'd still be in Carchester, not stuck out here. On the other hand, she thought, she wouldn't have met Mark. And Mark was nice, and seventeen, and had money. In fact, Mark was a lot nicer than anyone she'd met in Carchester. Not that she knew many boys. And neither did her friends, because they went to a stuffy all-girls' school. Wait till she got back and told Debbo about him. She'd be so green. Feeling better, she snuggled down and wondered if it would be too obvious to find a reason to go to the village shop in the morning. Then, just as she was drifting off to sleep, she remembered the next day was Sunday. Blow, she thought sleepily, I'll have to wait till Monday now.

'You didn't tell me you'd nearly had an accident last night.'
Claire had only just walked into the kitchen to get a mug of early-morning tea, when her mother rounded on her. 'No, I didn't. And the operative word is "nearly". The guy missed us. Well, almost.'
'Almost?'
Pammy tried to calm things down. 'He clipped my wing mirror. I expect it's the sort of accident that happens all the time in a big city. It was no big deal. Really.'
'How much will it cost to repair?'
'I've no idea. It's only a cracked mirror.'
'Well, find out and let me know. Claire can pay for it.'
'Mum!'
'The accident wouldn't have happened if Pammy hadn't been giving you a lift.'
Claire abandoned the idea of tea, and went to have a shower. She stomped out, just resisting the urge to slam the kitchen door. That wouldn't have been fair on Pammy, but if it had been her mother's door . . . God! Her mother was the limit.
She took her time washing and dressing – at least in the bathroom her mother couldn't have a go at her – but she couldn't spend all day there. After she had spent an age apply-

181

ing her make-up – well, she might run into Mark around the place – she finally exited.

She went back to the kitchen, where her mother was behind the newspaper. Pammy had disappeared, perhaps out of tact, so that Claire and Yvie could sort things out in private. But Claire didn't want to sort things out. She was in a lousy mood and it was all her mother's fault. She pointedly ignored the cause of her bad temper and stamped across to the furthest corner to switch on the kettle and the radio. Yvie rattled the paper. Claire was tempted to turn it up out of spite, but she decided that it would be foolhardy to irritate her mother further. The kettle boiled and, as Claire poured the hot water on to a tea bag, the pips signalled the start of the nine o'clock news. Claire cradled the warm mug and leaned against the work surface staring out of the kitchen window at the lowering clouds and steady drizzle. The weather matched her black mood. She listened to the start of the headlines with half an ear, the usual litany of death, destruction, gloom and doom, then let her attention wander to thoughts of Mark. The news droned on. She reached out to switch the radio to the local station. At least that would be jollier than this – well, anything would be jollier than this.

'Leave it!' snapped Yvie.

'But you're reading the paper.'

'No. There's something I want to listen to.'

Claire shrugged. Her body language made it obvious that she thought her mother was just being vexing, and she started to open her mouth to object, when her mother shushed her.

'More news has come in,' droned the newscaster, 'about the explosion near Carchester . . .'

'Ohmigod!' said Claire. She looked at her mother, whose face was ashen.

' . . . police have confirmed the victim was a retired member of the RUC, although they haven't released a name.'

'It can't be daddy,' said Claire in an unsteady voice. 'He was never anything to do with the RUC.'

'Journalists get things wrong. They make mistakes. Army, RUC – it's all the same to most of them.'

'It's not him,' said Claire, with a conviction she certainly didn't feel. 'That's too big an error.' She realized she was

182

shaking, her tea was slopping in the mug. She put it down on the work surface before she made a mess.

'Error or not, I have to find out for sure.'

'How?'

'I'll ring home.' Yvie almost ran across the kitchen to the phone, and dialled their home number.

'Come on, come on,' she muttered into the mouthpiece. She must have let the phone ring for over a minute before she pressed the button to sever the connection. 'He should be at home, it's Sunday.'

'Yeah, but Mum, with something like this, mightn't work want him in? You know what it's like.'

Yvie tried Richard's office number. Again nothing. She replaced the receiver shakily.

'His mobile?' said Claire.

Again Yvie dialled. Nothing. 'He's got it switched off,' she said. But Claire knew they were both wondering if it was really switched off or if it were no longer functioning.

'What about trying Daddy's boss?' suggested Claire.

Yvie nodded. 'Good idea. Trouble is, I don't know the number. I know where to find it – on Daddy's desk at home . . .'

'But doesn't Adam know Mr Hayman? Doesn't Dad always say that he got the job because of Adam?'

Yvie's annoyance with her daughter was forgotten under the pressure of the current turn of events. 'Yes, of course. Run and get it for me, please.'

Claire raced off, calling Adam's name, thankful to be able to do something constructive. She charged round the flat. He was nowhere, and Pammy wasn't around either. Perhaps he was at the estate office. She thundered down the stairs at a reckless speed, taking them two at a time, and ran across the kitchen yard. Without knocking, she burst into the office.

'Claire, what on earth's the matter?' he asked.

Claire gulped, trying to get her breath. 'There's been an explosion – in Wiltshire. We can't get hold of Daddy. Mummy wants to ring Rupert Hayman to see what he knows.'

Adam leapt to his feet. 'You don't mean that—'

'We don't know. Mummy couldn't get an answer at home.'

He pulled open a desk drawer and took out his Filofax. Not

even pausing to push the drawer shut again, Adam ran from the office. A couple of minutes later, the two of them piled into the kitchen.

'Here's the number, Yvie. Do you want me to make the call, or would you rather do it?'

Wordlessly, Yvie passed Adam the phone. Adam grabbed it and dialled.

'Come on, come on,' he muttered as the phone rang. After what seemed like an age, it was answered.

'Hi,' said Adam. 'It's Adam Clifton here, Hilary. I'm sorry to bother you on a Sunday, but I'm trying to track down Richard Maxwell . . . Oh, is he . . . ?' He grinned at Yvie and Claire and put his thumb up. Yvie sank on to a chair and Claire felt as if she might burst into tears with relief. 'No. It's just we heard the news about the explosion . . . Yes, terrible . . . Oh, right. Well, gas could be a quite likely cause . . . Of course, when we couldn't get hold of him . . . Yes, I'll tell her. Thanks. Bye.' He replaced the receiver. 'As you gathered, he's OK. The reason he didn't answer his phone is because he's round at Rupert's place because Rupert and his wife are about to have an enormous barbecue for all sorts of clients and Richard is helping out. Hilary will get him to phone you in a minute or two.'

Bang on cue, the phone rang. 'Richard, Richard . . .' Yvie said, a catch of relief obvious in her voice.

Adam came round the kitchen table and gave Claire a hug.

'False alarm,' he said. 'It seems it was gas. Nothing to do with our man. What a relief, eh? Just one of those dreadful coincidences.'

Claire nodded. She still felt very shaky and wasn't quite sure that she might not cry. She excused herself and went to the bedroom. Apart from anything else, she felt guilty about the bad thoughts she'd had about her father the night before – blaming him for her predicament. The last hideous ten minutes, wondering if her father might have been blown to smithereens by some stranger out for revenge, had put things into perspective. What did it matter if she was a bit unhappy here, if life wasn't going quite perfectly? It was all such trivia compared to the big things in life, and she'd just thought she would have to confront one of the biggest – losing a parent.

Despite the fact that she wasn't the least religious, she still felt the need to offer up a little prayer to whichever higher being it was that was keeping her father safe, to ask for continued vigilance.

She wandered back into the kitchen about ten minutes later.

'Mum,' she said. 'I'm sorry I was such a cow earlier. And for being unreasonable last night.'

Yvie came round the kitchen table and gave her a hug. 'And I'm sorry too. I know you're bored out of your skull here. If Pammy is happy to give you the odd lift, then it's no business of mine.'

'I'll pay for the mirror.'

'For heaven's sake. I expect we can work something out.'

Pammy came into the kitchen, looking worried. 'I heard the news. Adam says Richard was not involved.'

'No,' said Yvie. 'Richard doesn't know much more than us at the moment, except that it was a gas explosion. The poor bugger caught up in it had worked for the RUC though. Bit ironic that he left Ulster to get away from explosions, only to get caught up in one on the mainland.'

'And they're sure that's all it was? That he had no connection with Lynch?'

'They're looking into it, but it looks as though it was just one of those things.'

'But you told us that two of the other victims looked like they were victims of tragic accidents.'

'I know. I'm just keeping everything crossed that this one really is.'

'Shit,' said Pammy. 'It's scary, isn't it?'

'Frankly, yes,' said Yvie. 'I mean, I really want to believe, for my own peace of mind, that this accident is all quite innocent, but . . .'

'Exactly,' said Pammy.

Yvie sounded bleak. 'I don't see why he feels he has to stay there like a tethered goat. Why can't he come away up here with us? Why does it have to be him?'

Claire thought her mother sounded very close to tears. Yvie swung round, her arms folded, to stare out of the window.

'I'm sure the police know what they're doing,' said Pammy soothingly.

185

But Claire could see Pammy's face, and she thought Pammy didn't look the least bit sure. Quite the opposite, in fact.

As they ate a delicious Sunday roast, cooked by Pammy with Claire's help, the weather took a turn for the worse to such an extent that Pammy turned the dining-room light on.

'That's a shame,' said Yvie. 'I was hoping it would clear so I could have a little hobble about in the fresh air this afternoon.'

'Well, skin's waterproof,' said Adam. 'If you wrap up well, there's no reason why you shouldn't go out to blow some of the cobwebs away.'

Claire shuddered. 'No way I'm going out in the rain. Frankly, I'd rather stick red-hot pins in my eyes.'

'And I'm going to make a cake for tea,' said Pammy. 'You can help me if you like, Claire.'

'Ooh, yes please.'

'Perhaps I'll scrap the idea,' said Yvie, not fancying a solitary stroll.

'I'll come with you if you like,' said Adam casually.

Yvie glanced up at him, wondering if his offer was as innocent as it sounded, or whether there was another agenda.

'You don't want to be dragged out of a nice warm house on a day like this. Forget it. I'll go for a walk another day.'

'Don't be such a wuss,' said Adam. 'The exercise will do you good. Come on. Besides which, if there's going to be cake for tea, I would suggest that we need to make space for it.'

Yvie didn't think she could go on protesting that she didn't want a walk – especially as it had been her idea in the first place.

'Oh, all right. I'll help clear away and then we can go.'

'You leave that,' said Pammy. 'There's not much to do, and Claire will help me.'

Claire nodded, looking almost eager, Yvie noted with a touch of annoyance. Whenever she asked Claire to help with any domestic chores back in Carchester, Claire always found any number of excuses as to why she couldn't: too busy, too much homework, period pain, appointment elsewhere, phone calls to make . . . Huh! But when Pammy asked, it was a whole different ball game. Yvie tried to shove her ungracious thoughts to the back of her mind, but it was difficult not to feel a little resentful. Claire's willingness to help Pammy had gone beyond the good manners that Yvie had troubled to instil into her. Now it was as if she was desperate to please. Yvie was certain, though, that the instant they got back to Carchester – whenever that might be – this desire to be the perfect little helper would vanish into thin air. What was it that Pammy had that she didn't, Yvie wondered.

She stomped off to her bedroom to get herself togged up against the drizzle outside. She pulled a thick sock over her toes sticking out of the plaster cast, and then tied a plastic carrier bag over the whole thing to protect it. Not stylish, but practical, she thought as she slipped into her waxed jacket and then pulled a woolly hat down over her ears.

She met Adam at the top of the stairs to the back door. He gave her an ironic wolf whistle.

'Shut up,' said Yvie. 'I know I look like a freak.' She meant the words to come out like she was joking, but from the slapped look on Adam's face she'd got it all wrong. Obviously she was still in a mood over Claire's eagerness to please Pammy. To cover up, she said, 'Aren't we taking the dogs?'

'Pammy wore them out this morning. Besides, if they get excited, they might get under your feet. We don't want another accident, do we?'

Yvie grabbed her crutches and headed off down the stairs. She'd got much better at negotiating these now, and was able to descend with a degree of skill. At the back door, she paused to fasten her jacket properly and turn the collar up.

'All set?' said Adam, joining her. 'You set the pace, I don't know how fast you want to go.'

Yvie was getting much more adept with her crutches, and Adam didn't have to alter his usual stride very much at all to keep alongside her.

'You're getting good at this,' he said.

'I'm getting biceps like a Russian shot-putter.'

Adam laughed. 'Well, as long as you don't develop a moustache to go with it. Although,' he added with a grin, 'it might be an improvement.'

'You bastard,' said Yvie, taking a mock swing at him with

187

a crutch. Adam easily dodged out of the way. 'That's not fair. I can't retaliate.' She waved her crutch at him. 'Just you wait, Clifton. I'll get you when you're not expecting it.'

'That's better,' said Adam.

'What is?'

'You're smiling.'

'So?'

'So, you haven't been doing a lot of it lately. I know,' he said putting his hand up to stop the obvious explanation. 'I know, things haven't been easy. I mean, this morning was a case in point. That news story was horrid and must have given you a terrible jolt.'

'Adam,' said Yvie, stopping and turning to face him. 'Do you know, for about ten minutes today, I thought I was a widow. I really thought that Richard was dead, and I can't tell you how terrified and alone I felt. It was like one of those dreadful falling dreams when you lose all control and you know it'll be better if only you can wake up, but you can't, and the fear just gets worse and worse. Only, I knew that it wasn't a dream. I knew that the fear wouldn't go away if I opened my eyes, because I was already awake.'

'You poor kid,' said Adam. 'I didn't realize how bad it was. I mean, I knew it was a shock – it was a shock to us all – but, you know, once it was all straightened out . . .'

'Well, it took a while for the awful sick feeling to go away. It seemed such a close call at the time. I suppose I feel a bit foolish now, but I really thought that the news had got it wrong. I mean, how many explosions do you hear about – and one in the same county? I just couldn't believe it could be anything else.' She could feel tears welling up again in her eyes, and was grateful that her face was already wet from the fine drizzle. Around them, fatter drops had collected on the leaves and were pattering on to the ground, a small breeze sometimes shifting a flurry of drips. The fine rain had deadened all the other sounds. Even the birds had stopped singing. They were surrounded by silence.

Adam leaned forward to give Yvie a hug, but she pushed him away.

'No, Adam. I'm too vulnerable at the moment. Please don't.'

He moved back, looking hurt again. 'I don't mean . . .'

'No, I know.' They stared at each other for a brief instant. 'Come on. I'm getting wet and cold. Let's keep moving.'

Yvie set off again, along the track that led towards the cottage and the path to the village. They sploshed through puddles, side by side in silence, both deep in thought. The rain began to get heavier. It was falling straight from the sky like stair rods, and even though Yvie was wearing a wax jacket, she could feel it penetrating the defences round her neck and beginning to trickle down her spine.

'I'm getting soaked,' she said.

'Me too.'

'Let's go back.'

'What about the cottage? It's only round the corner now.'

'I left the key at the Hall.'

'Just as well I know where there's one hidden.'

'What?'

'Come on, I'll show you.'

They speeded up and, in a minute or so, they rounded the corner and there was the cottage. Adam lifted up a mossy stone from the top of the drystone wall and pulled out a key.

'That's not a practice recommended by your local police force, is it?' said Yvie.

'For heaven's sake. Everyone does it round here.'

'You wouldn't if you lived in Carchester.'

Adam led the way to the front door and unlocked it. 'It won't be warm, but at least it'll be dry,' he said, holding the door to allow Yvie through first.

Yvie shook the worst of the rain off her jacket and then hung it up on the peg by the door. She pulled off her sodden woolly hat and chucked it on to a worktop. It landed with a wet splat. Her hair underneath was damp.

'Ugh!' she said. She hobbled through into the kitchen. 'Shame there isn't any milk, or we could have some tea.' Then a thought struck her. 'Wait a min.' She rummaged in a cupboard. 'Look. Hot chocolate. How about a cup of that?'

'Sounds wonderful. I'd have settled for black tea – anything hot and wet – but this'll be a real treat.'

Yvie got busy with the kettle and the mugs.

'How about a fire?' asked Adam.

'Don't be silly. We're only sheltering from the rain, not moving in.'

Adam walked across the sitting room and leaned on the breakfast bar. 'I don't want you catching cold. You've enough to contend with at the moment without being laid low by some nasty bug.'

'You don't catch colds from walking in the rain.'

'I still think you'd better dry yourself properly. There'll be towels upstairs. I'll go and fetch some.' Adam pottered off and Yvie waited for the kettle to boil. Adam was back in no time with two thick fluffy towels.

'Sorry they're not warm but the heating's off.'

Yvie took one and rubbed her wet face and neck. 'Never mind.' The hissing of the kettle reached a crescendo and then it clicked off. Yvie poured the water on to the chocolate powder in two mugs. Instantly the smell of cocoa filled the small room.

'Here,' she said, holding a mug out to Adam. 'Drink this while it's hot.'

'Give me both mugs,' he said. 'You can't carry hot drinks and manage your crutches.'

Yvie didn't argue. Adam took the drinks and put them on the coffee table. Yvie noticed he sat on the wing chair, leaving the sofa for her. She swung across the room on her crutches and sank into it gratefully. She propped her crutches against the arm and, having settled herself, she picked up her steaming mug.

'Ooh, this is nice.' She took a sip.

'Isn't it?' said Adam, staring at her over the rim of his mug. 'I should have lit a fire though. That would have made this moment perfect.'

Yvie regarded him. What was he implying? She had a feeling he wasn't talking about the quality of the cocoa. She held her tongue; partly through not knowing quite what to say, and partly because she was afraid that Adam might purposely misinterpret anything that she did say. She took another sip.

'Flames flickering up the walls, this room warm and cosy, the rain pattering on the windows, you and I snuggled up on the sofa together—'

Yvie held her hand up to stop him. 'Well, apart from the rain on the windows, none of the rest of that little scenario is going to take place, so you can dismiss that particular fantasy.' As she said it, Adam rose out of his chair, took two steps across the room and sat down next to Yvie. 'There, you see. You're wrong. My picture is starting to come together after all.'

Yvie shuffled along the cushion a few inches. 'No it isn't. We're not snuggling. And no,' she added hastily, 'we're not going to either.'

Adam bent towards her. 'Aren't we?'

Yvie slammed her cocoa down on the table. 'Adam Clifton, how often do I have to tell you? It's over. I'm not going back to you. Forget it.'

Adam moved closer and grabbed Yvie's wrist. 'And how often do I have to say that I know you still want me. Goddammit, Yvie, you've even told me you still love me.'

Yvie leaned back to get as much space between them as was humanly possible. 'Well, I shouldn't have done. My mistake.' She looked coldly at Adam. 'Let go of my arm please.'

But Adam gripped it tighter and pulled her towards him. He was looking angry too now. 'You know you're kidding yourself. You know how, when I left you alone all last week, you missed my attentions. Admit it, you did, didn't you? I could tell. You kept looking at me. Why else did you suggest going for a walk? You guessed the other two wouldn't come.'

'No I didn't,' said Yvie, her voice rising with indignation.

'Huh. And I didn't see you refusing my offer of accompanying you.'

'Yes I did.'

'Hardly. I could tell you were just doing it for form's sake.'

His face was very close to hers now, and Yvie had no escape route. She was pinned against the big saggy cushions of the sofa. Even if she'd been fully fit, it would have been difficult to wriggle away from Adam, but with a cast on her leg it was nigh on impossible. He leaned forward and began to kiss her roughly. Yvie could feel her lips being bruised against her teeth. She tried to turn her face away, but Adam's free hand

191

caught her chin and forced it back. She felt him release her wrist and his hand move to her skirt.

'No,' she mumbled. But he completely ignored her. She could feel him pushing the fabric up her leg. If it hadn't been for the blasted plaster cast, she'd have been wearing tights – that would have slowed him down, she thought – but as it was, her legs were bare. She felt his fingers reach the edge of her knicker elastic and fumble their way underneath it. She squirmed. Once she would have melted at his touch, but now she felt violated and scared. Was he planning on raping her?

She freed her mouth from his. 'Get off, you bastard!' she hissed. 'Get *off*!'

She could feel his fingers assaulting her. She wriggled and managed to slide half off the sofa. Adam suddenly shifted his weight to try to get on top of her, but as he did so, it gave Yvie the chance to escape. She slid right off and landed on her bottom. She ducked sideways to avoid his attempt to grab her again and, using her good leg, she pushed herself along the carpet and away from him. As she passed her crutches, she grabbed one. 'You shit!' she yelled at him, brandishing the crutch. 'What on earth do you think you're playing at?' She was angry and frightened. She stood up and instantly became aware that her legs were trembling violently. She steadied herself by holding the back of the wing chair.

'You know perfectly well what I was up to, you prick-tease,' he snarled.

Yvie had never seen Adam like this. It was terrifying.

'Is this what you do to Richard? Lead him on and then go all coy. Pretend you're some sort of little virgin, too precious to be touched. Is that what you do?'

Yvie hardly knew how to respond. 'Of course I don't. But you had no right—'

'But I have every right. You're not in love with Richard. How could you be? You're in love with me. We both know it.'

'You're wrong. And after what has just happened, I never want to be alone with you again. You're contemptible.'

'*I'm* contemptible? What about you? I didn't notice you baulking at the idea of coming into the cottage with me.'

'I assumed we were getting out of the rain. Call me naïve, but I took the offer of shelter at face value.'

'Huh. You miss sex with me. Admit it. You came in here because you knew we'd be alone, but then you got cold feet. I don't remember you having such touching sensibilities in Germany. You couldn't keep your hands off me then. Remember?'

Yvie had had as much as she was going to take. She hobbled across to the sofa and grabbed her crutches, then took her coat off the peg. 'Don't you dare bring up our affair. It was over years ago. You can stay here with your sad little fantasies and delusions that you're God's gift, but I'm off back to the Hall. And if you ever come near me again, I'll . . . I'll . . .' But she couldn't think of a suitable threat, so she just stormed off out of the cottage, slamming the door behind her so hard the glass pane rattled.

She was so angry on the return journey, she barely noticed the rain. 'Bastard, bastard, bastard!' she mumbled like some sort of mantra. How could she have let herself get into that situation? She trusted him. She thought he was a gentleman, but he was nothing of the sort. However, one thing was certain. She and Claire would have to move back to the cottage. There was no way she was going to risk being stuck in the Hall with Adam on her own. Heaven only knew what he might try again. Now she was good with her crutches, she could probably cope. The spiral stairs would be a bit of a problem, but if all else failed, she could go up and down them on her bum. The trouble was, how was she going to tell Pammy? Was she going to be able to do it without Pammy guessing that something had happened between her and Adam?

'You're back sooner than I thought,' said Pammy when Yvie walked into the kitchen.

'Well, I can't go terribly far. Adam wanted a proper walk. I think he got bored with my pace. I don't suppose he'll be much longer. It isn't half tipping it down now.' Yvie was surprised at how normal she sounded. No one would guess that she had just had a blazing row, nor that the row had been caused by an attempted sexual assault. And although she knew that she wasn't at fault on this occasion, she was still guilty about how her best friend's husband felt about her.

'Where did you walk to?'

'Only as far as the cottage. Actually, when I saw it, I had

a thought. You know, I think I could manage there now. I'm good on stairs, and Claire can help me in the kitchen and pop to the shop for essentials. We'd be fine back there.'

Pammy looked doubtful. 'I really don't like the idea. What if you had a fall again when Claire was up here for lessons?'

'What if I fell here when everyone was out?'

'Well . . .'

'Precisely. I'll carry my mobile at all times, then, if anything happens, I can ring for help.'

'And what about the shopping?'

'Well, I admit that'll be a problem, but Claire can go to the shop for bread and milk and stuff. I'm afraid I'd have to ask you to do the odd bit for me in Keswick – meat and such-like.'

'Wouldn't it be easier if you stayed here?'

Yvie shrugged apologetically.

'You want your own space. That's it, isn't it?'

'I seem so ungrateful. After all you've done.'

'Not at all. I know how you feel. You can never really relax in someone else's home, can you? But I want you to know that if it proves too much for you, just give me a shout and you can come back here in a trice.'

'That's great. I was so worried that you would think really badly of me.'

'Never. I can't imagine anyone I am less likely to think ill of.'

If only you knew, thought Yvie, feeling even more treacherous.

When Adam returned, Yvie did her best to keep out of his way without making it too obvious, but in a small flat there was only so much space that she could put between them.

'Pammy tells me you are escaping,' he said, catching Yvie on her own in the sitting room.

'Do you blame me?' she retorted. 'I don't feel safe with you around.'

'Don't flatter yourself that I'll try again.'

'Good.'

But later, when she was in bed, she was unable to account for a sense of loss.

Claire was surprisingly pleased about the return to the cottage, and was more than happy to pop to the shop to get some basic foodstuffs for her mum. Of course, she didn't tell her mum that it gave her an excuse to see Mark, which was one reason why she was so happy to run the errand.

For once the sun was shining as Claire swung herself over the stile and set out on the footpath, armed with a shopping list and her mother's purse. The walk to the village seemed shorter than she remembered, but then, in the past she always seemed to have done it in the rain. Perhaps that was the difference. Or perhaps it was because her goal wasn't just the shop but the possibility of an encounter with Mark.

The bell over the door pinged cheerily as she went in, and she cast a quick look round to see if she could spot Mark, pushing the door shut behind her with her foot. He didn't seem to be around, so she lingered over her purchases, hoping he'd appear from the stock room or wherever he was. She became aware of a couple of local ladies gossiping by the till. They kept glancing in her direction, and Claire realized, somewhat uncomfortably, that she was the topic of their conversation. She drifted closer, pretending to choose some biscuits from the display.

'I was out walking Shep,' said the younger of the two in the sort of whisper that carried more clearly than a normal voice. 'I thought I'd take him for a quick run along the lake. I was just passing them 'oliday cottages and I heard voices raised, I couldn't help overhearing what was said.'

Yeah, right, thought Claire. She could just imagine the old biddy creeping as close as she could to make sure she didn't miss anything.

'Then her mum stormed out. In a rare old temper she was. Anyway, not long after, Mr Clifton came out looking like thunder.'

'He never did!'

'Anyway . . .' But Claire didn't catch the rest, as the young one dropped her voice to a proper whisper and turned slightly away from Claire. Whatever gossip was being imparted wasn't intended to reach anyone else's ears.

'Never!' shrieked the older one, followed by a burst of laughter. 'Fancy that, a lover's tiff. Well, from what I've heard, it's not the first time. My George caught him with his trousers down, so to speak, in the estate office with some woman who had come up to stay with the owner. They were going at it like rattlesnakes. And I've heard similar from others. He's got more notches on his bedpost than Casanova, from what I've heard.'

Claire put the biscuits down and moved to the back of the shop. She didn't want to hear any more. She could guess what the bit of the exchange that she hadn't overheard had been about. Her mother. How could she? And Adam. And he'd bonked his way through half of Cumbria, if the village gossip was to be believed. Claire felt sick. The idea was gross. My God, she wondered, how long had they been at it? Was it just the once, or had it been going on since they'd arrived? So much for thinking her mum didn't like Adam. What a liar! She did the rest of the shopping on autopilot, mechanically finding the items on the list and dumping them in the wire shopping basket. She paid, not caring that she hadn't run into Mark, and trudged home. The joy and happiness she had felt on the way to the village was replaced by a pall of anger and disgust. She turned the snippet of gossip over and over in her head. Perhaps she had misheard. Perhaps they hadn't been talking about her mother and Adam. Perhaps it was some other holiday cottages that the old bag had been passing. But Claire knew her mother and Adam had been there on Sunday. And then there had been that sudden decision to move out of the Hall. Whichever way Claire looked at it, she knew that the gossip made sense: her mum and Adam were having, or had had, an affair. And now half the village seemed to know about it.

'Hiya,' said her mum when she got back. 'You took your time.' Yvie took the shopping and the purse off Claire. 'What's the matter? You look upset.'

'You tell me what the matter is, Mum,' said Claire, her anger spilling out. 'Why don't you tell me about the "lover's tiff" you had with Adam on Sunday?'

'I'm not with you,' said Yvie.

'Don't lie to me. It's the talk of the village.'

Yvie flushed bright red. 'I don't understand.'

Claire recounted the overheard conversation with heavy

emphasis on the 'lover's tiff' and the 'trousers down' bit. As she did, her mum went from pink to white.

'You don't want to believe gossip,' she said shakily.

'Why not? Your face tells me it's true.'

'But it isn't. Adam and I never . . . We didn't . . .'

'Mum, I'm not a kid. The woman in the shop knew what she heard. She had no reason to make it up.'

Yvie sighed. 'I'm not denying we had a row. And yes, it was about sex. But we rowed because I wouldn't . . . I pushed him away. He was angry. Said I'd led him on.'

'And did you?' Claire couldn't believe that she was asking her mother this, but why else would he think his luck was in?

'No.' Her mother sounded genuinely indignant.

Claire stared at her mother. She wanted to believe her, she wanted this to be the truth, but she simply wasn't sure. A thought hit her. Had her mother been so wary of Adam when she'd arrived because he had tried it on with her before? No wonder she hated him. 'Why didn't you tell Pammy?'

'What? Are you mad? And what good would it do? All I'd do is wreck her marriage and our friendship.'

''Spose.' Claire suddenly felt embarrassed. She believed her mother now. This made more sense than the conversation the old biddies had been having in the shop. And now she'd accused her mother of something hateful and she'd been wrong.

'So that's why I was desperate to get back down here. I really don't want to be left alone with Adam again.'

'No.' Claire didn't think she wanted to be alone with him either. What a creep. And to think she'd really quite liked him to start with. She shuddered.

'You won't tell Dad anything about this, will you?'

'I think he should know.'

'No – for the same reasons that I'm not telling Pammy. And besides which, he's got enough to worry about at the moment without adding anything else.'

Claire didn't agree, but she held her tongue. 'But what happens if Pammy hears the gossip too? I mean, all those other women . . .'

'I don't know. Presumably she doesn't know anything about what he gets up to. I can't see her staying with Adam if she suspected.'

'You going to tell her?'

Yvie thought for a bit. 'I really don't think so. I can see there being only one outcome if I did, and would Pammy thank me for it? If she's happy living in ignorance, why should I spoil it?'

Claire shrugged. 'Look, Mum, I'm sorry about what I said earlier. It was just so horrid hearing that sort of stuff from complete strangers.'

'And I'm sorry you heard it too. But please believe me, Adam and I were not doing anything. Trust me, if the nosy old cow had got there a bit earlier, she would have known the whole story and not needed to make half of it up.'

'Will you be all right, here on your own, when I go for lessons?'

'I'll be fine. I don't think he'll try anything again. I'll keep the door locked when I'm on my own, just in case.'

'Promise?'

'Promise.'

'Right, well, I've got some homework to do for tomorrow, so I'd better get on with it.' Claire turned and went off to her room.

Before she went to her phone, Yvie waited until she heard the thump of a pop beat thudding from upstairs. She dialled the number of the estate office.

'I just thought you ought to know,' she said when the phone was answered, 'that our little exchange on Sunday was overheard by the village gossip.'

'It's not a good time right now,' said Adam with studied casualness. 'Can I call you back?'

'OK.' Yvie replaced the receiver.

Claire was still up in her room, immersed in homework, judging by the heavy beat that continued to permeate the cottage, when the phone rang about ten minutes later.

'Adam,' said the voice curtly when Yvie answered. 'Sorry I couldn't talk earlier, but I had Pammy with me.'

'No wonder you didn't want me to say more. Pammy might have overheard.'

'Precisely.'

'I just rang to warn you about the gossip in the village.' Yvie recounted Claire's report.

'Shit!'

'Yes, you are. A prize one.'

'I'm sorry?'

'All that bollocks about not seducing anyone, "not even Pammy", in that little love nest at the back of the office.'

'But I didn't . . .' Adam tried to bluster.

'That's not what the village thinks, is it? In fact, it's the talk of the village that you were caught with your trousers down, and not just the once, from the sound of it.'

'Look, Yvie. Be reasonable.'

Yvie noticed he didn't deny anything. 'Why? Why should I be reasonable for a man who just has to make those conquests? How many have there been, Adam? And where did I figure in your tally? Was I the first in a line of mistresses or were there others before me? And how many since, huh? And what about Pammy? You've got a lot of explaining to do, and not just to me.' Yvie punched the 'end call' button on her phone. 'Bastard!' she muttered.

Yvie felt suddenly energized. She got the mop and bucket out of the kitchen cupboard and set about mopping the down-stairs of the cottage. When she'd done that, she started on the windows.

'Blimey,' said Claire, coming down for a sustaining cuppa a little while later. 'You've been busy.'

'Yup,' said Yvie. 'There's nothing like a good clean-out once in a while. Makes you feel like you've got a new lease of life.'

Claire looked at her with raised eyebrows and shook her head. Her mother had obviously lost it.

'I thought about going into Keswick this morning,' said Pammy over the phone. 'After your visit to the fracture clinic. Do you fancy it?'

'Why not? There's a couple of things I need, and I'm going stir crazy here.'

'And don't worry about Claire's education. I've got a project for her to be getting on with. Should take her most of the day.'

'OK. Do you want me to walk up to the house?'

'No. I'll pick you up.'

'See you later.'

Yvie put the phone down. For the first time in ages she was really looking forward to a trip out with Pammy. The trip to the hospital had been in the diary for a week and was hardly cause for excitement; the chance of sitting on a hard chair for hours in a dreary corridor for the sake of a check-up was hardly designed to make one's heart beat faster. But a trip to a town, shops, people, cafés; now, that was much more enticing. It would be nice to go out with a girlfriend – and, now she knew that her infatuation with Adam was over once and for all, she could meet Pammy with no guilt. Well, there was the little matter of the torrid affair fifteen years previously, but that was history. Yes, she thought, her discovery about Adam, even though it made her feel slightly foolish, was also strangely liberating. At least one thing was now certain: Adam was out of her system for good. He was a serial cheat and liar. The magic that had surrounded him, the desire she had felt, had gone completely. Free at last.

Yvie clambered into the front of the Range Rover and tucked her crutches out of Pammy's way beside her.

'Sorry about the smell of wet dog,' said Pammy. 'Adam took them out for a walk this morning and they all ended up in the lake.'

'Even Adam?' asked Yvie hopefully.

'No, he just stood on the shore throwing the sticks.'

Shame, thought Yvie. A dousing of cold water was exactly what the man needed.

Pammy drove steadily down the valley towards Keswick. The road was slick with water from an earlier shower, but otherwise conditions were pretty good. Yvie admired the countryside as they drove through it. Primroses dotted the grassy banks, the trees were still a vibrant green that would be lost once the heat and dust of summer took its toll; on the fells and in the tiny stone-walled fields, the lambs gambolled beside their mothers, and the green shoots of fresh bracken began to subsume the tawny fronds left from the previous year. She was jolted back to reality by Pammy swerving up the bank and jamming on the brakes.

'Bloody hell!' she exclaimed as a huge SUV thundered past.

'Road hog!' Yvie yelled after it ineffectually.

'Not a local plate,' said Pammy. 'It's some stupid townie who only drives one of those to make themselves feel superior. I don't think that was the same twerp who bashed the mirror over the weekend, but it's the same mentality. *I've got a bigger car than you, so you can give way to me.* I hate them. What on earth do they want a four-wheel drive for anyway – in case they are going to get bogged down in the Tesco car park? You only have to look at most of them to see they've never driven off a road in their lives.' She glanced across at Yvie. 'Sorry,' she said. 'Rant over.'

'Rant away. It's the same where we live. Dozens of women round us use the things for the school run. Why?'

'And the drivers always seem to be so aggressive. Part of me says I can't talk, as this old heap is a four-wheel-drive job, but we do actually need one. We often go off-road – especially in the shooting season.'

'And, being an "L" reg, you can hardly call it a status symbol.'

Pammy laughed. 'Hardly.'

They reached the bottom of the valley and turned on to the road that led to Keswick and then Carlisle.

'Just look at them all,' said Pammy as a stream of Discoveries and similar four-by-fours passed them going the other way. 'And not a local number amongst them.'

'But isn't that what your tourist board wants?' said Yvie.

'Yeah, but why do they want to snarl up our pretty little lanes with things the size of trucks?'

'All right, all right, I surrender.'

'I'm sorry. It's a bugbear of mine.'

'No kidding,' said Yvie with a grin.

Pammy had calmed down by the time they pulled the hospital car park. However, they were both pretty frazzled and fed up when they finally escaped again a couple of hours later.

'All that, to be told I have no problems. *I* could have told them that. God, what a waste of the NHS budget.'

'Still,' said Pammy, 'better safe than sorry.'

Yvie wondered what it was about Pammy that, regardless, she could always see the best in any situation.

'What do you want to do, split up and meet up again for a spot of lunch, or potter around together?' she asked Yvie as she parked in Keswick.

'I haven't got a terrific amount to do. If you don't mind sticking with me. Just, you know, in case.'

'Not at all. Let's get your stuff done, then have lunch. If you're not too knackered after that, we can do my errands together, or you can wait for me over a cup of tea.'

'That sounds perfect. I think I'm probably up to an hour or so on my pins, but I don't want to overdo things.'

'Right then, where to first?'

Yvie detailed her list of requirements, and she and Pammy set off to the various shops, Pammy carrying the shopping basket as Yvie conceded that basket and crutches was beyond her. They pottered round Keswick, dodging other shoppers and tourists, chatting about inconsequential matters and enjoying the bustle of the busy town. Lunch was a bowl of soup, crusty bread and a glass of wine in a local pub, and then, with Yvie rested and fit to carry on some more, they strolled round the town getting Pammy's shopping. They were heading back to the car park when they were startled by blaring horns. At a narrow junction, two large off-road vehicles were bull-bar to bull-bar, neither giving way to the other, and totally blocking any movement for all the other traffic.

Pammy looked at Yvie and said, 'I rest my case, M'lud.'

On their return, Yvie declined the offer of tea up at the Hall, using tiredness as an excuse. It was a legitimate and truthful excuse, but she was wary about meeting Adam again, despite her new-found sense of liberation from his thrall. She didn't think she could face him glowering across the room at her, or being cornered when Pammy was out of the way, and being bombarded with tacky excuses and explanations about his alley-cat behaviour. Pammy dropped her off at the cottage and helped Yvie in with her purchases.

She was just relaxing on the sofa with a much needed cuppa when Claire burst in.

'Mum, Mum, can I go to a gig with Mark at the weekend? Pammy says she'll drive. Please, Mum, please?'

Yvie put her cup down on a mat slowly. 'And the gig is where?'

'Same place as last time. Mark says the group is good. They've performed at Brampton Live.'

'Well, it would be hard to perform dead,' said Yvie.

Claire raised her eyebrows. 'Pardon me while I die laughing.'

'I'm not with you; I didn't know I was making a joke.'

'Brampton Live is the name of a huge folk festival in the area. A bit like Cropredy.'

'Cropredy? Since when did you know anything about folk festivals?'

'Well . . .'

'Since Mark has been on the scene,' prompted Yvie.

'Maybe.'

'Look. I don't mind you going, but I really think Pammy shouldn't have to turn out. What about Mark's folks?'

'Ahh.'

'Ahh?'

'His dad doesn't have a licence at the mo, and his mum doesn't drive.'

'Ahh. Drink-drive?' Claire nodded. 'God, it must be tricky round here without a car.'

'Mark's learning but his test isn't for ages.'

A thought crossed Yvie's mind. 'Look, call me an interfering old bag if you wish, but Mark's interest in having your company doesn't have anything to do with transport problems? I don't want to ruin things, but it's a thought.'

'Mum, how could you?'

'Because I'm an old cynic who has been around the block a couple of times.'

'He's not like that.'

'I hope not,' said Yvie with a slight edge to her voice, 'because I don't want to see either you getting hurt or Pammy being used.'

When Richard phoned that evening, Yvie voiced her doubts about Mark's motives for his interest in Claire.

'Look, I'm sure it's all very innocent,' said Richard. 'Going to a folk concert is hardly going to produce uncontrollable passion leading to under-age sex and teenage pregnancy – well, not at the venue anyway.'

'Don't exaggerate. That wasn't what I was suggesting was happening at all.'

'I know. Listen, she's a bright girl and I'm sure she can handle herself. Lots of girls have a boyfriend at her age.'

'She's not very worldly-wise though. An all-girls' school might be great academically, but it's not good for learning about real life. And she's only fourteen.'

'Nearly fifteen, and you like Mark. And so does Pammy.'

'He's a nice boy but it still doesn't guarantee that Claire isn't going to wind up hurt.'

'And if she does, she'll get over it. Dumping and being dumped is all part of growing up. We all go through it, we all survive.'

'Maybe.' Failing to get the support she wanted, Yvie changed the subject. 'So how are things going with you, the spooks and the enemy?'

'God, it's so boring. It's just playing the waiting game. And we've been waiting for a month now. I'm supposed to act as if everything is normal, but it's sodding difficult knowing that every move I make is under surveillance. And I'm supposed to trust the system implicitly, so I mustn't check under my car in the morning, I mustn't look behind me when I'm out in the town, and I'm scared stiff they're going to get it wrong or miss something. After all, I expect I'm much more interested in my safety than they are. Besides which, I miss you so much, Yvie.'

'It sounds really stressful. It must be hateful. Can't you come up here for a bit, get away from it all – take a long weekend?'

'I'd love to, but the spooks are worried that either I might put you in danger, or else he'll give up because I disappear.'

'That isn't very likely, is it?'

'Which?'

'Either, both. And what about that RUC man and the explosion? Was it all innocent?'

'Well, it's been established that he had nothing to do with Lynch. Their paths never crossed and the gas board are convinced it's an accident, so I think we have to believe that it was.'

'So, he was an accident, the two judges might have been accidents, which only leaves one incident as a definite hit by Lynch. What if they're overreacting? What if you're not in any danger at all? What if this is all a waste of time? What if he only wanted that lawyer and now he's finished?'

'And what if he isn't?' said Richard gently. 'It's a helluva risk to take if they're right and you're wrong.'

'But haven't they any hot int? Surely, if they are spending so much protecting you, they are moving heaven and earth to track Lynch down. For God's sake, he's wanted for murder, quite apart from anything he might get up to in the future.'

'I'm sure they're doing everything they can.'

'Bah!'

'You don't sound very happy, Yvie.'

'I'm not,' she said baldly. 'I've had enough. I want to come home. I want to see friends and shops. I'm pretty much housebound. I've discovered I really don't like the rain or the countryside. The view's stunning – when the sun shines – but a view isn't any company. And anyway, I've seen it now. Plus, I've imposed on the Cliftons long enough, and I now seem to be surplus to requirements as far as Claire is concerned.'

'So we're back to Mark again.'

'Actually, no. She worships the ground Pammy walks on. Spends as much of her time as possible up at the Hall – she's there right now, as a matter of fact – she'll walk through fire for Pammy, but if I ask her to do anything, all I get is "in a minute", like she used to do at home.'

'You do sound pissed off.'

'Frankly, I am.'

'But at least you and Claire are safe.'

'Yeah, at least we're safe.'

When Yvie replaced the receiver, she wondered about whether being safe was worth everything else. And it wasn't just her safety, was it? She had to think about Claire. This was the place where people left spare keys where anyone would find them, that's if they bothered to lock their doors at all; where everyone knew their neighbours and could spot a stranger a mile off; where the local shopkeeper trusted the probity of your cheque without resorting to bank guarantees. Claire was safer here than she ever could be in Carchester, and that was without taking into consideration the attentions of Malachi Lynch. Yvie sighed deeply and resolved to sit it out in the Lakes.

* * *

205

Claire was staring at her reflection in the mirror in her room and trying to make up her mind about what to wear to the gig. Her jeans looked great with the laced-up blouse, but the trouble was the blouse was so stunning that she was certain everyone would remember she'd worn it to the last concert. No, not right, she thought. She took them off and let them drop on to a pile of other tried and discarded outfits, and picked some other clothes out of her wardrobe: her new skirt with a plain T-shirt. Again the skirt looked fantastic, but not half as good as it had with the blouse. She dithered with the idea of just wearing jeans and a plain top, but it wouldn't look as if she'd made much of an effort, and the last thing she wanted Mark to think was that she was taking him for granted. Besides which, she wanted to look her best for him. She wasn't going to risk some other girl taking his fancy. She took her skirt and top off and dumped them on the pile of clothes. Once again she opened her wardrobe and rifled through the hangers. It was hopeless. She had hardly anything at all to wear. If she'd been at home, she would have had twice as much to choose from, but here . . . And there was no point in complaining to her mum, she thought morosely. All she would do would be to bang on about how, when she was a girl, she only had two pairs of shoes and about three skirts and tops, plus a pair of jeans for playing in. Yeah, well, that was back in the dark ages when no one knew about fashion. It was different now. Pammy would understand. Claire wondered, if she dropped a heavy hint, whether Pammy would take her into Keswick again. She sighed, looked at the pile of clothes on the floor, and then at her watch. Clearing them up would have to wait now till she got back from the Hall, but her mum would go ballistic if she saw the mess. She slithered back into her jeans and T-shirt, then picked up an armful of garments and dumped them in the bottom of her wardrobe. When she'd banged the door shut on them, her room didn't look too bad at all. She rummaged in her dressing-table drawer and found her bank book. If she did manage to wangle a lift into town, she'd need some dosh. It was one thing hoping to persuade Pammy to drive her there, but she couldn't expect her to fork out for clothes a second time. That would be pushing her luck just too far.

'I'm off, Mum,' she called when she got to the bottom of the spiral stairs.

Her mum looked up from reading the newspaper which was spread out on one of the kitchen worktops.

'OK, sweetheart. Will you come home for lunch, or do you think you'll grab a bite with Pammy?'

'I'll probably stay there if that's OK with you.' Claire picked up her bag of schoolwork, which lay by the front door.

'Yes, fine. It looks as though it's going to be a nice day, so I thought I'd do some sketching by the lake.'

'Don't go too far, Mum. We don't want to have to send out any more search parties.'

'Oh yeah, like I'm likely to go miles with a crocked leg. I don't even think I'll go much further than the bottom of the garden.'

Claire blew her mum a kiss and swung out of the front door. On her way up to the Hall, she wondered what the best way of engineering a trip to Keswick was going to be. She didn't think the direct approach would work. What she needed was an excuse. Birthdays? No, her parents' were both later in the year. Their wedding anniversary wasn't for a couple of months. Frankly, there didn't seem any reason for them to take a trip down the valley. Perhaps if she asked about bus times on Saturday? That might be the way to go. She knew they were pretty hopeless, next to non-existent; Mark had told her, but she needn't let on that she knew. If Pammy thought she was going to be struggling with public transport, she might just take pity on her. Feeling happy with her strategy, Claire gave a little skip, then looked about her to make sure no one had witnessed her deviation from 'cool'.

'You look cheerful,' said Pammy when Claire appeared at the kitchen door.

'Do I?'

'So, what's the good news?'

'There isn't any. I suppose I'm just glad it's a nice day and nearly the weekend.'

'And nearly Saturday evening?'

Claire couldn't suppress a grin. 'Well, that might have some-thing to do with it,' she conceded, trying to sound casual.

'Have you decided what to wear?'

'Not really. In fact, I haven't really thought about it yet.'

Pammy looked quizzical. 'Really?'

Claire grinned. 'Well . . .'

'I thought as much. And the answer is . . . ?'

'I dunno. I thought I might go into Keswick on Saturday and have a mooch round. See if I can find a new top.'

'How are you getting in?'

'Bus.'

Pammy burst out laughing. 'So, either you're going to be spending five minutes in town or you don't want to come back till Monday.'

'It can't be that bad.'

'Trust me.'

'Oh.'

'I expect Adam or I will be going in on Saturday. We'll give you a lift if you like.'

'Would you?' Yes, result. She hoped that Adam wouldn't be joining them, but she'd have to put up with him if he came. The important thing was to get to Keswick.

''Course. We go in most Saturdays. If you need to go into town, always let us know. We're more than happy to give you a lift. Now, how did you get on with that history essay I asked you to do?'

'And you're sure Adam and Pammy don't mind?' asked Yvie.

'For heaven's sake, Mum! They wouldn't have offered if there was a problem. And anyway, Pammy says they go in most Saturdays.'

'Yes, that's as may be, but I just feel that we really impose on them sometimes.'

Claire sighed. 'They don't mind. Pammy offered.'

'Yeah, but I'm not keen.'

'Is it because of Adam?'

'Well . . .'

'Look, I think he's a creep too, but with Pammy around he'll be OK. Anyway, he may not come with us.'

'I suppose. But I'm not over the moon about it. I really don't want to owe Adam anything.'

'No, well, I see your point.'

After Claire had trotted off up to the Hall to get her lift

into town, Yvie was left at a loose end. She flicked idly through a day-old paper and considered doing the crossword, but then decided she couldn't raise the enthusiasm to cudgel her brains with the cryptic clues. She stumped up the stairs and fetched the washing and stuffed it in the machine, then she tidied the kitchen, but when she looked at her watch it was still only ten thirty.

She looked out the window but the weather was threatening rain – what a turn-up, she thought sourly – so going out sketching wasn't a likely option. She thought about phoning Richard but they'd chatted for ages the night before. Yvie flopped on to the sofa and sighed. All the day to kill and nothing to do.

Claire breezed along the track that led to the Hall. A day with Pammy shopping, how good was that going to be? It didn't matter that the weather didn't look promising. What the heck? She was in a great mood and nothing was going to spoil it. She swung round to the back of the Hall, through the courtyard and up the back stairs.

'Cooee!' she called as she got to the top.

'Hi there!' Pammy called back.

Claire went into the warm kitchen, where Pammy was finishing off some housework.

'Here, be a lamb and shake these out for me,' said Pammy, handing Claire a couple of blankets from the dog beds.

'Sure.' Claire took them and ran back down the stairs to the courtyard, where she flapped the dusty rugs about with gusto, causing hairs and other debris to fly off in a cloud. Adam, emerging through the archway from the direction of the estate office, made an exaggerated play of avoiding it. Creep, thought Claire, but she smiled and looked pleasant. Only manners, after all, and she didn't want to nark him before the lift.

'Are you coming into Keswick with us?' asked Claire as they returned to the flat together.

'Thought I might. Need to keep an eye on how much you two are going to deplete my wallet.'

Damn, thought Claire. Oh well. 'I shan't spend any money but my own,' she said primly. Besides, I wouldn't take money

209

off you if I was on my uppers, she thought. Not after what you did to Mum.

Adam followed Claire up the stairs and she was acutely aware that her bum was at his eye level. She came up in goose-bumps of disgust as she thought about him looking at it. Ugh.

When she reached the kitchen, Pammy was hauling wash-ing out of the machine and stuffing it in the tumble-dryer.

'No point in hanging it out on a day like today,' she muttered, checking out of the window as she said it.

'No,' agreed Claire. 'It does rain a lot up here, doesn't it?' she added.

'Certainly does. You get used to it though. Right.' Pammy looked about her. 'I think that's everything. Are you all set?'

Claire nodded and Adam grabbed the keys off the hook on the wall.

The three of them clattered down the stairs and clambered into the shabby old Range Rover. Claire sat in the centre seat in the back and did up her lap strap so she could get the bene-fit of the view through the windscreen As they set off, the weather broke and rain spattered on to the vehicle and the ground.

In the cottage, Yvie had another half-hearted attempt at the crossword puzzle, but the light was poor. She got up to switch on the lamp and noticed that the rain that had been threaten-ing had now started. And what's more, from the way the clouds were hanging in the valley, it looked as though it had set in for the foreseeable future.

'Typical,' she muttered under her breath. 'That's put the kybosh on getting *any* sketching done today.' She flopped back on to the sofa and wondered what she could do to occupy herself.

Of course, there had been times in her life when she'd made a science out of loafing; Germany being a case in point. But since that year, she had seriously tried to keep herself occu-pied, to make every day productive, to keep active. Trouble was, it was darned difficult right now. If she hadn't had the gammy foot, she'd have driven Claire into town and she'd have helped her choose some new clothes. Hell, she could have even taken herself to the library, so that, when there

210

wasn't much to do, she could at least have read. She sighed again, got up and clumped over to the window. Bored, bored, bored. At this rate she'd have to do something domesticated like make a cake.

At least that was an idea. She stomped into the kitchen and had a look in the cupboards and the fridge. There were flour, eggs, milk and sugar; Yvie couldn't think any more was needed, and she thought she could pretty well remember how to make a Victoria sandwich. She cast about vaguely for a recipe book but couldn't find one. No matter. From some deep recess, she remembered she ought to pre-heat the oven, but to what temperature? She took a guess – 150°C sounded about right. Or should it be 200°C? Oh, what the heck. She'd go for something in between. She set the dial and got to work. She greased a cake tin and then set to creaming some butter and sugar together. She did it with gusto but it was hard work. She needed something to give her some energy; she flicked on the radio and tuned to a local radio station. A catchy tune blared out. That was more like it. As she got busy with the ingredients and a wooden spoon, she hummed along to a recent pop song and shuffled her feet in time to the beat, or shuffled them as much as you could with a cast on one. The mixture didn't look quite right, and Yvie wasn't sure whether to add more sugar or try beating in the egg. She decided on the egg. Ugh, now it had curdled. She whacked the gooey mess briskly with a whisk and then considered the result. It looked disgusting, but the ingredients were good. Surely it would taste all right when it was cooked and finished? Yvie began to spoon some flour out of the packet into the mixing bowl. As each spoonful went in, she gave it a stir. It certainly began to improve its appearance. The glistening lumps of curdled egg, sugar and fat began to get incorporated into something that resembled cake mixture. She gave it a good beating with the wooden spoon and then allowed the shiny, cream-coloured concoction to dollop off it, back into the bowl with a satisfying splat. She stuck her finger in the mix and licked it. Well, it looked right and it tasted right, perhaps it was right. Only one way to find out. Yvie slopped it into the cake tin and pushed the whole lot into the oven and slammed the door.

The kitchen looked like a disaster area. She must have been more enthusiastic than she had realized with the beating. There were little splatters of cake mix all over the walls and work surface. Yvie giggled and began to mop up the evidence with a damp cloth. The radio played, the warm, sweet smell of baking began to fill the kitchen, and Yvie's earlier disconsolate mood lifted. Perhaps there's something to be said for being a domestic goddess, she thought.

The music on the radio played on, interrupted now and again by the presenter, Yvie finished clearing up and checked the cake. It didn't look as if it had risen much, but it smelt right. She stuck a knife into it – not cooked, she thought, looking at the gooey deposit on the blade. She decided to give it another five minutes and check again.

While Yvie was practicing her domestic skills, Adam drove the Range Rover down the valley towards Keswick. The cloud was low and the visibility wasn't great, but the inside of the car was warm and they all chatted animatedly about the folk scene in the Lake District. In the background, the local radio station played some catchy tunes.

'I didn't realize that folk music had such a following,' said Pammy.

'Not surprising when you consider the image it has,' said Adam with a laugh. 'Sandals, cagoules—'

'It's not like that at all,' interrupted Claire indignantly. 'And some of the people involved are really nice.'

'I'm joking,' said Adam. As he said this, he slowed the vehicle down. Ahead were two caravans trying to pass each other in the narrow lane. 'Oh God, bloody tourists!' he muttered, watching as the two drivers tried to manoeuvre between the drystone walls and soggy grassy verges. He switched the engine off. 'We could be here some time,' he added as it became apparent that neither driver seemed to be inclined to reverse.

Pammy sighed. 'It's like this every year.' She shook her head. 'I don't know which is worse – the four-by-four drivers who race around like they own the roads, or the caravan-towers who block everything up.'

'But we grin and bear it because we want their money. We

212

didn't half notice it the year we had foot and mouth and no one came.'

'True, but the roads were nice and clear.'

Yvie checked her cake again. It still didn't look as though it had risen, but it was the right colour and the smell was delicious. She poked it with a knife and this time the blade was clean. Grabbing a cooling tray with one hand and an oven cloth with the other, Yvie deftly turned it out. Well, she thought, inspecting it, it wasn't much to look at, but proof of the pudding and all that. She picked a few crumbs off the side. It tasted fine. Perhaps if she had a recipe book, she could make another one that looked right too.

Yvie thought about icing it, but then realized she didn't have any icing sugar. Damn. And a trip to the village shop wasn't really an option. Firstly she didn't think she'd be able to negotiate the stile, and also she didn't fancy her chances with a plaster cast, crutches and a wet muddy path. Icing would have to wait. So now what? All that beckoned was another look at the crossword puzzle. She turned up the radio, and returned to the sofa for some more boredom and loafing.

Adam drummed his fingers impatiently on the steering wheel.

'It's not going to make this pair of geeks get out of our way any faster,' said Pammy.

'Oh, for God's sake!' snorted Adam in disgust as, yet again, the two caravaners cocked up a manoeuvre that just might have succeeded in clearing the road.

'Why don't you get out and help?' said Pammy reasonably.

'Because they're such dimwits, I might just feel the need to slap one or other of them. Or even both,' he added grimly.

'Oh, go on,' said Pammy. 'We'll be here all day else.'

'Why don't you go?'

'Because both the drivers are men and there's no way they'll listen to my advice.'

'They might.'

Pammy raised an eyebrow and Adam sighed and got out of the car. Pammy undid her safety belt and swivelled round in her seat. 'Really!' she said to Claire. 'You would have thought he'd have thought about offering to help for himself. Men!'

Claire giggled. 'Dad's the same. He drives Mum nuts too sometimes.' As she spoke, she saw Pammy's eyes widen in horror and she glanced backwards. Filling the entire rear window was a huge car, thundering along the road directly towards them. The last thing Claire remembered was the sight of the horror-struck face of the male driver. Claire didn't even have time to scream before it ploughed into the back of the old Range Rover, throwing it forward. Pammy, unrestrained, was slung with huge force against the windscreen, and Claire was propelled between the seats until she connected with the gear lever, which smashed into her skull. Before the aged Range Rover came to a halt, both women in the car were unconscious. The momentum was such that the Cliftons' car was shunted ten feet, but it did not move in a straight line. After a couple of feet, the car began to drift off to the left and the nearside front wheel began to dig into the soft grass of the verge, making the slewing even more pronounced. The force of the big SUV continued unabated until the Range Rover began to tip. And as it tipped, it continued heading towards Adam, standing in the middle of the road. He tried to leap backwards but he wasn't quick enough, and the big car caught him as it toppled. He fell backwards, hitting his head with a sickening crack on the wet tarmac and then the vehicle, almost out of momentum, slowly settled on top of his inert torso. If the blow to his head hadn't killed him, then this did.

The silence after the crash was almost tangible. Then one of the women caravaners started to scream.

Yvie threw the crossword back on to the table. It was no good. Her brain just didn't work in the right way to make any sense of cryptic clues. '"Author about to receive printout (four, four)," she muttered. 'What in God's name is that going to be?' She put the paper down in disgust, lay back on the cushions and closed her eyes. She was *so* bored.

The music on the radio stopped. 'We have news of a bad accident on the B5289 to Keswick,' said the radio presenter. 'The police say that a number of vehicles were involved and there are some serious casualties. The road is likely to be blocked for some time, so would motorists please avoid the area till further notice. Now, with the time just coming up to

214

eleven forty-five, here are the Kinks with that old favourite, "Waterloo Sunset".' Yvie let herself drift as the song took her back to her youth and memories of Reading. Before the record had ended, she'd drifted off into sleep.

She was roused by someone hammering on her door. She glanced at her watch as she jumped up to see who her visitor was. Good grief, it was almost lunch time. It couldn't be Claire, she thought. They wouldn't even be on their way back from Keswick. She opened the door and was startled to see a policewoman standing there.

'Oh!' she said in surprise. She felt her heart rate race. Was this something to do with Richard? Oh God, please, no.

'Mrs Maxwell?' said the woman.

'Y–yes.'

'May I come in?'

Feeling mounting panic, Yvie couldn't speak, she just pulled the door open and stood back. The policewoman didn't say anything reassuring, no comforting words like *this is just a routine visit*, or *nothing to worry about*.

The policewoman stepped into the sitting room. Yvie followed her, shaking with fear.

'Let's sit down,' said the policewoman. They did. 'There's been an accident.'

Yvie nodded. She knew what was coming. 'Is Richard dead?' She had to know. She didn't want the news dressed up. It wasn't going to make it any easier.

The policewoman frowned slightly. 'Um, I don't think so. I thought Mr Clifton was called Adam.'

It was Yvie's turn to be perplexed. 'What's Adam got to do with this?'

There was a slight pause as the policewoman mentally checked the facts as she knew them. 'Mrs Maxwell, does Mr Clifton drive an "L" reg Range Rover?' Yvie nodded. 'It's been involved in a serious car crash.'

'Oh my God.' The one on the radio. Her hand went to her mouth. 'Oh my God, Claire.'

The policewoman nodded. 'I am so sorry, Mrs Maxwell, but she's in a very serious condition. I've come to take you to the hospital.'

'Oh my God.'

'I think it might be an idea if we grabbed a few things for both yourself and your daughter.'

'Yes, yes, of course.' But Yvie continued to sit on the sofa, thoughts tumbling about in her head, questions she knew she ought to ask, but there were so many, she didn't know where to start.

'Can I help you get some things together?'

'Umm, yes.'

'Mrs Maxwell,' said the policewoman gently, 'could you show me where to find Claire's clothes?'

Yvie looked up. Yes, right, clothes. God, what would they need? What should she pack? How long for? She knew she was losing control. She had to get a grip. Think, she told herself. Be rational.

'What about Pammy and Adam?'

'Mrs Clifton sustained a serious head injury. I'm afraid her husband was pronounced dead at the scene.'

'Oh my God.' Yvie leaned against the wall of the stairwell. Adam dead. It couldn't be true. For some bizarre reason, she began to worry about the dogs. 'The dogs, you'll have to get someone to sort the dogs out.'

'Mrs Maxwell, please don't worry. It's all taken care of. A friend of the family, Mark, has taken them. He told us where to find you. Now, we really need to get some things together and get you to the hospital.'

Yvie led the way to Claire's room and opened the door of her wardrobe. A heap of clothes tumbled on to the floor. On the top was the lace-up blouse. Yvie picked it up and held it against her face and then she began to cry.

The policewoman took a handful of tissues from the box on Claire's dressing table and held them out to her. Yvie dabbed her eyes and blew her nose.

'Yes,' she said, getting control of herself again. 'You're right. There isn't time for this.' She put the blouse down and grabbed some undies, a clean nightie and Claire's dressing gown and slippers. 'Her toothbrush and stuff are in the bathroom.' She pointed it out. 'There's a washbag on the side you can put it all in.'

'Right. I think you should take some things for yourself. You may want to stay in Carlisle.'

Yvie went to her room and grabbed a few bits for herself and hauled the suitcase off the top of the wardrobe. She plonked her things in it and took it back to Claire's room.

'I need to tell my husband.'

'Where is he? We can—'

'He's not here. He's in Carchester.'

'I could arrange—'

'It'd be better coming from me.'

She sat on the edge of the bed and pressed some buttons on her mobile while the constable folded Claire's things and packed the case.

'Richard,' said Yvie when he answered the phone. 'Claire's been in a terrible car crash. She's in hospital. The police are about to take me to Carlisle to be with her. Pammy's there too.' A sob escaped. 'Oh Richard, Adam's been killed.' There was silence on the line. 'Richard?'

'I'm here. How bad is Claire?'

'I don't know. Serious, I think.' She glanced at the police-woman, who nodded. 'We need you here.'

'Yes, yes, I understand. I'll get up as soon as I can.'

'What do you mean *as soon as you can*?'

'It's all kicking off here. Lynch is in Carchester.'

'So? Your daughter is in hospital. Special Branch can shove it. We need you more than they do.' Yvie was aware that the policewoman beside her was listening to this exchange unashamedly.

'I'll see what I can do. But what is happening here is impor-tant too, Yvie. What Claire needs is nursing. I can't do that. But I'll come as soon as I can.'

'Well, I hope to God it's not too late.' Even if Richard wasn't going to be able to do anything for Claire, Yvie needed him. She wanted support, she wanted someone to help her through this. She wanted Richard.

Yvie saw the constable glance at her watch.

'I'm sure we need you more than they do, but I need to get going. Claire needs at least one of us to be with her. I'll ring you when I know more.'

Yvie's goodbye verged on the perfunctory but, what with her anger at Special Branch's hold over her husband and her worry about her daughter, she didn't care.

'Special Branch?' asked the constable as she snapped the case shut and picked it up.

'I'll tell you in the car.'

'You look as though you've been in the wars yourself,' she observed as Yvie shoved her crutches on to the back seat before climbing in the car herself.

'Broken ankle – out hillwalking.'

'Then this isn't turning out to be much of a holiday.'

Yvie nearly snapped that this stay had never been a holiday in the first place, and now it was a sodding nightmare, but she bit her tongue. This poor young constable hadn't done anything to deserve such vitriol. The even younger-looking male driver drew away from the cottage and took them swiftly down the valley. The wreckage of the crash had been removed, but it was obvious where it had happened. With a feeling of sick fascination, Yvie gazed at the mangled verge and splinters of broken glass, swept to the side of the road.

'I think Mr Clifton died instantly,' said Paula, the constable. 'He didn't suffer.'

'How did it happen?'

Paula recounted what the witnesses had reported. Yvie couldn't believe that three people had almost been wiped out in such a random way.

'Sadly, all too often it's the innocent who suffer in accidents. It's the drunk or reckless driver who gets out of it unscathed.'

'Was he?'

'What?'

'Drunk or reckless.'

'I don't know. But if he was we'll find out. There were witnesses, and we can deduce a lot from skid marks and the like. It's all being properly investigated.' There was silence for a mile or two, then Paula spoke again. 'So,' she said conversationally, 'what's your husband's connection with Special Branch?'

Yvie told her.

'My God! This is all you need.'

Yvie nodded bleakly. 'Just when things don't seem to be able to get any worse.'

'So, is he going to get up here?'

218

Yvie shrugged. 'If Special Branch will let him. Trouble is, I think he thinks he should see this affair through – some misguided sense of duty or loyalty – so I don't know how hard he'll try to persuade them. And he's right.'

'What about?'

'There's not much he can do here. I mean, what will I be doing at the hospital? Waiting for news, worrying, pacing about. If Claire is really bad . . .' Yvie stopped.

'I'm sure she'll know you're there.'

Yvie shook her head. She wasn't convinced.

When they arrived at the hospital this time, there was no faff with parking tickets, no Job's Worth moving them on. The police car swept up to the front and Yvie was met by a nurse, who took her case and escorted her to an office where a very tired-looking young man in a white coat was waiting. In fact, Yvie thought he looked beyond tired – exhausted. She wondered how long he had been on duty.

'How is she?' said Yvie before they'd even finished shaking hands.

'Claire is in a serious condition. There is some internal bleeding and we'll be taking her down to the operating theatre shortly to deal with it. She also has a fractured skull and a number of broken ribs. She's very poorly, but we have every expectation that she will pull through.' Yvie sagged with relief. 'Of course, it's going to be a long haul, and we're not out of the woods yet. She is in good hands, but . . .'

'I understand.' She did, only too well. She was being told her daughter should make it but it wasn't a done deal. 'When can I see her?'

'I'm afraid you're going to have to wait now till she comes out of theatre.'

'How long will that be?'

'I can't tell.' The doctor gave the hint of a shrug 'The trouble is,' he said gently, 'although we have a pretty good idea what Claire's injuries are, we can never be quite sure until . . . Well, until we get to look inside. If it's all straightforward, it'll be over quite quickly. If not –' another shrug, not uncaring, just the body language of someone who is being asked to predict the future with nothing more to go on than a professional hunch – 'it could be several hours, I expect.

We'll keep you informed though, of course.' He looked directly at Yvie. 'Mrs Maxwell, I don't want to make you more anxious, but I have to be honest with you. Claire was in a very bad car crash. We're doing everything we can.'

'Right.' Yvie didn't know what else to say. She was sure there were questions she should be asking, things she needed to know, but it was all so terrible. The situation was so frightening and it was so unexpected she felt more dazed and numb than anything.

'A nurse will take you to where you can wait in comfort. And I promise to let you know as soon as we have any more news.'

Yvie grabbed her crutches and stood up to go. 'Just one thing, how's Pammy Clifton?'

'I haven't been involved in her treatment, so I don't know. Are you and she related?'

'We're friends. She and her husband were taking my daughter shopping, because . . . Well . . .' Yvie moved a crutch and shrugged her shoulders. 'Driving isn't something I'm capable of at the mo.'

'I'll get someone to find out and tell you. She was still alive when she got here, that much I do know.'

Yvie supposed that was positive news.

She was taken to wait in a small room with bland soft furnishings and a stack of magazines. Not that Yvie wanted to read. She sat on the sofa, shredding a tissue that she had pulled out from her sleeve and watching the second hand of the wall clock tick round. In fraught silence, Yvie watched the seconds and minutes pass. A nurse came and offered her tea, which Yvie accepted – something to do, she thought. Every time she heard footsteps outside the door, she stiffened, preparing herself to receive news, good or bad. Half an hour after her tea had been delivered, she was told Pammy was out of theatre and that her prognosis was good, but there was no progress report on Claire. Richard phoned and Yvie felt impotent, as she had no news beyond a report on the extent of her injuries.

'You will ring me as soon as you hear anything? Anything at all.'

'Of course. When will you be able to get away?'

'I can't say.'

Yvie wondered how forcefully he had put his case. Should she insist that Richard joined her? Should she throw a tantrum?

'Yvie?'

She sighed. No, there was no point in two of them sitting here doing nothing but worry. 'Yes, I'm here.'

'I'll come as soon as I can. I promise.'

'But what if . . .' She couldn't voice her worst fear.

This time the pause in the conversation was at Richard's end. Then, 'Even if I set out now, it'll be hours before I'm with you.'

Yvie understood his implication. If Claire lived that long, the chances were she'd make it. 'Yeah, you're right.' Yvie heard footsteps outside the door. She spun round and saw a nurse coming in. 'Hang on . . . Yes,' she said, holding the phone away from her face.

'Claire's out of surgery. We've taken her to the ITU. She's serious but stable, and we want to monitor her overnight.

Yvie felt herself sag with relief. 'Richard? Did you hear that?'

'Most of it. Thank God for that. I'll let you go. I imagine you'll want to see her. Keep me posted.'

Yvie rang off. 'Can I see her now?'

The nurse nodded. Yvie grabbed her crutches and hobbled after her. When they finally arrived at the unit, Yvie was startled by the level of noise and light. There were bleeps and buzzers competing for the nurses' attention, and the strip lighting was harsh and bright. Yvie tried not to stare at the other patients as she walked to where Claire lay, but it was difficult not to glance at the men and women who were suffering from dreadful conditions and wonder what had been the cause. She reached Claire's bed and was shocked to see the number of tubes, sensors, and other medical rigmarole attached to her daughter. She sat down on the chair and tentatively took Claire's hand.

A nurse came over. 'Hello, I'm Siobhan. I know this all looks alarming,' she said, gesturing to the monitoring equipment. Yvie nodded. 'We just like to keep an eye on everything, and this makes life easier for us. Claire is quite poorly at the moment, so we've got her sedated to keep her quiet.

Like that, her body can concentrate on healing itself.'

'Oh.' Yvie patted Claire's hand distractedly.

'We'll keep her like that for a couple of days, and then we'll slowly reduce the level of sedation until she wakes up.'

'Right.'

'Is there anything you'd like to ask?'

Yvie was sure there were dozens of things she should know, but her mind was a virtual blank. But there was one thing she wanted to know. 'What are her chances?'

'Pretty good. It would be unfair of me to say more than that, but she's young and healthy and the odds are in her favour.'

Yvie wished she could wave a wand and make Claire instantly better.

'Would you like a tea or coffee?'

Yvie shook her head. There was only one thing she wanted and no one was going to be able to deliver that for some time.

Siobhan moved round the bed and explained what the equipment did. 'If you understand a bit of what's going on, it's much less scary.'

Yvie supposed she was right, but half the information about the drips and drugs and monitors went over her head.

'Right,' said Siobhan when she had finished the guided tour. 'I'll show you round the unit now, so you know where the phone is and where you can get a coffee and suchlike. Do you live locally?'

Yvie briefly explained her circumstances.

'Then we need to get you fixed up with somewhere to sleep. Leave it with me.' Siobhan took Yvie around the unit, explained where she could find the hospital canteen to get a proper meal, rather than a snack or a sandwich, and then went to the nurses' station to organize somewhere for Yvie to stay.

'We've rooms for relatives here. They're not palatial, but it does mean you can stay close to Claire.'

Well, that's one thing less to worry about, thought Yvie, who hadn't relished the prospect of spending the night in a chair. She returned to her daughter's bedside and took her hand again. She wished she wasn't so pale and still. If it wasn't for the bleeping and the flicking needles recording her vital signs, it would be difficult to know she was still alive.

222

But she was, and Yvie had to cling to the hope that she would stay that way.

Yvie had been sitting with Claire for over an hour when she remembered about Pammy. She hurried to find Siobhan, feeling guilty that she hadn't done anything about finding out how she was sooner.

Siobhan made a phone call to discover which ward Pammy was on.

'Why don't you go and see her?' she suggested.

Yvie glanced at Claire and shook her head. No, she couldn't leave her.

'I can give you a pager,' said Siobhan. 'If Claire's condition changes in any way, I'll page you and you can be back here in a trice.'

Yvie wasn't sure.

'You needn't be away long, but I'm sure your friend would appreciate it.'

That was certainly true. And Yvie knew in her heart that one of the reasons why she was so diffident about visiting Pammy was that she didn't know what to say to her about Adam. But putting it off wasn't going to make it any easier. She took the pager, clipped it on to her waistband and made her way to Pammy's ward.

Before she went to find Pammy's bed, she made her way to the nurses' station and explained who she was.

'Does she know about her husband?' she inquired.

The nurse nodded. 'Dreadful, isn't it?'

'How is she?'

'Well, she's conscious but very shocked by everything. You can see her for a few minutes. Try not to upset her or tire her.'

Yvie nodded and followed the nurse to Pammy's bed, trying to prepare what to say as she went.

Pammy was sitting up, a bandage round her head, and with a neck brace on. Her face was ashen and expressionless. She was staring across the ward, ignoring everything going on around her. Even the sound of their approaching footsteps didn't make her turn and look in their direction. Yvie stopped by Pammy's bed.

'Pammy?' she said. She moved to the pillow end and took

one of Pammy's hands. Finally Pammy looked at her, and a tear rolled out of the corner of her eye.

'Is Claire . . . ?'

'Claire's in intensive care. But she's made it this far,' said Yvie gently. She sat down by the bed, still holding Pammy's hand. She rubbed the back of it with her thumb.

Pammy nodded as much as the neck brace would allow. 'That's something.' Her voice was flat, devoid of emotion.

'I heard about Adam,' said Yvie. 'I am so sorry.'

'It was my fault. If I hadn't made him get out of the car . . .'

'You can't think that. Of course it's not your fault. It was a ghastly accident.'

Pammy shook her head. 'But I made him go and help the caravanners. If he'd stayed in the car, he'd probably still be alive.' More tears rolled down her face.

Yvie felt helpless. She clasped Pammy's hand in both of hers and squeezed it. 'You mustn't think like that. It's not good for you.'

'What does it matter?' said Pammy bleakly. She gazed at Yvie. 'Who cares what is good for me? I wish I had died too.'

Over the next couple of days Yvie divided her time between her daughter and Pammy. There was no doubt that Claire was the sicker physically, but Pammy was mentally very fragile. Most times, when Yvie entered the ward, Pammy was staring ahead of her, just as she had been when Yvie had first visited her on the Saturday. She seemed to be living in a private inner world, a world where grief and guilt and pain were the only emotions allowed.

'How's Claire?' Pammy asked dully, when Yvie arrived by her bed on Monday evening.

'Still sedated, but the nurses are pleased with her progress. They're going to lessen the dose, so she should wake up some time tomorrow.'

'Good.' But the single syllable came out flat and toneless.

'I phoned Mark this morning, to find out about the dogs,' Yvie tried, brightly. Perhaps Pammy would show an interest in her pets. 'They're fine. He's been taking them on lots of long walks.'

'I'll have to do that now. Adam used to do most of it. He'd

224

take them out when he went round the estate. The dogs are going to miss their walks with him.'

Yvie nodded.

'I suppose someone else'll be brought in to run the estate. It'll be odd having a stranger in Adam's office.' There was a pause. 'I wonder if I'll be allowed to stay on.'

'I'm sure you will. If they can find someone local to run the estate, there's no reason for you to have to leave.'

'No.' Another pause. 'It'd be different if I'd had kids. I wanted to, you know, but Adam, well . . . I think he thought that if we couldn't do it ourselves . . .'

Yvie could imagine exactly what Adam would have thought. There was no way someone like him would have allowed himself to be subjected to all that intimate medical intervention. And now he was gone and Pammy hadn't a relation to call her own in the world.

'I loved him so much. He was so good to me,' said Pammy.

Yvie kept her mouth shut and looked away from her friend. She supposed it was probably a blessing that Pammy was so utterly in the dark about Adam's infidelity.

'Everyone loved him. He was so popular. And he was so good with the boss and his guests.'

'He was.' That wasn't a lie, thought Yvie with relief. At that moment her pager bleeped. Yvie looked at it as her heart rate accelerated. With slightly shaky hands, she switched it off.

'What's that about?' asked Pammy.

'I have to get back to Claire. They need me there.'

'Oh.'

Yvie leaned over Pammy's bed and gave her a quick peck on the cheek. 'I'll come and see you again soon.'

She sped out of the ward as fast as she could on crutches, and along the lengths of corridors that led her back to the ITU. She tried not to panic, but she couldn't get the idea out of her head that they wouldn't page her for anything other than an emergency. She rushed into the ward and went straight to Claire's bed. Bemused, Yvie looked around. Claire's machines all indicated that everything was OK. Perhaps she was missing something. But no, when she checked again, it was all fine. Besides which, if Claire had taken a turn for the worse, there would be a team of nurses and doctors here, working on her, trying to sort the problem out. Yvie had seen it happen a number of times with other patients: that frenzy of activity and complicated medical terminology, as the team calmly but swiftly coped with some sort of crisis.

'Hello, Yvie,' said Richard behind her.

Yvie spun round, nearly losing her balance as a crutch got caught in a chair leg.

'Richard!' she squealed. 'Oh, thank God.' She leaned forward so he could embrace her. 'How . . . ? Is it . . . ? I mean . . . ?' Oh hell, what did she mean?

'I tried to call you before I left, but your phone is switched off and the ward phone always seemed to be engaged. In the end I thought I might just as well surprise you.'

'Oh, it's so good to see you.' She nuzzled against his shoulder. 'I have missed you so much.'

'I've missed you too, darling. You have no idea how good it is to see you again. And Claire.'

'Things are looking pretty hopeful.'

'The nurse told me. And Pammy?'

'I was with her when they paged me. She's not good. I mean, physically she's on the mend, but all the life, all the spark has gone out of her.'

Richard sighed. 'It's not surprising really, is it? I mean, one minute she's on her way to the shops and the next she's in hospital and a widow.'

'She was saying that she had wanted kids, but when they discovered Adam couldn't, that was that.'

'He always was a selfish bastard in some ways.'

Yvie looked at him in surprise. Adam had been Richard's great friend. What on earth had brought this on? Unaccountably, she felt the need to defend him.

'It was hardly his fault that he got wiped out in that crash, though. It isn't as if he planned to leave Pammy on her own and childless.'

'No, and I shouldn't speak ill of the dead, but Pammy was wasted on Adam. I could never understand why such a lovely person as her would marry him.'

Yvie frowned and shook her head. 'Because she loved him very much? Have you thought of that one?'

'Yeah, you're right. I'm being mean about the poor bloke. But he was pretty selfish, for all that.' Richard moved closer to Claire's bed. 'I'm sorry I wasn't here for you at the start.' 'You're here now. And I'm sorry for being so angry with you about it. You were right. There wasn't much you could have done – well, except sit here and worry with me. But I imagine you were doing enough worrying of your own back at home.'

Richard picked up one of Claire's limp hands. 'Worry didn't even come close to describing what I went through. I kept imagining the worst and having to restrain myself from ringing the hospital every five minutes.'

Yvie sat on a chair on the other side of the bed. 'We'd have phoned you instantly if anything had changed.'

'I know, but it's not the same as being there.'

'Let's go and get a coffee and have a proper chat. I need to know what went on back at home. I expect you've got questions too, and perhaps we can visit Pammy on the way back.'

'Yes, I'd like that.'

Yvie told the nursing staff where she was going as she left the ward.

'I bet you're glad your husband is here now,' said Siobhan. 'And here in time for when Claire wakes up.'

Richard looked puzzled. 'How? I'm not Prince Charming, you know.'

'I'll explain over coffee,' said Yvie with a grin. 'Medical magic, not fairy-tale magic. I can't tell you how much jargon I've picked up over the last few days.'

'She could almost qualify for a nursing certificate herself,' said Siobhan.

Richard and Yvie made their way along corridors and down stairs to the coffee shop near the entrance to the hospital.

'I tell you,' said Yvie as they queued, 'I have become more familiar with this hospital than I ever dreamed. What with my foot and now this . . .'

'God,' said Richard thumping his forehead. 'I haven't even asked how that is.'

'Fine. Really it is. The plaster comes off soon.'

They shuffled forward a pace or two. 'I turn my back on you and Claire for a minute and both of you wind up crocked.'

'Best you don't let us out of your sight again then.'

'Like I'm going to.'

They reached the front of the queue, got two coffees and paid. Richard carried the tray and followed Yvie over to an empty table.

'So now I want to know all about what went on back home,' said Yvie as they settled down.

'Not much to tell really. I mean, I expect the guys really involved in the operation have plenty to say, but I didn't seem to be much in the loop.'

'But surely—'

'No, honestly. My job was to carry on as normal. That meant going to work, coming home, going to the pub occasionally, off to meet a couple of friends, that sort of thing. Not hobnobbing with undercover policemen and spooks.'

'So you didn't see them.'

'Oh, I saw them all right, I knew where to look. For a start, there were roadworks on the corner of the close for weeks, complete with a little red and white striped tent, workmen came and went, but I don't think a spade or pickaxe was wielded in anger once. And I certainly wasn't allowed to exchange the time of day with them, let alone ask for information.'

'Weren't you scared?'

'Shitless some of the time, especially after they found a fingerprint belonging to Lynch in Carchester.'

Yvie was puzzled. Carchester was a biggish sort of place – how many millions of fingerprints would there have been to choose from? 'How did they know where to look?'

'It all came down to a complete stroke of luck. He was in a cheap hotel near the station. The management had had complaints of a few things going missing from residents' rooms. They worked out one of the chambermaids was a bit light-fingered, so they got the police to search her digs. Amongst the stuff she'd lifted was an attaché case, which no one had reported stolen. The police wondered why, and had a good look at it. When they opened it, they discovered not only Lynch's fingerprints but also really strong traces of explosive. Of course, he'd checked out of the hotel when they went to get him. Losing his case obviously spooked him, so he legged it. However, a couple of the staff were able to furnish half-decent descriptions.'

'I suppose then it was just a question of time.'

'With half of Special Branch after him, to say nothing of the local constabulary, it was pretty much a done deal. But it was like knowing there's a wasp in the room and not being able to see it. I have to say I was very twitchy. It didn't help matters knowing that he'd recently handled a lot of explosive.'

'And then I ring up and give you grief for not being here to hold my hand.'

'I couldn't blame you for that.' Richard shook his head thoughtfully. 'What with one thing and another, it's not been easy for either of us.'

'And now we're all right and it's Pammy going through it.' Yvie took a sip of her coffee.

'Let's finish our coffee and go and see her.'

If Richard was shocked by the blank, empty look on Pammy's face when he got to the ward, he didn't show it. He hugged her gently and drew up a chair by her bed. Yvie hobbled around to the other side of the bed and sat on the chair that side.

'Hello, my dear,' he said. 'I shan't ask how you are, because I can't imagine the hell you must be going through.'

Pammy turned her face towards him. 'Richard. What are you doing here?'

'I've come to see you and Claire, of course.'

Pammy gave a tight, wan little smile. 'If you'd come a week earlier, you might have seen Adam.'

'And that is something I've been beating myself up about for a couple of days now. I would have liked to have seen the old bugger one last time.'

'And he would have liked to have seen you. He really admired you, you know.'

'I'm flattered.'

'He always said you were so steady and grounded.'

'Doesn't sound like admiration to me. Sounds more like he thought I was a boring old fart.'

Pammy smiled. 'You could never be that, Richard. Not with a smashing family like yours.'

In the little silence that followed, Yvie exchanged a look

across the bed with Richard. She knew what he was thinking – that if life had been the least bit fair, Pammy should have had a smashing family too, but now she was facing life on her own.

'Yeah, well . . . So when are they going to let you go home?' said Richard, trying to lighten the sombre mood.

'It's all to do with the fact that I'll have to be able to cope on my—' Pammy's voice choked on a sob. She blinked and cleared her throat. 'I'll have to be able to manage for myself.'

'Well, we're here to look after you now. Will that make a difference?'

'Suppose so,' said Pammy with no enthusiasm.

'Pammy, you're going to have to face going home soon,' said Yvie gently.

'I know, but I don't think I'll be able to cope. There'll be too many memories. All Adam's things. I don't think I can face dealing with everything.'

'We'll be with you.'

'I know you will, but Adam won't be, will he?'

Richard booked them into a hotel for the night. Yvie was concerned about leaving Claire, but the nurses insisted that they would ring Yvie's mobile if there was the least change.

'Besides, you need a proper night's sleep in a decent bed,' said Siobhan. 'You look worn out. Get that lovely husband of yours to take you out for a nice meal, have a couple of glasses of wine and then get an early night.'

Yvie agreed, and she and Richard left the ward. They were barely through the door when Richard whispered to Yvie that the early night was certainly something he had in mind, but sleeping wasn't on the agenda.

'Ooh, you randy old man,' said Yvie with a chortle.

'And don't you tell me you weren't thinking the same thing.'

'As if.'

'Yeah, right.

As Yvie stepped out of the hospital and into the fresh air, she realized that it was the first time she had left it since she had arrived on Saturday. Despite the nippy breeze and the grey clouds, she felt her spirits rise. Claire was almost out of the woods, Richard was with her, Lynch was in jug, and they

230

could soon go home to Carchester. Then, as quickly as her morale had soared, it plummeted. Pammy. Poor Pammy had so little to look forward to. Oh God, she thought. What a selfish moo I am.

Richard pulled a key from his pocket as they walked through the car park, and pressed the button. The indicator lights of a small Corsa blipped.

'What's this?'

'Hire car. I flew up. Quicker.'

Yvie shoved her crutches on the back seat and clambered in. As she did so, she saw a paper on the passenger seat. The screamer on the front page announced the arrest of Lynch, wanted for the murder of the lawyer. She read the story with a sense of unreality – that they, as a family, had been mixed up with all of it. But it was over now, she thought, as she tossed it behind her. If she hadn't come to stay with Pammy, if she hadn't broken her leg, if Claire hadn't wanted to go shopping, would the awful accident have happened? She felt that she was the catalyst in this string of events. It was her fault. So, if she was the cause for all this misery in Pammy's life, what could she do to make amends? As Richard manoeuvred the vehicle out of the car park, he glanced across at her.

'Penny for them.'

'I was thinking about Pammy. I was wondering what we might be able to do to help her get over this.'

'Tough one. I know it'll sound brutal, but I don't think there'll be that much that we can do. I think time is the only thing that'll really help her.'

'We could have her to stay.'

'Of course we could. In fact, it's a lovely idea and well overdue. Was it Claire's christening when she and Adam last stayed?'

'Yes.'

'I can't imagine why we didn't see more of them,' said Richard.

Yvie could, perfectly well, but she stayed silent.

'I suppose it's my fault. I should have made more of an effort to get them to come and see us.' Richard eased the little car out of the hospital complex and on to the main road that led to Carlisle. 'But it's usually a girl thing, isn't it, making those sort of arrangements.' He smoothly changed up the gears of the car.

'Well, don't blame me, just because you couldn't be bothered.'

'I didn't mean it like that. Just that you and Pammy had got on so well in Germany, I sort of assumed you'd be bosom buddies for ever.'

'We are.'

'But we hardly ever saw them.' Richard swung the car off the road and into the forecourt of a small hotel. 'I hope this is OK? I booked it on the Internet when I was waiting for my flight.'

'I'm sure it'll be fine. Just as long as it has a bath and a bar.'

'And a bed?'

'And a *double* bed.' Yes, that was very important.

They arrived back at the hospital bright and early the next day. Claire was still unconscious, but the duty nurse assured them that Claire's prognosis was still excellent and that, given the level of sedation she was now on, she should be coming round in the not too distant future.

'That is such good news,' said Richard, stroking his daughter's face. 'Just a question of being patient now.'

'And when she does come round, we'll move her to an ordinary ward,' continued the nurse. 'The one your other friend is on. That'll be nice for them, won't it?' She bustled off to check on another patient, leaving Richard and Yvie alone by their daughter's bed.

'Well, it'll make visiting easier for us, but I'm not so sure that Claire will think it's such a good idea,' said Richard. 'I mean, how is she going to cope when she hears the news about Adam? Apart from the fact he was her godfather, it always sounded as though she got on with him almost as well as she did with Pammy.'

'Hmm, yes,' said Yvie. She could hardly tell Richard that, just before the accident, Claire had completely revised her opinion of Adam, or why she had. 'Tell you what,' she said, to change the subject. 'I'll get a pager and pop down and see Pammy. If Claire does start to wake up, bleep me.'

232

'But don't you want to sit with her? I could go.'

'Of course I'd like to, but you're here now. Besides, not being horrid, but I think Pammy finds it easier to cry on my shoulder than yours.'

Richard nodded. 'OK. And I'll let you know the instant there's the slightest hint of a flicker.'

Pammy was sitting up with headphones clamped over her ears when Yvie got to her ward. She thought Pammy looked slightly less drawn than she had on previous days, but perhaps that was because her own good mood, the result of her reunion with her husband, was projecting that slant on to what she saw.

'Hi, Pammy,' she said, trying to assume a more sober manner. The last thing she wanted to appear was overly happy, that would be thoughtless.

Pammy turned her head. 'Hi, Yvie,' she said emotionlessly. She removed the phones and unplugged them so the faint tch-tch-tch of the music disappeared. 'How's Claire?'

'Progressing nicely. When she comes round, they're planning on moving her down here.'

'Oh.'

'It'll be some company for you both when Richard and I aren't around.'

'Great.'

Yvie lapsed into silence. She poured herself a glass of water from Pammy's carafe, just for something to do. 'I thought I'd take Richard over to see where we've been staying for the past weeks. I expect he'll be blown away by your place.'

'I'll give you a key if you like. You can give him a guided tour.'

'Oh, I don't know about that.'

'Why not? It's not like you're going to be in anyone's way. The place'll be empty.'

'What about alarms and suchlike? It's all too complicated.'

'Please yourself.'

Yvie wanted to placate Pammy. 'I was just going to show him the cottage and the grounds. I don't think he's really into stately piles.'

'Not like Adam. He loved pretending the place was his. The lord of the manor bit really suited him.'

233

'I'm sure.'

'The estate workers liked him too.'

'I'd heard,' said Yvie. Some of them a bit too much, from what she'd gathered. 'Difficult not to like him. He was always such a live wire.' She sipped her water.

'I couldn't believe it when he took an interest in me. The girls he seemed to go for were the flamboyant types. We'd met at parties a few times before he asked me out, and he'd always had some stunningly pretty or outrageously rich girl hanging on his arm on those occasions. I never thought he'd look twice at me.'

'But he did. And look what a gorgeous couple you made.'

Pammy didn't look at Yvie, but twisted the plain gold band on her left hand. 'You know, I once asked him why he chose me. I mean, compared to the girls he could have had, I'm not much cop. He said it was because I'd look after him the best. So I always tried to. But I failed, didn't I?'

'Pammy, you can't blame yourself like this. And the girls you're comparing yourself with were probably shallow or self-obsessed. That sort often are. Adam knew he'd found a winner when he met you. No one could have cared for him better or loved him more.'

'I was always scared he'd want to go back to that sort, though. I tried so hard to make life wonderful for him, so he'd stay with me.'

'And you *did* make life wonderful for him.'

'It didn't work though, did it?'

Yvie thought she was referring to the fact that he was gone now, but there was something in the way Pammy sounded that worried her, a note of anguish. She sipped her water to cover her silence.

'I knew. He didn't know I did, but I knew,' said Pammy in a low voice.

Yvie nearly choked. 'Knew what?'

'About Adam's affairs.'

Shit, thought Yvie. How? Adam must have told her, and all this time Pammy had known and hadn't said anything. She felt her face burning, but luckily Pammy was staring ahead, in that sightless way she had these days.

'I heard the rumours in the village about him.'

'What rumours were those?' Yvie hoped her voice sounded steady, as her heart was beating so hard she was sure the pounding must affect it.

'About him and the village girls.' Pammy turned and looked at her defiantly, as if she was daring Yvie to comment. 'And with some of the house guests.'

Yvie swallowed. Please God, Pammy didn't say that she knew about her and Adam. She stared at Pammy, but Pammy gave no hint of saying anything else. Oh, thank God! How shallow and self-obsessed did that make her, but she couldn't help feeling relieved. 'Were the rumours true?'

'I don't know. All I could do was pretend I never heard them.' Her voice almost squeaked as a sob constricted her throat. She swallowed and regained control. 'When we found out we couldn't have kids, I even wondered about confronting him. That way I could get a divorce and then maybe I'd marry again and there'd be a baby. But –' she shrugged – 'I just couldn't do it. I loved him too much. So I carried on pretending there were no rumours, and that way I could pretend that he still loved *me*.' The tears rolled again.

'But he did. Very much. He adored you.' She was certain about that. After all, he hadn't left Pammy for her all those years ago, though she could hardly tell Pammy that Adam's affairs were just about sex, not commitment.

Pammy stared at Yvie as if by doing so she'd find some sort of confirmation on her face. Yvie wanted to tell her she knew for sure, but how could she explain the source of her knowledge? What was the point of ruining Pammy's memories? They were all she had left now. Pammy's memories might have been flawed, Adam might have been serially unfaithful, but if Yvie could just convince Pammy that his flings meant nothing, then Pammy could carry on believing that Adam had loved only her. So Yvie told Pammy all the things she had noticed about Adam that had convinced her that he had truly loved his wife. Slowly, she felt that Pammy believed her and that his affairs were assuming less of an importance in her mind. As Yvie worked on convincing Pammy about Adam's love, at the back of her mind she was aware of a feeling of relief. If Adam hadn't told Pammy about him and Yvie, and as Pammy appeared not to have heard on the grapevine, then the odds were that he hadn't told anyone else either. And unless Laura plumbed to unlikely depths of spite, Richard would never know now. Yvie couldn't believe that here she was, sitting by her best friend's sickbed feeling relief that Adam was dead. And yet she was.

When she returned to Claire's bedside, Richard was sitting reading a newspaper, glancing over at his daughter every now and again. Yvie pulled a chair up and plonked herself down beside him. She wondered if she ought to tell Richard about Pammy's revelation about Adam. She realized that if she hadn't been one of Adam's conquests she would certainly tell him. It was only her guilty conscience making her dither. But Adam wasn't the most important thing on the agenda right now. Her daughter was.

'How's Claire?'

'The same, as far as I can tell.'

'Shouldn't we see signs – movement or something?'

'I asked, but all they could say was that every patient is different. Some come round relatively quickly after they come off the sedatives, some are woozy for ages. There's no rhyme or reason apparently.'

'Right, as long as there's nothing to worry about.' Casually she added, 'I've just been chatting to Pammy.'

'And?'

'Well, it's a bit sad really, but it seems Adam was a bit of a rake.'

'Oh.' But there was no surprise in Richard's voice, which Yvie thought was a bit odd. 'So, marriage to a good woman didn't change him?'

'How do you mean? You told me he was selfish but this is something else entirely.'

'He was like a tomcat when he was single. Even when he was engaged to Pammy, I heard that he was still putting it about. Part of being selfish. What Adam wanted, Adam took, and no consideration for anyone else.'

Yvie prayed to God her face wasn't going to redden. That about summed up in one sentence what had happened in Germany, and then again, nearly, in the cottage. She swallowed. She had to make some sort of response – it would look odd if she didn't. 'But how could he? Poor Pammy.'

236

'He reckoned what she didn't know wouldn't hurt her.'

'Well, it seems she did know.'

'He must have got lax in his old age. Probably the result of living in a small and isolated community. I'm certain she never knew about some of his earlier conquests. He could be very discreet.' Richard looked Yvie straight in the eyes as he said that, as if he was challenging her – or was she imagining it?

Yvie dropped her gaze. Guilt pumped through every fibre of her body. She stood up and busied herself checking the machines by Claire's bed.

'I wouldn't have thought you could have been friends with a bloke like that.' She still didn't look at him.

'He was a good laugh and there was never a dull moment with old Adam around.'

'That's as maybe, but the man was obviously amoral.'

'You liked him.'

'Yes but . . .' She could hardly say that she'd liked him because she hadn't known he was an adulterer. She'd known only too well that he was. She changed the subject. 'I'm parched. You couldn't be a honey and get me a tea from the machine?'

'No sweat.'

Richard went to find the vending machine. Yvie let herself sag. All this endless economy with the truth was exhausting. She hauled herself back to her chair and slumped on to it. She would be *so* glad when they were back in Carchester, away from anything to do with Adam, and she could put the whole mess of her affair behind her once and for all.

She took Claire's hand and patted it absent-mindedly. She nearly leapt off her chair when she felt the fingers, which for days had lain motionless in her palm, stir.

'Claire? Claire!'

Not a flicker on her face, but the movement was definitely there again, she was sure. She looked around to see if she could catch Richard's eye, but he was busy feeding coins into the machine by the nurses' station. She tried squeezing Claire's hand again and, yes, there was the sensation again. Barely more than the faintest butterfly fluttering, but it really was there. She hadn't imagined it.

As Richard approached with the two paper cups, Yvie couldn't contain her excitement any longer. 'Richard!' she squealed. 'Claire's hand moved.'

Richard's face broke into the most enormous smile. He dumped the cups on a nearby surface and took his daughter's other hand.

'Yes, you're right. Oh, thank God.' The look of relief on his face said more than words could. A nurse came over to see what the commotion was.

'She's coming round,' explained Yvie.

The nurse scanned the machines' readings and made a few checks of her own. She smiled and nodded. 'I would think she'll be back with us well and truly by tea time tonight. She'll come and go a bit for a few hours, I expect, but it won't be long now. When she does come to, it'll probably be best if you don't tell her too much about the accident. The details can wait till tomorrow.'

Yvie and Richard both nodded to show they'd understood, and then grinned inanely at each other, thrilled by the thought that Claire was properly on the road to recovery.

'I think I should break the news about Adam to Claire,' said Yvie in a way that she hoped wasn't going to cause an argument. 'It'd be better coming from me.' They were on their way up to the ITU after what they hoped was their final night in the local hotel.

'If you think so. Do you want me there while you do it?'

Yvie shook her head. 'Perhaps not. It's going to be a bit of an emotional moment. I think Claire might find it easier if it's just her and me.'

'Well, I'll nip off to see Pammy and leave you to it. I'll come to find you in about fifteen minutes.'

'That should be fine.'

Richard peeled off towards Pammy's ward and Yvie clumped on towards Claire's, going over in her mind exactly what she was going to say. Of course, it was a whole lot easier now she'd got shot of Richard. If Claire seemed pleased about Adam's death – which, given the acrimony she'd felt about him just before the accident, might be the case – there was going to be no need for any difficult explanations for her

238

father's benefit. The last thing Richard needed to know about right now was Adam's fumbled assault on her. God only knew what recriminations that might lead to. Yvie decided on the direct approach.

Claire was sitting up in bed looking amazingly perky when Yvie arrived.

'Hi, Mum,' she said brightly. 'Where's Dad?'

'He's gone to see how Pammy is. He'll be along shortly. And how are you?'

'OK. It's weird missing out on a big chunk of time like I did.' She frowned. 'And I know everyone's told me I was in a car crash, but I can't remember anything about it.'

'I think that's nature's way of looking after you. Some things are best not to remember.'

'Was it really bad?'

'I think so. In fact, it was terrible. Claire . . . Adam was killed.'

Claire looked completely bemused. She frowned and shook her head in utter disbelief. 'But he couldn't have been. He wasn't even *in* the car. That's the last thing I can remember: Pammy made him get out to help sort out a caravan that had got stuck.'

'I know, but he was. The car that hit you was going so fast it shunted the Range Rover right down the road. Adam was in the way.'

'Oh.' She considered this information and let out a long breath. 'That's gross.' Another pause. 'How has Pammy taken the news?'

'She's heartbroken.'

Claire considered this too. After a few seconds, she said, 'So, she didn't know about . . .'

'She knew lots of stuff, but not what happened in the cottage. And,' said Yvie emphatically, 'we must never let on about that. But she knew about the rumours in the village. She told me.'

'What? And she still loved him?' Claire was incredulous.

Yvie nodded.

Claire shook her head in disbelief. 'How could she have done?'

'It's difficult to believe, I know, but she did.'

239

'But he was a creep.'

'Look, whatever you or I felt about him is immaterial. And we mustn't let those feelings show, as it'll make Daddy and Pammy ask too many questions. What they don't know won't hurt them. As far as the rest of the world is concerned, we are both devastated that Adam is dead. We may have heard rumours about his personal life, but we have no direct reason to believe them.'

'OK.' Claire tipped her head back on her pillow and studied the ceiling. 'We're doing this to protect Pammy, right?'

'Right.'

'Just as long as you understand that I'm not doing it to protect Adam.'

'That's fine.'

When Richard arrived, Yvie was brushing Claire's hair.

'You're looking chipper,' he said, leaning over to give her a kiss on the cheek. More soberly, he added, 'Has Mummy told you the bad news?'

'Yes, it's dreadful.' She looked steadily at her father. 'But I'm being brave, aren't I, Mummy?'

That afternoon, life took a big step on the road to normality. Claire was moved out of ITU and into a bed next to Pammy, and Yvie and Richard finally felt relaxed enough to consider being more than a few minutes away from the hospital. They decided they could go and spend the night in the cottage.

'We'll have to get supplies en route. The village shop'll be closed by the time we get there, but we ought to go there just to let Mark and his dad know that Pammy will be coming home soon, and that Claire is on the mend.'

'I'm looking forward to seeing the place for myself. I have to say that being stuck inside Carlisle hospital for a couple of days has done nothing for my appreciation of the Lake District.'

'It's beautiful, when the sun shines.'

Richard grinned. 'So, judging by what you told me on the phone, I may get lucky and see it at it's best, *if* I stay here long enough.'

'Was I that grumpy about the weather?'

'Unbelievably.'

They stopped in Keswick at a supermarket and grabbed some basics, then drove on towards the estate.

'Blimey!' said Richard as he drove through the vast gates at the entrance.

'Wait till you see the house,' said Yvie. 'And you will have to wait, it's miles along this drive.'

'When you said the place was big, I had no idea . . . Who owns it?'

'I've no idea – some rich American is all I know. Pammy always referred to him as Mr Big or the Boss.'

Richard slowed the car down to negotiate yet another cattle grid. 'And Adam used to look after all this?'

'Adam and a team of estate workers. I think his role was more managerial than hands on. I never saw him in wellies.'

The trees that crowded the drive gave way to parkland, and in the pale light of an overcast dusk, Richard saw the house on the hill. 'Good grief.'

'Impressive, isn't it?'

They drove on in silence along the avenue of beech trees and up the hill. As the trees gave way to the vast expanse of gravel at the front of the house, both Richard and Yvie were agog to see a helicopter parked on the lawn to the side of the house. Richard stopped the car.

Yvie whistled. 'And who the bloody hell does that belong to?'

'Adam and Pammy's Mr Big, I assume.'

'Should we find him and tell him about the accident?'

'I imagine he already knows. It may be why he's here. Presumably he needs to find someone to look after things now Adam is . . .'

'He couldn't be that heartless, surely? Pammy hasn't even buried him yet.'

But Richard didn't answer, he was staring intently at the helicopter. 'Oh, for God's sake, how stupid have I been? Check the logo on the chopper.'

Yvie looked perplexed. 'You've lost me there.'

'It's not "Mr Big", it's Mr Bigge.' He spelled it out. 'You know, the tycoon. "Bigge Buildings", "Bigge Boats", "Bigge Business".'

'You're joking.'

241

'I don't think so.'

Yvie's jaw dropped. 'No wonder he can afford this place then.'

'And if I'm not very much mistaken, you're about to meet the man himself.'

Approaching them from the front of the Hall was a fifty-something man wearing a loud check shirt and sky-blue slacks. He had to be American. Richard and Yvie both got out of the car.

'Can I help you?' he called, the American accent clear even at thirty paces.

'My name is Richard Maxwell,' Richard called back. 'I'm a friend of Pammy and Adam.'

Mr Bigge strode towards them, but now with his arm outstretched. He reached Richard, grabbed his hand and pumped it up and down. 'Glad to meet you. And you must be Yvie,' he said, turning to her.

'Umm, yes.' Yvie was completely perplexed that he knew her name. Rich, successful and clairvoyant.

'Pammy and Adam have told me so much about you. Jeez, but what a tragic accident. Terrible, just terrible. I can't believe such a thing could happen to such a lovely couple.' He stopped in mid-flow and looked horrified. 'And what an asshole I am. Your daughter was in the crash too. How is she?'

'Almost better,' said Yvie, still feeling that the whole situation had become completely bizarre.

'I am so very glad to hear that.' He sounded really, genuinely pleased. 'And Richard, this business with the IRA is all over? I read the paper on the way over from the States.' Richard nodded, looking as confused and bemused as Yvie felt. 'Look, come on into the Hall. I want to talk to you guys about everything. I want to know exactly what happened. Yvie, will you be able to manage with your leg and all?'

Yvie nodded, too stunned to make a sensible reply.

He led the way into the Hall. 'Come in, come in.' He stood aside and let them go through the big oak door ahead of him. Yvie smiled when she noted Richard's reaction. 'We'll go through to the den. I'll have someone bring us some tea.' He stopped in mid-stride and turned. 'Tea is OK?'

'Tea would be lovely,' said Yvie. They followed him across

the massive hall and through a door in the panelling. Behind it was a room, lined with bookshelves, thickly carpeted and with a suite of extremely comfortable-looking leather chairs and sofas. In the large fireplace, a fire crackled brightly.

'The trouble with this goddam house is that it's always cold. I love it, but after Florida . . . I have to have fires in every room, even in summer. Take a seat. I'll organize tea.'

Yvie sank into a wing chair by the fire; Richard sat opposite her. The chair was as luxurious as it looked. She rubbed her hands over the soft leather on the arms and wondered how much it had cost. Across the room, Mr Bigge spoke into an intercom system and then came and joined them.

'If Pammy were here, it would be tea and scones or tea and cake, but sadly . . . Mrs Bostock from the village will do her best, but I just know it won't be the same.'

'No,' said Yvie. 'Pammy, is a great cook. I put on pounds staying with her.'

'But I thought I told Adam you were to have the holiday cottage.'

'Thank you. Claire and I did stay there, but when I broke my ankle, Pammy insisted I came and stayed in her flat. The spiral stairs in the cottage were a bit tricky.'

'Of course. How did the accident happen?'

Yvie recounted a potted version of her adventure.

The door to the den opened and a lady, who Yvie knew she'd seen in the village, brought in a tray laden with a silver tea service and some beautiful china. She put it on the table in front of the fire.

'Anything else?' she asked.

'Nothing at the moment,' said Mr Bigge.

She left the room.

'Shall I pour, Mr Bigge?' asked Yvie.

'It's Charlie. Call me Charlie, please. Yes do.'

Yvie did the honours and handed the cups round.

'I expect you two are wondering how I know so much about you.'

'I was rather,' said Richard, stirring his tea.

'I talk to Adam every week. I like to know what is going on round here. I have houses all over the place, but none that I like as much as this. And I like the people here too. Adam tells me what's happening in the village; who's had a baby, who did well at the village flower show. Stuff like that. I love it. Anyway, when he told me a friend of his and her daughter had had to rush up here, and the reason why, I was keen to see if I could make life easier for you. Hence the cottage.'

'And the cottage was great, thank you, till I went and fell over.'

'So now, tell me what happened on Saturday.'

Yvie recounted the details as she understood them, answering questions from Charlie as best as she could. 'But that's all I know,' she finished. 'I wasn't there and Claire can't remember anything. And I haven't asked Pammy about it.'

'No, I understand.'

'So how did you hear about it?' asked Richard.

'I rang the house and the office several times and couldn't get a reply. In the end, I rang that lad at the shop who sometimes works for Adam – Mark? Is that his name?' Yvie nodded. 'He told me. Naturally I got the next flight over.'

Before she could stop herself, Yvie blurted out, 'Naturally?'

'I think of the Cliftons as more than employees – they're my friends too.'

'I'm sorry,' said Yvie. 'I didn't mean—'

Charlie held his hand up to silence her. 'This may be my house, but they have made it my home. I don't get to spend much time here, but I value the time I do, more than I can tell you. Pammy looks after me like no one else ever has since my mom died.'

Yvie smiled. 'That's Pammy all right.'

'So she sure didn't deserve a tough break like the one she's just had.'

'No.'

Silence fell. They sipped their tea.

'So,' said Charlie, clattering his delicate cup into its saucer. 'What have you folks got planned for this evening?'

'We were just going back to the cottage to have a quiet supper.'

'Well, I'd be honoured if you'd join me for dinner here. Hell, why don't you stay here?'

'No, no, we couldn't impose,' said Yvie quickly. She glanced at Richard to check he agreed with her.

244

'Absolutely not,' he concurred.

'Besides,' said Yvie. 'I haven't got anything clean to wear. When the police whisked me off to the hospital, I only took stuff for a day or two. I didn't expect to be stuck in Carlisle till now.'

'Richard can go over to the cottage and get you some things.'

'No, really . . .'

Charlie looked crestfallen. 'I'm sorry. I should have realized. You two have hardly seen each other for an age. I shouldn't have asked. Forget it. It's just this is a big old place to be on one's own in.'

Richard and Yvie glanced at each other. Richard made a little moue which clearly indicated that he didn't mind if she didn't. Yvie raised an eyebrow. *Really?* Richard responded with the subtlest of nods.

'Well,' said Yvie. 'It's not that we're not grateful. I just felt I'd done enough freeloading.'

'Freeloading? Hell no! What are friends for? We are friends, aren't we? I feel as if I've know you for weeks.' Yvie smiled.

'Great, well that's settled then.' Charlie Bigge rubbed his hands, clearly delighted at the prospect of some company. 'Richard, let's go to your car and I'll show you the track that leads to the cottage. You can manage to get some things for your lovely wife, can't you? I'm really not happy with the thought of her on those spiral stairs.'

'I just need one complete change,' said Yvie. 'But make sure it's something I can get over my cast.'

'And don't bother with anything fancy. I'm not a dressy kinda guy.'

Charlie returned after he had pointed out the track to Richard. 'Now then, young lady,' he said. 'I'll show you to your room.'

Young lady, thought Yvie. It was a while since anyone had called her that! He lead the way up the grand staircase and then round to the left. He opened a door and stood back.

'This should be OK. When I knew I was coming over, I had Mrs Bostock make up a couple of extra beds and turn on the heating in the rooms in case anyone dropped by.'

Yvie went in. The room was palatial, with the biggest bed she had ever seen dominating the far end. Charlie walked across the room and opened a door near the window. 'There's your own bathroom in here, and here –' he opened another door – 'there's a dressing room for your husband.'

'Wow.'

'Is there anything you need?'

'I shouldn't think so.'

'It's just Pammy is so good at looking after my guests. She always puts flowers in the rooms, and books she thinks my friends will enjoy by their beds. I'm afraid Mrs Bostock . . .'

'No, it's fine as it is. Pammy is a wonderful hostess. Mrs Bostock would be hard put to be in her league.'

'I gather you and Pammy go way back.'

'We used to live next door to each other, in army married quarters in Germany. We were both newlyweds, so yes, she's one of my oldest friends. As was Adam.'

'Yeah, poor Adam.' But the way Charlie said it, it came out more as if he felt he ought to express some sort of sorrow than that he really meant it. 'We'd better go back downstairs. Richard'll wonder where we are.'

They returned to the den. The tea things had been cleared away.

'I don't know about you, but I think I could do with something stronger than tea right now. Can I get you something?' Charlie opened a concealed door, disguised as part of the bookcase, to reveal a well-stocked bar.

'I'd love a gin and tonic, please.'

Charlie mixed the drink and brought it over, then poured himself a large slug of bourbon.

'Cheers,' he said.

Yvie responded.

'You know,' said Charlie, 'what worries me most is that Pammy will want to leave now Adam isn't here to support her. Do you think she will?'

'Charlie, I honestly don't know. A couple of days ago she said something about being worried that you might not want her to stay. I imagine it was because you employed them as a couple. Perhaps you should go and see her in hospital. Talk to her about it. I think if you want her to stay on, she might be persuaded to quite easily.'

'You're right. I'll do just that tomorrow.'

'What will you do about an estate manager?'

'There'll be someone local who could probably do it in the short term. I'll get my secretary to advertise. It's my housekeeper I need to live in. The estate manager can have a cottage.'

How swish, thought Yvie. Secretaries, housekeepers, estate managers . . . Charlie took another swig of his drink. 'But I worry about Pammy being here on her own. It would be different if she had kids to keep her busy when I'm away somewhere else, but she will get terribly lonely here.'

'I think she's got quite a few friends in the village.'

'It's not the same.'

'No.'

Charlie thought for a moment, took a sip of his bourbon and said, 'You know, I always thought she was wasted on Adam. I always thought he took her for granted.'

'Oh?' First Richard not rating Adam, and now this guy. Yvie had never given much thought to the Cliftons' marriage, but then, she'd always had a slightly skewed agenda as far as Adam was concerned.

'I mean, I'm no great shakes as husbands go—'

'I didn't know you were married.'

'I'm not – now. I felt Adam never really appreciated what a great woman Pammy is.'

Yvie sipped her drink. Well, Charlie obviously appreciated her. Yvie had heard nothing but Charlie singing her praises since she'd met him. 'Pammy is a saint.'

'She sure is that.'

The door to the den opened and Richard returned, so the conversation changed tack. During the rest of the evening, over a delicious dinner, cooked by an invisible chef and served by Mrs Bostock, accompanied by some exquisite wines, they talked of many things: baseball and cricket – no one really understanding the other's explanation of the games – world politics and local issues, gardening and big business, and, naturally, Adam and Pammy.

After a second, and possibly unwise, brandy, Richard and Yvie tottered off to bed in their vast room.

After Yvie had shut the door, Richard flopped back on the king-size bed. He lay, spreadeagled, looking at the ceiling.

'Blimey, I could get used to this.'

247

Yvie began undoing the buttons on her blouse. 'I wouldn't bank on it – not on our earnings. Did you clock the quality of everything? I don't think anything in this house is in our league.'

'If you've got it, flaunt it, I suppose. I'll tell you something else I noticed. He certainly likes Pammy, doesn't he?'

'I got that impression too. I'm glad. It means that he won't be looking to get rid of her. It would be bad enough that she's lost Adam without losing her home too.'

'No, I mean he *really* likes Pammy.'

Yvie stopped undressing. 'Are you sure?'

'Absolutely certain.'

'Well, perhaps I'll stop worrying quite so much about her after all.'

'I think you can be quite certain that when Pammy comes out of hospital, Charlie will make sure she wants for nothing and has his complete support. And the village will rally round, too. Everyone seems to like her – regardless of what Adam got up to. It'll take a while, but I think, in the long run, Pammy will be fine.'

'I do hope so.'

'Now, hurry up and get your kit off, Mrs Maxwell. I've never made love to anyone in a king-sized bed, and I think tonight's the night I'm going to break my duck.'

Giggling, Yvie threw off the rest of her clothes. '"Breaking my duck." Is that rhyming slang?'

Two days later, Richard and Yvie had finally persuaded Charlie that they would be able to manage at the cottage, and returned there, apart from anything else, to clear up the stale cake and other chaos left by Yvie's precipitate departure to Claire's bedside. They had only been there a matter of hours when Charlie phoned to say that he was about to drive to Carlisle, as Pammy was being discharged.

'That's great news,' said Yvie.

'And there's no way she's going to live in that poky servants' flat while she convalesces. I've told Mrs Bostock to make up a room for her here. I want to make sure she is properly looked after till she's completely better.'

'Told you Charlie would take care of her,' said Richard with a grin, when Yvie relayed the news to him.

'But what about all his businesses? He's been away from his head office for a week now.'

'I expect he can keep tabs on everything from here. This is the modern age, Yvie. He's not running it using carrier pigeons. Besides, he has minions.'

It was only a couple of days after Pammy's return that the hospital said that Claire could go home too. She would have to visit outpatients as soon as possible after her arrival in Carchester, and had a list of instructions about what she was and was not going to be able to do in the immediate future. However, the nursing staff were of the opinion that she would be happier at home, and would therefore make faster progress, than if she remained in Carlisle.

'I can't believe we're finally able to go home. I came here just after Easter and now it's June,' said Yvie, shutting another brimming case.

'It's been a long haul,' agreed Richard. 'And considering I was supposed to be the one who was in danger, the fact that not only my wife but also my daughter ended up in hospital seems to indicate that maybe I wasn't the one who needed round-the-clock looking after.'

'Yeah well . . . I reckon it's because Claire and I are both townies at heart, and you shouldn't have tried to introduce us to the wild. All this open space and countryside – dangerous stuff for city slickers like us.'

'I promise I won't take you away from shops and pavements ever again. No more "north of Watford" for you. No more "exposure to the elements". When an invitation to one of Charlie's house parties arrives, we'll decline.'

'You mean there will be one?'

Richard shrugged. 'Well, Charlie has told me that he wants to see us again. Apart from anything else, he's told me that Global Solutions is probably going to get the contract for consulting and advising on all his Middle East and Asian projects. But what does it matter if you don't want to leave Carchester again?'

Yvie gave a little whimper. 'But a house party at the Hall isn't like being exposed to the elements, and it's only just north of Watford.'

Richard grinned. 'If you say so.' He took her in his arms

249

and gave her a hug. 'You know, there was only one thing I worried about when I sent you up here, and it certainly didn't involve fell walking or car crashes.'

Yvie nuzzled his neck. 'And what was that?'

'Adam.'

Involuntarily, Yvie stiffened. 'Oh?' She tried to sound unconcerned.

'Given what I knew about him, I did worry he'd try his charms on with you. But I reckoned that, even if I couldn't trust him, you'd tell him where to go if he tried anything on. So did he?'

Yvie drew back so she could look Richard in the eyes. Adam and the past were dead. Her loyalty lay with Richard, the present and the future – no question.

'No. Nothing happened at all.'